REBECCA CANTRELL

A City of
Broken Glass

A TOM DOHERTY ASSOCIATES BOOK
NEW YORK

A CITY OF BROKEN GLASS

A Forge Book
Published by Tom Doherty Associates, LLC
175 Fifth Avenue
New York, NY 10010

www.tor-forge.com

Forge® is a registered trademark of Tom Doherty Associates, LLC.

The Library of Congress has cataloged the hardcover edition as follows:

Cantrell, Rebecca.
    A city of broken glass / Rebecca Cantrell.—1st ed.
        p. cm.
    "A Tom Doherty Associates book."
    ISBN 978-0-7653-2734-5 (hardcover)
    ISBN 978-1-4299-4643-8 (e-book)
    1. Women journalists—Fiction. 2. World War, 1939–1945—Refugees—
Fiction. 3. Jewish refugees—Fiction. 4. Kristallnacht, 1938—Fiction.
5. Germany—History—1933–1945—Fiction. I. Title.
PS3603.A599C58 2012
813'.6—dc23

                                                        2012011652

ISBN 978-0-7653-2736-9 (trade paperback)

Forge books may be purchased for educational, business, or promotional use.
For information on bulk purchases, please contact Macmillan Corporate and
Premium Sales Department at 1-800-221-7945, extension 5442, or write
specialmarkets@macmillan.com.

First Edition: July 2012
First Trade Paperback Edition: January 2014

Printed in the United States of America

0 9 8 7 6 5 4 3 2 1

To my husband, my son,
and those whose lives were shattered in November 1938

Acknowledgments

Thank you to all who labor in the background to help bring the Hannah Vogel books into the light, including my fantastic agents, Elizabeth Evans, Mary Alice Kier, and Anna Cottle; and the wonderful staff at Tor/Forge: my clever and particular editor, Kristin Sevick, and my perspicacious publicist, Alexis Saarela.

This novel required extensive research, and I was ably aided by Robert Coleman at the U.S. Holocaust Memorial Museum. This novel, and my other novels, have been much improved by the crackerjack Kona Ink writing group of Karen Hollinger, Judith Heath, Kathryn Wadsworth, and David Deardorff. Thanks also to the writer directors, Mischa Livingstone and Richard Gorey, for bringing their unique perspectives to the work. Finally, I would like to thank Mr. Sutherland for being such a great teacher to my son. A great teacher makes a profound difference in the life of a child, and I'm glad that my son found your classroom.

But the biggest thanks of all go to those who make it all happen and make it all matter: my mother, my tireless and supportive Iron-man husband, and the most wonderful son in the world.

A City of
Broken Glass

1

A herd of black and white Friesian cattle, a pair of mismatched draft horses, and a blacksmith's shop passed by the Fiat's windows. Nothing looked any different from any other Polish village. Yet today there were twelve thousand reasons why Zbąszyń was no longer a simple farming town. If only I could find them.

"Where do we go, Frau Zinsli?" Our driver, Fräulein Ivona, used the only name of mine she knew, my Swiss alias. My real name was Hannah Vogel, but in all of Poland, luckily, only my son Anton knew it.

"On." I pointed forward, although I had no idea where the refugees were housed.

Once I found them, I would talk to as many as possible, then the local doctor, the townspeople, and the mayor if I could. Getting quotes should not be a problem, as I warranted that many in Zbąszyń spoke German. Less than twenty years had passed since it was ceded from Germany to Poland in the Treaty of Versailles.

We approached a large brick stable with armed Polish soldiers clustered in front. They stood awkwardly, as if not certain why they were there, and kept stealing glances inside. Somehow, I did not think they guarded horses so closely.

I directed Fräulein Ivona to stop. She rolled the car to a halt next to a cluster of military vehicles. Clad in a tight white dress and jacket and high-heeled pumps, shoulder-length ash blond hair perfectly combed, and China red lips made up into a Cupid's bow, she stroked a languid hand over her hair, checking that every strand was in place before she turned off the engine.

"Anton," I said. "Wait in the car."

He gave me a look of utter disbelief before ordering his features. "All right."

I stopped, fingers on the door handle. He never gave in so readily. I studied him. He had no intention of staying put. The moment I was out of sight, he would follow. My thirteen-year-old daredevil would plunge straight into trouble and stoically bear the punishment later. As if reading my thoughts, he gave me a deceptively innocent smile. Freckles danced on the bridge of his nose.

I had to smile back.

I had brought him to Poland to enjoy time together while I researched a light feature piece about the Saint Martin's Day festival. Every November 11, Poznań held Europe's largest parade to celebrate the saint, known for his kindness to the poor. 1938's event promised to be grand.

The assignment should have been fun, but I viewed it as punishment. I had been banished to this backwater from Switzerland because my recent anti-Nazi articles had resulted in a series of threatening letters, and my editor at Zürich's *Neue Zürcher Zeitung* did not want to risk anything happening to me. If I had been a man, he would not have cared.

But I was not, so I had resigned myself to enduring my sentence quietly until I read the newspapers this morning and discovered that Germany had arrested more than twelve thousand Polish Jews and deported them across the border. I could not let that pass unnoticed, so I had headed to Zbąszyń to see the refugees myself. The paper had no one nearer. My editor would grumble, but he would also be grateful.

At least I hoped that he would.

Anton rubbed two fingers down the clean stick he had whittled. He pursed his lips as if about to whistle a jaunty tune to prove how innocent his intentions were.

"Fine." He was safer where I could see him. "Come with me. Stay close."

He clambered out eagerly. "Will there be riding?"

He loved to ride. In Switzerland, the stables were his second home. This would be like no stable he had ever seen. Suddenly cold, I turned up the collar on my wool coat. "I think not."

I pulled my Leica out of my satchel and snapped shots of the stable and soldiers. Their silver buttons and the silver braid on their dark uniform collars gleamed in the weak autumn sun.

I turned my attention to the stout brick building. Its tall doors measured more than twice the height of the men. Thick, too, with sturdy hinges and wrought iron bands fastened on the outside of the wood. They could safely contain horses. Or people.

Behind me, the Fiat's door slammed. I winced at the sound, and as one, all the Polish soldiers in front of the stable swiveled in our direction. So much for doing a quick walk around unnoticed. I wished that I had procured a car without a driver.

I hung my camera around my neck and hefted my satchel's leather strap higher on my shoulder. We walked to the stable and the soldiers guarding it. The soldiers admired Fräulein Ivona as she sashayed up.

Perhaps she would choose to use her assets to our advantage.

"Dzień dobry!" she said brightly.

The soldiers answered enthusiastically and tipped their queer uniform caps to her. The caps were round where they fit the head, but the top was square and the corners extended out an extra centimeter, like a combination soldier's cap and professor's mortarboard.

I looked through the half-open door behind them. The stable teemed with people. Most had a suitcase or small bundle, but I saw no food. A few souls peered out, looking as confused as the soldiers in front.

I itched to take notes.

The autumn breeze carried the smell of horse manure and the unpleasant odor of human waste. Presumably, no one had had time to set up toilet facilities for those packed inside.

Next to me, Fräulein Ivona wrinkled her nose. "We can't go in there. It's full of vermin."

"It is full of human beings," I reminded her.

"It's a stable." She shuddered. "It's also full of rats."

"There are worse things than rats," I said.

A young boy wearing a thick overcoat two sizes too big waved from inside the dark building. I put his age at around four. Anton waved back and took a step toward him.

When a soldier blocked Anton's way, he stumbled back in surprise. In Switzerland, stables did not have armed guards. Yesterday, in Poland, they had not, either.

Touching the shoulder of Anton's brown coat, now almost too small for him, I said, "Wait."

I handed the soldier on the right my press credential. He turned the document over with puzzlement. A small-town soldier, he had probably never seen anything like it. It sported an official-looking Swiss seal that I hoped might sway him into letting us pass.

"I am authorized to go inside," I told him.

Fräulein Ivona raised one perfectly shaped eyebrow skeptically. I had no such authorization, of course, as she well knew.

"I don't know," he said in German. He handed the credentials to the soldier next to him, and they discussed my case in Polish.

If I did not get in, the view into the stable might be all I had to write about. I snapped pictures of people on the other side of the open door. Because of the lighting, the quality would be poor, but it would be better than nothing. The soldiers shifted uneasily, but did not stop me.

When I had finished, I turned impatiently, as if late for a most important appointment. "Well?" I used my most officious tone. "Will you give way or must I speak to your superior?"

I hated using that tone, but it was often effective on soldiers, a hint that perhaps I had authority somewhere.

The soldier handed me my papers. "A quick visit."

A look of surprised respect flashed in Fräulein Ivona's eyes.

Anton walked toward the stable with his shoulders back as if he expected a fight. I quickened my steps to catch up. Together we stepped across the threshold.

Fräulein Ivona lagged behind, exchanging flirtatious words with the soldiers before following.

The long rows of horse stalls had not been cleaned. I suspected from the smell that the animals had been turned out only minutes before they herded in the refugees. Horses and manure smelled fresh compared to the odor of unwashed bodies and human waste.

Fräulein Ivona wrinkled her nose again, Anton clamped his jaws together, and I breathed through my mouth. I paused, waiting for my eyes to adjust to the gloom.

So many people. When I tried to do a quick head count, I realized that too many people crowded into the small space for me to do more than guess. A few stood, but most sat dejectedly on the dirty wooden floor, mud-spattered long coats drawn close against the cold. The women wore torn stockings and proper hats; the men fashionable woolen coats and fedoras. These were city people. They had not expected to exchange their urban apartments for a Polish barn.

"The guards say we may stay inside the stable for a moment only." Fräulein Ivona shifted in her white pumps. Mud smudged the once immaculate heels. "Your press credentials worried them."

I photographed as fast as I could, hoping that the dim light would be enough. Pictures would show what had happened more convincingly than any words I could muster. No one took notice of me as I clicked away. The tall ceiling absorbed sounds, and the refugees spoke in hushed tones.

Anton kept close and quiet. I wished that I had insisted he stay in the car so that he would not see what had happened to these people.

But he lived in this world, and he was not keen on any attempt to protect him from it.

Yet I never would have brought him here had I known it was this bad.

I stopped in front of a woman sitting on the dirt floor, back propped against the edge of a stall. She cradled a baby inside her long black coat. I knelt next to her in the dirty straw.

"My name is Adelheid Zinsli." I used my best fake Swiss accent. "Do you speak German?"

"Of course I do." She sounded nettled, her accent pure Berlin. "I was born in Kreuzberg. In spite of what my passport says, I've never even been to Poland." She looked around the filthy stable and hugged her baby close. "I can't say I like it much."

"I am a reporter for a Swiss newspaper. The *Neue Zürcher Zeitung*. I want to tell your story."

She looked at me suspiciously, then shrugged. "What more have I to lose?"

"What is your name?"

"Ada Warski. This is my daughter, Esther Warksi. I don't imagine you much care, but my husband, Uriah Warski, is in Dachau for the newfound crime of being a Jewish man in Germany."

I pulled out my notebook and fountain pen. Anton knelt next to me, so close that his pant leg touched my dress. I wanted to send him away somewhere safe, but where would that be? "How long have you and Esther been traveling?"

"Three days. They took us from our apartment at night and arrested us. They gave me only a few minutes to put together a bag for the baby and a few more to pack up a lifetime of possessions." Frau Warski's voice shook with outrage. I wrote as quickly as I could. I did not want to forget a single detail.

"They took us to a train station under guard. Neighbors I'd known all my life stood in the streets, yelling 'Jews to Palestine!' although we were only going to Poland. The candy man who used to give me sweets when I was a girl was there, too. Yelling." She stared at the muddy floor. I thought of Berlin, my own home, having come to this and clenched the smooth shaft of my pen more tightly. I would tell this to the world.

"After that," she went on, "they made us stand for hours in the station. Many of the old fainted. Some people were lying down by the stairs, but we were too packed together to see much."

She rocked the baby. Anton watched with wide eyes. When I put my free hand on his shoulder, he let it rest there.

Fräulein Ivona seemed to cave in on herself as if she tried to make herself as little as possible. She wanted nothing to do with this place. I wondered why she did not simply leave.

"Trains came, and they ordered us in at gunpoint. More trains came behind ours. I can't speak for the others, but our car had two SS men. They stood guard, to keep us from escaping. As if we would jump off and run back into Germany." Frau Warski spit on the floor.

Anton started in surprise. In Switzerland, women did not spit—but then again, they did not have as much cause as Frau Warski did. "We ended up at the station at Neu Bentschen. What day is today?"

"Sunday, about noon," I said quietly.

She stroked the baby's soft black curls. "Saturday, then. They searched us and took all our money. They let us keep only ten Reichsmarks. They said, 'That's all you brought into Germany, and that's all you can take out.' My father came into Germany with much more than that, as I imagine most of us did. But we did not argue."

She looked up at me. "What will I do now? Ten Reichsmarks is enough for only a few meals. Here there isn't even food to spend it on."

Anton shifted closer to me.

"Did they bring you here in lorries?" I asked.

She sniffed. "No. When they'd taken all they could, they told us we had to march to the border on foot. Two kilometers, they said. Some people, the very old, couldn't walk, so—" She broke off and hugged her baby close. Its blanket looked pitifully thin in the cold stable.

"So, they beat them. I held Esther in one arm and my suitcase in the other, and I ran as if the Devil were at my heels." She shuddered.

"It was raining and very cold. I put Esther in my coat, but I worried that she would get sick."

I swallowed, not daring to make a sound.

"When we got to the border, someone fired guns. I don't know if it was Poles or Germans, although I don't suppose it would have mattered much if you'd been hit by one. A Polish bullet kills as well as a German one."

I scratched away at my notes. I would tell her story, but I wondered if it would help her, or the others here.

She took a deep breath before continuing, calmer now. "The Poles were surprised to see us here. I gave my papers to a Polish officer, and at first I thought that he would send us back toward the SS. I hear that some were marched back and forth through the rain. But not me. They let me through. Maybe because of Esther. They sent us here. We walked all the way in the rain." She shook her glossy dark hair, cut into a bob like my blond one. "I thought that the Third Reich would come and go and things would go back to the way they were before. Now I know they won't. Not ever."

"When did you last eat?" I did not see how such a small town could provide for this many refugees. Zbąszyń had only about five thousand inhabitants.

"Bread this morning. Nothing for the first two days." She brushed her fingers through the baby's curly hair again. "I'm glad Esther is still nursing. It has been difficult for the very young and the old."

Anton fished in his coat pocket and brought out a chocolate bar. He handed it to her.

"Thank you," she said, surprised.

"It's all I have," he said with a note of apology.

Shamed, I reached into my satchel and handed her the bread and salami that Fräulein Ivona had brought for our lunch.

"How many of you are there?" I asked.

She nibbled a corner of the chocolate. "I don't know. Thousands, I think. I heard that they arrested twelve thousand people. Some died on the journey. I don't know how many. The Polish government let some into the rest of the country, but I've heard there are about seven thousand of us trapped in Zbąszyń."

Dirty white pumps shifted in my peripheral vision. I glanced up at Fräulein Ivona. She looked as if she might be sick on the floor, either from the smell or from the enormity of the situation.

"Thank you," I said. "Your story will be heard."

"It will make no difference," Frau Warski said bitterly. "Since Évian, we have known that no one cares."

I had no ready answer. Months ago, the world had held an international conference in Évian, France, with the charter of addressing the burgeoning Jewish refugee problem. The only outcome had been a near consensus that no country wanted to take them in. The conference went so badly that the Nazis had been able to use it in their anti-Semitic propaganda.

"Please!" screeched a voice from across the stable.

A short woman dressed all in black called again. I looked at her more closely and drew in a quick breath. I knew her, and she knew my real identity, the one I struggled so hard to hide.

The one that could get me killed.

2

As I hurried to the woman's side, I hoped that she would be discreet. Her name was Miriam Keller, and although she was married to my longtime friend Paul, she did not much like me. I did not see him as I stepped through the crowd of refugees, but that was unsurprising. Only Polish Jews had been targeted so far, and Paul was German.

Her face shone pale in the stable's gloom. Although it was cold, beads of sweat stood out on her forehead. Like the last time I saw her, two years ago, she was pregnant. She lay curled on her side on the floor. Her stomach humped through her coat. She looked ready to deliver again.

A woman with blond hair tied back in a dark blue kerchief pillowed Miriam's sweaty head in her lap. Miriam's belly heaved. She was in labor. The poor woman might deliver her child on the filthy stable floor.

"Hello, Miriam." I knelt and took her hand. Even through my glove, it felt cold. "It's Adelheid."

She jabbered weakly in Polish. I wiped her forehead with my green scarf, a gift from my late brother. With her free hand she clutched a gold locket that hung around her neck. I had once worn it myself, but I had returned it to Paul after I decided not to marry him. He had kept it, then given it to the woman who became his wife. Where was he?

"Fräulein Ivona!" I called.

She came over. Her dazed expression told me that she had become overwhelmed by people and suffering.

I put my hand on her arm and squeezed. "Can you please translate?"

Her frightened blue eyes met mine. "I—"

"You can do this. Soon we will be back in Poznań. They will not." I gestured around the stable with my free hand. "We must glean what information we can so that their plight can be publicized, their suffering alleviated."

"I don't speak Polish," she said. "Beyond a few words."

She had made no claims of being a translator when she presented herself at my hotel that morning, claiming only to be a driver hired by the newspaper. I had assumed that whoever hired her had thought to ask if she could also translate.

A flood of urgent words poured out of Miriam.

"Miriam," I said. "In German?"

The woman with Miriam spoke in broken German with an accent more French than Polish. "She left Ruth. In a case. No, a cupboard. By the door. Ruth is good girl. Very strong."

"Who is Ruth? What cupboard?"

The woman spoke to Miriam, and Miriam gasped out a few syllables.

"Yes?" I asked when Miriam stopped talking.

"In Berlin," the woman said. "In the apartment. She says you know where it is."

"I do," I said.

Miriam's eyes fluttered closed. The metallic odor of blood spilled into the air.

"Is there a doctor or a midwife here?" I asked the woman.

"No," she said. "I asked."

Miriam spoke again, and the woman translated. "She says Ruth is her daughter. She's two."

My heart sped up. Unless someone had rescued her, a two-year-old girl had been stuck in a cupboard for three days. The poor child might be dead already. I swallowed. "Ask her where Paul is."

"Paul?" Fräulein Ivona asked. "That's a Christian name."

"He had a Christian father," I said.

Her companion did not bother to translate. "Gone. Many days."

I thought of Miriam, dragged off alone and pregnant, locking her daughter in a cupboard. It was too horrible to contemplate. Yet it was clearly true. She clutched her companion and spoke urgently.

"Get Ruth. Promise."

Miriam's bloodshot eyes bored into mine. *"Proszę!"* she pleaded.

"Please," the woman translated.

"Tell her I cannot go back." Going to Berlin was out of the question. The Gestapo had a file on me. If they caught me, they would kill me. Anton, too. But I wavered for a moment, wondering how I could abandon the little girl.

"Why can't you go back?" Fräulein Ivona asked.

"For reasons of my own."

The woman holding Miriam's head begged me with her eyes. "Promise anyway."

I stared into Miriam's frightened dark eyes and opened my mouth to lie. "I promise." I did not have to go back to Berlin to find Ruth. I still had friends there who could bring her to safety.

Miriam's body relaxed, and she gave me a huge smile of relief. I was probably her first hope that her daughter might be saved.

What had happened to Paul? She seemed to expect no help from him. Was he dead, or in prison or a concentration camp? Or was he somehow alive and free?

The woman holding Miriam's hand bowed her head in a quick thank-you.

Fräulein Ivona turned away quickly.

Behind me I heard shouting, first in Polish, then German. "All members of the press must leave!"

I was the only member of the press in the stable. I started to stand, but Miriam grasped my hand.

"Stay," the woman translated. "Not safe here for her. For the baby."

"I will fetch a doctor," I said. "From town."

The woman gestured around. "She does not want the baby to be born in a stall. Like an animal."

"I will try," I said.

A hard hand settled on my shoulder. I looked into the face of a stolid Polish officer.

"This woman needs medical help." I shook off his hand and stood. "She is having a baby. Could you send her to the local doctor?"

He shrugged. "She has no valid passport, so she can't leave the stable. I can put her on a list for medical care, but it may be long in coming. What's her number?"

"I do not know her number. But she is right here." I pointed to Miriam. "She is a person, not a number. If she does not get medical care soon, she might die. And her baby with her. Will those numbers matter then?"

He shook his head.

I knelt next to Miriam again. "I need your number."

I hated to help them to reduce her and the others to numbers instead of names, like prisoners. But there was no other way Miriam might get medical care. "Did someone give you—?"

Miriam held up her hand. On the back, someone had written a number in black ink. I copied it into a page of my journal. "I will get you a doctor. Don't worry."

The woman next to her translated my words. Miriam's eyes widened in fear. She whispered a few words.

"Soon," she said. "She says come back soon."

I copied the number onto a second page and then tore it out and handed it to the soldier. "Her condition is serious," I told him. "The baby could come at any moment."

He took the number from me, then hooked his thumbs in his wide leather belt.

"She will have to wait," Fräulein Ivona said, "like the other Jews."

"People," I said, "like the other people."

Two more soldiers arrived.

I turned to the soldiers. "Please put her on your list for medical care. A mother and a baby might die right here in the stable. Surely, as Christians—"

The new soldiers seized me by the elbows and started dragging me out. I struggled to pull free. "I will not leave her."

"Don't," Fräulein Ivona said. "They will arrest you. You can do her no good in jail. And what becomes of your boy?"

Anton looked from me to the soldiers, ready to fight.

The soldier on my left said, "Listen to your sister."

I looked at him, surprised. Fräulein Ivona as my sister? We did look strikingly alike, slight and blond with Aryan blue eyes. She was around the same age my brother, Ernst, would have been, had he lived. She could have been my sister.

She rested her white gloved hand on my shoulder. "Do listen to your sister. You cannot win this, but you can lose."

I let the soldiers lead me outside. I would find a doctor in town and bring him here to argue for Miriam's release. Perhaps they would listen to him. At the very least, he could help to deliver the baby.

We returned to the hired Fiat. Fräulein Ivona had not given up her bread to the refugees. With a dramatic sigh, she broke it into three pieces and shared them around. I had no appetite, but I ate a few bites of my portion anyway, so that Anton would eat his.

Then we drove through the village. At the inn, they directed me to a doctor's office nearby. The doctor's wife, Mrs. Volonoski, listened to my entreaty, round face more grave with each word.

"Anka!" she called.

A young girl of no more than ten rushed in. Honey blond braids bounced against her shoulders. Mrs. Volonoski rapped out quick instructions in Polish, and Anka sprinted down the hall and out the front door.

Mrs. Volonoski led us to an empty waiting room full of solid Polish furniture, walls painted forest green above dark oak wainscoting. A fire crackled in the fireplace.

"Where are the other patients?" I asked.

"I sent them away," Mrs. Volonoski said. "He will not be back here today, not with so many refugees to treat. Probably without pay, too. You sit now."

We each took a straight-backed spindle chair. Mrs. Volonoski said something in Polish to Fräulein Ivona and disappeared. She returned a moment later with three cups of strong black tea.

A knock sounded at the door.

"All day!" She wiped her long fingers on her striped dress. "Excuse me."

She trotted down the hall to answer the door to a blond girl carrying a baby bundled up against the cold.

Anton wrapped himself in his coat and curled up in his chair. I wondered if he, too, revisited the morning's events. His eyes closed, and I hoped that he slept.

I wished that I had left him in Switzerland. He would not soon forget today. But I had expected only to write an easy feature. I had not known that Poland was too close to the Nazis now.

Fräulein Ivona looked at Anton, then to me. "Do you know the woman in the stable well?"

"I met her once before, but I do not know her well," I said.

"Then why did she expect you to help her?" Her carefully outlined lips made a moue of surprise.

"She had no alternative." I stared out the window at a pair of chickens scratching in the brown grass of the front yard. "And I will help her, if I can. A child's life is at stake."

"You can't save them." She drew out a silver lipstick tube. "There are too many."

"I can save this one," I said.

"I thought you said you could not go back to Berlin." She applied her lipstick in two sure strokes.

"I know people in Berlin," I said. "I have written stories from there." The articles had been published in the paper, so I had no reason to deny it.

"Then why not go back yourself? Are you wanted by the Gestapo? Is that why you cannot go back?" Her question held too much curiosity.

I forced out a laugh. "Nothing so complicated as that. The newspaper has paid me to be here. If I leave, I could lose my job."

"Good that you are not wanted," she said. "The Gestapo are most persistent."

"Are you familiar with the Gestapo, then?" I glanced through the window at the yard. Chickens pecked in a desultory way at the dust, searching without much hope.

"No more than anyone else," she said. "I have heard stories."

"I, too, have heard stories." I left it at that.

"The man I am seeing? I think he worked for the Gestapo once, although he's never said."

"I imagine he would not." And I had no intention of telling her anything either.

"He is a curious type." She drew off her white gloves and tucked them in her pocket. "He speaks little of his past, even when drunk. I think he has dark secrets he drinks to contain."

"Drinking seems a poor way to keep secrets." I sensed that she spoke from nervousness. After what we had seen, she probably did not trust herself to be alone with her thoughts. I sympathized and tried to concentrate on what she said, but my thoughts strayed back to Miriam. She was so young, not much older than Fräulein Ivona.

Where was Paul? The Paul I remembered would never have abandoned his pregnant wife and child. But he had changed since the Nazis came to power and robbed him of his citizenship, his livelihood, and his freedom. When last we met, we had fought. He had accused me of being in league with the Nazis and refused to help me to investigate the death of a close friend. I no longer knew what he was capable of. Tellingly, Miriam herself did not seem to expect him to return to rescue their daughter.

Was she still alive to be rescued? Did she still have a mother? I looked out the door and down the empty road. No sign of Anka.

Fräulein Ivona moved her chair close to the fire and picked up the heavy poker. The firelight shone on thick red scars that ran up the back of her hand.

Anton sat up. "How did you hurt your hand?"

An impertinent question. I opened my mouth to scold him, but she answered before I spoke.

"My father—" She shook her head. "A long story."

I gave Anton a quelling look, and, chastened, he sat back.

"Do you like your father?" she asked him.

Anton nodded uncertainly. It was a complicated question, as we did not know who his father was.

"Mine died a few years ago." She rubbed the scars on the back of her hand. "And I miss him every day."

"I am sorry to hear of such a loss for you." The words sounded stiff, but I meant them.

She stared into the flames for a long time before answering. "I failed him too often, because I was weak, like my mother. Like many mothers."

My mind strayed to Ruth, trapped in a dark cupboard, Miriam terrified in the stable, and all I had been through with Anton. Motherhood was not for the weak.

"Some mothers are strong." Anton glanced at me meaningfully.

"Thank you, Anton." I smiled at him.

"Some mothers get up to all sorts of mischief." She shot me a furtive glance before returning her gaze to the shifting flames.

What mischief had her mother gotten up to?

We all watched the fire. My thoughts returned to Miriam and her daughter. As soon as I brought Miriam a doctor, I would call Bella Fromm in Berlin. A Jewish aristocrat, she had strong connections within the diplomatic community and had opted to stay and help others safely out of Germany. If she had remained in Berlin, I could trust her to check the cupboard and help the little girl. She also had worked with Paul and had met Miriam. Things had become so much worse in Germany in the past months that perhaps she, too, had left. For her sake, I hoped so.

If Bella was gone, I could call a Jewish physician friend. She would look for Ruth if she could. If both had managed to flee, however, I could think of no one else to send. My contacts in Berlin had not fared well under the Nazis.

"It is our fathers who shape us." Fräulein Ivona poked a burning log so hard, it split. The log atop it rolled off the andiron and into the back of the fireplace.

Anton blurted, "Not always. Sometimes—"

Anka burst into the room. She jabbered breathlessly, in Polish. Her mother hurried in behind her.

"She says that her father is at the old flour mill. He is helping people there," Frau Volonoski said.

I stood. "Where?"

She gave me careful directions. It was not close.

"Thank you!" I sprinted to the car, Fräulein Ivona and Anton close behind. Chickens in the yard fled from us.

"I am no good at directions," Fräulein Ivona said.

"May I drive?" I hoped that she would allow me, as she was a slow driver. All in all, she had been a terrible hire. I wondered how she made a living at it, but I supposed that her male passengers might overlook a great deal.

She seemed relieved as she handed me the keys. "Please."

I pulled out onto the rutted road.

3

Fräulein Ivona stripped off her gloves and lit a cigarette. She watched the flame burn down almost to her fingers before she blew it out. Then she took a deep drag. "Why do you take the boy on these excursions instead of leaving him with his father?"

I wrestled the car around a pothole before answering. "I did not know this trip would have excursions of this nature. And I cannot leave him with his father, because he is dead."

"I am sorry to hear that. I just assumed when I saw the wedding band that your husband was still alive." She sucked in another drag from her cigarette. "It must be difficult for you, a woman alone."

"Anton and I manage just fine." I floored it down a straight stretch of road.

"So there is no man since the father? No man now?"

"No."

She cocked her head to the side and said teasingly, "I cannot believe such a thing. You are a beautiful woman. You must have toyed with the hearts of many men."

"Toyed? No."

She tapped ash off her cigarette onto the floor of the car. I resisted the urge to chastise her. It was her car, after all. "I think you have more experience with the hearts of men than you admit."

"Have I?" I acted surprised, but perhaps she was correct. I'd had six opportunities to marry, which seemed extravagant when I thought about it. I ran through my suitors in my head. First, Walter. While still in my teens we were engaged, but he died in the Great War. My life would have been different had he lived.

Second, Paul. A few years after the War, he had asked me to marry him. I had declined. I had realized that I did not want marriage, but I was unsuited for lighthearted casual relationships with men. For years I avoided them.

My third and fourth proposals came from the same man. In 1931, and again in 1934, a powerful Nazi officer named Ernst Röhm had tried to force me to marry him to provide cover for his homosexual activities and claim Anton as his own. The adventure had brought Anton into my life and had helped me to solve my brother's murder. And both times we had eluded Röhm. I shuddered to think what would have happened otherwise.

Then, I had lived in Switzerland with a banker named Boris Krause, the man I probably should have married. A kind, stable man—with him I had enjoyed the happiest, most peaceful time of my life. Eventually he, too, asked for my hand in marriage, but only if I settled down as a proper wife and mother and gave up spying for the British against the Nazis. I had been tempted, but I refused his offer, too. Ironically, my career as a courier came quickly to an end. By then he had moved on to someone else, and I thought I had as well.

My sixth and final chance came by an accidental marriage on paper to a former SS officer named Lars Lang. He had been my contact when I worked against the Nazis. Together we had smuggled many secret documents to the British. We had been listed as married on a set of false paperwork created to help us escape Germany. Still, the feelings we had for each other were not false. I had been willing to turn that piece of paper into a real marriage, but he vanished on a trip to Russia two years ago. I assumed that he was dead, but I still wore his ring.

Fräulein Ivona turned and blew out a lungful of smoke. I coughed.

"Apologies," she said without looking contrite. "So, you have no man?"

I suspected she wanted to talk about her own man. She had alluded to him several times on the way to Zbąszyń. I decided to humor her before she suffocated me in her smoke. "Have you?"

"I do." She flapped her hand in the air as if that would chase the smoke out of the car. "But I am not certain if he is a good man or a bad one. How does one tell?"

"It is rarely that simple," I said.

"But surely you know about men. You were married, after all."

"Being married did not help to understand men better."

Fräulein Ivona flicked her cigarette out the window. "Even if he has done bad things, I think mine is a good man. I think he might have been led astray at times. Anyone can be led astray, can't they?"

"Perhaps." I braked to avoid a gray goose waddling across the road. "Although I do believe that we are responsible for our own actions. And that someone who has been led astray once may be led astray again."

The goose honked angrily as I eased past it.

Fräulein Ivona drew another cigarette out of a metal case. This time, she offered me one. I shook my head. "In spite of that, he's a good man."

"Indeed?"

"He is kind, handsome . . ." Ivona ticked points off on her fingers. Lars used to do that. I swallowed. I had not expected that I would still miss him as much as I did. Two years was not as long as it seemed. She prattled on. "He is reliable. And he is a very excellent lover."

Women had not spoken so frankly about men in my day. "How fortunate for you."

She nodded and unfolded a fifth finger. "That counts double."

I laughed.

"But," she announced. "He is not really mine. He is married to someone else. And yesterday . . . yesterday I saw him look at another woman, and I knew that he loved her, not me."

I pitied her, with her good man who was married to someone else and starting up a third dalliance. "A complicated situation."

She talked as if I had not spoken. "Soon—" She made a sound like *ffft*. "—he will be on to the next girl."

"He will?" She would probably be better off if he did move on.

She lit the second cigarette before answering. Again, she watched the flame creep close to her fingers before blowing it out or speaking. "He never stays with a girl longer than a month. He told me at the beginning that we had only a month."

I looked over at her, finally curious. "He gave you a deadline? Why did you choose him?"

"Because he is such an excellent lover, of course." She raised her arched eyebrows as if surprised that I could ask such a foolish question. "He is kind, too. After my mother died, I wanted that."

I turned a quick left at the large gray boulder, as Frau Volonoski had directed. I wished for street signs and hoped that this was the correct boulder. "When did your mother die?"

"A little more than a month ago now. Her heart gave out." She stared at the Fiat's dusty red hood. "The nuns were very kind to us through the end."

"I am sorry to hear of your recent loss. My mother has been dead many years, but I still think of her." Although I did not miss her.

"She had been ill for a long time, so it was for the best." Ivona leaned away from me. "Perhaps I shall be the one he settles on."

"If he is married, it seems that he has already settled on someone else." I kept my voice as gentle as I could. The girl was not so tough as her words.

"If he truly loved her," she said. "He would be with her, not dallying with others."

I did not want to second-guess the motivations of her philandering lover, but he sounded like trouble.

"You really have no man in your life?" she asked, as if surprised that a woman could exist in such a state.

"No." Since Lars's disappearance, I'd had no interest in dating men, and at thirty-nine, I had passed the age where they were interested in dating me. I had managed most of my life without them. I now hoped only to stay safely away from emotional attachments, besides Anton.

She clucked her tongue. "Why not?"

"Broken heart," I said lightly, although it was true.

"I think my man is broken. More than just his heart, but that, too. Still, I think it can be fixed." She took a long drag of her cigarette. "Don't you?"

"People are not clocks," I said. "It is difficult enough to know what is in someone else's heart, let alone fix it. But, as I said before, I am no expert."

"Didn't you find happiness, at least once?"

She sounded so sad that I hurried to answer her. "I did. More than once."

In the distance, the chimney of the flour mill loomed against a forbidding gray sky. The building was much bigger than I had expected, at least four stories tall. Like the stable, it was made of brick.

"It looks like a castle!" Anton said from the backseat.

"It does at that," I said. "With those crenellations along the roof."

"One thing I do know," I returned to my conversation with Fräulein Ivona, "there is much more to life than men and romantic love. It is part of the whole, of course. But it is not everything. Children, friends, work. I build my life on those things, too."

"It sounds like you have quit trying!" she said. "Did the man who broke your heart drive you away from love?"

"A man did not break my heart." I thought back to watching Lars board the train to Russia, fearing even then that he might not return. "Life did. But remember, life holds more than just men. Much more."

She pursed her lips and shook her head, clearly disbelieving my words.

I braked to a hasty stop in front of the mill. A cloud of dust roiled around us as we hurried to the front door.

As at the stable, soldiers surrounded the building. These could not be bullied. I showed them my press credentials. I told them again and again about Miriam and the baby, but they remained stony-faced.

Finally, Anton took matters into his own hands and darted past the soldiers and into the flour mill. I lunged toward him, but soldiers caught my arms.

"Anton!" I rounded on the soldier. "Anton Zinsli is a Swiss citizen, and if he comes to harm, there will be severe consequences."

A soldier broke off from the group and went into the mill after him. The others still held me fast.

"If I let you go, miss, can you behave yourself, as a sane adult?" The oldest soldier asked. He was about my own age.

"I will." I had spoken with precious few sane adults all day. Perhaps I could serve as a role model.

An eternity later, Anton reappeared at the door, accompanied by the soldier and a tall dark-haired man carrying a black bag. He had fetched the doctor.

I put my hand on Anton's shoulder. "You should not have gone in there."

He looked levelly into my eyes. "However you punish me, it will be worth it if the woman on the stable floor lives."

I caught him in a rough hug. "We shall discuss this later. But think for a moment. What if you could not have come back out? Watch your step, or you will not be able to help yourself or others."

The doctor held out his hand. "I believe I have another patient?" he said in German. "Doktor Volonoski."

I shook his hand. He had a firm, relaxed grip. "Frau Adelheid Zinsli. Thank you for coming out."

I opened the Fiat's passenger door for him. Fräulein Ivona climbed into the backseat, leaving me in the front seat with the doctor. Anton rode on the running board, arm looped over my window.

I drove more cautiously back toward the stable, mindful that Anton would pitch into the road if I was not careful. "There is a woman about to give birth in the stable. Could you get her released to a hospital?"

"Depends," he said. "Was the labor progressing normally, or was she in distress?"

"She was in distress." I lied to convince him to move Miriam elsewhere. Even if she could deliver her baby safely in the stable, that did not mean she should have to. "She is about twenty-eight years old. It is her second child. She was in full labor."

"Have you expertise in these matters?" the doctor asked.

"I was a nurse," I said. "During the War."

He gave me a tired smile. "Wonderful. Can you assist?"

Help to deliver a baby? I had worked with wounded soldiers, not expectant mothers. But there was no one else, so I must. "Of course."

When we arrived, I left Anton in the car. "Do not leave," I said. "Fräulein Ivona, please stay with him. Keep Anton in sight every second."

"Acting as a nanny was not in the terms of my hire," she said primly.

I gave her a handful of tattered Polish zlotys. She counted them, folded them, and tucked them into her pocket before answering. "Very well."

The doctor and I strode to the stable door.

"How bad is it?" I asked him. "In the mill."

"Very bad," he said. "Old and young were dragged from their homes and made to stand for days on platforms and in trains with no food and little water. Running through the forest at the end was too much for many of them. And the Germans set dogs on some and beat others. I studied medicine in Dresden, and I cannot believe what has happened to the German people." He shook his head sadly. "I've been treating heart attacks and strokes, although there's little enough I can do without medication."

"How can I help?" I asked.

"Could you be my nurse? Just for this afternoon? I believe that the Jewish council in Warsaw is sending doctors and food tomorrow."

"I can."

When we reached the soldiers, Doktor Volonoski started a weary-sounding speech. The young soldier's face remained impassive. He already acted tougher than he had that morning, getting used to his new role.

"Please," I said in Polish. *"Proszę."*

An older soldier with muddy knees came out of the stable. I turned to him, ready to start again. Bureaucratic rules would not be enough to keep us from Miriam.

He muttered a few words in an undertone to the young one. The young soldier's face softened when he spoke to the doctor, and they all took their hats off.

I knew what he would say before he spoke. "I am very sorry, miss. Your friend did not survive the labor."

My knees threatened to give way. "And the baby?"

He asked the soldier, and the soldier mumbled his answer to the ground, ashamed and sad. I understood his answer before the doctor translated it. "The baby was lost, too."

4

The older soldier pressed a set of cold keys and a heavy locket into my palm. "She said: For Ruth."

I dropped the keys into my pocket, certain that they belonged to Miriam's Berlin apartment. The locket rested in my palm, a design of leaves surrounding a sun etched in its surface. It shone gold in the watery sunlight. I had not held it for years. The last woman to wear it had died alone in a stable. I hung the thin chain around my neck.

"I want to see her." The reporter in me needed to verify it.

The soldier looked uneasy.

"Please," I said.

"I will go with her," the doctor said. "I will keep her out of trouble."

He would not be the first one who was wrong about that.

"Quick," the soldier answered.

Doktor Volonoski and I followed the soldier into the fetid barn. The soldier led us to a pregnant body stretched in a corner. Someone had removed Miriam's threadbare black coat and placed it over her face. I lifted it. Her eyes were closed, her unruly hair plastered to her forehead. Damp strands formed ringlets around her temples.

Her still, bluish face told me what I would find, but I took off my glove and dropped my fingers to her neck. Her oily skin felt icy. No pulse. She must have died soon after I left the stable.

"I do not understand," I told the doctor. "When I left she was fine."

"I thought you said that she was in distress." He looked reassuringly at the soldier, as if to vouch that I would not make a scene.

"In distress, yes, but not near death."

"I am sorry. But things can change quickly during a labor." He gestured around the filthy barn. "Especially in conditions like this."

I drew the coat over her face and opened the locket. It contained a picture of a two-year-old girl. She looked like neither Paul nor Miriam. A dark ribbon tied back her long blond hair. She glanced sideways at the photographer, eyes alight with mischief. She looked a little like me. Indeed, if things had worked out differently with Paul, perhaps she would have been mine.

The edge of the little girl's picture curled forward. I gently pried it out with my fingernail. Underneath was a picture of a blond man who looked very much like Ruth. Was it Miriam's brother? Or was it Ruth's father? If so, it might explain why Paul had not followed his wife into Poland.

I smoothed Ruth's picture on top of the man's. Then I closed the locket and clasped it between my palms. Let it keep its secrets, for now.

The doctor helped me to my feet.

"Thank you." I stared at Miriam's inert body. She had been so young, and the baby had never had a chance to live. Two more innocents claimed by the Nazis. I sighed.

The doctor's worried gray eyes looked into mine. "I feel sorrow for your loss."

I wiped the back of my hand across my eyes. "As do I."

I would find out more about her last minutes. I glanced around the stable, searching for the blond woman who had served as her translator. She was nowhere in sight.

"Excuse me," I said to the old woman sitting closest to Miriam's body. "Where is the woman who was with her?"

She, too, looked around the stable. "Gone."

"Where did she go?"

"Out." She pointed toward the half-open front door.

I had thought no refugees were allowed through there.

"You can stay here no longer." The soldier took my arm and began steering me toward the door, his grip just short of painful.

"Wait!" I called back to the old woman. "What's your name?"

She put her finger to her lips and turned away.

The soldier and Doktor Volonoski ushered me out of the stable. I would help Doktor Volonoski with the refugees in the mill today, but tomorrow I would come back here and find out what had happened to Miriam's translator.

Fräulein Ivona and Anton stood where I had left them. He had both eyes fixed on the door, waiting for me. She looked everywhere but at the stable. She clearly wanted to be far away. I did not blame her. No one else wanted to be here either.

"Is she all right?" Anton asked.

I wavered. I hated to leave him with this kind of news alone.

"I have to help the others, in the flour mill." I inclined my head toward the doctor.

Fräulein Ivona fussed with her fashionable jacket. She knew the answer, too. "Are you sure that you shouldn't get some lunch and come back?"

I shook my head. "No time for that. I can eat later."

She tilted her head to one side. "You care about them so, though they are strangers? And Jews?"

"They are human beings, some injured and sick. If I can help them, I must."

"So their pain is more important to you than your hunger?" It appeared as if this thought had not occurred to her before.

"I will survive, Fräulein Ivona." I put my hand on her arm. "They might not be so fortunate."

"Let me get you food before you go," she said.

"If you could have something ready for me later," I said, "that would be a tremendous help."

I dropped them at the sole hotel. I handed Anton my satchel. "Take good care of this for me."

He slung the strap across his body. "When will you be back?"

"When the doctor says we are finished."

"I will have her back for dinner, young man," Doktor Volonoski said.

I turned to Fräulein Ivona. "Please stay with him."

She tugged her wrinkled jacket into position. "Of course, Frau Zinsli."

"I do not want him left alone."

"How long, exactly?" Her china doll blue eyes narrowed.

"Until I return," I said. "And there will be a sizable bonus for you then."

She ran her hand over her sleek hair. "Very well."

I drove Doktor Volonoski back to the flour mill, where most of the wounded and ill had been brought. I set arms broken by truncheons, bandaged heads grazed by thrown rocks, and helped make those who had suffered strokes and heart attacks comfortable.

Doktor Volonoski found doctors and nurses among the refugees and put them to work, too. I soon supervised three nurses, glad that someone would remain with the refugees after we left.

Even with help, by the time we finished, we could barely stand. Despair weighed heavier than the work. It felt so in the Great War when I worked in triage, consigning some patients to death so that others might live. Here, who knew what awaited the living. I feared that their troubles had only begun.

The weak autumn sun had already dropped below the horizon by the time we finished. Frigid air stung my cheeks when we stepped outside. I thought of Frau Warski making a dinner of our sandwiches. The stable would be a cold place for her and baby Esther to spend tonight.

"I believe that my driver procured us rooms at the inn near your house." My breath formed clouds in the night air. "Could I offer you a lift home, Doktor Volonoski?"

"That would be most kind."

"It would be my privilege." He had worked hard and ceaselessly for hours without a trace of anti-Semitism. He might be more accustomed to working with the sick than I, but it had worn on him, too.

He opened my car door. I climbed in and pulled on my cold leather gloves.

He sat in the other side and closed his door with a soft thump. "You were very good in there. You should have stayed with nursing."

"I could not stand watching people die," I said.

He stared out across the hood at the darkened windows of the mill. "It's not as it was in the war. Usually, the patients don't die. If you're good at your job."

I mustered a smile. "You are good at your job."

"Thank you," he said. "I don't imagine you expected to spend your day like this either."

"I had this idea I would research croissants with poppy paste for an article on Saint Martin's Day."

We both sighed.

I started the car and turned on the headlights.

"I can be good at my job only when it is possible," he said. "I fear I have months of an impossible job ahead of me."

"How long do you think the refugees will be stranded in Zbąszyń?" I pulled away from the flour mill and drove down the rutted dirt track toward town.

He stared at the dashboard for a long time before speaking. "Poland does not want them. Germany does not want them. I think it might take months to sort out."

Months. Thousands of people living through the end of winter outside or in stables and a flour mill.

We drove in silence.

"It's there." He pointed to a modest wooden house surrounded by a wall and an arched entryway that probably supported roses in summer. I had left that house hours before, but it felt like weeks.

"Thank you, Frau Zinsli," he said. "If your companion could not find rooms for you and your son, my wife can make up a room. You are in no condition to drive to Poznań tonight."

"Thank you, Doktor Volonoski," I said, touched. "If I do not have a warm bed waiting for me, my son and I shall knock on your door."

I drove the few houses to the inn and turned off the ignition, but I did not get out. I rested my forehead on the hard steering wheel, trying not to remember the day's events. Miriam. The baby. The wounded refugees. And Ruth. Cold cut through my coat. I shivered.

I raised my head and climbed out. Exhaustion dragged down my limbs, but I had to call in the refugees' story to my paper and also telephone Bella. Only then could I sleep.

I stumbled into the smoky inn, grateful for its warmth. I rubbed my eyes with the back of my wrist. At the front desk the thin clerk recognized me immediately.

"Your sister got you a room. She and the boy wait in the dining room." He gestured toward the left, then pulled his arm back to adjust its too-short sleeve.

"Thank you," I said. "Is there a telephone? I must make a few calls. Private ones."

He pointed to a wooden booth in the corner of the lobby. I stumbled over, suddenly light-headed. I realized that I had eaten only bites of bread since I left the hotel in Poznań.

The telephone was an old-fashioned wooden box hanging from the wall. I had not seen one like it in years. It took a few moments for the Polish operator to understand me. Eventually she did, and the exchange rang through to Bella's number. An unfamiliar male voice answered Bella's phone. "Fromm."

"Frau Fromm, please," I said,

"May I ask who is calling?" The twinge of Berlin accent gave me pause. Bella's servants tended to speak perfect High German.

"Frau Petra Weill." I used a variation on my pseudonym from my days as a reporter for the *Berliner Zeitung* before I had fled in 1931. Bella would recognize it, and there would be no record of that name that the Gestapo might trace, as Petra Weill was never a real person.

"Frau Fromm is engaged." The butler's deep voice was impassive. "Where may she reach you?"

I paused. I hated to give the name of my Polish hotel, but surely the Gestapo's reach did not extend all the way to Poland? And if it did, Petra Weill was not wanted by anyone. Even if the name was noted in my Gestapo files, it seemed unlikely that it would be linked to Bella or that someone would bother to look it up. Bella had literally hundreds of troublemaking friends. She and I had spent little time together where we might be observed. Still, there was a risk.

"Frau Weill?" His voice rumbled patiently.

I had to leave a message. If Ruth had not been rescued by Paul or by neighbors, she had been locked in a cupboard for three days. Every minute mattered. I told him the inn's name and telephone number and hung up. She would know that my message was urgent. We had not spoken in over two years. She knew I would not telephone unless I needed to.

Next, I called a Jewish physician friend in Berlin, Frau Doktor Spiegel, but she did not answer either. Perhaps she had fled Germany, or perhaps she simply attended a patient.

The reedy desk clerk seemed occupied paging through a thick green ledger, but his attention looked staged. I wondered if I was being paranoid. I was in Poland, after all, not Germany.

Finally, I called the newspaper in Switzerland. Lucien Marceau answered. Smart, fast, and liberal, he would not censor my words, but he would not be pleased that I was on the scene reporting this story. He fancied himself the top political correspondent at the *Neue Zürcher Zeitung* and had been cool toward me for the past month, ever since my first political piece came out.

I quickly explained the situation. I told him what I had learned of the deportations, Ada and Esther Warski, and the wounded patients I had treated. I finished with Miriam, dying with her unborn child inside her in the icy stable.

"Good god," he said. "Come home."

"I intend to stay here a few more days to cover the story."

"Of course you do." Disapproval permeated his words.

"Tell Herr Knecht that he will have to wait for his Saint Martin's coverage."

"He will rail about it," he said. "But he will be happy that you have such a solid story. And perhaps a trifle worried about you. Perhaps he should assign someone more experienced."

By which he meant himself. "I am no fashion reporter. I shall be fine."

He snorted. "How could anyone doubt that you might have troubles going up against the Polish army?"

"It is not the entire army," I said. "Just a few soldiers."

"Oh, god," he groaned. "Herr Knecht will be unbearable if something happens to you."

"More so than usual? Impossible!"

"He sent you to Poland to write about saints and cakes, not refugees and Nazis," he snapped.

"He sent me here to find news," I retorted. "And I found some."

"The police called today about your last letter." His words dripped vile glee. He enjoyed the amount of trouble the letters had caused.

I groaned. Ever since a secretary at the paper had accidentally opened the first threatening letter to me a month before, Herr Knecht had turned into an overprotective mother bear. "He sent the letters to the police?"

"Of course he did." I pictured him shaking his finger at the telephone, as he would a naughty child. "The police recovered fingerprints. You are to stop by the station to give yours up for comparison."

That was a disaster. If the Swiss ever shared fingerprint cards with the Germans, they might discover that I was wanted for kidnapping Anton and, perhaps, in connection with the murder of four Gestapo men in 1936. "I certainly shall not. He never sends the letters that the men receive to the police. Some of theirs are as bad as mine."

"They're not as bad as yours." He huffed with indignation. "Even if they were, you are not a man. Herr Knecht does not want responsibility for a woman being injured because of his paper. This brings me back to my original suggestion: Come home."

"Tell Herr Knecht—"

"I imagine you're tired," he said. "So I shall stop fighting Herr Knecht's battles for him and ring off."

He disconnected so quickly, I had no time to reply. Let him be angry. I did not have time to have it out with him anyway. My stomach rumbled, and my eyes ached. Tomorrow would be another long day.

I asked the clerk to be alert for messages for Petra Weill, explaining it as newspaper business, and asking to be notified immediately if a call came, to wake me even in the middle of the night. Hopefully Bella would call soon.

I visited the washroom off the lobby. Icy water sputtered from the tap. I scrubbed my hands again and again with their hard soap, trying to scrape the blood of strangers from under my nails. My dress looked fairly clean, but mud, blood, and who knew what else spattered my coat. At least the coat's black color made it look clean.

I dried my hands on the rough towel, then smoothed them across my face. The bulb's harsh glare showed my exhaustion. Dark circles stood out against my pale skin, a tracery of red capillaries filled the whites of my eyes, and my hair hung limp. My brother's voice echoed in my mind: *I hope you had a good time to earn a face like that!* I smiled at the memory and hung up the towel. As usual, I had not earned my face by having too much of a good time.

5

I trudged to the dining room. It held four dark wooden tables and a bar with a handful of stools, most occupied. At one table a group of men played cards and smoked foul-smelling Polish cigarettes. Two tables were empty. Anton and Fräulein Ivona occupied the fourth.

Anton leaped to his feet when he saw me. He still wore the satchel with the strap across his narrow chest. "I waited to have dinner with you."

I embraced him and held him a second longer than usual. He was almost as tall as I. I reminded myself to lecture him for entering the flour mill without my permission, but after dinner.

Fräulein Ivona stood. "I will have them prepare a meal for both of you."

"I appreciate it," I said. "I have had nothing since lunch."

"Which you did not eat." She flounced across the room to the bar, skirt and jacket rumpled, but still shapely enough to draw the men's eyes from their card game. She stopped at the bar and began an animated conversation with a tall handsome man seated there. Was he her lover? He was attractive enough to cause many women to forget their better judgment.

I chose a chair with a view of the front desk so I would be ready if the call came. What if Bella did not call? Berlin lay only three hours away, but I dared not chance a trip. Still, Ruth was alone. As a mother, how could I leave a two-year-old child to die alone in a cupboard? As I had left her mother to die alone in a stable.

"Mother," Anton asked, and the tone of his voice told that it was a serious question. "Is Sweetie Pie dead?"

He never asked about his real mother. I was grateful for that, because she had been a drug-addicted prostitute. She abandoned him with me when my brother's death stopped him from delivering money for Anton's care. I tried to decide what to tell him and what to spare him. "Yes. She is."

"Are you certain?" He brushed his fingers through his tousled blond hair, and it stuck up crazily. I resisted the urge to stroke it back into place.

"I read the police report of her death, and also saw it verified by a different policeman." Lars had added it to the file he compiled on me. Thorough, he had researched Anton back to his birth.

I put a hand on his shoulder, but he shifted it off. "How did she die?"

She had been found dead in the public toilets at Wittenbergplatz subway station. I had to tell him the truth, but I would omit what details I could. "Of a drug overdose."

"Cocaine?"

He had been only six, but he knew. Shocked, I answered. "How do you remember that?"

"I wasn't a child," he said indignantly. "I remember a lot from those years."

He had been a child, indeed he still was one, but I did not contradict him. "I see."

"Will you rescue the little girl in the cupboard?" he asked. "As you rescued me?"

He, too, had spent time locked in a cupboard. That was where his mother put him while she transacted business with her clients, probably when he was as young as Ruth. I gazed into his serious blue eyes. "I will try. I called two friends in Berlin to see if they can find her."

"If they can't, what then?" He fidgeted with his latest carving, tapping what looked like large webbed feet.

"I hope they can. If not, I think there might be a Jewish orphanage I can call." Although how I could find them in Poland was an open question.

"If none of them will help her, will you go back to Berlin?" He leaned forward in the round wooden chair, clearly ready to leave right now.

I did not lie to him, but in this case I did not know the truth. "It would be complicated for me."

"Because of your trip during the Olympics?" He folded his arms.

How much did he know or guess of my actions there? More than I wanted him to. "Because of that, too."

"And because you took me away," he said.

"You are too smart for your own good."

He smiled, and I noticed how grown up his face had become. He had lost the softness of his early boyhood. His features were sharpening toward the face he would wear as a man. "So, why can't you go back?"

He never relented. He would make a fine journalist, or a prosecuting attorney.

"Because." I chose my words with care. "Near the end of my last Berlin trip, the Gestapo arrested me and a colleague. We managed to escape, but I might not be so lucky again."

I did not tell him that I had a clean passport, one that identified me as Hannah Schmidt. I had it made to escape Germany in 1936, but had not needed it. Since then I kept it sewn into the thin lining of my satchel. If I had not been with Anton, I would already have cut it out and risked a quick trip into Berlin to find Ruth myself.

One of the men won the card game, to a loud roar from the others. He smiled bashfully, clearly unused to winning. Anton smiled back at him before firing another question at me. "Do the Gestapo have a file on me?"

"Yes." I gave him a stern glance. "You could not get in and out safely, if that is what you are thinking."

His surprised expression told me he had been thinking exactly that. "But if they don't know who I am—"

"They know who you are," I said. As Anton Röhm, he was still a liability to the Nazi government. "And in any case, you cannot cross the border alone. You are only thirteen. They would never let you through." At least not without a sheaf of papers I had no intention of filling out.

He set his chin mutinously, a bad sign. Anton never stopped searching for wrongs to right.

Before I could marshal an argument, someone tapped my shoulder.

It would have to be a convincing argument. I turned to see who it was.

My breath caught in my throat.

It was Lars Lang.

His eyes looked dazed. Mine probably did, too. Anton's face swung from me to Lars.

I stared at Lars. Relief flooded me. He was alive. I wanted to throw myself in his arms. But doubt burnt away the relief. For two years I had mourned his death. Where had he been?

A new scar intersected his right eyebrow. His dark hair was longer than I had ever seen it, and a strand curled into his forehead. His face, always sharp featured, was thinner than I had ever seen it, almost gaunt. Seems he had not enjoyed the last two years much. Neither had I.

He clicked his heels and bowed, as he had so long ago in the police station at Alexanderplatz when we met for the first time. He stood erect, hands clasped behind him, like the military man he had once been. His posture reminded me of my father's. I went still inside.

"How do you do, Frau Zinsli?" I felt his wedding band when he shook my hand. Was it the one he put there on the day we pretended to marry, or from a more recent, and equally faithless, liaison?

I dropped his hand and sat straight in my chair, too shocked to speak.

He touched the back of the chair next to mine. "May I?"

I had many things I wished to say to him, to shout at him, but not in front of Anton. I stared, unable to think of a single appropriate word. Without waiting for my permission, he sat.

Would he try to explain his absence? How? I tried to imagine what could constitute an adequate explanation, but my mind came up with only one: He had lied to me in Berlin. He had never intended to rejoin me in Switzerland. It had been a trick to get me into his bed, and I had been completely taken in.

Anton gave me a worried look.

"Struck dumb?" Lars said. "I know how difficult that is to achieve."

I cleared my throat. "It is not every day I see a ghost."

"A ghost?"

I swallowed. "I thought you were dead."

"Did you?"

"Yes." I clenched my trembling hands in my lap. I would not let him see how upset I was. That, at least, I could spare myself.

Anton watched us as if we were the most entrancing film he had ever seen.

"Anton," I said. "Please wait for me at the bar. I will be along in a moment."

He hiked my satchel up on his shoulder and went. He knew better than to argue with that tone. He took a seat a few stools away from Fräulein Ivona's handsome man.

The bashful man at the other table paused in his game, probably sensing something amiss, but with a quick shrug he went back to his cards.

"What is your name these days?" I asked.

"Lars Lang," he said. "Same as ever."

So he was not using the false identity under which we were married. It was as if I never existed. "Do you still work for the SS?"

"Discharged," he said with a grimace. "Under a personal cloud but not, in case you are worried, a criminal one."

"How did you find me?"

"Your Swiss paper said that you would be going to Poznań to cover the festival."

Of course. A teaser for my upcoming story had appeared in the newspaper. Since he knew my pseudonym, finding me must not have been that difficult. My hotel in Poznań had probably directed him here. "Why did you find me? And why now?"

"I am glad to see that you are well." His tone was matter-of-fact as he dodged these two questions. "Are you glad to see me?"

"I thought you had betrayed me or died." The hours wasted mourning when I should have been angry instead. "I suppose, for your sake, I should be happy it was the former."

The smell of alcohol drifted across the table. I gauged his state—neither visibly drunk nor completely sober. Hopefully sober enough to avoid causing a scene. "I've missed you, Spatz."

His term of endearment cut. "Really?"

He pulled on the cuffs of his white shirt. "What brings you here?"

"The refugees," I said. "You?"

"It is the last stop on my delivery route before Berlin."

I looked into his dark eyes. I had much I wanted to discuss with him, but I was so angry that nothing came to mind. Then one thing did. Ruth. She might still be locked alone in a cupboard, and so far no one had returned my calls. "Could you run an errand for me in Berlin? Tonight?"

"For you," he said. "Anything."

I bit back a retort. Ruth had no time for my hurt feelings. I summarized the happenings in the stable and gave him Paul's address. I also told him that Miriam's death had made me uneasy, so he should be careful.

"I am always careful." His lips curved up into a hollow smile. "I can leave immediately, once we have solved the question of my fee."

The Lars I remembered had never been interested in money. But then again, perhaps that man had never existed outside of my memory.

"What is your fee for saving a child's life, Herr Lang?" My tone rang colder than the air outside.

"I'm certain that you and your banker can come up with something commensurate with my exertions." He cocked his head to the side, clearly expecting me to name a figure.

"I am afraid my pockets are not so deep as you seem to think. A reporter's salary is meager, but as you know, I have a few objects of value I could sell, if you were willing to wait for your payment." I still had some of my brother's jewelry, although with so many selling their possessions and fleeing Germany, that was worth less every day.

He rocked back in his seat. "The banker won't pay?"

"Why would he?" I had ended my relationship with Boris more than two years ago, before I had taken up with Lars. Boris continued to be a presence in Anton's life, but he was no longer a presence in mine.

I read surprise in Lars's eyes, something I had rarely seen there.

Fräulein Ivona walked into the dining room carrying two plates. She smiled at the man at the bar and set a plate in front of Anton. Then she came to our table and placed a thick white plate in front of me, looking smug.

She turned to Lars. "I see that you found my employer."

Lars's mouth dropped open.

"Fräulein Ivona." My words came out high and strained. "What is the meaning of this?"

She sat across from me and folded her hands in her lap like a schoolgirl. "I believe that you are acquainted with Herr Lang?"

"What is the meaning of this?" I repeated. No other useful words came to mind.

"I followed you," she said to Lars. "To the train station in Poznań yesterday."

That was the day that Anton and I had arrived.

Lars rubbed his forehead. "Why?"

"Because, my darling," she said. "I wanted to see where you were going."

Darling? I thought back to her conversation earlier in the day. Lars was the excellent lover with the one-month deadline. I had been mourning him for two years while he was sleeping his way across Poland. I pressed my dry lips together and watched him squirm.

"I saw how you looked at her." Disdain toward me was clear in her tone. Fair enough. I did not like her much right now, either. "And I realized that my month had ended early."

"I told you the very first night that I was not free," Lars said calmly.

Fräulein Ivona directed her ice blue eyes to me. "You're not the first. And you won't be the last."

"I am not in the race at all," I said. "Luckily."

"I spent the day with you, trying to see what he could possibly desire in you," Fräulein Ivona sneered. "But I saw nothing."

Lars cleared his throat.

"Good-bye." She stood and kissed him hard on the mouth. I looked toward Anton. He had stopped pretending to eat his soup with his spoon halfway to his mouth.

She strolled to the bar, where the handsome man handed her a glass. I longed for a shot of something myself. But I had a few things to resolve with Lars first. "Are you certain that she knows nothing incriminating about me?"

"I do not believe so." Face impassive, he watched her wrap her arms around the man at the bar. "I've never spoken of you to her, so I imagine that all she knows is that she saw me watching you at the train station and then whatever she has learned since you've been dragging her around all day."

I forced down a flash of rage. "Where the hell have you been for the last two years?"

"I'm sorry, Spatz. Things became rather complicated for me in Russia." He brushed a lock of black hair, too long in the front, out of his eyes and shifted on his chair.

"Somehow—" I gestured toward the bar. "—you manage to amuse yourself."

"I doubt that you have been idle yourself."

I had, in fact, been completely idle, but I had no intention of telling him that. I gritted my teeth. "Are you certain she poses no risk to me, or to Anton?"

"Yes." A muscle twitched under his eye, as it always did when he was angry. Let him be.

I took a deep breath. "How did you meet her?"

"In a bar. Late. I was drunk and she was beautiful. A familiar refrain."

Two men in dark coats entered the lobby, but I paid them little attention.

"And there was nothing odd in her wanting to take up with you?" She was much younger than he and very attractive. Surely that had made him suspicious. Suspicious was his natural state.

He smiled mechanically. "She wasn't the first, Spatz. I'm quite competent in bars."

I tried to ignore that. Apparently, that was none of my concern.

Lars leaned forward and reached for my hands. I pushed my chair back with a screech.

He sat back. "She's no risk to you. I checked her out shortly after I started sleeping with her. She's not involved in the Party and has no connections that are in any way suspicious."

"She strikes me as a very vulnerable young woman, Lars. You should not be toying with her affections." I thought of her mother's recent death and the eerie way she stared at the flames. She was not entirely stable.

"So, you two are friends?" he asked. "You wouldn't like her if you knew her. She's the most anti-Semitic woman I know, and my circle of Nazi acquaintances is quite wide, as you know."

The men rang the bell for the clerk. I realized with a start that under their dark coats they wore Gestapo uniforms. Gestapo in Poland? I stood to fetch Anton from the bar. We had to leave.

But the Gestapo officers already crossed the dining room, making a beeline for my table. Anton was now safer if I left him there. I sank back into my seat.

"Spatz?" Lars asked. "Why are you jumping up and down like a jack-in-the-box?"

A hand closed cruelly over my shoulder. I looked up into the lumpish face of a Gestapo officer. Another stood next to him, practically quivering with excitement. My stomach clenched.

"I beg your pardon." I tried to pry his massive fingers off, but he would not let go. My shoulder resembled a child's in his huge paw.

"I believe that you are Hannah Vogel?" he asked in a gravelly voice.

I tried to think. I had crossed the Polish border as Adelheid Zinsli. I had registered at the hotel as Adelheid Zinsli. The only living people in Poland who knew my real identity were Anton and Lars. Anton, I trusted. I wanted to blame this on Fräulein Ivona, but did not see how she could have known, unless Lars had told her. Had Lars turned me in?

"I am afraid that you are mistaken," I said. "My name is Adelheid Zinsli. I am a reporter for the *Neue Zürcher Zeitung*."

He jerked me to my feet as easily as if I were made of straw. Physical resistance was impossible.

My eyes darted around the table, looking for weapons. Two teacups, two saucers, and two spoons. And a plate of sausage and kraut. A laughable arsenal.

His smaller companion moved to the side, flanking us, perhaps worried that I would snatch up a spoon. Lars stood, too, but he stumbled as he did. How drunk was he? Not that it mattered. Even sober, he could do little against two armed and alert Gestapo men.

"I am a Swiss citizen," I said.

Anton swiveled on his barstool and caught sight of me.

Gravel Voice stuck a hard metal object in my back, where no one could see. A gun. I winced. Lars's face tightened. I trusted that he knew of the gun, and I hoped he would do nothing to get me shot.

Although perhaps he would enjoy it. I had no idea what he might be capable of, I reminded myself.

I looked up into Gravel Voice's impassive ash gray eyes. He dug the gun farther into my ribs. He would have no problem shooting me. My avenues were closing down fast.

"Let's not make a scene, Fräulein," he said. I did not think he would care if I did make a scene. It would give him a chance to hurt me.

"Could you please fetch my coat?" I asked Lars. Both he and the Gestapo men looked confused. *Lars,* I pleaded silently. *Get Anton out of here.* I had to trust that Lars would do that. That I had not been wrong about everything with him. "I gave it to that boy at the bar."

"Certainly." Lars bowed, clicked his heels, and limped toward Anton. When had he developed a limp? Before I had time to think on that, my captor dragged me toward the dining room door. His partner followed.

Anton walked toward me. He would not let me be taken without a fight. My heart quickened. Lars had to stop him.

"Why are you arresting me?" I spoke quietly so as not to cause a scene. I needed to keep them calm, and to keep their attention focused on me, instead of on Anton.

Lars pinned Anton against the wall and dropped a hand over his mouth. I closed my eyes so that the Gestapo men would not see my relief. But would Lars take Anton safely back to Switzerland? Anton's chances had to be better with Lars than with the Gestapo. I straightened my back and talked up to Gravel Voice. "I am a Swiss citizen. And you have no authority in Poland."

"I make the authority I need." His gravelly voice sounded matter-of-fact. For him, today was another ordinary day. Only for me was it a unique disaster.

We quick-marched across the lobby, his fingers digging painfully into my upper arm. Surprised murmurs followed us to the door. My body screamed to fight, but I could not. If I did, Anton would try to help, and even if he were not hurt, they would take him back to Germany, too. I had to prevent that, whatever the cost.

Gravel Voice's colleague opened the hotel door, and he shoved me through it into the night. Gooseflesh sprang up on my arms. The air felt only a few degrees above freezing, and my coat hung in my hotel room. If I lived to be thrown into their car, I had a cold ride ahead.

Gravel Voice yanked my hands in front of me and snapped on tight handcuffs.

"You are a traitor to Germany." Outrage covered the pockmarked face of Gravel Voice's friend. His words lisped out in white clouds. "You are wanted for murder. For consorting with traitors and Jews."

"That is nonsense," I blustered. "I am a reporter for a Swiss newspaper. A Swiss citizen. You cannot—"

Gravel Voice picked me up like a toy and dropped me into the trunk.

6

He threw a blanket over me and slammed the trunk lid before I could move. I thrashed under the blanket. The car juddered to life, then jounced into motion.

We shot forward, and I bounced painfully around the trunk. Hoping that we would reach a paved road soon, I shielded my face with my cuffed hands. Would they take me into the woods and shoot me, or did they intend to drive me back to Berlin and interrogate me? A quick murder in the woods seemed the better option for me.

We stopped. I kicked against the trunk lid and shouted, but to no avail. Seconds later we started again, the road considerably smoother now. The stop could not have been the border. Surely the Polish border guards would take longer than that to let us across. As minutes passed and we did not stop again, I realized that it must have been.

For the first time in two years, I was in Germany.

I felt carefully around with my cuffed hands for a way to open the trunk, but I was securely entombed in the darkness.

I wrapped myself in the scratchy blanket as best I could. I wanted to sleep. Best to face the Gestapo rested. Just a few minutes' sleep would help. My eyelids grew heavier.

Gas must be leaking in from the car's exhaust system. I fought to stay awake. Each blink lasted longer than the one before.

I woke shivering. My teeth chattered. My head ached, my heart pounded, and my breaths came quick and shallow. A nursing lecture came back to me, on hypothermia, and I mechanically checked off symptoms.

I felt sluggish. How close were we to Berlin? It was a three- to four-hour drive from Zbąszyń, but I had no sense of how long I had been out.

If only the border guards had heard me, I might have had a chance. In spite of dragging me out of the hotel, the Gestapo had no authority there. People might shelter me. The police might protect me. But we had crossed into Germany. Matters were much more complicated. Here I could rely on no one, especially not the police.

The car slowed, crunched over gravel, and rolled to a stop. Doors slammed. Voices rumbled outside. Liquid pattered against the ground. They must be relieving themselves.

I pounded the trunk lid with numb fists.

The lid opened into night.

I squinted at the shape above me and cleared my throat. "P-p-ardon." My teeth chattered together so hard, I thought they would crack. "P-p-please. B-b-bathroom."

Two things stood between me and freedom: the men who had taken me. I must escape them before we got to Berlin. If not, I would die.

Gravel Voice called forward. "The traitor is awake."

"Not trait-t-t-or." I forced out. "Mistaken."

In actual fact, I took pride in being a traitor to the Nazi regime, but this did not seem the best time to bring that to their attention.

"We should let you lie in your own filth," he sneered.

"Your t-t-trunk." I shivered so hard, I could barely sit upright. I did not know how I could stand, let alone overpower one or both of them. But I must. My sluggish brain tried to formulate a plan.

"I don't fancy cleaning it." The pockmarked driver came around. "Get her taken care of. It's more than an hour to Berlin."

I struggled to control my panic. An hour away. And I was in the woods in Nazi Germany. Even if I got out of their car alive, no one would help me.

I took several deep breaths. My immediate options had not changed. I had to escape from two men. After that, I would do what I could to get the handcuffs off and get back to Poland. One step at a time.

"Your problem." Gravel Voice yanked me out and dropped me on the roadside. I skidded on gravel on my hands and knees. I imagined the stones must be sharp, but I felt nothing. I stood awkwardly, still shivering, and stamped my numb feet, trying to get blood flowing into them.

If I slipped away, they might not be able to find me in the dark.

Gravel Voice walked back to the front seat, shaking his head. The driver stayed by me. He was barely taller than I. I felt a surge of relief that the larger man had returned to the car.

The running motor's exhaust puffed out in a cloud of blue. The headlamps cut through mist to reveal empty road in front. We were alone.

"P-p-rivacy?" If I got away from the car, they might not find me if I ran.

"It's no ladies' club," he said. "Piss where I can see you."

I would have no chance to run. Whatever happened, I would have to do it alone and right here. I pointed to the ditch a few meters away. "There?"

He shoved me toward the ditch. When we reached it, we both stopped.

"Get on with it," he said.

I looked past his head. Gravel Voice's silhouette faced forward in the passenger seat, back bent as if he leaned to adjust the radio. The driver moved his head to follow my gaze, turning his back to me.

I dared not think about what I had to do. I had one chance to survive. I swung my handcuffs over his head and pulled the chain that held my cuffs together taut across his warm throat. He scrabbled at it with both hands. I kicked the backs of his knees. He fell, landing hard against my chest. I collapsed onto the ground with his weight atop me. My head struck a rock. The world swam in and out of focus. I struggled to retain consciousness.

He forced his fingers under the handcuffs. He twisted to the side. I yanked as hard as I could. With a crunch, his trachea collapsed under the metal encircling my wrists. He groaned. Even if he escaped, he would not be able to breathe properly.

His fingers tore at the metal. I forced my knees up behind his shoulders and yanked harder. His shoes kicked against sodden leaves in the ditch. I hoped that the radio would distract Gravel Voice a few more precious seconds.

The driver kicked convulsively. His head smashed my arm against the rock. I heard a crack as the bone broke. Hot pain shot up from my wrist. I bit my lips and did not let go. Soon, he went limp.

His chest stilled. I shifted my fingertips to the side of his bruised neck and felt for his pulse. None. I remembered checking Miriam's cold neck hours before and shuddered.

Grimacing, I lifted the handcuffs over his head and felt for the holster on his hip. If I had a gun, I could force Gravel Voice out and drive away. No one else need die. My fingers slid to the bottom of the holster. They ran along cold leather. Empty.

What options were left? Fight, flee, hide.

A gunshot cracked. Gravel Voice.

He was armed. I was not. That eliminated fight.

I rolled sideways into the shelter of the wet ditch. Cuffed hands in front of my face, I belly-crawled toward a stand of trees faintly visible in the murk. A second shot broke the muffled stillness, then silence.

I crawled past an oak and pushed myself into a standing position, hiding behind the trunk. I shook so that I could hardly stand. Any advantage I received from adrenaline had ended where I left the driver on the ground. I had killed him. My mind sheered away from that thought and tried to focus on the tree, the car, and Gravel Voice. I could regret my decisions, if I lived. Right now, I did not have that luxury.

I peered between gray trunks. He would have trouble finding me if I stayed still, but even if I eluded him, I could well freeze to death. Warmth trickled down the nape of my neck. Blood from where I had bashed my head, but I had no time to worry about it.

The engine of the Gestapo car still ran; its headlamps flooded the empty road with light. The driver lay on gravel next to the car, neck twisted into an unnatural angle. The car looked empty, but the dark made it hard to be certain. Where was Gravel Voice?

A twig cracked next to me. I bolted.

I told myself it was blind panic, and I should stop, but my legs had their own mission. A figure crashed painfully into me. We fell toward the ground together. At the last instant, he twisted and took the force of the fall on his own body. An odd thing for a Gestapo officer. Instinctive kindness? Or perhaps he wished to spare me for something worse later. We rolled when we hit the ground, and he pinned me under him.

My handcuffed hands were smashed between our bodies. I had nothing to fight with. I thrashed under him, trying to free my hands. My arm reminded me that it was hurt and badly. I groaned.

"Easy, Spatz!"

Lars. I stopped struggling, suddenly conscious of his familiar weight atop my body. I wriggled out from under him and struggled to a sitting position.

"Anton?" I asked.

"Safe in the lorry." He brushed wet leaves off my back.

"The other Gestapo man?" I asked.

"Dead," he said. "Both of them."

The gunshots I had heard were Lars killing Gravel Voice. Lars had come after me. But why?

He ran his bare hands along my arms. "You are frozen."

"You neglected to fetch my coat." I shook in earnest.

"How inconsiderate of me." I heard the familiar smile in his voice. "Would you attack me if I offered you mine?"

"I am f-f-fine." I hated that I could not speak.

A warm coat settled around my shoulders. Years before, he had given me his coat, back when I thought it meant something. I reached up to push it off.

"Don't interpret this as an amorous advance, but I fear that you are in no shape to walk to the road yet." He wrapped his arms around me.

My mind tried to argue about the wisdom of getting close to him, but my body only noticed how warm he felt. He smelled the same as he used to. I closed my eyes and tried not to think about the last time I had been in his arms, when I had wanted never to leave them.

"My god, Spatz!" he said. "You are cold clear through."

He pulled me closer and rubbed his hands up and down my back under the coat. I tried to push away from him. I would rather freeze to death than owe him.

"Damn it," he said. Long ago, he had always apologized for swearing in front of me. It seemed quaint now. "Why must you fight everything?"

He was correct, as usual. My pride would not get me out of this forest and back to Anton. I stopped struggling and relaxed against him. The shaking subsided to shivers. I tried to think about something other than the feel of his arms around me, his chest pressed close against mine. I reminded myself that he had not come to Zürich. He had not contacted me to explain why. I had been in mourning for two years for a man who was still very much alive.

Slowly, even the shivering stopped. I felt warm, relaxed, almost drugged. Now, I thought, is when trouble starts. I stayed put.

"Better?" His voice sounded soft, as it used to.

I nodded, not trusting myself to speak.

"Anyone else would have welcomed help," he said. "Instead of freezing to death."

"I am not anyone else," I whispered. A ridiculous point to make.

"No," he said. "You're not."

His lips found mine, and the last two years melted away. My heart beat so hard that I suspected he must feel it, too.

I thought of Fräulein Ivona and drew my head back. "No." I pushed away, gasping when my arm moved. Cuffed hands awkward in front of me, I struggled to my feet. "Thank you for keeping Anton out of danger," I said. "And for coming for me."

"It's become a habit," he said from his position on the ground.

"Not all the time," I said, bitterness strong in my words.

"Quite." He stood next to me. "Let's get back to the car. We have much to do."

"Where is your lorry?" I asked.

"Behind the car. You can't see it, but it's there."

I strained my eyes, but I could not see the lorry. I stumbled and slammed against a tree trunk. After that, I kept my eyes on the ground as we walked to the road. I did not want to fall down in front of Lars.

When we were within range of the car's headlamps, he stopped. A waltz now played from the car's radio. How curious that I had not noticed it until now.

He lifted my cuffed hands and winced when he examined my wrists. Blood coated my hands and ran halfway to my elbows. Metal must have sliced my skin during my struggle with the Gestapo driver. It looked dramatic, but was not so serious as the broken arm.

"I hope I did not stain your shirt." A dark smear ran along the front of his white shirt.

"I have a woman who washes them."

"You seem to have a woman for everything."

He released my hands and pulled on a pair of leather gloves. He stepped over the driver on the ground. I stared down at the body. A swollen tongue protruded between his teeth, and his sightless eyes stared at the stars. I had done that.

Revulsion climbed my throat. I turned from the body and vomited. The world darkened around me, but I was still awake and crouching by the roadside. Lars must have shut off the headlamps.

I wiped my mouth on my sleeve and sank back on my haunches. Lars appeared in front of me and with a quick movement unlocked my handcuffs. Years of experience as a policeman. When he took the cuff off my right wrist, I smothered a yelp.

I gasped when I tried to rotate my swollen wrist.

"Broken?" he asked gently.

"I am no doctor." It was broken. As soon as I had a moment away from him, I intended to splint it. "We will have to see. But first, I think we must get away from this car."

"We need to move it off the road. I know a place nearby where it might never be found. If you can drive one of the automobiles, I'd like to bring the Gestapo car there. Can you drive?" He gestured to my swollen wrist.

"Of course." I pulled my injured arm up under the coat.

His face relaxed in relief. "Good. Once the sun rises, anyone who comes by will see it here otherwise. Would you prefer to drive the lorry?" He pointed back down the road to a barely visible rectangular shape. "Or this one?"

I looked at the dead man in the passenger's seat and realized that Lars had saved my life. I looked again at the dead man on the ground. The bodies would be traveling in the car. "I prefer the lorry."

He heaved the former driver into the backseat. He knelt and smoothed the gravel and leaves by the side of the road. I slid my hand inside Gravel Voice's still warm jacket and withdrew my Adelheid Zinsli passport from his pocket. As I suspected, he had retrieved it from the hotel manager before he arrested me.

"Follow me," Lars said. "I'll turn in about two kilometers, then drive along a dirt road. When I stop and turn off my headlamps, stop and turn off yours. I will keep driving and dispose of the car. In about fifteen minutes, I should be back at the lorry. If it takes longer, leave without me. Poland is a few hours away. Do you understand?"

"I am not deaf, despite everything." I slipped his coat from my shoulders.

"Keep it," he said. "You'll need it."

"As will you," I pointed out.

"The fewer foreign objects we bring into the Gestapo's car, the better."

He argued because he wanted me to keep the coat, but he was also correct. I let him help me put my arms into the sleeves, gentle with the broken one.

He walked me back to the lorry, both of us holding our hands in the air. "That's the signal," he said. "So Anton won't shoot us."

"Anton has a gun?" I asked.

Before he could answer, Anton sprinted across the road. He threw his arms around me and held on tight, for the moment not worried whether thirteen-year-old boys still hugged their mothers. Blinking back tears, I kissed him on the forehead.

"I thought you were gone," Anton said.

"It is much harder to get rid of me," I said, "than most people think."

Next to me, Lars chuckled.

When we arrived at the lorry, Lars helped me inside. I let him. For all my brave façade, I was exhausted. My wrist ached, my head throbbed, I had started shivering again, and I wanted nothing more than to curl up in a ball and sleep the clock around.

Lars leaned across me to pick up a pistol off the seat, probably not trusting me with it. With a practiced gesture, he stuck it in his belt.

"We'll drop the car off and go straight back to Zbąszyń," he said. "I have a compartment you can hide in while we cross the border. I promise to get you and Anton out safely."

What exactly were his promises worth? I took a deep breath. "Thank you."

"Getting you out of the Gestapo's hands is in my own best interest."

"How fortunate for me that saving your own skin will help me to save mine." I cradled my broken arm against my chest.

"Are you certain you can drive?" he asked.

"Have I ever given you cause to doubt me?" My voice shook at the end of the sentence. I bit my tongue. Even if I was tired and in pain, I would not lose control in front of him.

He slammed the door and stomped back toward the car, limp more pronounced now that he was upset.

7

I fit the key into the ignition left-handed and started the lorry. I turned on the headlights awkwardly. Ahead of me, Lars started the Gestapo car.

"Anton," I said. "You must help me to shift the gears."

"I will," he said. "I've practiced on Boris's Mercedes. I could drive this by myself."

"Perhaps if both my arms were broken," I told him. "But not yet." He smiled. I felt better.

I explained how and when to move the shift lever. If Anton could not manage it, I would have to shift with my left hand while he steered. He concentrated ferociously as I spoke, tip of his tongue sticking out the corner of his mouth, as it had since he was five.

We managed to shift into first. I pulled onto the road and followed Lars's taillights, closer than I would have liked, because I could not see far through the fog. Second gear went fairly well, too. I rested my broken arm on my chest and steered left-handed.

"He was amazing!" Anton said. "I tried to get to you when they first took you, but he grabbed me and promised we would take them on the road."

"He has promised many things." Such as his promise to return from Russia.

Anton shook his head, his hand resting on the gear shift. "He was furious that they had you. I could tell. I knew that he would get you back."

"I see." Steering the heavy vehicle took more strength than I had expected. I hoped Lars had chosen a straight road. I gritted my teeth and turned the wheel. When did he ever choose the straight road?

"Then another car was ahead of us at the border, so we got farther behind. Plus we had to stop so I could hide to get across the border. He has a special compartment. He's very clever."

"Indeed," I said. A compartment? For smuggling people, or something else? Lars had certainly been busy the past two years.

"He planned to shoot out your tires," Anton said. "Soon, but your car stopped so he stopped, too."

"How thoughtful of him." On either side of the road, bare trees loomed out of the gloom and quickly vanished again. I was weaving more than I should, and Lars must see it, too. I concentrated on ignoring the pain in my arm and keeping the lorry steady.

"He pulled us over and jumped out practically before the lorry stopped moving. He can be very fast when he tries."

"Can he?" My head throbbed. The back of my throat burned. I would not vomit. I would not. I yanked the wheel straight. I could not drive the car one-handed much longer.

"I saw a flash of light from his gun, but he was too far away, and it was too dark for me to see much else."

I thought about strangling the driver, the dead face of Gravel Voice, and Lars kissing me in the woods. "That is just as well."

Almost exactly two kilometers from where the Gestapo men had died, we turned onto a rutted gravel road. Each bump worsened the pain in my head. When we hit a deep pothole, my broken bones grated against each other. I cursed.

"You said a curse word!"

"I may say quite a few before we stop." I risked a glance at him. Instead of looking shocked, he looked pleased.

When Lars turned off his headlamps, I stopped the lorry so suddenly, it stalled. My head throbbed, and I vomited bile out the side window. Not good. How bad was my head injury? I extinguished our headlamps, too. Darkness rushed in around us.

I opened the door and looked down. My seat seemed farther from the ground than it had when I got into the lorry. The sound of Lars's engine receded. I climbed out, careful to avoid my mess.

Anton scooted to the edge of the seat and jumped to the ground. He landed next to me, missing the vomit. I leaned against the cold metal door, uncertain if I could stand much longer. I had not expected my head and arm to hurt this much.

"I can track him," he said. "Report on his movements."

"I have other uses for your woodcraft." I gestured with my good arm. "I need a flat stick to splint my arm. About this long. Two if you can find them."

I slipped down and sat on the running board. I had to stay conscious until Lars came back or fifteen minutes elapsed, and I had to drive to Poland without him, as agreed. But how would I get us across the border? Our passports had not been stamped. I closed my eyes.

"Mother!" Anton sounded frightened. I hauled my eyelids open. My ears protested against the volume of his voice. I ran off another checklist in my head. Symptoms of head injury: pain, nausea, sensitivity to light and noises, strong desire to sleep.

He shook my good arm.

"Awake," I said. "Hand me the stick."

With clumsy hands, I positioned the broad stick across my legs, then rested the back of my arm on top of it. "The perfect size. Thank you."

"The brave knows his woodcraft," he said. "I could light it on fire for you, if you'd like."

I forced a smile to keep him from worrying. "Just this is fine."

"If I don't light it, you'll miss my circus act." He crouched in front of me. Despite his light tone, I could see how upset he was. Me, too.

He handed me the second stick and I aligned it along my arm from palm toward elbow.

"Need something to tie this," I said.

He unlaced his shoes and proudly held up the laces.

"Smart young man." I was glad that he had taken first aid at school.

I ducked my head to tie the splint on with my left hand and my teeth. Hot pain shot up my arm. I jerked backwards and smashed my injured head into the lorry, but my arm stayed straight.

"Do you need help?" he asked.

"No." I spoke around the shoelace. "I have splinted quite a few arms in my life, including today. I can manage."

I tugged the knot snug. My stomach clenched against the pain. Cold sweat broke out on my forehead. Once I tied the splint and rested my arm against my chest, the pain changed to a steady, sickening ache. The ulna was not set, but at least it was stabilized.

I leaned against the lorry. Held at bay while setting my arm, my headache pounded back to life.

He examined my left wrist. "You're bleeding, too!"

"Cuts from the handcuffs," I said. "Nothing serious."

"You were handcuffed?" His clear young voice rang with outrage.

"Yes. I—" I fell to my knees and retched.

"How many times has she vomited?" Lars asked from behind me.

Anton jumped. So neither of us had noticed his approach.

"Twice, sir," Anton said. "Once before she splinted her arm and just now."

Three times, but he had not seen the first one by the Gestapo car. I thought to chastise them for speaking about me as if I were not there, but decided to save my strength to crawl away from my mess one-handed.

"You splinted your own arm?" Lars knelt next to me. "I could have helped you."

I pushed hair off my forehead with my good hand, sweating in the cold air.

He brushed his fingertips across the nape of my neck. "What happened to the back of your head?"

"Hit a rock," I said. "Behind the Gestapo car."

"You might have mentioned it sooner."

My head spun. The ground rushed toward my face. I could not get my arms up in time.

Lars scooped me up. Pain stabbed in my arm. My stomach lurched again.

"Get the door, Anton," Lars said.

I fought going to sleep. Lars bundled me into a blanket, and I felt more bumping. Then, nothing.

Pain grated in my arm. I moaned and tried to wrench it away, but someone held it fast. I struggled to open my eyes. I lay on something soft in a brightly lit room. A man I did not know held my arm.

Lars stood on my other side. He cradled my head in one hand; with the other he stroked hair off my forehead. "Easy." He soothed. "He's set your arm. The worst is over."

Wetness slapped against my wrist. A plaster cast. My arm would heal. My head I was not so certain of. My heart I did not even want to think about.

I tried to push pain aside and figure out where I was. This was no time for weakness. I tried to speak.

"Don't move," Lars said. "Everything will be fine."

"Anton." I forced out the word.

"Here." The voice came from somewhere on my left. I turned my head but could not see him. My eyes watered in the glare. I closed them.

I had seen that I lay in a bedroom, on a bed. A man I did not know applied plaster to my arm. My head ached, and I wanted only to sleep again. I fought it.

"Switzerland," I said. "To Boris."

"Don't worry about that," Lars said.

"Promise." Every word took a hundred years to say.

"I promise," he said softly. "I will take him home for you, if it comes to that. Which it will not."

"Thank you," I said, and I was gone again.

* * *

I awoke to darkness. Where was I?

My head hurt worse than it ever had. My cheek rested against a stale pillowcase that smelled of Khasana perfume. When I lifted my aching right arm, it felt heavy and hard. What had happened to it?

Someone else lowered my arm back down to my side. "Shh," said a voice. "Sleep."

I turned my head to the voice. It belonged to Lars Lang. I lay in a bed with him. It must be a dream. I struggled to wake up.

"Lars?" My voice sounded thick.

"I'm here," he said. "You had nightmares, and I didn't want you to injure yourself thrashing around."

I touched his face with my heavy hand. I felt stubble on his cheek. It seemed real.

"Am I dead?" I asked.

He tightened his arms around me. "No."

"But you are dead." I wriggled out of his grasp. "I remember."

"No, Spatz." Worry tinged his words.

"Where is the little girl?" I remembered a little girl was in danger. I pushed myself into a sitting position. A mistake. My stomach heaved, and I vomited on the duvet.

"Fetch a basin," he called. "Her name is Ruth. She's fine."

I wiped my mouth on a clean corner of the duvet. I shook. My stomach twitched again. I looked around the room. Empty except for the bed and shadows that must have been nightstands. A heavy curtain covered the window, so I could not tell if it was night or day. Artificial light fell through the doorway. "I am sorry about the blanket."

Lars folded the duvet one-handed, his other arm tight around my shoulder. "It can be washed."

Anton stood suddenly next to the bed and handed Lars a white ceramic bowl. Anton wore a nightshirt too large for him. It must be the middle of the night. Lars took the basin with his free hand.

"Anton!" I said in shock. "You should not be here."

"Why not?" He rubbed his eyes with his fist.

"Because, then I have failed at everything." I tried to move toward him, but Lars eased me back against the mattress. Gray shapes swirled above my head.

My head throbbed. Later, a man came to shine a bright light into my eyes and speak in a rumbling voice that I could not understand. I slept.

My eyes opened. The sun was up, but half-drawn curtains dimmed the light. A stranger in a white coat sat on a chair next to me. I looked around. A bedroom, sparely furnished with a double bed, a wardrobe, a muted rug, and two nightstands, plus the chair upon which the stranger sat.

I cleared my throat. My head ached, but it was manageable.

"Ah, good," said the stranger. "You are awake." He held a glass of water to my lips. "I am a doctor."

He had not given his name. Neither should I.

8

A figure appeared in the doorway. I turned toward it. "Mother?" Anton said.

"Anton!" Relief flooded through me. Wherever I was, Anton was safe.

He came and sat on the edge of the bed. He took my hand in his warm one. "How are you?" He spoke with the Berlin accent he had used as a young child, not the Swiss one he used now.

"My head hurts." I used the same accent as he. "But I think I shall be fine."

Guardedly, I turned my head. I feared moving quickly, as if my head might come loose. The man in the chair was tall and spare, dressed in a well-tailored dark suit under his doctor's coat. He had an old-fashioned long mustache and a pink indentation on his nose where he must usually set his pince-nez. Near his shoes sat a black leather doctor's bag. "What do you think, Doktor Anonymous?"

"You remembered my name," he said in a delighted tone. "That's very promising."

"Where am I?" I asked.

Anton opened his mouth to answer, but the doctor shook his head. "Where do you think you are?"

"In a room, in a house." I struggled to recall. Switzerland? We usually lived in Switzerland, but I remembered a vacation. A vacation with a promise of a white horse and fragrant pastry with almond paste and poppy seed. Poland. But Anton's accent led me to think we were no longer there. "Berlin?"

"Yes, Mother," Anton said. "We're in Berlin."

My head spun. Berlin was the most dangerous place in the world for us. "I see."

"Do you know how you came to be here?" The doctor settled his pince-nez on his nose.

I had no idea. But should I admit it?

"I think that's enough questions," someone spoke from the doorway.

I looked over at it. Lars? That made no sense. He was dead. Relief surged through me, then confusion. Why had he not come back from Russia? I closed my eyes. Anton squeezed my hand.

I had taken Anton on a holiday to Poland to cover Saint Martin's Day. Remembering that detail made me feel better. Fragments of my trip to Zbąszyń came back to me.

"Ruth." I opened my eyes. I did not know how I had gotten here or how Lars had become involved, but I knew why I was here. I had to find that little girl.

"Later, Spatz," Lars said. "Once you are finished with the doctor."

I stared at him. "Where have you been?"

"Later," he insisted. I sensed that he had a good reason for wanting my silence, that he did not trust the doctor. I kept my questions to myself. His quiet awareness of others was something I had once loved about him. It had saved our lives many times.

The doctor looked from Lars to me. "How do you feel?"

I described my headache and, to get rid of the doctor, lied when I answered no to questions about nausea, pain, and vision disturbances.

The doctor turned to Lars. "Physically, she is much improved. I would like to ask questions to ascertain how much of her memory is gone—"

Lars shook his head once.

The doctor polished his pince-nez on the edge of his white coat. "So," he said peevishly. "The questions you should ask are things about what she last remembers. If she has lost more than twenty-four hours before the incident and loses time again now, I would be concerned."

"What should we do?" Lars asked.

"Rest," he said. "And quiet. Nothing stressful."

I stifled a laugh. Anton and I were in Nazi Germany, and I was not to feel any stress about it.

"Can she be moved?" Lars asked.

He made me sound like a piece of furniture.

"I would advise against it," the doctor said. "I believe she lied to me about the state of her injuries."

Lars's lips curved into a smile. "Indeed?"

I did not see how a protestation of innocence would help my case, so I stayed silent while Lars saw the doctor out.

I pushed myself to a sitting position even though my head warned me that it was a mistake. "Anton, how long have I been here?"

Lars came back into the room, and Anton looked toward him before answering. I pushed down my irritation. He owed no loyalty to Lars. Did he?

"It's November fifth." Lars walked to the heavy curtains and pulled them open. Midday sun jumped into the room. "We arrived late last night."

"What happened?" I asked Anton.

"You slept, mostly." A closed look dropped over Anton's eyes. I recognized that look from my own face in the mirror. I would get no further information from him. But why not?

Lars sat on the bed and took my good hand. When I yanked it back, both he and Anton looked startled. What did they know that I had forgotten?

"Ruth," I said. "Please tell me."

"I went to Paul's apartment," Lars said. "No one was there so I let myself in."

The former police *kommissar* was skilled with lockpicks. "Did you have a key, Herr Kommissar?"

He gave me a conspiratorial look. Anton wrinkled his brow in annoyance. He did not like it that his mother had a life he knew nothing about.

"Once inside," Lars continued, "I checked all the cupboards, including the one by the door. I saw evidence that a small child had been in it, but no child."

I let out my breath. My head hurt so that I had trouble thinking. "Where is she?"

"I don't know. I couldn't do much more than look."

"Why not?" I sounded more irritated than I should have.

"Because, Spatz," he said gently. "You were hurt. No one knew if you would live or die. My place was here."

"Was it that bad?" I read the answer from his eyes. For the first time I realized how terrible he looked. He looked as if he had not slept, his clothes hung on him as if he had lost weight, and he had missed a patch shaving. I longed to reach over and trace the new scar in his eyebrow. And if he had not abandoned me for two years without a word, if I had not spent months grieving his death, I would have.

I turned to Anton. He, too, looked pale, but not so bad as Lars. Either he had more faith in my ability to recover than Lars did, or Lars had hidden the extent of my injury from him. Perhaps both. "How are you?"

"I am much better than either of you," Anton said. "Except I've been shut up in here since last night. So I cleaned Lars's guns and practiced on the flute."

I wondered how many guns he had, but all I said was, "The flute?"

"Lars has a flute." Anton pulled a long wooden instrument out from behind his back. "I learned a new song."

He started playing "O Tannenbaum." I stared at him, astonished. He did a creditable job. However, the sound burrowed into the pit of my stomach. I struggled not to clap my hands over my ears. Another sign of a concussion: sensitivity to sounds.

"Nicely done," I managed when he finished.

"Your mother needs rest," Lars said. "This is the longest she's been awake yet."

Anton returned the flute to a long velvet sack and sat quietly.

Lars did not let me rest. He quizzed me on what I remembered: Gestapo men taking me from the hotel and disjointed images from a car's trunk. I thought I remembered waking up in Lars's arms.

"Anton," I said. "Could you please give us a moment of privacy?"

He grimaced but walked out twirling his flute sack.

As soon as he closed the door, I turned to Lars. "Were you in this bed with me?"

He suddenly became very interested in the floor. "I did not mean to presume, but the doctor said to tie you down, and I didn't have the heart."

"Next time," I said, "listen to the doctor."

"As you wish." He sounded hurt. Well, perhaps he should have come back two years ago.

"Please tell me what happened after I got out of the trunk."

He quickly filled me in on my abduction. How I managed to free myself by murdering a man. How could I have done such a thing? And how could I have forgotten it afterwards? Shame and horror filled me. I had taken away a life. Indirectly, I had taken two. My head ached. Tears pricked my eyelids.

He put his hand over mine. "They would have killed you."

"Does that make me better than they?" The man's family was slowly beginning to realize he would never come home. I had ensured that he would not. Worse still, I did not remember his death. I drew my hand back.

Lars talked, but I barely heard the words. Death surrounded me every time I came near Germany, and now I had dealt it out myself. I shivered.

He gently eased me from a sitting position to lying back down. I lifted the covers up to my chin. "So, after all that, when we got here I put you in that bed, and there you have mostly stayed since," he finished.

Mostly? He concealed something from me. "Did I wake at all?"

"You did, from time to time." He gave me a half smile. "You had a great deal to say."

I winced. I hated to think what I might have spilled. Once again, he knew more than I wanted him to. Only this time the fault was mine. "I wish to make sure that Ruth is with her father. Then, Anton and I return to Switzerland."

"How?" He crossed his legs. "Your Hannah Vogel and Adelheid Zinsli identities are compromised. And Anton has no papers."

I still had my Hannah Schmidt papers, but I did not tell him so. My old colleague, Herr Silbert the forger, could produce papers for Anton for the proper price. I only hoped that he still lived in Berlin and had not been arrested, and that I had enough money. "We cannot stay in Berlin with no papers either."

"I have a clean identity." He leaned closer and began to speak more quickly. "Lars Schmidt. I can use it to drive you and Anton across any border but Zbąszyń. I have a false gas tank in the lorry that I've used for smuggling. I'll put you both in it."

"Thank you." I hated to owe him more, but I would pay whatever price he asked to get myself and Anton out of Germany. "You have done much already."

"I am your husband," he said. "It's my duty."

I glanced quickly at the door to make certain that Anton had not heard. "Please do not jest about that, Lars. I am grateful for what you have done for us, but we both know that your actions clearly indicate you have no interest in assuming that role. I would prefer that you not confuse Anton." *As you once confused me,* I wanted to add.

"You were easier to deal with when you were raving," he said.

"That is because I could not remember."

"On the contrary. You remembered a great deal."

My head throbbed. "I—"

"Rest. You are in no condition to fight with me." He smiled wryly. "And I'm in no condition to fight with you, either."

"Then let me get dressed. We can fight in Switzerland," I said.

He grinned. "I agree."

I hauled my legs over the side of the bed and waited for the world to stop sloshing. My head injury was not going to make any of this easier.

"May I help you?" he asked.

"I can manage."

Lars raised a skeptical eyebrow, but he knew better than to object, as he must recall the hospital beds I had climbed out of over his objections. He handed me a dress. "I had it cleaned and mended."

"Thank you." I took it. I wore an unfamiliar slip. I tried not to think who had undressed me. It had to have been Lars. I closed my eyes and swallowed.

To my surprise, I felt better standing up. I dragged myself to the bathroom with my dress clenched in my good hand. Where had Lars been for the last two years, and what was he doing now? Could I trust him? He had risked his life to save mine and Anton's. That worked in his favor.

I raised my hand to my head. My dress. I shook out the sage green linen. I must have worn it when I was abducted, but I did not remember doing so. I turned it over in my hands, hoping it would spark memories. It did not.

While bathing, I recalled Fräulein Ivona's words in Doktor Volonoski's office. She claimed to be one in a string of Lars's lovers. My stomach clenched. *Think about it later,* I told myself. *First, get out of Germany.* Someone had rescued Ruth—probably Paul, or the mystery man from the locket. Even if Miriam's death was suspicious, there was little I could do about it. I had to get myself and Anton out of Germany as soon as I could.

I bathed and brushed my teeth before I chanced a glance in the mirror. I looked better than I had expected. My skin, always pale, looked nearly translucent. I had the cast on my arm, of course, and dark purple circles smudged under my bloodshot eyes, but otherwise I did not look as if I had come into Germany in the trunk of a car. I also did not look like I could have killed a Gestapo man by the roadside. I remembered his face now, but I did not let myself speculate about his life outside of the night I had met him. I would not think about the wife and children he might have had. The mother who waited at home for him.

I pushed the thoughts down and busied my hands. I teased the gauze bandage from my hair. The wound was so small that it did not warrant a new bandage. I threw away the gauze, wondering how much damage had been done to my head where I could not see it.

I donned the green dress. Buttoning the front took time because I had only one hand. But when I was finished, I was satisfied with the results. The long sleeves hid most of the cast on my right arm and the bandages on my left wrist. I peeled back the bandages and checked. Lacerations and bruising, but nothing serious. I must have been handcuffed.

How had the Gestapo known to find me at the inn? They had called me Hannah Vogel. That left out Fräulein Ivona and the Polish soldiers, since they knew me as Adelheid Zinsli. So my message to Bella had tipped them off.

Unless someone had linked my Hannah Vogel identity with my Adelheid Zinsli one. Last time I left Germany, no one had known that I was both women, except Lars's old chief, Sturmbannführer Hahn. But it could not have been him. When last I saw him, he lay dead on a warehouse floor. By my hand.

I had since checked my sources to see if Hahn had left notes, and they had turned up nothing to link Hannah Vogel to Adelheid Zinsli. Much could change in two years. Perhaps new evidence had been unearthed.

I found my satchel near the bed and walked more or less steadily to the front room. Anton and Lars stretched out on the floor playing backgammon.

"You're up!" Anton cried. "You look wonderful!"

He leaped to his feet and hugged me. When I kissed his forehead, he gave me an aggrieved look, but he did not step back.

Lars put away the game before standing. "Indeed you do."

"When can we leave?"

"Now," Lars said. "I could take you to a restaurant to wait and eat while I fetch the lorry and my passport."

"That sounds like a fine plan," I said.

"Are you certain that the trip won't overtax you?" He studied my face.

"Staying here would also be taxing." My legs wobbled as I walked toward the door.

Lars helped me into a woman's coat, his hands lingering longer than they should have. As much as I did not want to, I stepped away. I stroked my palm down the dark blue wool. The coat did not belong to me, and I did not wish to know its provenance. Another of his conquests, no doubt.

What had happened to my own coat? It hung in my hotel room in Zbąszyń. I felt proud that I had found the memory in my battered head. I now remembered arriving at the hotel. A little less time remained lost to me.

I drew on a pair of black leather gloves I found in the coat pocket.

Lars shrugged into a dark brown overcoat. He pulled his fedora low over his eyes, like a police detective hiding his expression from a suspect. An old habit from the days when it was true. Anton put on his own coat and took my satchel.

Anton bounced next to me down the hall and into the street. He studied shops and people with interest. He had not been back in the country of his birth in four years, an eternity in, now Nazi, Berlin.

The neighborhood felt decidedly working class, very different from Lars's previous apartment. Soot streaked dark brick buildings thrown together decades ago to house workers. Bare trees cowered in hard dirt squares in the sidewalk. The branches did not look as if they would leaf out even in summer. Holes left by missing cobblestones gaped in a street with more horse-drawn wagons than cars. I was not certain where we were, but it looked like a bad patch of the district of Moabit.

"Mind your step." Lars led me around a broken beer bottle. I tried to avoid a squashy white object that I hoped was a sodden newspaper.

Anton stopped next to a battered wooden door. "What about this restaurant?"

It did not look promising. Grime caked dark windows, and dirty ocher paint outside did not speak to clean conditions indoors. Its battered sign read HAUS HUBERTUS.

Lars shook his head quickly. "That one is no good."

Although I agreed with him, something in his tone gave me pause. "Why not?"

He glanced at the windows. "The quality of the food is—"

A chubby blond woman in her early thirties bustled out the restaurant's door. She wore a waitress uniform, a black dress with a white apron and cap.

"Lars!" she screeched, grasping his arm. "It's been more than a week!"

He peeled her hand off his arm. I clenched my good hand in my pocket, but kept my face impassive and waited to see what would happen next.

Lars turned a pleading gaze on me. I gave him a stiff smile. I had no intention of helping him to resolve this. It was painful enough for me already.

His scowled. "Adelheid, may I present Fräulein Gretl? She works here. Gretl, this is my wife, Frau Lang."

Gretl's face fell. Anton's mouth dropped open. My headache returned full force.

"How do you do, Fräulein Gretl?" I thought of denying that I was Lars's wife, but that might lead to more complications. "Is this a favorite restaurant, Lars?"

Anton started. He knew that tone meant trouble. I took a deep breath.

"I have dined here from time to time." Lars's gaze fixed somewhere beyond my left ear.

"I see that," I said.

"Should we ask Gretl to find us a table?" Lars asked me.

Gretl looked at me with sympathy. She would certainly be correct to pity Lars's wife. However, I was not.

"I think not," I said. "Although I enjoyed meeting you, Fräulein Gretl."

She blushed and curtseyed.

Lars reached for my arm, but I set off down the street without him, my hand on Anton's shoulder. Out of the corner of my eye, I watched Lars bow to Gretl and follow.

My head ached so much, I wanted to curl up in a ball in a dark room, but I would not give Lars the satisfaction of knowing how upset I was. To think that I had believed this situation could not become more intolerable. I cursed my paucity of imagination. Why did I care? Once I knew he had lied to me and betrayed me while I mourned in Switzerland, why should I care if he slept with one woman or one hundred? Yet, I cared.

I had to stop letting my emotions distract me. What did all this mean? It meant that Lars had relationships and loyalties I knew nothing about. Still, he had kept Anton away from the Gestapo in Poland, and risked his life to help rescue me.

"Lars," I said when he caught up. "Perhaps we could skip lunch and go straight to the lorry?"

"Spatz," he said. "I—"

"Please," I said. "Just get us to the lorry."

Lars turned on his heel and led us in the opposite direction. "As you wish."

Anton spoke up. "Are you really married?"

"No." I wished my head did not hurt so much. I might have been able to think of a way to explain it to him. "When I was in Berlin last—" I stopped when I saw the expression on Anton's face.

"1936?" Anton asked in a small voice.

"Yes," Lars said. "And—"

Anton drew back his fist and punched Lars full force in the groin. Lars folded to the ground. Anton ran.

I followed him, trying to suppress my feeling of immense satisfaction at Lars writhing on the cobblestones.

"Anton!" I ran out of breath. "Stop!"

I stumbled to a streetcar stop and held on to the streetlamp. Black paint peeled off the stem in curls. "Anton! Please!"

What if he kept running and disappeared in the streets of Berlin? He could get stuck in an orphanage or worse. Panic rose in my throat. Red and white lights blinked at the edges of my vision. I sagged against the lamppost.

I would not faint in the street in front of Lars. I would pull myself together and catch Anton.

Anton hurried back to me, shaking with rage.

"Need to catch—breath." I owed him an explanation, but I could not give it here, with Lars hobbling toward us, only meters away.

Anton waited, blue eyes turned from angry to anxious. I tried to think what to do. If I had a few hours' rest and a good meal, I would think of something.

Lars's limp was more pronounced than usual. Not surprisingly, he looked furious. He brushed off his coat. The ground rippled as if made of water. I knew the ground stood still, and that my perception was faulty, but the knowledge did me no good. Not for the first time.

Lars approached us both cautiously. "What was that for?"

Anton set his jaw and glared at Lars.

"Anton. Please apologize to Lars for your behavior," I said.

Anton looked at me hanging on to the streetlamp. He unclenched his jaw. "I apologize for what I did."

I recognized that he apologized only out of sympathy to me, and I doubted that any of us thought he meant it, but I suspected that it was the best we would get.

"I did not start a fight with you," Lars said to him. "And I do not want one."

I met Lars's dark eyes. "Our fight started two years ago. Anton is not to become part of it."

Lars held up both palms in a placating gesture. "Apologies all around."

I pushed off the lamppost.

"Are you all right?" Lars asked me.

"Are you?" I asked.

Lars grimaced. "I've taken worse." He looked over my shoulder. His eyes went cold.

"What is it?" I asked.

Lars took my arm and pulled me in the opposite direction. Under his breath, he said, "The lorry is gone."

"Stolen?" I whispered. Without the lorry, we were trapped.

"Or the Gestapo has a good idea what I was up to in the woods last night." Lars's face was expressionless, which meant real trouble.

The ground kept moving, but I tried not to stumble. "Should we separate?"

"Can you get yourself to safety?"

"Of course," I said, irritated. "I am not an invalid."

"For all that you have been conscious for less than an hour," he reminded.

"I will take care of her," Anton said.

"We will be fine," I said.

"I will check my apartment, and my sources," Lars said. "Where can we meet tomorrow?"

"Anhalter Bahnhof, track three. At noon," I said. The train station would be packed with people then. With luck, no one would notice us. "I have my own resources. If I am not there, you can assume that we are safely in Switzerland and you can get yourself out as well."

Lars smiled. "You cannot imagine how much I have missed you, Spatz."

"Perhaps," I said, "I can."

Lars looked surprised again, and I wondered what else he was not telling me.

Just then, a streetcar rattled up. Lars pushed a handful of German marks in my palm. I had only Swiss francs and Polish zloty. "Safe journeys," he said.

"Likewise," I answered. He leaned forward as if to kiss me good-bye. I stepped back and herded Anton onto the streetcar.

9

The streetcar pulled off. Lars had already walked away.

We were now on our own, in Nazi Germany.

I sank onto the nearest empty bench. My legs shook. Doctor's orders: no stress. I stifled a bitter laugh.

Anton sat next to me on the wooden bench. His eyes were wide and frightened.

"Anton," I said, trying to tease him to lighten the mood. "Would Winnetou have hit his opponent there?"

His hero as a young boy had been Winnetou, the honorable Apache brave from the Karl May series. He relaxed a little. "If his opponent was that much bigger, he might have."

"Might have?" I had read every book aloud to him. Winnetou had never hit anyone in the groin.

"Winnetou's honor didn't help to save the Apache from the white man. Did it?" He stuck out his pointy chin.

As usual, his logic was irrefutable. "You know that it was inappropriate to hit Lars."

But I knew why he had. He had seen my grief when Lars did not return from Russia, as much as I had tried to hide it from him. And he blamed Lars. Well, so did I.

I gave him a stern lecture about being respectful to adults, but I knew he did not regret his action.

The streetcar jolted. I gritted my teeth and struggled to convince myself that my head did not hurt.

We traveled south. Eventually we would end up at a major station. I would find my way from there. It looked as if I was correct, and we traveled through Moabit. I felt better. This streetcar should end up at Alexanderplatz. We could walk from there.

I watched out the back window until reasonably certain that no one followed, then relaxed against the hard oak seat. The streetcar's rocking reassured me, and I closed my eyes.

"Were you two really married?" Anton asked.

I sat back up and examined the other passengers. A tired woman rested a string shopping bag between her shoes. A mother balanced a dirty two-year-old on her lap, a three-year-old fidgeted next to her. Two young girls chattered on the seat behind. No one seemed a threat, but caution was my watchword.

"This is not the place," I said.

"Where, then?"

Stung by his tone, I lowered my voice. "We will be going to the Jewish quarter. It is not a safe place, but I know of an empty apartment there."

"Miriam's?" He was a step ahead.

"Yes. I have her key. We can stay there until I sort things out."

"How?"

"I know someone who might help us." Herr Silbert could procure papers for Anton. "Then, we take a train home."

"What about our things in Poznań?"

"I will see if I can have them shipped to the newspaper," I said. "If not, we will do without them."

At the next stop, an SS man in full black and silver uniform boarded. We had no papers. If his suspicion should fall on us, I hated to think of the consequences. I hoped that our blue eyes and blond hair would shield us from notice.

Tension blew through the car like a cold wind. The chattering girls fell silent. As everyone else did, I watched the man in the black uniform until he chose a seat. He faced forward, seemingly unconcerned about those of us in the car with him. The girls resumed their conversation in subdued tones.

Anton said not another word until we arrived at our destination, and neither did I. My headache lessened. The rest did me good.

At Alexanderplatz, I steeled myself against glancing at the imposing police headquarters. In the late 1920s, I visited weekly to gather information for stories I wrote as crime reporter Peter Weill. In fact, I had met Lars in that building when he was still a police *kommissar*. I had not liked him on first meeting. I thought of Gretl. Clearly, I should have trusted my instincts.

Once, I had valuable sources in the building, but now it held only danger. Anyone who recognized me knew that I was wanted by the Gestapo for kidnapping and, perhaps now, murder.

The SS man from our streetcar approached the main entrance. He probably had offices there. Since the police and the Gestapo had merged, the only justice was Nazi justice.

Walkers jostled us as we crossed the busy intersection. I hurried into the deserted streets of the Jewish quarter. Thousands lived here, but they stayed indoors, probably to avoid attacks. Ada Warski had walked down these Berlin streets carrying her baby while German friends screamed slurs. We, too, had best get inside—and soon.

Although I had expected it, the anti-Semitic graffiti shocked me. *Der Stürmer* vented anti-Semitic hate from specially built display boxes. Black paint outlined a cartoon figure with a huge nose and yarmulke. JEWS OUT! was scrawled on one wall. I looked around. Every building had been defiled.

Anton stared at large white letters on a brick wall that read DEATH OF THE JEWS, WOULD BE THE BEST NEWS. I had seen anti-Semitic graffiti before, but it felt worse to read it on every wall in my home city. Once these buildings were covered with honest soot.

"Control your expression," I said. "If you truly lived in Berlin, you would be inured to this."

He looked down at the dirty sidewalk. "Let's get inside."

We walked down the once bustling street to the apartment that had belonged to my Jewish friend Sarah. After she and her son fled in 1931, she lent it to Paul and Miriam. The door to the apartment building had been freshly painted black. I shuddered to think of the foul graffiti the paint concealed.

I took Miriam's key out of my satchel and fitted it clumsily in the lock with my left hand. It took three tries, but I managed. When I tried to turn the key, it caught, and I wondered if she had given me a key to something else entirely. I rattled the key, and the door opened.

We stepped into the lobby. A single bare bulb illuminated the well-cared-for room. I spotted the mailbox where I had hidden Röhm's incriminating letters in 1931. Would revealing them have changed the course of Germany's catastrophe?

"Mother?" Anton was already halfway up the first flight of stairs. I walked quickly up to him. We had no time for thinking about things that might have been. We lived in what was.

The stairwell itself was clean, but the paint was dingy. It looked as if it had not been repainted in years. Presumably they used their available paint on the building's outside, covering insults.

"We came here when I was little," he said. "Once when you were looking for something and once after your apartment was destroyed. They were beating a man in the street."

He forgot nothing, poor child. "Yes. A good friend lived here, but she left before I met you."

"Is this where Miriam lived, too?" he asked.

"Until they deported her." *And killed her,* I added silently.

Someone had wrenched the mezuzah from Sarah's doorframe. It had taken with it several layers of paint. Before unlocking the door, I touched the splintered wood where the mezuzah had been.

Inside the hall smelled of stale cabbage, as it had on my last visit. I closed the door and turned on the light.

As Miriam had said, in the hall near the front door was a cupboard. It had two doors. Both had been torn from their hinges and thrown to the floor. The little girl was gone.

I motioned to Anton to stand quietly by the front door, then did a quick pass through the apartment to see that it was empty, and that Paul and Miriam had no telephone. The Gestapo often opened a line and listened to occupants' conversations. But as I suspected, Paul and Miriam could not afford such a luxury.

I returned to the hall. "You can talk now. There is no telephone to listen in on what we say."

In my mind, I drew a half circle around the cupboard. I dropped to my hands and knees and searched that half circle.

"What are you doing?" Anton asked.

"Looking," I said. "Please keep out of the light."

"She's not here."

"I know." I picked up a door. "Let's see what is. Perhaps something will give us a clue to her whereabouts."

The door had little dents hammered on the inside near the bottom. Had the little girl tried to kick herself free? I stared at the smooth depressions and admired her grit. It must have hurt to kick the wood that hard, but she had kept at it. The dents were in a nearly straight line across the back of the door, showing determination as much as desperation.

A scrap of white fabric dangled from a broken hinge. I carefully picked it free and held it in my open palm.

"What is that?" he asked.

"I would guess that it belonged to Ruth, or to the person who freed her from the cupboard." I studied the cloth. Thick cotton and expensive looking.

"A piece of a dress? Or a shirt?" he asked.

I rubbed the cloth between my fingertips. "It feels thicker than that. Perhaps a jacket?"

"Not a warm one," he said.

I opened my satchel, pulled out my notebook, and pressed the cloth between the pages.

He pointed to a dark mark in the middle of a door. "What made that mark?"

"Something small," I said. "Perhaps a pen."

"Or a screwdriver."

"Could be." I ran my fingertips over the mark. Whoever had opened these doors had no key and had not bothered to look for one. Surely that boded well for Ruth. She was with someone who cared more for her than for the furniture and worries about the noise of wrenching off the doors. I stacked the doors atop the cupboard, not sure what else to do with them.

Why had Miriam not left the key here? If she had a key, she would have given it to me at the stable, with her house key and locket. I checked atop the cupboard. The key rested there, in plain sight.

I searched the rest of my imaginary half circle. Shoes lined up near the door: a pair of old slippers that probably belonged to Miriam, worn patent leathers for Ruth, and brown slippers for Paul.

Who had ripped the doors off? It could have been Lars. I regretted not asking him for more details. Where he was concerned, I regretted much, I reminded myself, and cupboard keys were the least of it.

With any luck, she was with Paul. I told myself that, but I did not believe it. Miriam had not thought so.

The cupboard smelled of urine. The little girl had wet herself. No matter how brave she was, she was only two years old. The terror that she must have felt while sitting in the dark, listening to them take away her mother.

The last thing the cupboard held was a soft green blanket. I sniffed it—Miriam's perfume and urine. I folded it and set it on top of the ruined doors.

There was no sign that whoever had rescued the girl had brought her back inside the apartment.

We checked the bedroom that my friend Sarah had used for her son, Tobias. It probably belonged to Ruth now. The white-painted wardrobe held little girl's clothing, neatly hung or folded on the shelves. Most of the dresses had stains on the knees. I thought of the many pair of pants that I had mended for Anton. I was proud of

Miriam and Paul for letting their daughter get dirty. My own dresses had been pristine at that age. Even then I feared my father.

No evidence of hasty packing, so the person who took her away had taken their time and packed carefully, or they had taken nothing at all. I searched for a urine-soaked dress. That, too, was gone. Was she still wearing it?

I saw nothing that would explain who had taken Ruth, or why her mother had thought that she might be safer locked in a cupboard than on a train to Poland. Did she fear what the Nazis would do to her, or someone else?

I gave up, for now, and went to the kitchen where I found stale bread, butter, and honey. I heated water for tea and found eggs to boil.

I cut a piece of hard bread and handed it to Anton. He smeared it with butter and honey and devoured it. I sat at the table and ate a piece myself, more slowly.

"So," he said. "Are you and Lars married?"

"We are not married." I struggled to decide how much to tell him. He might as well know most of it. "When I was last in Berlin, Lars and I ran afoul of the Gestapo. We had fake identities made and the man who made them, for reasons of his own, decided it would be easiest to make us married."

He looked unconvinced. "Why would he do that?"

I sighed. There would be no peace until I had explained it to his satisfaction.

Stalling, I removed the eggs from the stove and poured water for tea. As on my last visit, they had only odious nettle tea. They must have gathered the leaves themselves because they could afford no other tea. "Lars and I had been pretending to be engaged."

"Why?"

"To make my visits to Berlin have a reason besides the obvious one: spying. And you may not tell anyone this."

He gave an exasperated sigh. "I am not a child."

I did not point out that he was, in fact, a child. "Do you have your pocketknife?"

He drew a bone-handled folding knife out of his coat pocket and dropped it in my palm. It smelled faintly of sawdust, probably from his pocket.

I set my satchel on the table and emptied its contents. I snapped open his knife and slit the satchel's lining.

"What's in there?" he asked.

I plucked my Hannah Schmidt passport out with a sigh of relief. At least now I had valid papers, even if they were not properly stamped.

I handed him the passport. He read it. "You're Hannah Schmidt?"

"You are Anton Schmidt," I said. "We shall get you proper papers tomorrow."

"Who is my father?"

I hesitated, but it was there on the passport. "My husband, Lars Schmidt."

"From Lars Lang?"

"Yes." I threaded a needle from my sewing kit and began to stitch up the satchel's thin lining.

He put the passport back on the table. "Do you love him?"

"I am certainly grateful that he rescued me from the Gestapo yesterday." I kept my eyes on my needlework, partially so I did not have to look at Anton, but also because I wanted to make the stitches as small as I could so that they would not be visible to a casual searcher.

"That is no answer," he said, as I had so often said to him.

I pulled the next stitch taut. I did not know the answer. I had loved Lars very much. I still did. But acting on that was another matter. "I did."

"Is that why you've been so sad since you came back from Berlin last time?"

"What do you think?" It was, but I did not wish to talk about it.

"I'm glad I punched him." Anton took a defiant gulp of tea.

"It was completely inappropriate to hit him," I said. "Whatever happened between Lars and me is my concern, not yours."

"But you would never hit him yourself." He put his teacup down on the table.

"No," I said. "Because it is an inappropriate way to solve problems."

"Isn't Gretl inappropriate?"

I tied off the last stitch and cut it with a little pair of folding scissors.

"Did Fräulein Ivona turn you in, back in Poland?" he asked.

"Did she seem surprised when the Gestapo came in and took me?"

"I wasn't paying attention." He leaned forward on his elbows and looked away guiltily. "I was trying to listen to you and Lars, and then I was trying to help you."

"You did the correct thing to listen to Lars."

I stood and took a hot egg from the pan. I placed it in an egg cup for him, then fished out one for myself.

"So, did she turn you in?"

"I think not," I said. "But only because the Gestapo arrested me for being Hannah Vogel, not Adelheid Zinsli, and I believe Fräulein Ivona did not know my real name."

We finished our eggs and bread in silence. Anton looked at my cast. He stood to do the washing up.

I went to the living room to see if Ruth's savior had left a note. I riffled through papers on Paul's desk. Handwritten letters in a language I did not know, but I guessed it was Polish. The other letters were official looking, and they came from the Reich. A letter stating that Paul must append the name Israel to his identity card, officially changing his name to Paul Israel Keller. A Jewish Asset Inventory Form where he and Miriam had been required to list their possessions. I skimmed it. It included even the locket I now wore around my neck.

Anton came into the living room wiping his hands on his pants. "Any clues in there?"

I shook my head. "Receipts, paperwork for various visas, and notifications from the Reich announcing further restrictions against Jews."

I opened the drawer and sorted through pens, pots of ink, and rubber bands. At the back, folded into a square, was a sheet of paper.

I unfolded it and smoothed it flat. The undated and unsigned type-written note read:

Enough. I will not continue paying. I cannot do what you ask. It ends now.

I turned on Sarah's old desk lamp and held the paper under it. The watermark was the same as on the letters I had been receiving from Berlin. The paper trembled in my hand.

"Mother?" Anton asked. "What does it say?"

I handed it to him.

He skimmed it and gave it back. I folded it up and returned it to its place at the back of the desk. I did not mention that it matched my other letters. Anton did not know about them. And he did not need to.

"What does it mean?"

"I am not certain," I said slowly. "But I think it might be a reason for Miriam to leave Ruth here instead of taking her along. Perhaps she was being threatened."

My heart beat faster. It did not matter what I found in the desk. I had to get Anton and myself out of Germany. Ruth was no longer in the cupboard, and there was little I could do for her now.

Should I chance going to Herr Silbert's tonight? The sky outside was already growing dark, which made it around four. His shop would close before we got there. First thing tomorrow morning, I would get Anton a Swiss passport and get mine stamped. We might be on a train to Zürich by lunch. But what of Ruth? What if the person who typed the letter had taken her? What if she had not been rescued at all?

10

The lock in the front door clicked.

I pushed Anton ahead of me into the kitchen, where we would not be visible from the front door, and took a carving knife from the drawer by the sink. I had a quick memory of the last time we had stayed here. Then, too, I had drawn this knife to defend myself against a mysterious late-night threat. I hoped this one would prove as harmless. I pushed Anton behind me, knowing he would hate it.

The front door closed quietly.

"Miriam's boots are gone," said a deep voice. Paul. I relaxed. He belonged here. "She must be at her mother's."

"Thank god for small mercies," said a woman. Maria? Paul and Maria had been lovers before he married Miriam and, perhaps, after. Had Maria broken the Nuremberg Laws forbidding sexual relations between Germans and Jews? She hated to risk herself, but I thought that she did love Paul as much as she could love anyone. So perhaps she had.

"I'd hate to run into her so soon after our two-week trip," Paul said. "It takes some time to adjust."

"Since she's not here . . . ," Maria said.

I put down the knife on the table so that the tablecloth would muffle the sound. "He is Miriam's husband," I whispered to Anton. "We are old friends, but stay here, just in case."

Paul and Maria stood next to the sofa with their arms wrapped around each other. A small suitcase rested on the floor next to Paul's stocking feet. I cleared my throat loudly and felt gratified when both jumped. They turned to look at me. Paul ran his elegant hand quickly through his thick dark hair, straightening it where Maria has mussed it.

"Hannah?" said Maria. "What the hell are you doing here?"

"I could ask you the same." My voice shook with anger. He had been off gallivanting with his mistress while his daughter crouched, terrified, in a cupboard and his pregnant wife died alone in a stable.

"Hannah," Paul broke in. "I don't understand."

"Have you any idea where your daughter is?" I had no time for social niceties.

"It's not your concern." Paul leaned against the arm of the sofa and angled his long legs to the side. He still carried shrapnel in his leg from the War, and it pained him to stand for long.

"Nor, obviously, are you concerned about the whereabouts of her mother," I said.

"I don't know what you are implying," he said, "but that is not your concern either."

"I saw Miriam," I said. "Yesterday."

Maria scrutinized me.

"In Poland," I said.

Paul's eyes dropped to the locket around my neck. He must have last seen it around his wife's neck. He could not know that I had taken it from the soldier who had removed it from her corpse, but he had to know that she never would have given it to me unless the situation were dire.

"Where were you?" I asked. "Where is your daughter?"

He dropped onto Sarah's old purple sofa. The wood groaned. Maria stayed put.

"Why was Miriam in Poland?" he said.

"Deported. With the other Polish Jews." Now that I saw his worry, I regretted my hostile tone. I would have to tell him his wife and unborn child were dead. I should not do that from a place of anger. And if Ruth was not his, perhaps he had expected someone else to stand by her and Miriam.

"How was she?" He picked at his cuticles.

I stood next to the sofa. "She went into labor there. The refugees were quartered in a stable."

His burnt umber eyes stared into the distance. "How is she? Is the baby a boy or a girl?"

"I am so sorry, Paul." I hesitated, hating to finish the sentence. Maria watched avidly. "Miriam. She . . ."

A smile twitched on Maria's lips and was quickly hidden.

I took a deep breath. "Miriam did not survive the birth."

He gulped. "The baby?"

I shook my head.

Maria stood stock-still. I tilted my head to indicate that she should sit by Paul and comfort him. Not surprisingly, she did not.

"Ruth?" he said hoarsely.

"She left Ruth here," I said. "Locked in the cupboard by the front door."

He leaped to his feet. Maria and I jumped. He raced to the broken cupboard and threw himself on his knees in front of it.

"Where is she?" His voice rose in panic.

"I arrived here not long ago," I said. "I had hoped that you had come home and found her."

Someone else had taken Ruth.

"The neighbors, Maria," he said. "We must ask the neighbors."

She backed away from him. "You can't expect me to be seen with you. I can't traipse around announcing my presence to your neighbors."

He gaped at her as if he did not know her. But I did. She would not help him. She did not know how.

"I think it's best if I leave." She collected her hat and coat and fled without closing the door.

He slumped to the floor and stared at the empty cupboard.

I eased the front door closed.

Anton appeared in the hall and looked from the cupboard to Paul. Every day he witnessed more than I would ever want him to. I squeezed his hand and quickly let go.

"Paul." I knelt and put my hand on his shoulder. "We should ask the neighbors now. Perhaps one of them has Ruth. If so, she needs her father. She needs you."

He looked up. His eyes had gone blank. I had seen that look in his eyes long ago, when I was a nurse. He had been brought back from the trenches as the only survivor in his battalion, carried in, nearly comatose, with a badly wounded leg. It had taken a week before he spoke, months before he learned to walk again. He had to recover faster this time.

I left him on the floor and crossed back into the living room. I poured out a glass of schnapps and brought it to him. He had not moved. When I handed him the glass, he tossed the schnapps back in one swallow and dropped the glass onto the floor.

"Anton," I said. "Please finish washing up in the kitchen."

He shot me a worried look and backed out of the hall.

I knelt beside Paul again. "Paul?"

He clenched the stained green blanket in his fist. I sat next to him, keeping one hand on his arm. I waited.

An hour passed. Still he remained silent. I wondered if I should go to the kitchen for Anton, but he would be all right. He had seen much in the past days, but he was strong. Paul was not.

I touched Paul's shoulder and spoke his name once more. "Paul?"

Without looking at me, he stood and shambled to his bedroom. I followed a few paces behind. He threw himself on his marriage bed face-first. I covered him with a well-worn quilt.

"Should I stay?" I asked. When he did not respond, I closed the door. I could not leave him alone with the knowledge that his wife and baby were dead and that two-year-old Ruth was lost. We would spend the night here.

I went to the kitchen. Anton sat on the floor, whittling what resembled a duck from a stick he picked up on the way to Zbąszyń.

"A duck?" I asked.

"A duck-billed platypus." He held it up. I recognized the plump shape of the mammal now, with webbed flippers and a bill. A creature caught between two worlds, like us.

"Very lifelike," I said. "Are you hungry? How was the tea?"

He made a gagging noise. "What kind of tea was that?"

"Nettle," I said. "I never liked it either."

"Should we go ask the neighbors about Ruth?"

I sat next to him. "I think not yet."

He leaned his head against me. "But shouldn't we find her?"

"Tomorrow." I had been thinking about this while waiting for Paul to speak. "If the neighbors were kind enough to rescue her, she is better off there tonight than with her father. And I doubt they would give her up to me if they had her. I am a stranger to them. And an Aryan German to boot. They will view me as the enemy."

"Will your friend be all right?"

He had lost his wife and baby, perhaps his daughter as well. He would never be all right again. "He will manage as best he can."

Anton blew shavings off the platypus bill.

"Let's see if we can find some nightclothes and a place to sleep," I said. "But first you must clean up the wood shavings."

I found an old straw broom in the corner where Sarah had always kept it and Anton swept the shavings into a pile. He deposited them in the stove in the living room. Although it was cold in the apartment, I hated to light it, worried about using up Paul's winter coal.

Anton followed me to Ruth's bedroom. The corner held old boxes. One contained clothes that once belonged to Sarah's son, Tobias. I pulled out a nightshirt and handed it to Anton. Last time he wore Tobias's undershirt, it hung to the floor. I bet now it would fit.

While he changed, I stripped to my slip and inspected the box. It contained a pair of trousers, a shirt a few sizes too big for Anton, and a single Karl May book from Tobias's old collection, too dog-eared to sell. The book was *Deadly Dust*, and it featured Winnetou.

I bedded down on the sofa and spread blankets for Anton on the floor next to me. I tucked him in and read him stories about Winnetou, the Apache brave, written by a man who had never been to the American West. Anton had surely outgrown it, and probably knew it by heart, but he did not object. The familiar words soothed us both.

After he fell asleep, I stared at the photograph in my Hannah Schmidt passport, remembering the day that Herr Silbert took it. Not surprisingly, I looked exhausted. The day before, I had been struck by a car, then almost succumbed to Lars's charms. I should have stayed that course. I closed the passport. Tomorrow the inestimable Herr Silbert would make a new one for Anton, stamp them both, and we could leave. The neighbors must have Ruth, and soon she would be reunited with her father.

I rolled over on the sofa, trying to wriggle away from a sharp spring. In the days following my fiancé Walter's death in the War, I had slept here often, but nothing felt the same, except my sense of grief and worries for the future. I fell asleep with my hand dangling over the edge, centimeters above Anton's head, just to make certain that he could not move without my noticing.

Much later, bare feet scuffed across the floor. I opened my eyes, my heartbeat pounding in my head. Paul stumbled past into the kitchen, wearing only an undershirt and his pants from yesterday.

I slid off the sofa, careful not to wake Anton, and went to talk to Paul. The day felt early still, but a hint of gray in the sky told me that it was getting on toward morning.

Paul busied himself shaking leaves of undrinkable tea into Sarah's familiar blue and white teapot.

"Paul?" I asked from the doorway. My head ached, and I rubbed my temple.

He turned. Red rimmed his eyes. Sorrow rested there, but they were no longer blank. I let out my breath.

"Thank you, Hannah," he said. "For coming here to check on my daughter and for not leaving me alone last night."

"Of course," I said. "You would have done the same for me."

"I doubt that. I am not you, Hannah. I should not have let you go."

Hardly a comment to make mere hours after learning of his wife's death. "You did not let me go. I left against your advice, remember?"

His lips twitched in a reflexive smile that did not reach his eyes. "Quite." He turned to the sink with the kettle in his hand. His shoulders shook.

I went to him. Whatever he had been doing with Maria, he had lost his wife, his baby, and his daughter. He turned into my arms, and held on to me so tightly, it hurt. I had no words to comfort him. His life was irretrievably damaged.

Eventually, he loosened his arms, and I looked up into his familiar brown eyes. It had been a long time since we had stood so. He caressed my cheek. I closed my eyes.

Behind me someone coughed. We jumped apart as if caught by disapproving parents.

I turned to face the intruder. Lars. I realized that I wore only my slip. I crossed my arms across my chest.

"Who are you?" Paul asked with the fear of a Jewish man who had just been caught with an Aryan in arms.

"A friend of Hannah's." Lars looked ready to hit us both. A paper bag in his hand crackled. In spite of his half dozen interchangeable lovers, he was jealous of my standing here with Paul.

"I was making tea," Paul forced out. "Please join us."

Lars walked past me and sat at Paul's table. I backstepped away from him.

"Why did you come here?" I asked through gritted teeth. "We were to meet at noon. Elsewhere."

He looked embarrassed. "I—I came to see how you were. To explain a few things, but perhaps outside?" Paul looked from Lars to me.

I remembered my manners. "Paul, this is Lars." I did not say his last name, not certain which to use. "Lars, this is Paul Keller. This is his apartment. His wife was Miriam."

Lars's expression softened. "I am sorry to hear of your loss."

Paul went very still. Lars was the first one who had offered him condolences, not counting me. I walked over, took the full kettle from him, and placed it on the stove.

"Paul?" I asked softly.

"I must go speak with the neighbors." He wiped his eyes with the back of his hand. "Enjoy your tea."

It was early to be calling on the neighbors, but I did not stop him.

He walked straight to the front door, still in his socks and undershirt, Paul, the man who was always impeccably dressed. When he came back through it, Ruth would be with him. One of the neighbors must have heard her crying after Miriam's departure and come in to free her.

"Excuse me, Lars." I went to wash and dress.

As I walked through the living room, Anton sat up, looking sleepy. "What's going on?"

"Nothing," I said. "You can go back to sleep."

He slumped back down, and I tucked the blanket around his shoulders. He was probably asleep before I reached the bathroom. I felt a strong desire to be thirteen years old.

I completed my toilet hastily. When I returned to the kitchen, the kettle had begun to whistle. Lars poured steaming water into the teapot and brought it to the table, which he had set with items from his bag: rolls, butter, and jam. He had brought breakfast, either as an apology or a tactic to ensure that I spent time sitting at the table with him while he pumped me for information.

"Nettle tea?" he asked. "I thought you hated that."

I sat and folded my hands in my lap. "Why did you break into Paul's apartment to meet early?"

"Where was he when they took his wife and daughter?" he asked.

"With his mistress." I clenched my hands together. "A situation I am certain you have faced yourself."

Lars checked the tea. It probably needed more time to steep, but then again, I did not want it to have a stronger flavor. I poured myself a cup with my left hand without offering to pour for Lars.

I spooned in honey awkwardly, cradled the warm cup against my cast and my left hand, and waited, but he stayed silent, so I gave up and asked. "Why are you here now?"

He lowered his gaze to the table. "My lorry is definitely gone. My apartment is under surveillance by the Gestapo."

"I am sorry I landed you in this mess, Lars," I said. "If you had not come after me, you would be safe and happy in Poland."

"Safe, perhaps," he said.

I took a quick sip of too-hot tea. "I have a few questions about Fräulein Ivona."

"Have you?" He poured his own tea, looked at it as if it might be poisoned, then grimly took a sip. I hoped he would hate it as much as I did.

"I want to be certain that she did not turn me in to the Gestapo," I said. "I have enough enemies already."

"If she is your enemy, then she's my enemy as well, now." He held up his cup in a mock toast.

I did not lift mine. "Sun Tzu said to keep your friends close and your enemies closer."

"How fortunate when my enemies are attractive twenty-five-year-olds." He took a long sip of tea to punctuate his words.

That hurt. I dropped my gaze to my disgusting tea. His visit changed nothing. I must visit Herr Silbert at nine, the moment his store opened, so we could leave Germany. Still, I was curious. "Did you send her to drive for me, and to spy on me?"

"As I said earlier, no," he said. I wondered how true that might be. "But she is a very jealous woman, so I'm not surprised that she sought you out to make a scene after she saw you on the station platform."

I toyed with my spoon. I longed to ask him what he had been doing on the station platform watching me arrive in Poland after

abandoning me for two years, but I did not want to give him another chance to say something hurtful. "How do you know that she
is not a danger to us?"

He pressed his lips together in irritation. "I investigated her, of
course. A colleague in Berlin checked out her file. She worked as
a secretary in some minor department having to do with road building and then came to Poland to study engineering. She is unmarried.
She has never been under investigation for anything. None of her
associates are suspicious either."

Lars had been, as usual, thorough. So Fräulein Ivona posed no
official threat, although perhaps a personal one. "Do you think she
turned me in to the Gestapo in Poland?"

"I checked with my contacts this morning before I came here.
According to the file, you were arrested based on a phone call to a
Bella Fromm, whose telephone was answered by an informant. I am
under suspicion because I crossed the border so soon after you were
arrested and taken across. The detectives investigating the disappearance of the Gestapo agents feel that, based on our previous engagement, I might have been tempted to help you."

So, we were both wanted, and all because of my indiscreet
telephone call. I should have been more careful. "I am sorry that
you are under investigation. I should have—"

He sipped his tea. "Do not concern yourself overly. It's not the
first time."

"How did you find us here? Were you followed?" I itched to peer
out the closed kitchen curtains and into the street. But then if someone was down there, they would know that I was looking for them.

"Don't insult my intelligence, Spatz. I knew you would not trust
my assessment, that you would let no time elapse before coming to
check on the girl yourself."

I hated being predictable, especially to him. My head throbbed.
"Clever, Herr Kommissar."

"You looked pale when we parted, so I assumed that you might
have to spend the night. Are you feeling better this morning?"

"Much," I lied. I took my gold pocket watch from my pocket. Still too early for Herr Silbert.

"Do you have an appointment?" he asked testily. "Or have I overstayed my already tenuous welcome?"

"Lars," I said. "I appreciate all you have done for us. I am certain it has been a burden—"

"Not at all." He set his cup on the table and sat up.

"How gallant of you to say."

"I did it for quite selfish reasons." He gave me a flirtatious smile. "I can assure you of that."

Looking at him, I lost my train of thought. I well remembered where that smile led. I forged on. "Be that as it may, it was very kind—"

He smiled with half his mouth. "I sense a *but* coming."

He had always known me too well. I twisted my hands in my lap. "But I think it might be best if you and I have no further contact."

"Where will you stay?" he asked. "I could—"

"I believe where I sleep is as much my affair as where you sleep is yours." My head spun, and I swallowed. I would not get upset and throw up on the table.

"I'm sorry about this, Spatz," he said. "I am not without resources, perhaps I—"

"You are too kind," I said. "But I believe we are safer without you, thank you."

"Will you stay here? With a Jewish man?" He stood. "You will be charged with race defilement. It's not safe." He paced around the kitchen, trying, I knew, to think of an argument to change my mind.

"Lars." In spite of myself, I spoke too loudly. "Even though you have apparently been thriving here for the past two years, Anton and I cannot call anywhere in Germany safe."

"As for the matter of the last two years. I hardly think that you—"

Anton appeared in the doorway, rubbing his eyes with his fists. "Mother?"

"Good morning, Anton," I said.

Anton pulled out a chair and sat. He looked greedily at the food, probably hungry after last night's pitiful dinner. "May I start breakfast?"

"Yes," I said. "I must pack."

Lars sat across from him and picked up a roll. He handed the basket of rolls to Anton. "Did you sleep well?"

I left them sitting at the kitchen table and walked to Paul's empty bedroom. I found a box in the corner with Sarah's things. They were out of fashion, but many women in Germany these days could not afford to keep up with the latest fashions. I packed dresses and underthings for me and Tobias's hand-me-downs for Anton into an oversized bag I found in the closet. Sarah would not care if we took them, and we would look less suspicious on the train if we had luggage.

When I returned to the kitchen, Lars and Anton chatted companionably. I made myself a roll while standing. "Has Paul returned?"

"No." Lars gestured to the satchel on my shoulder and the bag in my hand. "Where are you off to?"

I hesitated. "Shopping."

"I shall accompany you."

"No."

He gave me a long-suffering look. "I can walk with you, or tail you from a distance, but I am not letting you out of my protection until you are safe on Swiss soil."

I bit back a sarcastic comment about the value of his protection. I wanted nothing more to do with him, but it might not be a bad idea to keep him where I could see him. Just as Sun Tzu said, friends close, and enemies closer.

I finished my roll. We left the table set for Paul and, hopefully, Ruth.

I wrote a note for Paul, thanking him for the use of his house and saying that we most likely would not be returning. I gave him my number in Switzerland, although I suspected that he would not call it. I would try to check in on him again before we left Germany, to make sure that he and Ruth were all right, but I could do little else.

I turned to Anton. "Let's go."

He rose and shrugged apologetically to Lars. Apparently they had moved past the groin-punching incident. As I had told Fräulein Ivona, I did not understand men.

Before we got to the door, Anton tapped my cast and reached for the bag. "It's my job to carry the heavy things."

I gave him the bag, and kept the heaviest burden for myself.

11

We rode to Kreuzberg in the same subway car. Lars sat at a bench opposite and did a credible job of pretending we did not exist by reading the *Völkischer Beobachter*. I tried my best to ignore him and his Nazi newspaper. Anton looked at the two of us as if we were insane, probably grasping the subtleties of the situation better than we did.

I had thought of trying to evade Lars, but Anton's presence complicated the situation. In any case, yesterday's chase after Anton had proved that I was not up to running. Lars probably already assumed that Herr Silbert's store was my first stop, and he had been there before, so I revealed nothing by taking him there.

Besides, he might need Herr Silbert's services to get out of Germany. No matter how angry I was at Lars, I owed him. He would not be stuck here if I had not been arrested, and he had not followed to help me.

The subway stopped, and we bustled up the stairs with a crowd of workers starting their day. The men wore suits and hats, but few women joined them on their way to work. The Nazis' efforts to force women back into the kitchen seemed to be working. I turned up my collar, wishing I did not stick out against this background of men, and wondering how I would have survived here had I stayed. How I might have to survive if we could not leave.

Outside, the streetlights' glow fought against the cold gray sky. Anton stayed close. I did not see Lars, but he was there. I did not have the luck for him to have lost interest.

My steps quickened when I spotted the familiar cobalt blue storefront. When I stopped in front of the door, I paused. GERMAN BOOKSTORE flowed in gold Gothic-style letters across the plate glass front window, not SILBERT AND SONS. Panic fluttered in my stomach. Perhaps he used such nationalistic language only to keep the Nazis at bay.

I glanced up as I stepped across the threshold. The brass bell that Herr Silbert usually hung over the door was gone. I took a step into the store, then turned to Anton.

"Could you please wait for me at the candy shop across the street?" I pressed coins into his palm. "I would like a packet of mints."

He wanted to come in with me, but he understood my tone and left for the candy store.

I walked past a giant exhibit of *Mein Kampf* topped by a black-and-white glamour photo of Hitler staring pensively out a window.

A stranger stood behind the counter. His white shirtsleeves gleamed, and his green eyes had a questioning look.

"Excuse me." I mustered a polite smile.

"Good morning, madam," he said. "How may I be of service to you on this fine German morning?"

So the Nazis now used their nationalistic terminology on even the weather.

I pulled my jade green fountain pen out of my satchel. "I bought this here years ago. Lately, it keeps getting clogged. Can you fix it?"

My brother had given me the pen as a gift. I had no idea where he had purchased it, but it seemed a safe way to start a conversation. In addition to his illegal activities, Herr Silbert had sold and repaired fountain pens.

The man took a pince-nez up out of his pocket and settled it on his round nose. He peered down at the pen in my hand.

Behind me, the door opened and closed. I hoped for Lars and not someone worse.

"We don't repair pens here anymore," he said. "We only sell books."

I stuck the pen back into my satchel. "Do you know where the previous owner has set up shop? He was so meticulous."

The man put his palms flat on the counter. "Prison."

"Oh, dear." I sounded like my grandmother.

He regarded me coldly.

"I suppose I shall have to find another place to repair my pen. Is there a shop nearby that does that sort of thing?"

"No," the man said.

Lars put a firm hand on my elbow. "There you are, my dear! I'm glad I found you. We are so very late."

I looked up at him. "Are we?"

He led me onto the sidewalk. As we passed the candy store across the street, Lars waved, and Anton came out. As if by some unspoken plan, Anton did not cross the street but kept pace with us on the other side. Lars and I did not speak.

Anton caught up with us at the station. Lars bought tickets; then we stepped into a crammed subway car. I held on to a leather strap and wondered what to do next. Herr Silbert had been my only hope.

Anton offered me a mint from a brown paper bag. I shook my head. Lars took one.

"Did you get what you needed?" Anton asked.

"No," I said without explaining. Anton sucked a mint and stared out the window. I looked at Lars. Perhaps he had a useful contact. "Do you have a source?"

He looked pained. "No."

I had not expected him to, but having it confirmed was still a blow. The car carried us forward through a dark tunnel. We stopped at a station, but I did not bother to read the name on the wall. They were all the same to me now. My shoulders sagged as the implications of Herr Silbert's absence came home to me. I tried to come up with a new strategy, but my head would not comply.

Anton rose at Alexanderplatz, and I followed, feeling dizzy and nauseated. Lars stuck close by my side, no longer pretending that he was not with us. I felt grateful for his presence. Berlin felt different now that we were trapped here.

Anton led the way back to Paul's apartment. We had nowhere else to go. I tried not to notice the graffiti. A nearby shop window had been broken the night before, and our shoe soles crunched on shards of glass.

Again I had trouble working the key with my left hand. Lars held out his hand for it, but I gave it to Anton instead.

"You hold on to the key, Anton," I said when he tried to return it. He dropped it into his pocket.

We reached Paul's door without exchanging another word.

I walked straight to the kitchen and swallowed four bitter aspirin. I did not expect them to help my headache, but I had to try something. Lars watched from the doorway.

"How much does it hurt?" he asked.

"More than I want it to."

I walked past him into the living room. Paul sat on the sofa with his head in his hands, still wearing only his undershirt and rumpled pants.

I sat next to him. "News?"

"No one has her. No one knows where she is, or no one's telling." He sounded beaten. Stubble lined his cheeks. He had not bothered to shave or dress.

"Why not?" I supposed his desertion of his pregnant wife had earned him enemies.

"I imagine you know," he said. "But I truly think they do not know where she is."

I itched to question the neighbors myself, but they would reveal nothing to me. "Perhaps we could ask Bella to intervene?" And I needed to warn her that someone in her household was an informant.

"You are losing your touch, Hannah," he said.

"Pardon?"

"Bella left over a month ago. She's in New York now. Last I heard she was making gloves in a factory."

"Bella, working in a factory?" It saddened me to think of aristocratic Bella laboring in an American factory. She must have been forced to flee without her assets. She deserved better. "I left a message for her when I was in Poland."

"That was foolish," Paul said. "They've been rounding up her friends."

That confirmed what Lars had told me. My call to Bella had landed us here.

Anton peeked out the window. "May I go out? They are playing football down there."

I peered over his shoulder. A group of children around his age kicked a raggedy brown ball around the back courtyard. My every instinct screamed to keep Anton where I could touch him.

"Please," he begged. "I can't sit around all day."

"I could come and watch you," I began.

"You will cause me trouble." He crossed his arms. "I bet some of their parents know you. They know you're not Jewish."

"You are not Jewish either," I said.

"I've decided on a story to tell." Anton was full of stories. And the telling often ended with problems for me. "I'm a Jewish boy from Switzerland. I was sent here to visit my uncle Paul with my mother. I need a good Jewish boy name."

"Aaron," Paul said woodenly. "Aaron Baumgartner."

I glared at Paul. Lars stifled a smile, probably grateful to see someone else in disfavor.

"I have a cousin named Aaron," Paul said.

"Aaron," Anton said. "That will do. Please?"

His pleading blue eyes softened my heart, as he knew they would. What was the sense in keeping him inside worrying with me? If we were trapped here, who knew how long it would be before he got to play again?

"Be careful," I said. "Stick to your story. And stay in the courtyard. I will be watching from up here."

He was halfway to the front door before I finished my admonitions.

"Your coat!" I called.

He snagged it from the hook by the door and dashed out without a second glance.

"You cannot wrap him up in cotton wool," Lars said.

"Thank you for that bit of wisdom from your vast treasury of child-rearing experience," I snapped. Lars smiled, but I ignored him.

I fetched a chair from the kitchen. I sat it next to the window, where I waited with held breath until Anton appeared in the courtyard below. He ran to join the group and in less than a minute was part of the game. How would I safely get him out of here? I rested my forehead against the glass, hoping that the cool would soothe my head.

"Do you have a picture of your daughter?" Lars asked Paul.

I turned to see. Paul took down a picture of a blond girl with light-colored eyes and handed it to Lars. It was the same as the picture in the locket. "It's only a few months old. We had a devil of a time getting her to be still during the sitting. Ruth is a feisty girl. She knows her own mind."

Lars looked sidelong at me. "That can be a challenge."

Paul stared at the picture. "She's a tough one. Smart, too."

Lars drew the corner of his mouth down slightly. A small change of expression, but it usually meant that something did not make sense. "She does not resemble you. Does she favor her mother?"

I thought of Miriam's dark eyes and hair and the man in the locket. I glanced back out the window without saying anything. Anton ran with the ball across the courtyard.

Paul took the photograph from Lars. "She looks like my father's side of the family. The Aryans."

I winced at the pain and bitterness there. I stood and gestured to my chair. Lars sat in it and stared down at the courtyard while I took his place on the sofa, next to Paul.

Paul stroked the glass with one fingertip, eyes far away. I took his free hand and waited. Lars kept his head pointed toward the window, his back rapier straight. I wished for words to comfort Paul.

"We will find her," I said.

"There's not much point to anything otherwise," Paul said.

"Don't talk like that." I stroked the back of his hand. Lars twitched but did not turn his head. "We have uncovered many things over the years, Paul. We are reporters, remember?"

"I was a reporter," Paul said. "I was many things. But now . . ."

"What now?"

"I don't know." He stared at the floor. "I don't know if I can be anything now."

"You can. You will."

Paul was silent for a long time.

"Thank you for those years after the war," he said finally. "They were good years."

"I like to think I was at least better for you than Maria," I said. "I mean, honestly, whatever possessed you?"

His surprised brown eyes met mine. "The challenge."

"Like Russian roulette," I said.

Paul gave me a ghost of a smile. I viewed it as a victory. He could not slide into despair. I had to do something.

Lars coughed.

"Did Miriam have any enemies?" I asked.

"Not that I know of." Paul's left eyebrow raised a millimeter. He was lying.

"When I spoke to her in Poland, she seemed concerned that she was not safe, and I wondered if that is why she did not take Ruth with her when she left."

"Things happened to Miriam in Poland." Paul ran his hands along his face. "She was terrified about going back."

Lars spoke without turning his head. "And you just left her?"

Paul dropped his head into his hands.

"You are a fine one to talk," I said to Lars.

"I hardly think a privileged life in Switzerland can compare to a stable in Poland," Lars said.

I stood up from the sofa and went to the window. Anton ran back and forth as lightly as if we were in Switzerland and not in the Jewish quarter of an anti-Semitic country with no identity papers. He seemed to fit in with the group, but I wished that he were with me instead.

"You have clearly not seen my life in Switzerland," I said quietly.

"Haven't I?"

I peeked at Lars out of the corner of my eye. He looked tired and surprisingly handsome. I quickly looked back into the courtyard so that he could not see my expression.

Paul came to stand behind me. "I think I'll fetch Anton."

Relief shot through me. "Thank you, Uncle Paul."

He touched my nose with one finger. "You're welcome."

Seconds later the front door closed.

"Did you pry open the cupboard doors?" I asked Lars.

He looked as if he were about to say something, but changed his mind. "They were like that when I arrived. Both cupboard doors were off their hinges and on the floor. The front door was locked. No sign of forced entry."

"So whoever took Ruth had a key to the front door?" I wondered who had a key. That might narrow it down.

"It seems that way. But it may have been left open. If I were Miriam, I would have left it open."

The boys below stopped playing and lay in a circle in the dirt. I could not tell, but it looked as if they played marbles. Anton's confident head turned from side to side, probably telling them Indian stories. Unlike me, he had always been accepted by his peers.

Lars leaned close to me. The scent of starch rose out of his warm shirt. Obviously the woman who washed them for him did exemplary work. "What will you do now, Spatz?"

I leaned away. "Same as before. Flee Germany as soon as we can." I had no idea how. "If Herr Silbert had been able to provide us papers, we would already be on a train to Switzerland."

"What about your friend?" He lingered over the last word.

"Why is Paul your concern?" I glared at him.

"Because," he said. "I suspect you will look for that little girl and try to fix her father's broken heart."

"And why is that your concern?" I clipped off each word.

He sighed. "We are linked. In the eyes of the Gestapo if nothing else. I intend to get you out of Germany without your implicating me."

"I have yet to betray you." I could not help where the emphasis fell on that sentence. "My decisions are my own. You have no claim on me."

He looked down at Anton's figure far below. "There are those who do."

"You will not tell me how to raise my son, either."

"Spatz, I—"

A woman called down into the courtyard. A boy stood and raced toward the building. Another woman called and another boy left. The others stood and moved as a pack toward the door.

Paul appeared below and beckoned to Anton. Anton waved at the window where he must know I sat vigil before trotting over to Paul.

"I have no intention of implicating you," I said to Lars. "As you well know, I have had many opportunities to do so in the past, and I have not succumbed to the temptation. Although perhaps it was not so great then as it is now."

His lips twitched. "I appreciate the restraint."

"You should." Once again, my tone was more bitter than I would have liked. I clamped my mouth shut.

We stared down at the empty courtyard in stony silence.

"Perhaps you should exercise the same restraint regarding your friend Paul?" Lars said.

"What, exactly, do you mean by that?" My uncasted hand clenched into a fist.

"Only to ask if you are free to make those kinds of decisions." Lars enunciated each word carefully, as he always did when he was pretending that he was not angry.

"My life and my freedom are my own," I said. "You forfeited any right to be involved in either when you chose not to come back from Russia."

"Did I choose that?" he asked.

"You tell me."

Anton saved him from answering by bursting through the front door. "Hello!"

His eyes shone, and his cheeks were flushed from exercise. He looked better than he had since we left Poland. I was glad that I had let him play.

"I have news!" Anton sang out.

He reminded me of my old mentor, Peter Weill. He, too, always had news and announced it just so. Anton had never met him, so he must have heard the expression from me. What else slipped out when I was not thinking?

I looked at Lars. I did not trust him, but he probably knew more about how to find a missing person in Berlin than anyone else. "What news do you have?"

Anton shifted on the balls of his feet. Paul walked into the living room and stood behind him, arms loose by his sides as if he did not know what else to do.

"I asked them about my uncle Paul and my cousin Ruth."

Color drained from Paul's face at the sound of Ruth's name. I ached for him.

"And?" Lars leaned forward like a Bavarian mountain hound on a scent. "What did they say?"

"You should not have done that, Anton," I said at the same time. "We are not here for you to play detective."

Anton smiled his pirate smile. "But I did, and now I know something you don't."

"This is no game." I scolded. "We must be careful here, Anton."

"Aaron," he corrected. "And I was."

"Hannah." Paul raised a hand as if I were a teacher. "Please, could you chastise him after we find out his news about my daughter?"

For Paul's sake, I turned back to Anton. "Well, then, out with it."

"Say *please*." His eyes crinkled at the corners.

I drew in a breath to admonish him. This was no time for games.

"Please," Lars said. "Tell us."

"Reuben said that an Aryan man always used to visit Miriam," Anton said.

"What did the man look like?" Lars asked. "How did they know that he was Aryan?"

Anton grimaced in self-reproach. "I didn't ask."

"Did the man take Ruth?" Paul asked.

"Nobody saw him on the day of the deportations," Anton said. "But still."

"Do you know who the man is?" I asked Paul.

He shook his head.

"Yet he came often." Lars had a challenge in his voice.

Pain lingered in Paul's eyes. He lowered his head.

"Not everyone compiles a dossier on their friends, Lars." I glared at him. "And I rather suspect this man's visits were timed to match Paul's absences."

"Is it really so easy for a woman to betray her husband?" Lars asked sharply.

Paul looked at me, clearly waiting for a response. I did not answer. I had never betrayed any man, including the ones in this room. Not that it had done me any good.

12

I frowned at Paul and Lars. Neither of them had any right to speak of betrayal.

Anton rocked back on his heels and raised an eyebrow questioningly at me. I forced out a smile.

"I'm hungry," Anton said.

"As am I." I was grateful for the change of subject.

"I would be honored to invite all of you to a meal," Lars put in quickly.

"Because it was such a delightful experience last time." I thought of Gretl. "I think perhaps—"

"We don't have much money," Anton pointed out helpfully. "There's practically no food in the house."

I said, "I will remedy—"

Lars slipped my new coat onto my arms, gently moving it up over my cast. "I think it might be good to leave the apartment for a while. To help us all think. Will you join us, Paul?"

"No, thank you," Paul said.

"Please," Anton wheedled. "Mother won't go without you, and we'll all starve."

Paul looked at me uncertainly.

"Do come," I said. "There is nothing you can do here right now."

Paul glanced around the apartment as if realizing that there was, in fact, little he could do. "Very well."

We waited for Paul to shave and dress. When he rejoined us, he looked more like his old self.

I gathered up my satchel. Paul locked the door and took my arm. We followed Lars and Anton down the stairs.

Anton prattled about horses to Lars, who listened with every appearance of interest. He knew a great deal about the topic. In a long-ago conversation, he had told me that he spent much of his childhood on horseback. Anton, too, was obsessed with riding. He had learned trick riding when we were in Argentina, much to the vexation of his current Swiss riding instructors. They endured his showy maneuvers because he was the top rider in his school, and they needed him to win competitions for them.

"What is he to you?" Paul watched Lars.

"We have a complicated history," I answered. "The present even more so."

"Do you trust him?" he asked quietly. We both knew the dangers of misplaced trust.

"I used to."

We turned at the landing. The doors were closed, and I wondered about those inside. Whom did they trust?

"What happened to the banker?" Paul asked. "I quite liked him."

"Boris married someone else," I said quietly. Unfortunately, Anton had stopped talking, and my words fell into a moment of utter silence.

Lars stopped so abruptly that I ran into him.

I stumbled on my stair. "Pardon me."

Paul steadied me.

Lars looked back, face stricken.

Anton, unheeding, tugged Lars down the stairs. "I'm hungry."

"What was that about?" Paul released my arm.

"I have no idea," I said. "Until a few days ago, I had not seen Lars since the Olympics."

"That does not sound as complicated as you describe," Paul said. "Perhaps you are omitting details?"

Perhaps Lars regretted his earlier assumption that I was betraying my husband with Paul. But why had he assumed that I married Boris?

We arrived at the bottom of the stairs. When Anton opened the front door, the brisk air felt good against my face. Afternoon sunlight fought through high gray clouds. People bustled by, heads down. Anton darted toward the sidewalk.

"Hannah," Paul said before we stepped outside. "You must take Lars's arm before we go onto the street."

Lars turned and stiffly extended me his arm. "Shall we?"

"We shall not," I said. "I am fine on my own, thank you."

"It would not do for you to be seen walking around with a Jew," Paul said.

"Paul!" I said. "You know full well that I do not—"

"Hannah," he said. "I have no desire to be arrested because someone suspects that we are having . . . relations."

I gulped.

"Certainly"—Paul guided my hand to Lars's arm—"not without having the fun of actually doing so."

Lars tucked my gloved hand in his elbow and pivoted toward the door like a machine.

Out on the sidewalk, Anton called, "Come on!"

Lars and I walked out together, Paul a few paces behind. Lars looked straight ahead as if I were not there. We certainly did not make a convincing portrait of a couple out for a stroll.

When Anton, waiting outside, saw that we were on the sidewalk, he raced ahead.

"Go left," Paul called to him.

Anton turned left, and we followed. Paul stepped up and walked on the other side of Lars. We walked past apartment blocks defaced with anti-Semitic graffiti. Here and there, glass glittered on cobblestones, probably knocked out by a Nazi with a rock. I thought of families inside, sleeping, eating, and going about their normal lives when their windows shattered, reminding them that nowhere was safe.

"Do you have a place in mind?" I asked Paul.

"To the right are the Aryan-only restaurants. As a Jew, I'm no longer allowed to enter them, so we must go left." He spoke matter-of-factly, used to these circumstances.

I thought of the many years that we had spent in Berlin, researching stories and eating out. In those days, we could go anywhere we could afford. "I am sorry, Paul."

"You say that often," he said. "Yet, is it your fault?"

I wondered how much blame was mine to carry. I was a German, an Aryan, and I had not done all I could to stop the Nazis from coming to power. I carried more blame than most. As if he knew what I thought, Lars tightened his grip on my arm.

Anton stopped in front of a bright storefront with a large yellow star painted on the window. Inside stood four empty tables covered with dark green cloths, set for lunch. "How about this one?"

The waitress, in a black dress with a white apron and cap similar to Gretl's, wiped her hands on her apron and watched us suspiciously. Anton looked at Lars, probably thinking of our last restaurant incident.

I looked at him, too. "Does your collection of women extend this far?"

Paul tilted his head to the side. He clearly wanted to know the rest of that story.

"Paul." Lars spoke with an obvious effort. "Is this acceptable?"

"Certainly." Paul led us inside and procured a table near the back. I hung my coat over the back of my chair. When I tucked my gloves into the pocket, I realized that they did not match. Lars must have substituted one of his gloves for my right one so that it would fit over my cast. For someone who claimed to care about getting me out of the country only to save his own skin, he was surprisingly thoughtful.

Lars did not say a single word during the meal. Anton sat to my right and went on about his football game, reliving each play. Paul sat next to him and tried to put in a desultory word or two. My headache grew as I watched them. I ate chicken soup with matzo balls, happy to have something familiar and well cooked in my stomach. Lars ate mechanically and paid the check without looking at it.

I reached for my coat. Paul rose quickly. "Thank you, Lars. Anton, let's go see if they have candy at the counter."

As Paul stepped by, he shot me a meaningful look before propelling Anton toward the front of the restaurant where a long glass counter displayed colorful candies in trays. I pursed my lips in exasperation. I understood his intent. Busybody.

"Lars," I said quietly. "What is wrong?"

When his dark eyes met mine, a wall had gone up behind them. Nothing came through—not anger, not worry—nothing at all. "Could I prevail upon you to remain at Paul's until tomorrow morning?"

I hesitated. "Why is it suddenly your concern where I sleep?"

"Promise me you won't disappear before then," he said. "Just that. Promise."

"This afternoon you told me I had to leave Paul's." And he had no right to dictate where I slept. I donned my gloves.

"Where would you go?" A muscle jumped under his eye.

"I do not see how it is any of your concern. We discussed this earlier." I picked up my coat.

"Promise." His voice broke. "Please."

"Lars." I put my hand on his arm. "Tell me why."

"Promise you won't disappear."

"Like you did?"

He closed his eyes.

"Lars?"

"Like I did," he whispered. "Yes."

Behind his head, I watched Paul and Anton heading toward us. When they got close enough for Paul to see Lars's face, he took Anton by the shoulder and led him away.

Pain knifed through my head. This was not the calm suggested by Doktor Anonymous. I massaged my temples. "Why do you care now?"

Lars opened his eyes. "Spatz, please. One night. I'll be back tomorrow morning. I will explain then."

"One night," I told him.

Instead of answering, he stood. I rose, and he helped me into my coat. His hand lingered on the small of my back. "Thank you."

Anton came over with a paper bag of candy. "Cat's tongue licorice! Would you like one?"

I took a strong black lozenge from his bag. When I glanced back, Lars and Paul were speaking by the door. By the time I reached them, Lars had limped down the street.

"Now what?" Anton asked. "There's an afternoon football game back at Herr Keller's."

"Lars suggested I try the Jewish orphanage," Paul said. "He thought that the neighbors might have taken her there."

"We will come, too," I said.

"I can go on my own," Paul said. "I am quite grown up."

"I would prefer to go with you," I said, remembering his expression last night.

Paul and Anton looked at each other and shrugged. Both knew better than to argue.

Paul used his passport to change some of my Swiss francs for German marks, since my passport was still not properly stamped. I tucked the bills in my pocketbook and dropped it into my satchel. I felt better with my own money, although it would not last long.

We took the subway to Baruch Auerbach Orphanage, the most likely place for Ruth to have been taken if someone thought her an orphan. Paul carried her framed photograph, her birth certificate, and an expression of hope so fragile, it hurt to look at him.

The orphanage was only two stops on the subway, but the first one had been renamed to Horst-Wessel-Platz to celebrate a Nazi folk hero. I thought of Jewish orphans, many of whose parents had been killed or imprisoned by the Nazi regime, riding through that station every day. Bile rose in my throat. I stared down at my tightly locked hands to conceal my expression.

On the train I prepared a cover story about being a Swiss reporter interested in the deportations to Poland. I had my Adelheid Zinsli press credentials ready in my satchel. Unlike a German orphanage, a Jewish one would be unlikely to check my identity with the Gestapo, so I felt safe using my Adelheid Zinsli identity there.

We climbed out at Senenfelderplatz and walked up Schönhauser Allee to the orphanage. Gently arched windows welcomed light. It looked friendly, but the exposed bricks on the first floor were the same hue as those at the stable in Zbąszyń. A crudely painted yellow star on the front door ensured that no passersby could fail to treat the children with the expected contempt.

Gray trees rose on both sides of the stoop. Bare limbs rattled above our heads. In summer, these trees probably provided leafy green shade, but now their skeletal forms outlined the chill.

Paul took the broad steps to the front door three at a time.

A harried matron opened the door, wiping her square hands on a starched white apron. Her dark eyes skated over Paul and me and settled on Anton.

"We're not taking older boys." Her tightly coiled bun quivered with disapproval.

Anton seized my hand.

"We are not here to drop off a child," I said.

"I'm here to find my daughter." Paul showed her the picture of Ruth. "Her mother is Polish, and during the deportation they were . . . separated."

The matron stepped briskly out of the doorway and gestured for us to enter. "Follow me."

Her round form sped down the corridor, and I hastened to keep up. She stopped at a closed door. A rustling and squeaking sounded behind it. "A moment, please."

She flung the door open. I peered into the dark room. Shapes humped under blankets. They looked asleep, but judging from the sounds of a second before, most of them had just jumped into their squeaky beds.

"There will be no more horseplay," she said sternly. "It is nap time."

"Yes, Frau Goldberg," chorused several young voices.

She closed the door softly and herded us to an office at the end of the hall. We followed, as obedient as the children. She ushered us inside and sat us down.

Not a speck of dust had dared to settle on her gleaming desk. "Tell me about this child."

Paul handed her the picture again. "My wife was deported to Poland a few days ago. She and our daughter were separated, and I thought someone might have brought Ruth here."

"She has been missing for that long?" The matron scowled. "Yet you just now come?"

"I thought that she was with my wife." Paul wrung his hands. "I found out only last night that they were not together."

"How did you find out?" The matron straightened the blotter and lined an old-fashioned inkwell next to it.

He looked at me helplessly, too worried to come up with a good lie.

I held out my hand for the matron to shake. "I am Adelheid Zinsli, a reporter for the *Neue Zürcher Zeitung*. I was recently in Zbąszyń reporting on the plight of the refugees."

"I read your piece." The matron softened and shook my hand. She had a strong, confident grip. "On the young mother in the stable."

"And her curly-haired daughter." I gave her my official Swiss press pass, glad that she had broken the law and read foreign papers. "While I was interviewing refugees, I came across Herr Keller's wife, Miriam. She told me that her husband had been away during the deportations and that their daughter was left behind. So I traveled to Berlin to see for myself."

The matron held my press credentials at arm's length and scanned them. "You came all the way to Berlin for that?"

"Not just for that," I said. "I also intend to write a story on the situation here, about children left behind, the effect of the deportations on those who remained here, and so on." I stopped and looked at Paul's worried face. "But first I would very much like to see Herr Keller reunited with his daughter."

"How do I know that you are this girl's father and not someone intent on stealing a beautiful little girl?" She looked down her nose at us as if we were kidnappers or worse.

Paul handed her the documentation that he had brought. "She's mine."

I wondered if that was true. And did he know?

"She is just over two years old. She loves to play on the swings and her favorite food is turnips, because I once told her that children didn't like them. She's contrary. And she loves butterflies." He listed the facts desperately, as if their simple accrual would convince the matron.

She pulled a pair of reading glasses from a drawer and read each document thoroughly before handing them back.

"Very well. Let's go see." She unlocked the center desk drawer and took out a giant ring of metal keys. "While the little ones are down for their nap."

We bustled along behind her.

"I can't say that we have your daughter. We have had several children brought in, I'm sorry to say. Between parents being taken to the concentration camps, the deportations, and the suicides, we have more children here than ever before. It's becoming difficult to keep track of them."

Anton clung to my hand. I remembered his fear after I took him in that I would abandon him at an orphanage. "No need to worry," I whispered. "You leave with me."

His grip did not loosen. I stepped close to him.

The matron stopped in front of a light blue door. "This is the ward for girls under five. Please keep your voices down."

We followed her into a darkened room. Two dozen cribs lined the walls on either side. We walked between them, close enough to touch the cribs' slats. To the side of each crib stood a simple oaken wardrobe.

Anton and I stood in the center of the room while Paul and the matron checked each sleeping girl's face. No Ruth. Paul's shoulders slumped.

When the matron closed the door behind us, she turned to him. "Are there any more?" he asked. "Any more wards?"

She shook her head. "Not for girls that age."

"Where else might she have been brought?" I asked.

The matron's eyes fixed on Paul. "Nowhere."

He crumpled back against the wall.

"Could you make inquiries?" I asked.

The matron hesitated. "Of course. Do you have a telephone?"

"No," Paul said.

"I will telephone you tomorrow evening," I said.

She patted Paul's back and led him to her office, where she gave him a shot of schnapps. I declined. I should not be drinking with so recent a head injury.

He stared at his shoes while the matron reeled off statistics about the number of children they had taken in because of the deportations. I took notes and asked questions. Paul drank. Anton sat so quietly, I worried for him.

The matron caught my shoulder as we stepped through the front door. Anton and Paul walked forward, but I stayed.

"You realize"—she leaned forward to speak into my ear—"that there are no inquiries I could make?"

I had suspected as much. "Where is the harm if it gives him another day of hope?"

"Eventually he must face the truth." She put her hands on her ample hips. "His daughter is gone."

"Or perhaps we will find her." Paul had to have that hope.

She gave me a pitying look and stepped backwards into the hall.

Paul and Anton stood at the foot of the stairs, illuminated by pale golden light from inside the orphanage. The matron closed the door. Darkness swallowed them.

"Mother?" Anton's voice quavered.

I hurried toward him.

13

I embraced Anton. He hugged me back hard before stepping away.

"I told you that you would leave with me," I said.

Anton lightly punched my shoulder. "I know."

"I need to find a telephone booth," I told Paul. "It will take only a moment."

Paul's haunted eyes glanced once more at the dark front of the orphanage. He did not answer.

I quickly found a telephone booth and left them outside while I called in a story about the Berlin orphans to my Swiss paper. Herr Marceau dutifully took notes.

I already wrote under a pen name, but I could not take even the slightest chance that someone had connected that name to Adelheid Zinsli.

"I need this to come out under a different name," I said. "Until I leave Berlin, it is too dangerous to let anyone reading the paper know I am here."

"You are in Berlin?" His voice rose in astonishment.

"Yes."

Icy silence poured down the line. Herr Marceau was having an affair with a German actress and longed for a posting in Berlin. I knew that he viewed my filing stories from here as a personal affront, but I would not hide the orphans' story to mollify his ego. He said, "I see."

"I have no intention of staying longer than I need to." I glanced through the glass at Paul. He stood with his hands in his pockets, weight on both legs, even though I knew it must hurt him.

"You got another letter today from Berlin," he said. "It was no love note."

"Same author as before?" Nearby, Anton had crossed his arms and leaned against the side of the booth, staying as close to me as he could. And eavesdropping.

"Same as before, except that the author said something about how 'he wrote her and said that he would meet with you that day.' Does that make any sense?"

"No." But I wished that it did.

"Should I fetch the letter?" Herr Marceau asked. "I'm sure you will want to hear it in its entirety. It is quite . . . colorful."

I bet. I had no desire to spend even a second on such foolishness. Paul and Anton needed to get home. "I have to get off the line soon. But tell Herr Knecht that I did not intend to come here."

"So someone coshed you on the head and dragged you across the border?" he sneered.

"After a fashion," I said, "yes. Please, see if Herr Knecht can get me back out."

Astonishment crackled down the line. "You are not joking."

"I wish that I were." I pulled my wool coat tight against the cold. "Get a lawyer on this."

"Why not take the next train home? The paper could send someone else to cover the story." He meant himself, of course, and I would have been happy to give him this one.

"It is not about the stories. I was forced into the country illegally," I said. "And I am not certain they would let me leave again."

He sucked in a long breath. "The Swiss embassy?"

"Find out if Herr Knecht can get assurances that they will help me leave," I said. "And I will be on their doorstep in an hour."

"That sounds very dangerous." He did not believe me.

"I know," I said. "Can you get Herr Knecht?"

He hesitated. "He is not here."

I wondered if he told the truth.

"Are you certain you do not wish to hear the letter?"

"I have to get off the line now," I said. "If it is tapped by the Gestapo, they might be on their way."

"You sound like a spy film."

"I have stumbled into one," I said. "Take care, Herr Marceau."

I broke the connection and herded Paul and Anton into the nearest subway station.

Dark and cold pressed against us as we rode back to the apartment.

I massaged my temples. My head still ached, and I felt more tired than I should. Still, I had managed to stay awake the entire day, which had to be an encouraging sign.

Anton rode next to me, subdued by the trip to the orphanage. He was deeply shaken by what he had seen, aware that might have been his fate had I not taken him in. I wrapped an arm around his shoulder, and he leaned against me.

Paul sat in silence on a different bench. I suspected that he had not expected to find Ruth in the orphanage, but now he had no hope and no idea where to turn. His best source would be the mysterious man whom Anton had discovered, but who might know more about him? Miriam must have had friends, surely. Hopefully friends who had not been deported. Tomorrow we would find them.

We arrived at the apartment building. Paul insisted that Anton and I go in a few minutes before he did, so that no one would think that we were together. He had not been that careful when he had come in with Maria yesterday. Or perhaps he had.

I got ready for bed. Paul had pressed me to use Ruth's bed instead of spending another night on the tired sofa. Anton had already lain down on the blankets I spread for him on the floor next to me. Before I settled in to bed, I donned Sarah's old nightgown and robe and padded out to the living room, where Paul sat on the sofa in darkness. "Paul?"

He raised his head slowly. "Yes?"

"We will start fresh tomorrow. Someone will know this man who visited Miriam. And he might well know where Ruth is."

"That's kind of you to say, Hannah."

Helpless, I stared at him.

"Good night," he said, and I understood his tone of dismissal.

I left him sitting in the dark and returned to Ruth's room, where I stepped carefully over a sleeping Anton, who lay on his back, arms flung out to both sides as if he had to cover as much of the floor as possible. He had kicked off the blanket. I covered him again.

I lay on my side on the little bed and watched his boyish chest rise and fall. I could not imagine life without him, as I suspected that Paul could not imagine life without Ruth. He would not have to. We would find her.

Tomorrow morning, Lars would return from his mysterious errand. He would have some idea of what to do. He had been an effective police detective. He would think of things that we could not. He would help Paul to find Ruth.

Stop that, I told myself. *Do not rely on him. You should know better.*

A knock on the door interrupted my thoughts. Murmurs came from the front hall. Two men, by the sound of it. Paul and Lars, or someone else?

I peered out my door and down the hall. A man in a white coat stood behind the sofa, talking to Paul. Was he the mystery man and was that a scrap of his coat on the cupboard hinge?

I waited until he left before venturing out in my robe. Paul sat alone on the sofa, hands resting on his knees.

"Was it someone with news of Ruth?" I stood next to him.

He stared at his knees. "Yes."

"Where is she?" I asked. "Is she well?"

"She is in a safe place." He sounded defeated rather than relieved. "And she is fine."

My heart lightened. Ruth was well. "Where is she?"

"Somewhere where she is better off than she ever could be with me."

"What nonsense! Who told you that? You are her father."

He turned his hands palm up. "Perhaps she needs to start a new life, with a new identity."

"Paul—"

"What can I provide for her?" His words were angry, but his eyes were sad. "The same misery and death that her mother suffered? That's all I have to offer, Hannah. To her or myself."

"She is your daughter and she loves you. You cannot take away her father so soon after she lost her mother. Whom did you just speak to?"

"She is better off without me." He sank deeper into the sofa. "I wish it weren't true. But it is."

"Who was here?" I put my hands on my hips.

"I will not tell you, Hannah," he said. "So, please, stop asking."

"Then tell me where she is, so we can make certain that she is well." I felt like Paul's mother. I took my hands off my hips and sat next to him instead. The sofa creaked.

"She is my daughter. Not yours." He shifted until his leg was straight out in front of him

"Are you certain that—?"

"Any decisions about her welfare are mine alone. And she is better off without a Jewish father weighing her down. Everyone is." It was rare for Paul to speak with such authority, and I knew I would not be able to dissuade him. Not tonight, anyway.

"I hate to ask this, Paul." I hesitated. "Is Ruth yours?"

His shoulders slumped.

I pulled out the gold locket and removed Ruth's picture to reveal the blond man behind. "Do you know this man? Might he be Miriam's brother? Or a friend?"

"He is not her brother," Paul said. "Or a friend."

"But—"

"Enough, Hannah," he said. "Just . . . enough. Please, let me be. This is difficult enough without your meddling."

I shifted away from him on the sofa. He was correct.

"Don't be angry." He took my casted hand. "It's just all so hope-less."

"Sleep on it, Paul. Things will feel different in the morning."

"What if—?" His voice quavered, but he steadied it. "What if they don't?"

"Then we will see." I sounded brave, but I had no idea what we could do either.

He gathered me into his arms and rested his chin on my head, as he used to twenty years ago. Back then it felt hopeful, but tonight it felt lonely. Eventually, he kissed the top of my head and said, "It's late, my dear."

He disentangled himself and stood, extending a hand down to help me up. "Is your complicated friend Lars coming by tomorrow?"

"He says he is." I took his hand and let him pull me to my feet. "But he is not always reliable."

"Really? He strikes me as a very reliable man indeed, where you are concerned."

"That is exactly what I used to think," I said, "until I was proved wrong."

We walked back to our separate bedrooms.

"Best of luck with him," he said. "Thank you for all you have done for me."

"Of course," I said.

He touched my nose lightly with his fingertip. "Good night."

It sounded more like good-bye than good night. He turned and went into his room, pulling the door closed behind him. I stood uncertainly in the hall, staring at his closed door. I would talk to him again tomorrow, and make him see reason. If he just checked on Ruth once and made sure that she was safely settled, I would let it go.

I crept past Anton and settled into my child's sized bed. My head ached for a long time before I drifted off to sleep.

I awoke to the sound of a clatter, as if something had dropped to the floor. My heart raced. I lay still, listening. Silence shrouded the apartment.

The sound might have come from upstairs or outside, but I could not shake a feeling of dread. I sat up and listened. Nothing. I got quickly out of bed, driven by a sense of urgency I did not understand.

The streetlamp's dim light provided enough illumination for me to see Anton, still sound asleep. I dropped a hand to his warm head, stepped around him, and padded to the door, wood cold under my bare feet.

I crept through the living room, the bathroom, the kitchen, and the hall, searching for an intruder. All cloaked in late-night darkness, but empty. I paused in front of Paul's door. I thought of knocking, but decided instead to glance in without waking him.

I eased the door open. Hinges squeaked, and I froze. Paul's curtains stood open to the streetlamps, his room brighter than ours. His form lay at an angle under the quilt, taking up more than half the mattress. Years before, I had chided him about using more than his fair share of the bed.

One pale hand dangled off the mattress almost to the floor. Nothing looked out of place, but a compulsion rose up my spine. I pushed the door open and stepped into the room.

The floor was empty except for a small thin shape, centimeters below Paul's fingers. It rested in a pool of liquid. Had he spilled water?

I stepped closer. The familiar smell of blood filled my nostrils. It dripped from the tips of his fingers, landing on the small object. A straight razor. Had that caused the clattering that woke me? I wished I had gotten right out of bed and come straight here, before he'd had time to lose so much blood. Now that I looked for it, blood was everywhere. It stained the bedspread and pooled on the floor. Sadness unfolded in me like a giant bird.

I brushed it away and dashed to the bed. When I rolled him over, his eyelashes fluttered against his white skin. I felt for his pulse. Weak and thready.

"Paul," I said softly so as not to wake Anton. He did not move. I dropped to my knees next to the bed. How could he leave Ruth? Leave me?

I fumbled for a wrist, but the cast made me clumsy. His right arm seemed uninjured, but blood slicked the left. I lifted his wounded arm high above his heart and pressed hard against his wrist with my left hand.

I was slow, and every second counted. I cursed the Gestapo man who broke my arm.

Paul moaned and tried to pull his arm back down.

"Don't you dare fight me." I sounded harsh and angry, but I did not care. I smashed his arm against the wall and pressed on his wrist. He had missed the artery, but opened a large vein. He struggled weakly.

I tucked my chin to see better. A slit ran from his elbow to his wrist. I winced at the determination that the cut revealed. *Oh, Paul,* I thought. *Paul.*

I stared at the wound, trying to think as a nurse. He did not need stitches, I thought or hoped. I had no idea how I could get them into him if he did. He twisted his wounded arm. I pressed it harder against the wall with my good hand.

"Stay still," I said through gritted teeth. He collapsed, either because he understood or because he was too weak to fight.

With my casted hand, I yanked the frayed pillowcase off Miriam's pillow. I bit down on the edge and tore off a strip, the ripping sound loud in the quiet room. Even though my casted arm seared each time, I tore off another and another, dropping them awkwardly on the quilt and cursing my cast. Through it all, he barely stirred.

When the pillowcase lay in shreds, I bound up his arm. I worked from elbow to wrist. I had only one strong hand, so I had to tie the knots with my left hand and my teeth. Frau Doktor Spiegel would have marked me down on neatness, but by the time I finished, the bandage was secure.

When his arm was covered and the bleeding stopped, I wiped my hands on my nightdress, leaving streaks down the front. Both my hands were still sticky with blood. It had soaked into my nightgown at the knees when I knelt next to him. How much blood had he lost?

I felt for his pulse in his good arm. His heart beat steady and stronger than before. I let out a breath of relief, suddenly aware of the room's temperature, and that I had left Sarah's robe hanging next to my bed. Just as well, since it, too, would have been soaked in blood now. My headache returned full force, and I slid down to the floor by the bed. The wood felt cold on the backs of my legs.

He clutched my hand. "Hannah?"

"Here, Paul." The room whirled. Nausea grew in my stomach. I took a deep shuddering breath. I had to hold it together, for him.

"Why stop me?" he whispered.

"I am a nurse." I swallowed bile. "I could not help myself."

"Damn," he said. "Damn. Damn. Damn."

"We should get you to a doctor." Although I did not know if either of us could stand.

"Please," he said. "Let me stay here. Just don't leave me alone."

"I won't." I took his good hand and leaned my back against the side of his bed. It felt better to have something propping me up.

He stirred.

"Hush," I said, as if he were Anton, newly wakened from a nightmare. "Tomorrow."

He quieted.

Soon I would get up and call Frau Doktor Spiegel. I closed my eyes for a moment to rest. Only a moment.

14

Light seared my sleeping eyelids. I tried to open them, but they were too heavy. Was my injury to blame? A flame of panic ignited at the back of my skull, too small to help me.

"My god." A familiar voice.

Hands lifted me. I struggled through the pain in my head. Someone said the word *no* over and over, a litany.

Arms tightened around me, and the sound stopped.

"Not now," he whispered. "Please not now."

Arms crushed me. I conquered the pain in my head and pushed through to wakefulness. "Let me go!"

The arms did not release. Whoever held me rocked us both from side to side. Where was I? Why was I so cold?

"Can't breathe," I choked out.

The arms loosened. A fingertip trailed down my cheek. I wrenched open my eyelids. Lars had arrived and turned on the overhead light. He held me tightly.

"Forgive me," he said. "Please."

I focused on his familiar dark eyes, but a stranger looked back. As one had during my last visit, in 1936. Blood had triggered an episode in him, then. My blood. "Lars?"

He stared as if he truly could not believe that I spoke. He still did not recognize me. He was having another episode. I yanked my arms free and put my filthy hands on his warm cheeks. "Lars?"

Something stirred behind his eyes. Recognition? I held his face so that he could not look away. "Come back to me."

He blinked, but his expression did not change. I had not reached him. He fought his own demons, either the ones he had created as an interrogator for the SS or others I did not know.

"It's me, Hannah." I could barely move in his grip. I shivered, from cold and from fear.

Probably to warm me, he shifted me closer to his chest, hiking me into his lap. I felt him harden under my leg. Recognition dawned in his eyes. "Spatz?"

So that part remembered me best. Any other time, it would have been funny. I did not know whether to be offended or flattered. "Lars?"

His eyes cleared. He was back.

"Where?" He felt my head, my arms, my shoulders. "Where are you hurt?"

I put my hands over his, stopping his exploring. His eyes spoke a question. He was still there.

"I am not hurt." Or at least nothing new.

He pulled his hands free and went back to checking me. "But you're covered in blood. Where are you hurt, Spatz?"

"Not mine." I struggled to sit up. "Paul's."

Expressions chased across his face, ending with relief. He sagged against the side of Paul's bed. "Thank god." He kissed the top of my head, my forehead, my cheeks.

I leaned back before he could get to my lips.

He gently released his hold on me.

"What are you doing here?" I rested my palm on Paul's chest. He slept deeply. I took his pulse. Strong. He would make it through.

"I came back to . . ." Lars's gaze traveled around the room, noticing blood on the walls and dried in blotches on the floor. "What happened here?"

He noticed the razor. I had not bothered to move it. He picked it up. "I see."

"I need to clean up," I said.

He eased me off his lap and stood. Light-headed, I closed my eyes and leaned back against Paul's bed.

Lars put a hand down and helped me to my feet. I swayed.

"Your head?" he asked.

"Hurts. Dizzy." I read alarm in his eyes. "Not like right after."

His eyes said that he did not believe me, but at least his mouth stayed silent.

I took an unsteady step to the door. "I must wash up."

He walked next to me, opened the bathroom door, and watched while I sat on the vanity bench in front of the sink. When he clicked on the light, I stared into the mirror, shocked. Blood smeared my cheek. Blood crusted on my hands and cast. Blood streaked the front of my nightdress. No wonder he had thought me injured or worse.

He ran hot water into the sink and wet the washcloth. I watched him in the mirror as he stroked it gently across my face. His expression said he expected me to stop him. I touched his hand. "I can do the rest."

He bowed slightly, picked up another washcloth, and left the bathroom. I listened to his steps approaching Paul's room before I closed the bathroom door. I took another four headache tablets, hoping they might temper the pain.

I studied my bloodstained hands. Paul's blood. It was caked in my knuckles and under my nails. If I had gotten to him much later, he would not have survived. Paul, gone.

I savagely scrubbed my hands clean and pulled the nightdress over my head. I stared at the bloodstains. I shivered, but I had nothing else to put on.

As if on cue, Lars rapped on the door. "I have your robe."

I opened the door a slit, and he handed it through. "Thank you."

I closed Sarah's too-short robe tight around me. At least it was warm.

Although chilled through from sitting on the floor and from washing up, I lingered in the bathroom. I did not want to face Lars. He moved quietly around the living room, and I wondered what he was doing.

Eventually, Lars called softly. "Spatz?"

I stumbled out of the bathroom into the living room.

He led me to the white-tiled stove that Paul and Miriam used to heat the apartment. I touched the smooth tiles, warm under my icy fingertips, glad that he had built a fire in it. He helped me into one of the chairs drawn up close to the stove, wrapped a warmed blanket around me, and tucked it under my feet. I took a cup of hot tea from his hand, and he sat in the other chair, very close. "I made it while you were washing up."

I wrapped my cold hands around the warm cup. "Would I frighten Anton if he saw me now?"

Lars shook his head, eyes still worried. He handed me headache tablets, and I swallowed another two with a long sip of tea.

"I should sit with Paul, in case he wakes and tries to do himself harm again." Warmth soaked into me. I felt drowsy.

"I tied him to his bed," he said. "It seemed the best way for all of us to get some sleep."

"I thought you did not have the heart to tie someone down. Or so you told me."

He smiled with half his mouth. "I said I didn't have the heart to tie *you* down. I have no such qualms about Paul."

"Poor Paul," I said.

"And I would much rather climb into your bed than his."

I blushed and looked at the steaming tea. "I had better clean Paul's room before Anton sees it."

"I already did," Lars said. "As best as I could in the overhead light. You just sit."

I set down the tea and settled into my soft blankets, grateful that I had nothing else to do. "Thank you, Lars."

He took my hand. "How do you feel?"

"Tired," I said. "But my head feels much better."

He squeezed my hand. "I am relieved to hear that."

"Thank you," I said again.

Fingers lingering on my temple, he tucked a strand of hair behind my ear. "My pleasure. More than you know."

I grazed my fingertips down the line he had traced across my temple. I should get up and take myself to bed. I closed my eyes. I drifted off to sleep wondering what he was doing in Paul's apartment, in Paul's bedroom, in the middle of the night. Why had he not waited until morning to come around?

I awoke in Ruth's bed. Anton's blanket lay neatly folded on the floor. I touched my temple. For the first time since Poland, my head did not hurt. I lay there, savoring the absence of pain.

But I could not lie in bed forever. Judging by the light, it was late morning. I had slept long and deeply. I put on a dress, made my bed, and headed for the living room.

On the way, I peeked into Paul's empty room. Lars had cleaned away every trace of last night's disaster so thoroughly that I wondered if I had dreamed it. My glance fell on my cast. Blotches of blood stained its surface. No dream, then. Where was Paul? My heart beat faster.

In the living room, Lars and Anton sat on the sofa building a kite of brown paper and sticks. Lars had rolled up his shirtsleeves.

"Good morning!" called Anton. "Lars and I went shopping already. Your breakfast is laid out in the kitchen."

Lars looked up from the kite. He was tying a knot with his teeth, while he held the kite's ribs with both hands. He looked as carefree as Anton. My heart somersaulted in my chest. *No,* I told myself sternly, as if I spoke to a disobedient child. My feelings for Lars did not matter. Only my actions counted, and I had best mind them.

Lars finished the knot and handed the kite to Anton. "Good morning, Spatz. You look better than you have for days."

"As do you." He was shaved and showered and looked as if he'd had a good night's sleep, although he had to have slept less than I. "Where is Paul?"

"Kitchen," Lars said. "I rebandaged his arm."

"You are a full-service man."

He gave me a wicked grin. "Not all my services have been fully utilized."

In spite of myself, I smiled.

"But," he said, "it's early yet."

I shook my head at him and walked into the kitchen. My smile faded when I saw Paul. He hunched over the table, deathly pale, clutching a teacup with his right hand. Lars had done a neat job with the bandages, but I itched to take them off and see if Paul needed stitches. I did not think so last night, but it had been dark, and I had been too concerned with stopping the blood flow to worry about long-term healing. "How are you?"

Paul raised sunken eyes to me and grimaced.

I helped myself to a roll, drizzled it with honey, and poured a cup of tea. Lars and Anton talked in the living room about the best ways and places to fly a kite.

"Do you intend to try that again?" I asked Paul.

His lips thinned. "I think I'll take your friend Lars up on his offer instead."

I choked on a crumb and coughed. "What offer?"

"He said that you were badly injured a few days ago, that he will not let me make you another one of my casualties, and if I had any more drama I needed to exorcise, he would happily put me out of my misery somewhere quiet so you wouldn't be disturbed."

I stared at him openmouthed. I would have a word with Lars. He had no right to speak so to Paul. I started to stand.

"He was correct to be angry." Paul put his hand on my arm. I stopped. "I did not know that you were so ill. Are you all right?"

"I am fine." I sat. "I am more worried about you. I apologize for Lars—"

"I don't know your complicated history with him," he said. "But I'm starting to like him."

I grimaced. "It is not his right to tell you what you can or cannot do in your own home. With your own life."

"But you had the right to stop me from doing what I wanted with my own life?" He took a sip of tea.

"That was—"

"Different?" he interrupted. "Because you did it?"

"I am not going to apologize for trying to save your life," I snapped.

"Perhaps you should not make Lars apologize for trying to save yours." He splashed more tea into his cup, as if this ended the discussion.

I swallowed my retort. I slept in for a few hours, and suddenly everyone had befriended Lars.

I had to admit that he had taken good care of me last night, that he must have spent a great deal of time cleaning up blood in Paul's room, that breakfast was lovely, and that he had entertained Anton so that I could sleep in. If I were not careful, I would end up friends with him as well. Fräulein Ivona's red mouth appeared in my mind, and I took a deep breath. I remembered too well where befriending Lars led. I would not let him betray me again.

I tasted my tea: orange pekoe, my favorite. Lars again.

"Paul," I said finally. "What will you do?"

He picked at his bandage. "I don't know."

"You cannot try to take your own life again." I moved his fingers off the bandage before he unraveled it. He let me.

"You won't allow it?" He dropped his injured hand in his lap.

My teacup clanked into its saucer. "Think about Ruth. She needs a father more than ever."

"Perhaps she has a better one." His brown eyes held so much pain, it hurt to look at him.

"What does that mean?" I asked. "Who?"

"Enough, Hannah. As I said last night, I'm not going to explain myself to you." He sat up straighter. "I am no good to her here."

"Then leave Germany," I said. "Take her out. I know a man who might get you false papers—"

"Where would I go?"

"New York," I said. "Sarah would take you in. Herr Klein has a spare room."

Herr Klein was an ancient Jewish jeweler who had fled Berlin in 1931. He and Paul had been friends. He would help Paul, and Ruth, too.

Paul put his bandaged hand gently over mine. "Always working to solve the world's problems, aren't you?"

"I did not spend years of my life dragging you back after the War to lose you now, Paul."

He smiled, not a real smile, but something. "So I owe it to you?"

"You owe it to Ruth. And yourself. And some of it, yes, to me."

He squeezed my hand. "We'll see."

"See what?"

"What's next." He studied our joined hands.

"You have to see that she is well settled," I said. Hopefully, when he saw her, he would change his mind. "At least that."

"Do I?"

"Who once told me that one cannot make a decision without all the facts?" I said. He had told me that.

He smiled reflexively. "Some fool or other, I imagine."

"No fool like an old fool." I put my hand on top of his. "Let's find out the facts, Paul. Then you can make your decision."

"I'll go see," he said. "Happy?"

He meant it. I smiled with relief. "Yes."

"But alone." He took his hand back and stroked his bandaged arm. "I don't want either of us to do anything that might endanger Ruth in her current situation."

"What could we—?"

"Leave it." He sounded worried. "Please, Hannah. Trust me?"

I wanted to ask how I could trust him after last night, but when I looked into his eyes, all I could do was nod. I could not add to his burden.

I put away the breakfast things, hoping that the familiar domestic tasks would bring me peace. But they did not. Paul seemed safe for today, but tomorrow, I could not see. Then again, were any of us safe? Could I find someone to create false papers for all of us, including Paul and Ruth?

Herr Silbert was in prison. Or was he? I had only the shopkeeper's word. I looked at the sun outside. In a few hours, a good friend and police officer would be having his lunchtime cigar. I could catch up with him and ask him to check on Herr Silbert's whereabouts. I only hoped that this meeting would go better than my last meeting with the police officer, when he and his wife had expressed their loyalty to the Nazi government and summarily dismissed me after I had choked down a piece of strudel.

I ran water in the sink. Paul stood next to me. He picked up a plate. I took it out of his hand. "You cannot wash with your wounded arm."

"But you can?" he asked tiredly.

"We have two arms between us," I said.

"Like a three-legged race." He stepped closer and wrapped his wounded arm around my shoulder. "I have a right, you have a left."

I held a plate while he washed it and rinsed it, then passed it to him to place on the drainboard.

Behind us, Lars cleared his throat. Paul lifted his arm off my shoulder. I turned to face Lars, who gave me an icy look. I glanced up at Paul. Lars, with his different young girlfriend every week, dared to be jealous of my friendship with Paul? I stayed close to Paul's side.

"May we go to the park to fly my new kite?" Anton popped out from behind Lars. Perhaps not such a bad idea. The best concealment was pretending to be a normal German family doing normal family activities. Hiding in an apartment, particularly in the Jewish quarter, was likely to invite questions from the neighbors. Playing in the park was not.

But everything in Nazi Germany had risks.

I sighed. I might as well let Anton have a fun afternoon. I had a few hours to spare before I hoped to meet my friend with his lunchtime cigar and find out more about Herr Silbert.

"It will do us all good to get out into the fresh air." Lars nodded toward Anton, but he meant Paul.

"That sounds delightful." I said with forced enthusiasm.

Lars looked at Paul and me, still standing close together. He raised his teacup toward me as if in a toast. So, he thought I was interested in Paul now. Let him. I tilted my head to show that I acknowledged Lars's gesture.

"The paste is dry on the kite," Anton said. "See?"

He turned to show me. The kite's wooden rib jostled Lars's arm. Tea spilled down the front of Lars's white shirt.

He pulled the shirt away from his undershirt, but both were already soaked through.

"I'm sorry," Anton said.

"It serves to reinforce my point that indoors is no place for a kite." Lars unbuttoned his shirt. He slipped it off and hung it over his arm. "I'll go wash up."

He had always looked good in an undershirt. I turned back to the breakfast things so that he would not catch me looking.

"I have something you can borrow," Paul said.

But before he could fetch it, someone knocked on the front door.

"I'll get the door," Paul said. "Into my room. All three of you."

15

Anton, Lars, and I slunk down the hall to Paul's bedroom. My heart sped up when I stepped across the threshold. The clean bedspread, the light through the curtains. Everything felt warm and friendly, as if last night had never happened.

Lars rested his palm on my lower back, as if to keep me in balance, and I found myself leaning against it. I stood up straight. What did he feel in this room? What had he been thinking as he held me on the floor last night, soaked in blood? To whom did he think he apologized? It had not been to me; of that I was certain.

A little boy's voice piped up from the front door.

"Reuben." Anton stepped toward Paul's door. "May I go talk to him?"

"But stay in the apartment," I said.

Lars pulled his undershirt over his head and wiped the back of the shirt across his chest, which looked every bit as muscular as I remembered. He dropped the soiled undershirt on Paul's bed. Last night I had rested against the side of that bed in Lars's arms. I tried hard not to think about how much I wanted to be there again.

Instead, I stepped to Paul's wardrobe and opened the door one-handed. Shirts and undershirts were stacked neatly on the top shelf, where he had always kept them. I took out a white shirt and an undershirt and turned to give them to Lars.

He stood by the window with his back to me, looking at the street below.

Walking over with the shirts, I noticed his back. In 1936, it had a few shrapnel scars, but a new story of pain was inscribed on his skin now. Angry pink lines of scar tissue crisscrossed his back.

He caught my expression reflected in the window. "Quite a mess, isn't it?"

I offered him Paul's undershirt. "How?"

"Russian prison." The undershirt muffled his words as it went over his head. "About a week after we parted. Not a hospitable lot, I'm afraid."

I gasped.

He gently tilted my chin up so I had to look into his eyes. "You didn't think I was avoiding you on purpose, did you?"

Shame burned in my cheeks. I had thought just that. "Why were you arrested?"

"A charge of espionage," he said. "Carelessness."

If I had not uncovered the evidence that had sent him to Russia, he would never have been there to be arrested. "Lars—"

"Don't take responsibility for that." He released my chin and put on Paul's shirt. "You have enough already."

"How did you get out?"

"The prison decided to withdraw its hospitality in January." He quickly buttoned the front of the shirt. Paul was taller than he, so the shirt hung on him as if he were a boy dressing in his father's clothing. It looked strangely endearing. I folded one of his cuffs back, conscious of how close my fingers were to the soft skin of his wrist. He drew my hand up toward his lips.

Anton spoke from the doorway. "January was ten months ago."

I took my hand off his shirt and stepped back from Lars. Ten months was a long time. What had he been doing?

"You certainly did not teach him to hold his tongue," Lars said.

"I do not excel at that myself, so I find it difficult to teach." I rubbed my fingers across the top of the hand that he had almost kissed.

Lars tucked in the shirt. "I can imagine."

I turned to Anton. "Do not be impertinent, Anton."

Anton crossed his arms.

"What, exactly, have I done to make you both so angry with me?" Lars asked.

He had left me waiting in Switzerland, thinking him dead, and he wondered why I might be angry? My head started throbbing, and I took a shaky breath.

"One of these days," Lars said, "perhaps we can have a conversation when you have no injury to hide behind."

"Doubtful." I thought back to conversations we had after I had been shot, had a broken rib, and had been poisoned by toxic gas. "I so often come to harm around you."

"Due to your efforts and in spite of mine." He swept past me into the hall.

"What did Reuben want?" I folded Lars's tea-stained things.

"To play marbles," Anton said. "May I?"

"We are just about to leave," I said. "How about you two play in the stairwell? I will fetch you on my way out."

Anton ran back toward the living room. Still thinking about Lars in prison, I followed more slowly.

Lars and Anton chattered in the living room about the kite.

"Where is Paul?" I asked.

"He left to borrow the neighbor's telephone," Lars said. "He said that he had an important call to make."

"We must wait for him," I said.

"But can I go play with Reuben right now?" Anton asked.

"Go," I said. "Do not leave the building."

I stood awkwardly next to Lars. I wanted to apologize for implying that he caused the trouble in my life, but the words stuck in my throat.

He watched me for a long moment. "Spatz—"

Paul opened the front door and strode into the living room, his face relaxed.

Lars's brow furrowed in exasperation. I knew how he felt. But I also felt afraid to hear what else he might say.

"How did your call go?" I asked Paul.

"Good news," he said. "I have an appointment in an hour."

"With whom?" I asked.

"Someone," he said. "That's all you're getting, Miss Journalist."

"Come with us to the park," I said. "If only for a little while."

"It is on my way," Paul said. "I think that is a capital idea."

From the top of the doorless cupboard that Ruth had been hiding in, Lars took a gray wool blanket. He slung it over his arm.

"We are ready to go now," Lars said. "Right, Spatz?"

Paul helped me into my coat. As he slipped it over my shoulders, he whispered in my ear. "What happened while I was gone? You look as if you've seen a ghost."

I shook my head. The question was, what had happened to Lars in prison? More important, what had happened since his release?

We trooped downstairs. Lars several steps ahead, Paul and I lagging behind.

"I'll go with you to the park." Paul said quietly, probably to keep Lars from overhearing. "Because I think you and Lars might need time with someone else minding Anton. But I can stay only a few minutes before I go see about Ruth."

I squeezed his arm. "You can leave now. Lars and I can sort things out."

He raised one eyebrow. "I have a little time."

Lars slowed, but he did not turn around.

"Please," Paul said. "Let me do this for you."

I looked up into his eyes, trying to decide whether he needed to gather his courage, or perhaps he was correct that Lars and I would not manage to sort things out with Anton around. Or both. "If you wish."

Anton and Reuben started guiltily when they saw us. What were they up to?

Lars took my arm before we stepped into the street. To have a

Jewish friend in Germany was shameful, but not illegal. An Aryan with a Jewish lover, however, was breaking the law, and both partners could be sent to a concentration camp. Any of Paul's neighbors might turn him in. Paul fell back to walk with Anton. Dark clouds glowered overhead.

We had gone only a few steps when Anton said, "I have more news."

I turned around in time to see Paul's shoulders raise. Anton looked at him worriedly. We all stopped walking. Luckily the sidewalks in the Jewish quarter were deserted.

"Out with it," I commanded.

"Reuben said that he did see the man who visited Miriam on the day of the deportations." Anton rushed through his words. "Reuben saw him come after everyone else left."

"Did he take her?" Lars asked. "Or any kind of bundle at all?"

I winced, not wanting to think about that.

"Reuben didn't see," Anton said. "But he might have."

"What else did you find out?" Lars asked. "Any new details?"

"This time I asked what he looked like," Anton said proudly. He was learning to be a detective. "He was tall and very thin. Reuben said he was a doctor. He had blond hair and round glasses and a long white coat." He looked at me meaningfully.

I thought of the scrap of white cloth that had been caught on the cupboard hinges. It could have belonged to a doctor's coat. And what of the mysterious visitor in the white coat the night before?

"Reuben also said—" Anton shifted his feet. He gulped and kept going. "—that the doctor asked to buy a baby once from his mother—"

"I know about the doctor," Paul interrupted. "He doesn't have her."

"Really?" I asked him. "Perhaps he and Miriam—"

"She is my daughter," Paul said, "not yours. And, yes, I am certain."

He brushed past us and trotted up the sidewalk.

Anton hurried to catch him. Paul's reaction was another mystery to solve. But first I had some questions for Lars. He took my arm, and we followed the others.

A woman hurried out of a kosher butcher shop with a packet wrapped in white paper. Two small children hung on her skirt. She kept her eyes low and stepped into the street to pass us.

Lars gripped my arm.

"It is because you look like a policeman," I said.

"I do not." He pursed his lips in irritation.

I studied his straight posture and his low fedora. "I see."

We walked a few steps in silence.

"Why were you at Paul's apartment in the middle of the night?" I asked Lars.

He patted my hand. "I had an errand to run. I came back when I completed it."

I hated it when he patted my hand, and he knew it. "What errand?"

"The second we have privacy, Spatz, I shall reveal all." He raised his eyebrows dramatically.

"Reveal all?" I asked. "What about public decency laws?"

"I shall exercise what restraint I can." He leaned close to my ear. "Which isn't always much."

I held my tongue. We caught up with Paul and Anton. Paul gave me an apologetic smile for walking off. I smiled back.

Shop after shop sported the same sign in their front windows: JEWS ARE NOT WELCOME HERE. Crudely painted yellow stars adorned a few buildings. I could not accept that this was my Berlin. Even though I now lived in Switzerland, I considered Berlin my home, had always treasured a hope that the Nazis were wrong about their Thousand-Year Reich, and that I would return someday for good. But there seemed no way to undo this.

Paul caught my eye. "You can become accustomed to it."

"I hope not," I said.

"How can you get used to it?" asked Anton. "It's wrong."

"You do it because you have no choice," Paul said. "I've done nothing but try to emigrate since 1935. I can't get out. They canceled all the passports of German Jews in October, so I can't even take a trip and fail to come back."

Anton looked at me, as if he knew that he should not be listening.

Paul kept talking. "I have no relatives outside of Germany to sponsor me. And my job skills are useless abroad. Newspaper writing? In German?"

"What will you do?" Anton asked. I wondered what we would do and how we would get out ourselves.

"Get to Palestine," Paul said. "However I can."

I took a step toward him, but he sidestepped away. "You don't want to be seen as having any kind of relationship with a Jewish man, Hannah. Anything sets tongues to wagging."

As if to agree with him, Lars kissed the top of my head. I glared at him. Out of the corner of my eye, I saw Paul smile.

"There's the park!" Anton pointed ahead of us at a long stretch of dead brown grass surrounded on all sides by tall apartment buildings. On the edges, bare trees lifted heavy limbs up to the steely sky as if they never expected spring to return. Wind blew my hair across my cheek. I shivered. If nothing else, it was enough wind to get the kite aloft.

Anton shifted the kite to his other hand and tugged on Paul. "Let's go! You, too, Lars!"

"I think I will stay here and keep an eye on your mother," Lars said.

Paul and Anton headed farther into the park.

Lars spread a gray woolen blanket on dead grass and patted it. I sat, but left a wide stripe of space between us, trying not to think about the gray wool blanket we had spent so much time under in 1936. This might be the same blanket. I blushed.

"How are you feeling today?" Lars asked. "Is your head better?"

"I am not interested in small talk." I tucked my hair behind my ears. "I believe this counts as privacy. Tell me why you came to Paul's apartment so late?"

"You do seem back to your old self." He lay on his back on the blanket and laced his fingers behind his head. He would feed me his story at his own pace. "It took me some time to complete my errand, and I came as soon as I finished it. I came in the middle of the night because I wasn't entirely certain that you would be at Paul's if I waited till morning."

I turned to face him so that I could watch his expression, careful to maintain space between us. "And? What were you doing?"

He studied my face long enough to make me uncomfortable before answering. "The *kommissar* acquired another lorry last night." He smiled impishly. "With a bit of skill."

"Herr Kommissar is a felon at heart."

"I have many things in my heart, Spatz." His eyes turned serious. "What about you?"

For years, my heart had caused me nothing but pain. Instead of answering, I watched Anton sprint across the brown grass with his kite.

"I built the compartment in the first lorry," Lars said finally. "I know a warehouse where I can work undisturbed by official questions to build a compartment in this one. When I'm done, I can smuggle you and Anton into Switzerland."

I let out a sigh of relief. "Thank you."

"I love that expression on your face," he said. "Relaxed. I haven't seen enough of it lately."

"How long will it take to build the compartment?"

"A few days," he said. "I can work only at night, when the shop is closed."

I studied him. "Why are you doing this?"

"Three reasons." He rolled onto his side, closing the space between us. I stiffened, but stayed put anyway.

He propped his head on one hand and lifted the thumb of his other hand up to tick off his first reason. I stifled a smile at the familiar gesture. "One, if you are caught, things would go badly for me."

"Self-interest?" I did not believe it. His Lars Lang identity was already useless, and nothing I said would change that. His smartest course of action was to leave Germany himself as Lars Schmidt immediately, without waiting to build a compartment in the lorry.

"Something like it." He extended his index finger. "Two, I landed you in this mess by not turning straight around and driving to Poland after we killed the Gestapo men."

I winced at the bald words. But he spoke the truth. We had killed them. I had killed one myself. I swallowed. "Why did you press on to Berlin?"

"Because I thought you might not live through the trip back to Poland."

"That would have been an easy solution to problem one." I pointed to his thumb.

"Simple," he said. "Not easy."

I could not meet his eyes. Anton had the kite in the air now and ran with it. Paul limped a few steps, then stopped. His leg clearly pained him.

"Spatz?"

I did not know what to say to his last words. "I believe you said you had three reasons."

Lars drew in a shaky breath. I turned my full attention to him. This was the real reason. My heart sped up.

"And third, and probably most important . . ."

"Lars?" I prompted.

"I've spent the last six months trying to convince myself that I don't." He rolled and unrolled the edge of the blanket.

"Six months?" I asked.

Lars raised his head and met my eyes. "When I saw you in Poznań, I realized that I do. I . . ."

"Do what?"

"I love you."

I stopped breathing. I should have a reaction to his words, but I felt numb, as if I waited for my emotions to catch up. I had never stopped loving him, but that did not mean that I was ready to fall into his arms and forgive him for everything he had done, or not done, in the ten months since his release from prison.

He looked terrified, which was how I felt. "Spatz? Do you still—?"

"What happened six months ago?"

Before he could answer, across the field, Anton cried out. I jumped to my feet. I sprinted across dusty grass and around an obstacle course of molehills. In the mostly empty park, no one else seemed to notice that Anton scuffled with three boys in a tangle of arms and legs. Two were his size, one larger. Halfway across the field, Paul gazed up at the kite now caught in a tree. He turned slowly.

Behind me I heard Lars and Paul running, too, but I outdistanced them easily.

I grabbed the tallest boy's bony arm as he drew back his fist to strike Anton and yanked him to his feet. His friends stood, too. Two were taller than I, one only slightly smaller. All three were flushed pink with exertion or anger. None lowered their fists. Anton scrambled up and held his fists up, too.

I gulped and raised both hands, palm out. "Stop this at once."

In the dirt at their feet, a fourth boy of six or seven curled in a sobbing ball.

Paul and Lars arrived and waded in, and the boys dropped their fists.

"I am a police *kommissar,*" Lars said sternly. "You will tell me what this is about."

Blood ran out of Anton's nose and dripped onto his shirt. I fished a handkerchief from my pocket and handed it to him. I longed to sweep him up in my arms, but knew that he would not thank me for it.

"That boy didn't want to prove he was no Jew pig." The tallest boy pointed scornfully at the little boy, whom I now saw had no pants. The older boys must have removed them to see if he was circumcised. I looked at Paul. He held one of the larger boys by the collar and looked unsurprised by the revelation.

Lars snatched a pair of shorts from the second tallest boy's hand and dropped them on the little one.

I knelt beside him. "Are you all right?"

He unrolled and grabbed his shorts. He slid both legs in, yanked them up, and ran. No one tried to stop him.

"Was he Jewish?" Lars asked.

"No." The tallest boy kicked a dirt clod near where the little boy had cowered. "That would have been the end of it, if this kid hadn't stuck his long nose in."

Anton glared at him. A bruise darkened his cheekbone, but other than that and his nose, he seemed in fairly good shape, considering that there were three of them.

"Is that what it has come to?" I asked. "Big boys like you picking on a little boy still in short pants?"

"Don't matter what size he is. A Jew's a Jew."

"Yet he was not Jewish, correct?" Lars rebuked him. "So you beat up and humiliated another good German boy."

I winced at the easy way those words came out of his mouth. Good German boy, as opposed to a Jew. A former SS officer, he was adept at navigating Nazi speech.

"We didn't know." Chastened, the three boys shifted their feet.

"Be off home," Lars said. "Think better next time."

Muttering, the boys marched off.

"I believe I must take my leave as well," Paul said. "As we discussed earlier."

He was going to visit Ruth. "Do you want me to—?"

"No." He shook his head. "This will be painful enough without spectators."

Imagining the unpleasantness that lay ahead, I took a step toward him. Lars dropped his arm around my shoulder, establishing ownership for anyone who watched.

Paul stuck his hands in his pockets. "I am quite able to shift for myself, Hannah."

I thought about the night before.

"Stop by the apartment tonight," he said. "We can talk about the next step."

So, at least now, he thought that there was a next step. "See you then, Paul."

"Until then." He nodded to Lars and Anton and left.

As his tall form limped across the grass, I longed to follow, but I stayed put.

Anton wiped the back of his hand across his bloody nose. "Where is he going?"

"To visit Ruth. He knows where she is now." I reached for the handkerchief that Anton held.

"I can do it." He gingerly wiped his nose.

"Just your nose?" Lars asked.

"They didn't land a lot of punches," Anton said.

"Good man," Lars said. "Three against one, and all larger than you."

"Lars," I said. "I do not wish him to be encouraged in fighting."

"I didn't encourage him before," Lars said. "Merely congratulated him after."

Anton beamed.

"Anton," I said. "Learn to restrain yourself. Things are different here than at home. The consequences of your actions can be much more severe."

"Yes, Mother," Anton said in a singsong. "I shall."

He had no intention of following my advice.

Lars laughed heartily.

I rounded on him. "What, exactly, is humorous here?"

He stopped laughing, but still smiled. "Watching you beset by problems that usually face me."

"What does that mean?" Anton asked.

"Trying to get someone to change their nature because you worry about them," Lars said.

"I am not your child." I crossed my arms.

"That is not what I meant," he said. "Only that it is difficult watching the brave and sometimes foolish."

Anton looked from one of us to the other. "I'm going to get my kite."

He bounded across the grass.

I turned and searched the empty field for Paul. He was gone.

"He told you not to follow him," Lars reminded.

"His Jewishness is a liability," I muttered. "Something he, as a man, cannot hide."

"Of course it is," he said gently. "Have you forgotten where you are?"

But Ruth could hide. She looked Aryan. And, as a girl, she was not circumcised. As much as it pained me to think it, perhaps Paul was correct to let her go.

16

Lars and I came to the blanket. I took one end, Lars the other. We shook off the grass and folded it in half, then stepped close together. Our knuckles touched. I admired the way his eyes crinkled in a little arc in the corners when he smiled like that. It was his first real smile since before Poland. I smiled back.

"Spatz." His voice was low. "You never answered my question."

I glanced over his shoulder at Anton halfway up a tree.

I took the blanket from his hand and completed the final folds before giving it back. I did not know what to say, and I could not even begin to discuss it with Anton seconds away.

I cleared my throat. "I need someone who can make inquiries without being suspicious. A policeman."

"Despite what I just said," he said. "I am no longer a policeman."

"I know," I said.

He hung the blanket over his arm. "But I can make inquiries."

"Not you." I pulled my gold watch out of my satchel. "I need to run an errand, alone."

"Dare I ask what it is?" He straightened his hat again, a nervous habit.

"I want to talk to a friend and find out where Herr Silbert is. Can you mind Anton?"

"I have sources I could contact about Herr Silbert."

"As do I." I did not trust his sources, and I was still unsure if I trusted him, in spite of what he had said on the blanket. He had told me that he loved me before, but it had not been enough for him to meet me in Switzerland, or even to tell me that he was still alive.

I could see that he wanted to argue the point, but he merely said, "How long do you need?"

I watched Anton climb down the tree with the rescued kite. "A few hours?"

"Some days," Lars said, "I feel like an errand boy."

"But a reliable one?" I asked.

He smiled. "Full service. And don't forget it."

Anton jogged across the field, winding up the kite string. "Really?" I asked.

Lars touched my shoulder. "Oh, yes."

Anton reached us. "The rib cracked when it hit the ground."

"We can repair it later," Lars said. "I believe your mother has a mission."

"A mission?" Anton smiled conspiratorially. "What's my part?"

"Helping me take a stolen lorry to an illegal shop to have it painted," Lars said.

Anton looked delighted.

"Lars," I said, "could you not think of something more—?"

"You have errands to perform," he said. "As do I."

I put his Lars Lang and Lars Schmidt passports in my satchel. With luck, Herr Silbert could use the German entry stamp on the Lars Lang passport for both Schmidt passports, and Anton's. I had a goodly amount of Swiss francs. If I found Herr Silbert, it ought to be all he needed.

We arranged to meet at five o'clock at the Brandenburg Gate. I kissed Anton good-bye, and he let me. I did not kiss Lars, although I was tempted when he proffered his cheek.

Before I went down the stairs to the subway, I turned around to wave good-bye one last time.

When I got to Alexanderplatz, I checked my watch. I had ten minutes. Plenty of time. I took the steps up to the daylight, emerging a block from the police station. I sat on the bench at the bus stop, drew out my sketch pad, and sketched an old Alsatian dog resting under his master's table at a café across the street. White fur stippled the black on his muzzle. Careful to appear engrossed while watching the street, I took my time with the drawing. But because I could not control the pencil properly with my hand in a cast, the picture was terrible.

I had not sketched anything in a long time, and I missed it. When I worked in Berlin as Peter Weill, I drew courtroom sketches every day for the newspaper. All those criminals seemed small time, now that the real criminals were in charge.

If Fritz Waldheim followed his old patterns, he would come by soon, smoking his after-lunch cigar and taking his after-lunch walk. If he did not arrive, I would have to go to his home and leave a message with my friend, Bettina. I hoped it would not come to that, as on my last visit they had sung the praises of the Nazi regime, and I did not trust them not to turn me in. The memory still stung. The Nazis had robbed me of my oldest friend, and I would not forgive them for it.

But here he came. His rolling gait was unmistakable, even though he wore a long brown overcoat and a new fedora, pulled low like Lars's. My hand sketched a nervous line on the paper, ruining the shading. Out of the corner of my eye, I watched his approach. What came next had to be handled delicately.

"Excuse me," I said when he was only a few steps away. "Would you care to buy my drawing?"

"No, thank you." He touched his hat politely before he recognized me. He faltered, but covered for it by sitting next to me on the bench. "Perhaps I will have a look at it."

"It looks a bit like your dog, Caramel."

"He died." Fritz's gray eyes were hard.

I slid my palm across the paper. "How are Bettina and the children?"

"Better than you," he said. "Someone who knows that we were friends from before showed me your file. You are wanted for murder. Double murder."

"They threw me in the trunk of a car in Poland," I said. "They intended to kill me."

"I don't want to know any of that," he said. "Get the hell out of Germany."

"I cannot," I said. "My passport was not stamped when we crossed the border because I was, as I said, in the trunk."

He bit down on his cigar. "What do you need?"

"Information on the whereabouts of Herr Silbert, the forger I did that piece on in the twenties. Do you remember him?"

"I'll get a look at his file," he said. "Meet me two blocks farther south in half an hour."

"Thank you, Fritz," I said. "You might be saving my life."

"I might not be either." He took the cigar out of his mouth and pointed it at me. "Don't hold out too much hope. If he was arrested these days, he'd need a wily lawyer to get back out."

"How is it here?" I asked.

"It's bad. Loyalty to the Party is everything." A shadow passed across his eyes. "The children are part of the Nazi machine now. Soon enough, they'll send my boys off to war."

I ripped out the sketch. "Tell Bettina I said hello."

"I'd rather tell her you said good-bye." He took the sketch and handed me a ten-mark note before marching down the sidewalk toward Alexanderplatz.

I drew another sketch, this one of a young couple lingering late over coffee. The picture could have been drawn any time in the last twenty years. I liked that about it. If I had done a better job of it, I would have offered it to them.

Instead I closed the sketchbook and left for Fritz's suggested rendezvous point.

Once I arrived, I found little to draw to keep me occupied, but it would not do to be seen as loitering suspiciously, so I drew a section of cobblestones with a cigarette butt lodged between stones. I sketched and shaded happily, glad to be doing something innocent and mundane. I was getting better at working with the cast, too.

A shadow fell over my picture. I looked up to see Fritz's back retreating down the sidewalk. I stood to follow and noticed a scrap of white paper on the ground. I dropped my pencil next to the paper and picked up both. The paper contained only an address. And that, I suspected, was all I would get out of Fritz.

I packed everything back into my satchel and took the subway to Kreuzberg, and the address Fritz had left for me.

Dark trees stood sentinel on the sidewalk. I stood between them in front of a brown brick building of four stories capped by a high copper roof. The building was well kept, stoop newly swept, curtains drawn to keep in the warmth.

I scanned the names on the bells, stopping at SILBERT. I rang his bell and waited. No answer. I rang again and again. Perhaps he was away at a job; it was the middle of the day. I smiled at the thought of Herr Silbert toiling behind a desk at a legitimate job.

I rang the landlady's bell.

A woman with a back bowed with age came to the door. She held the door with one gnarled hand and stood in the threshold. "We have no free apartments."

"I am here looking for someone. A Herr Silbert."

She angled her head to look at me. Milky cataracts covered one blue eye, but I suspected that she saw fine out of the other. "What for?"

"We are old acquaintances," I answered. "May I leave him a message?"

"He's not here," she said. I could not tell if she told the truth. "Perhaps he'll pick it up when he gets back."

I scribbled a quick note on a page torn from my notebook, telling him that I was in town and would love to meet him. I wrote the number of the paper in Switzerland and asked him to leave a message with a suggested meeting time. I suspected that Herr Silbert, being rather an expert in the field, would recognize my handwriting, but I signed it only Weill. That, he would know for certain. He had saved the articles I wrote about him as Peter Weill in a scrapbook.

I folded the note and handed it to the old woman. Her swollen fingers unfolded it. She settled a pair of wire-framed glasses on her nose and read it in front of me while I stared at her incredulously. I had assumed she would read it, but had expected at least a pretense of privacy.

"Like Peter Weill, from the newspaper?" she asked.

I stepped back in shock, glad that she looked at the paper and not my face. "Similar."

"Paper's garbage now," she said. "Used to enjoy his stuff."

I wished that Maria could have heard that. I had written under the Peter Weill byline before her, and she wrote under it now, but all I said was, "I believe it is a pseudonym that the newspaper owns, so the writer can be changed."

"A good alias." She dropped the note into the pocket of her faded yellow dress.

"When is Herr Silbert expected to return?"

"Don't know," she said. "Before you ask, I don't know where he's gone. Keeps his own hours and keeps his business to himself. Pays his rent promptly."

"Will you see that he gets my note?" I wondered if she even knew Herr Silbert.

She studied me with her good eye before answering. "I will."

I thanked her and returned to the sidewalk. I leaned against a cold streetlamp and waited, in case Herr Silbert was inside and would come out in response to my note or send me a note himself.

I could not stand too long without attracting suspicion and had decided to find a stoop and pull out my sketch pad when curtains on a window on the fourth floor twitched. Someone watched the street, and me. I returned to the door and rang the Silbert bell again. This time the door swung open, and I stepped through.

The landlady stood in the hall. She held up four fingers and pointed to the stairs. I plodded up. My tired legs asked why he had to live on the top floor instead of the bottom. When I arrived at the landing, I hurried to the single door that stood ajar.

Suddenly conscious that it might be a trap, I hesitated. But I had to have valid papers. I went in.

No one stood in the darkness in the hall. I waited, one hand on the cold door handle.

Someone whispered my name.

"Herr Silbert?" I whispered back. I let out my held breath when I recognized him. He wore an immaculate white shirt, as always, although he had lost a great deal of weight.

"How did you find me?" His usually perfectly coiffed hair was longer than I had ever seen it. He had not been taking care of himself as well as he usually did.

"The police." I stayed near the door in case I needed to leave quickly. "An old police friend gave me this address."

"Who?"

"You know I cannot tell you that."

"Put down the satchel," he said. "Face the wall."

Fear coursed through my limbs. "Herr Silbert—"

"Quickly," he said. "I am no longer the patient man that you remember."

I slowly bent my knees and lowered my satchel to the ground, then turned to face the dingy gray wall.

He stepped close and ran trembling hands over my coat. I submitted. I could do little else.

He stepped back and held out his hand. When I shook it, his handshake had none of its usual strength.

"What do you need?" he asked.

"Exactly what I needed the last time I visited."

He wiped his hand on his fine tweed pants. They, too, hung loosely on his gaunt frame.

"Have you been ill?" I asked.

"I've been in a concentration camp," he said. "So I've been more than ill. Come along and leave the satchel there."

He led me out of the hallway and into a bare living room. It contained two leather club chairs and a coffee table, but none of the books or tools of his trade that I had expected.

He sank into one chair and gestured to the other.

I sat, aware that my satchel was not close to hand. When I was in Germany, it never left my side.

He leaned back in his chair with his eyes closed. He looked frail and weak. "I do not have the . . . facilities that I once had."

"What can I do for you?" I asked. "Do you have medication?"

He shook his head once and pointed his finger to a door. "Water?"

I hurried through that door and into a kitchen. In the cabinet I found a single glass, a single plate, and a single cup. He must live quite alone here. With growing uneasiness, I opened a bottle of mineral water and filled the glass.

When I brought it out and handed it to him, he took a sip and leaned back in his chair again.

"You should see a doctor," I said. "I can call a taxi and take you there myself."

He shook his grizzled head.

I knelt next to his chair and took his pulse. Fast, but slowing. "Do you have a heart condition?"

He slid his arm back so that I held his hand instead of his wrist. "Such a surprising one you are."

"Herr Silbert, your heartbeat is dangerously erratic, you must—"

"I know what you think I must do." He squeezed my hand. "Your kind heart will be your undoing."

"Your heart may be your undoing as well."

"Tell me why you are here," he asked.

"I have need of your expertise." I moved my fingers up to his wrist again to take his pulse. "I require passports for—"

"I no longer have the equipment for that."

I lifted my chin. "Can you recommend someone else?"

"No."

I could think of no other way to procure passports for Anton, and perhaps for Paul and Ruth. Perhaps, if Paul wanted to leave, they would all fit in the compartment Lars had promised to build. If so, I needed only to get my and Lars's passports stamped to show that we had entered Germany legally so that we could present them at the border. "Can you put stamps in existing passports?"

"For that I need only ink," he said. "Show me what you require."

I took out the Hannah and Lars Schmidt passports and handed them to him. He opened them and smiled. "You are still together. When I saw your reaction to the marriage certificate, I thought perhaps I had made a mistake."

I had no desire to explain my complicated relationship with Lars. I took out his Lars Lang passport and flipped it open to the last stamp, showing that he had entered Germany legally on the night I was kidnapped. "This is what I need to have copied."

Herr Silbert drew a pair of horn-rimmed spectacles from his shirt pocket and studied the stamp. "Of course."

We haggled over the price, as we so often had in the past. I paid him with Swiss francs that I had not yet exchanged.

"You may wait here, if you wish." He stood, seemingly steady on his feet.

"I think my time would be better spent making soup," I said.

"*Ach,* Frau Schmidt," he said. "You should have told me that before we agreed on the price."

I returned to his kitchen and made a quick soup, using a withered carrot, one old onion, potatoes, and a yellowed stalk of celery, seasoned with a couple of beef Maggi cubes. It was the first meal that I had cooked in days, and I realized how much I missed the everyday feeling. Setting the pot to simmer, I made a list of groceries that I thought he might eat and presented it to him.

"I have finished the passports." He handed them to me. "Would you care to stay for dinner? It smells wonderful."

"I have an appointment soon." I thought of Anton and Lars waiting for me. "But I can spare a few minutes."

I had dished him out a large bowl of soup, me a small one.

I remembered one more thing in my satchel. "On the way over, I picked up your favorite cigarettes," I said. "Ravenklaus."

I had brought him those cigarettes when he was in prison for forgery and I had visited him as Peter Weill. Cigarettes for interviews.

He smiled, and new, deep wrinkles appeared around his eyes. "Bless you, Fräulein Vogel."

We ate our soup with little conversation and he saw me to the door. "I will be leaving Germany soon, and for good," he said.

"Good for you." I did not think he would live long enough to leave Germany. "I shall, too."

"Thank you for the soup," he said.

"Not my best meal," I said. "But I work with what is at hand."

We shook hands. I wondered if I would ever see the charming criminal again.

It was dark when I reached the Brandenburg Gate. I turned my side to the cold rain and paced anxiously next to the stone pillars. Punctual, Lars drove up in a black Opel Blitz lorry. The streetlights showed a tarp tied tightly over the contents of the lorry's bed. When I got close, I smelled a whiff of new paint.

Lars got out, and I slid in the driver's side to the middle of the seat. He piled in and slammed the door.

"Hello!" Anton said. "Isn't the lorry beautiful?"

"You are an Opel man," I said to Lars, remembering the Opel Olympia he drove during the 1936 Olympics.

"I had little time to shop," he said.

"Every busy man's curse." I imagined him searching the streets late last night, looking for a convenient Opel to steal.

"They're reliable." Lars pulled into traffic. The windshield wipers worked to keep up with the rain.

"What did you do while I was gone?" I asked Anton.

"We went shooting!" Anton's eyes shone in the light from the streetlamps. "At the Wannsee shooting range."

"Did you, now?" I said, staring at Lars.

"He's quite a good shot," Lars said. "We practiced with different pistols, and he was good with all of them."

"Lars gave me a gun." Anton drew out a Luger. I had carried one around myself in 1934, and Boris had killed a woman with it in self-defense. She had stabbed me, and we were being shot at as well, but I knew Boris still regretted his actions. It was not easy to take a life, especially not in the days and years after.

I took the pistol out of Anton's hand. It smelled of gun oil. "You cleaned it, too?"

"It's part of owning a gun," Anton explained.

I turned the heavy weapon over in my hands. At thirteen, Anton was too young for it. Did Lars seek to buy his affection, or did he truly think Anton needed to be armed?

"Lars," I said, "we shall discuss this later."

"Don't make him be in trouble," Anton said. "I think it's a very logical decision."

"I bet you do." I stuck the gun in my satchel.

"How was your meeting?" Lars kept his eyes on the road.

"The Schmidt passports are stamped, but I could not get any new ones." I knew I sounded defeated. Anton still had no papers, and how could I help Paul and Ruth?

Lars briefly touched my shoulder. "Once we get the compartment built, that won't be a problem."

"Can we go shooting again tomorrow?" Anton fidgeted on the seat. "I need all the practice I can get."

"I think we shall have to leave that up to your mother," Lars said. "For now, where are we going?"

"Take us to Paul's," I said.

"This is a mistake, Spatz." Lars stopped at a red traffic light. "Stay anywhere else, but not there."

"I need to check on him, Lars." The streets were completely empty. It felt eerie, like wartime.

"We should keep out of the Jewish quarter. We've been over this before. You cannot live with Paul there or you run the risk of being arrested for breaking the Nuremberg Laws." Lars's voice sounded like a lecture.

I bristled. "Paul and I are not—"

"You know better than to believe that the truth will save you. Or him."

I did. "I agreed to meet him tonight." To find out what he had decided about Ruth.

"I'll go with you," Lars said. "When you are done, we should spend the night elsewhere. I have a safe place where you and Anton can sleep. It's not luxurious by any means, but it will do."

"How irresistible you make it sound."

He dropped his hand off the steering wheel onto my knee. "I could be irresistible, if you were so inclined."

I moved his hand. Lars drove to Paul's apartment and parked out front. Anton jumped down first, still full of energy from his time at the shooting range.

I stepped out and looked up at Paul's dark bedroom window. Perhaps he was not home.

A white light flashed from Paul's kitchen. A gunshot broke the silence.

17

Anton took off at a run toward the front door.

"Stop!" I yelled, already knowing that he would not.

He was at the door first and streaked through before I made it to the stairs. I wished that I had not given him the key.

Anton pounded up the inside stairs, with me close on his heels. Far behind us, Lars uttered a muffled curse.

Paul's front door stood open. Anton burst through and ran for the kitchen. I raced after him. Anton stopped in the living room, staring through the doorway.

I stepped past him and into the kitchen. Paul sat on a dining room chair, head back. A splash of darkness marred the wall behind him.

"Wait here," I told Anton.

He nodded, eyes on Paul. I put my hand on Anton's head and turned it so that it faced away from Paul. He let me. His neck drooped forward. I held him in a hug. I should have protected him from this. I should have protected Paul.

Lars appeared in the doorframe, gun drawn and held in front of him. "Touch nothing. If you listen to only one thing I say, let it be that."

"Yes, sir," Anton said.

Lars quickly surveyed the kitchen. "Stay here. Both of you."

"Yes, sir," Anton repeated. Lars looked at me.

"I am going to examine Paul," I said. "I will not leave this room."
Lars nodded and walked down the hall, gun still out. Did he think someone else was in the apartment?

I walked Anton a few paces into the room, still facing away from Paul's body.

I left him there and stepped past the chair where Paul and I had sat and talked only this morning. My shoe crunched on broken crockery. Someone had torn the tablecloth from the table and knocked the dishes to the floor.

Unheeding, I walked through the mess to reach Paul. His elegant hands dangled over the chair's arms, his head leaned back, his familiar brown eyes frozen wide in death.

Far behind me, I heard Lars walk through the apartment, opening and closing doors, but it seemed as if he must be in another house. Here there was only Paul and me.

I reached out and closed his eyes. His eyelids felt soft and warm under my fingertips. I stroked his cheek with the back of my hand. A long day's-worth of stubble roughened it. I thought back to when I first met him, after the War. The hours we had spent as nurse and patient, the hours we had spent as young lovers planning a future together. Even after our affair ended, we had stayed friends for two decades. Grief clogged my throat. Tears blurred my eyes.

Footsteps came into the room.

"Steady, Anton," Lars said. "We'll be leaving soon."

Lars wrapped an arm around my shoulders, squeezed, and let go. I could not stop studying Paul's face. Paul. Gone.

Lars squatted and investigated the floor. Ever the clinical police officer. Or so I hoped. What if the scene triggered an episode in Lars? His right hand held his gun by his leg. I glanced back at Anton, still facing the wall.

"Lars?" I had to keep myself under control, particularly if Lars could not.

"Spatz." His voice was matter-of-fact. "There's no gun."

Paul's hand hung over the side of the chair. No gun rested below it. He had not committed suicide. I took his left hand, running my fingertips along the bandage. His long legs angled off to the side as if he might stand up and walk away.

Lars examined the bullet hole in Paul's forehead and tilted his head forward to look at the back. He stepped to the broken kitchen window, careful to touch nothing. He nodded once, pulled a handkerchief out of his pocket, and opened my satchel.

"Lars?"

He touched one finger to his lips, put his hand into my satchel, and took out the Luger I had confiscated from Anton in the lorry. He opened the handkerchief and wiped the gun down thoroughly. He curled Paul's fingers around the stock. Then he dropped the Luger onto the floor. It landed with a clunk.

"Please, Spatz," Lars said quietly. "We must go."

"Good-bye," I whispered to Paul. Lars put one arm around my waist and guided me away. I dropped my head and let him lead me.

He stopped at the table and picked up the only thing on its surface—a sheet of paper. I stopped, too, head down. He folded the paper and slipped it into his pocket.

"Now," he said, with new urgency. "We must go at once."

He shoved us through the living room, gun drawn again.

"Back door or front?" Lars muttered.

"There's a cellar," Anton said. "Paul showed me. It has a door, too."

"Perfect," Lars said. "Lead the way. No talking."

We stepped out of Paul's apartment into the deserted hall. Lars wiped fingerprints off the handle and left the apartment door open, as we had found it.

Anton stealthily led the way down the stairs, past the lobby door to the cellar.

We walked between tall slatted compartments used by the apartment dwellers for extra storage. In the gloom, I recognized boxes, chairs, a tall lamp. One of these compartments stored Paul's medals from the Great War and the typewriter he had lent me to type my first stories as a reporter.

Anton scurried through the maze like a mouse, sure in his route. We kept close to him. Anton found the back door, and Miriam's key opened it. We stepped into the cold night. Far above, hung stars that Paul would never see again.

Lars herded us a few blocks before pushing us into a dark doorway.

Sirens grew louder.

He cursed. "Their response time is too quick. Something's wrong."

"We need to keep moving," I said.

"I have to go back and get the lorry." He fit his pistol into my palm. "This is a Vis. Polish. You have eight rounds."

I gripped the stock tightly, comforted by the heft of it, but worried about aiming it left-handed.

"If I'm not back in five minutes, you're on your own. Good luck." He brushed my lips with his and stepped away.

Anton and I huddled in the cold doorway behind a chained-up bicycle that leaned against the railing. Left there by someone who did not trust his neighbors. Probably right not to.

With my right arm, I hugged Anton close. He shuddered, but fought down his tears. A brave boy.

"Is it always like this?" he whispered.

"What?" I whispered back.

"When you come to Berlin?"

I thought of my last visit, when my friend Peter Weill had died in my arms, or when I had stumbled on a dying man in my search for Anton in 1934. Corpses and grief littered my trips to Berlin. "Sometimes."

"I see why Boris doesn't want you to go."

"Boris is a wise man." Wise enough to leave me when he realized that I would not change.

Sirens closed in. I longed to run, but I wanted to wait another minute for Lars.

"I know why you go anyway," Anton whispered.

"Why?"

"To see. To help. To do what's right."

The Opel Blitz stopped in front of us.

We ran to it and climbed through the passenger door. Lars held out his hand for the pistol. I gave it to him.

"No one on the street," Lars said. "I can't tell if anyone's in the other apartments, of course, but it's the best I can do."

"Were the police there yet?"

"Almost." He pulled into the street and set out at a sedate pace. "But I think we got away clean."

"What's next?" Anton asked.

"I know a warehouse." Lars sounded tired. "We can stay there nights, but we must be gone during the workday."

I hunched into my coat. Lars patted my knee.

Anton huddled close to my side.

I thought of the look of resignation on Paul's face. His killer had not surprised him. He had expected to die. I shivered.

Lars put his arm around me and drove one-handed. I remembered how difficult it had been for me to drive with only my left hand when I followed him in his car full of dead Gestapo agents. So much death.

"Thank you," I said.

"I haven't done much that's useful," he muttered through tight lips.

"Yes, you have!" Anton objected. "You saved my mother from the Gestapo. And you're helping us now."

"Thank you, Anton," Lars said. "It is kind of you to say."

We drove away from the Jewish quarter in silence, through the still-teeming streets around Alexanderplatz, and over to the warehouse district by the river.

"We're here." Lars stopped in front of a dark warehouse.

I glanced nervously around the lot, but I saw only the silhouettes of weeds.

"I'll open the door. Wait here." Lars left the lorry, and a blast of cold air entered.

"What are we going to do?" Anton asked.

"Lars is going to build a compartment into this lorry," I told him. "In a few days, we will be home."

"What about Paul?"

"He is dead," I said. "We can do nothing for him now."

"We could find out who killed him," he said.

"So can the police, better than we." I did not mention that Lars must have left his gun on the floor to make Paul's death look like a suicide. The police were unlikely to investigate it further. In fact, even if it were ruled a murder, I doubted that they would trouble themselves over the death of another Jew.

The door opened. Lars slid into the seat next to me. "Just a second now."

He drove into a mechanic's bay and turned off the engine. Darkness cloaked the room, but I got a sense of tall ceilings and faraway walls. When Lars opened the car door, smells of grease, metal, and turpentine filled the cab. He squeezed my hand once, then was gone. Anton moved to follow.

"Wait until he closes the door," I said.

Lars returned soon. "Door's closed. You can get out now."

Lars led the way across the darkened room. I barked my shins on a heavy angular object. Other mysterious shapes looked equally menacing.

Lars opened a door into an office, stretched his arm, lowered the blinds, and turned on the light. He looked pale but calm. Tears had left streaks on Anton's dirty face. I did not want to think about how I must look.

"Beds here." Lars gestured to two automobile seats that had been removed and set on the concrete floor. "Washroom in the back."

His gloved finger pointed to a half-open door. Then he left.

The office felt barely warmer than outside. I set Anton on the cleanest-looking car seat. "Tonight I think we skip washing up and tooth brushing and go straight to bed."

He craned his head to see a calendar with a girl in a red bathing suit hung on the wall. Even though it was November, the calendar read July. I shook my head. Obviously the calendar's function was not to help them keep track of the date.

I dug through the bag I had packed at Paul's apartment days before. I had no blanket in there, but I drew out a nightshirt for Anton and folded it into a pillow so that his face would not come in contact with the seat's cracked leather. I counted out headache tablets and dry-swallowed them without any belief that they would help.

I opened the blinds a crack so that I could see the warehouse floor. No one there.

Lars returned with a dark brown blanket that stank of beer and the gray one we had used at the park. "We can get better blankets tomorrow."

Anton took off his shoes and lay down on his side. I covered him with the gray blanket, tucking it around his legs, and spread his coat over him as well. I slipped my hand under the blanket and found his.

He gripped mine tightly. "Aren't you going to take the other seat?"

"I think I may sit here until you fall asleep," I said.

Anton smiled. "That would be nice."

He closed his eyes, and I stroked his hair, as I used to when he was little.

Through the glass I watched Lars. He took off Paul's too-large shirt, folded it, and hung it over the steering wheel. I looked back to Paul's shirt. It would be cold now without Lars's warmth. Paul's body would never warm it again.

I closed my eyes. Memories of Paul in clean white shirts through the years streamed through my mind. Too painful to see. I opened my eyes and blinked away tears.

Lars reached into the lorry for his overcoat. After he put it on, he drew the Vis from the pocket, checked it, and stuck it in his waistband. What kind of trouble did he expect here? I surveyed the empty-seeming warehouse again. Still no one.

Anton's grip on my hand loosened. He kicked once. I knew by the sound of his breathing that he slept. I watched him sleep for a full minute before going out to talk to Lars.

He rummaged through a stack of metal scraps in the corner, holding an electric torch awkwardly in his left hand. Why did he not use his right?

"Lars," I called softly across the room. He did not act as if he heard me.

I walked gingerly toward him. When I reached him, I tapped his shoulder. His right hand drew the gun from his waistband as he turned. Now I knew why he held the torch in his left.

"Lars!" I lifted both hands to shoulder height. "Don't shoot!"

He lowered the barrel. "Apologies."

I put down my hands, shaking.

He tucked the gun back into his waistband. "You startled me."

"I am sorry." I pulled my coat close against the chill.

"It has been a difficult evening."

"Yes," I said, "it has."

He led me back to the lorry, set the gun on the dash, climbed in, and handed me up beside him. I glanced toward the office where Anton slept.

"You should be working on the compartment," I said.

Lars tightened his lips. "I don't have the materials I need here. I'll make a list for my friend in the morning."

I wished that he could start sooner. But where would we find sheet metal in the middle of the night? Even Lars had limits.

"I would have talked to him earlier today," he said. "But I didn't want to meet the other workers."

His caution was warranted. "So, you start tomorrow?"

"Tomorrow night," he said. "I can't work here during the day without raising questions. I don't trust the men here."

"But you trust your friend?"

"I do." He removed a flat glass bottle from the glove box. He took a swig and handed it to me. I shifted it from the hand with a cast to my left hand and drank. Korn schnapps burned my throat.

"Show me the paper," I said.

"What paper?" He took another drink.

"The one that you nicked off Paul's table."

He hesitated, then drew a sheet of paper from his overcoat pocket. I turned on the lorry's overhead light. Block letters in familiar handwriting goose-stepped across the page.

TO ADELHEID ZINSLI,

   THE SUFFERING THAT JEW-FUCKERS LIKE YOU HAVE CAUSED THE GERMAN PEOPLE CAN NEVER BE UNDONE. JUST AS YOU STOLE A LIFE FROM ME, I STEAL ONE FROM YOU. THE JEWS ARE NOT DONE MURDERING THOUGH, ARE THEY? NOR AM I.

18

I gulped. The handwriting matched the threatening letters that had been mailed to the *Neue Zürcher Zeitung*. My head throbbed. Red and green lights flickered in my peripheral vision.

Lars pushed my head between my knees. "Breathe."

I breathed until the lights went away; then I sat up. "Paul's death was about me," I whispered. "It was my fault."

"You did not kill him."

"I brought him grief, then death," I said.

"You are missing the essential element in that note."

I stared at him.

"Someone wants to hurt you. It's why they killed Paul."

"It worked." Paul's life had ended because of something I had done. Or not done. I had never taken the letters seriously.

Lars put his arm around my shoulders to steady me. I leaned against him and closed my eyes. He stroked my hair. I stayed there, matching my breaths with his, calming down.

"Spatz?" He sounded sleepy.

I sat up. "I imagine they will not stop trying to hurt me either."

I looked again toward the office where Anton lay asleep.

"They know you are Adelheid Zinsli." Lars buttoned the top button on my coat. "When we leave, they'll know to look for you in Switzerland."

"Did anyone follow us here?" My heart raced as I scanned the dark warehouse, as if I could spot someone.

"No," he said with great finality. "I watched behind us, and we took a most circuitous route. I never saw anyone."

I struggled to pull myself together. He handed me the schnapps. I took a long swallow. I had to think. I had to get myself and Anton out of this. And I had to warn Lars that he might well be in danger, too. "I have received other letters."

"What?" He choked on the schnapps and coughed. "You didn't tell me."

"They came to the paper. In Switzerland. I get all kinds of crank letters. I have for years, even when I worked crime. Peter always used to say, 'If you're not getting letters, you're not writing pieces that move people.'" I shuddered. "Now I get political ones. I never take them seriously. But these were written in the same handwriting as—" I held up the letter that he had taken from Paul's table.

"How many letters? How long?" He rapped out questions.

"Ten or twelve, I think," I said. "They started coming a month ago, right after I wrote a piece criticizing the French and British governments for giving Hitler a giant swath of Czechoslovakia."

"You can't ever leave well enough alone?" His brow furrowed in irritation.

"I would not call that situation well enough." I took another drink of schnapps. It barely burned anymore. "What would you have me do, Lars, join the French throngs throwing roses?"

He pursed his lips. "Perhaps you could allow another journalist to draw attention to it."

"I will not sit by." I met his eyes calmly.

"My apologies, Spatz," he said. "You are correct, of course. Please tell me more about the letters."

I thought back to the last letter and the ones before, when I had been safe and warm in Switzerland. "When the first one came, a secretary opened it by mistake and took it to my editor. Since then, he has been confiscating them and giving them to the police. For my safety, he sent me to Poland to write a nonpolitical feature."

Lars raked his fingers through his hair. "That turned out well."

"Quite."

"What do the letters say?"

"They say—I—they." I took a long shuddering breath. "The letters call me a traitor and a whore and a Jew-fucker."

He winced, unused to hearing me swear.

I forged on. "They say that I will be called to answer for my crimes against Germany. And they urge me to come back to Germany to face my punishment, which they hint is to be a slow death."

"Where are they postmarked?" His unfocused eyes stared out the windshield. I knew that expression. He was thinking.

I took another drink of schnapps. "Berlin."

He took the flask off me, but he did not drink. "How often?"

"At first weekly, but lately almost daily. One arrived yesterday in Switzerland." I watched dark shapes in the warehouse. I had not taken the letters seriously, and now Paul was dead.

As usual, Lars read my mind. "Don't blame yourself, Spatz."

"I have no one else to blame, Lars. I did not warn Paul. And I left him alone." I looked longingly at the schnapps flask, but did not reach for it. I would not numb myself to this.

Lars took another drink. "What happened to you a month ago, when the letters started?"

"I have been over that again and again on my own and with Herr Knecht. Nothing significant happened to me."

"If the letter writer is indeed the killer, he is targeting you." He took a deep breath. "Who would want to kill you? Whose life did you steal?"

"I killed one of the Gestapo men who kidnapped me in Poland."

"Too recent to have written the letters," he said.

"The Röhms," I said. "Frau Röhm blamed me for her son's death back in 1934, and she was certainly willing to kill Anton and me to avenge him."

His eyes narrowed. "They are good candidates for something like this. They have no more political power, so they couldn't just have you arrested and shot. They'd have to do it themselves."

"Comforting." I shifted on the car seat. The smell of old leather wafted up.

"Who else?" Lars tapped his fingers on the steering wheel impatiently.

"Bauer's family. Or Hahn's. Or the other two," I said. A policeman named Bauer and Lars's former superior, Sturmbannführer Hahn, had died in a gun battle in 1936, along with two other men, moments before they would have killed us.

He sat quiet for a moment. "I don't know much about Bauer or the other two. Hahn was estranged from his wife for years before his death, I believe. They had a child, but I can't remember if it was a boy or a girl. I do know that Hahn often beat his wife so badly, she ended up in hospital."

I remembered how Hahn had broken Lars's nose and his ribs, and the plans he had stated that he had for me. I had killed him to stop him, and while I did not regret it, I still had nightmares about what I had done.

Lars kept talking. "I don't imagine his wife or child would search hard for his killer, except perhaps to give him a reward."

"Bauer?" He and Hahn were the only two whose names I knew.

"They are long shots," he said. "If it's Gestapo-related, they would have had you arrested at Paul's house and shot you, not him. Nor would they waste time with threatening letters."

"So, a civilian?" I held the letter up to the light in the lorry. "I found a letter in Paul's apartment typed on this same kind of paper."

Lars stared at the paper, thinking. "Do you think Paul could have written the letters? Or Miriam?"

"Paul?" I straightened up on the seat. "Never."

"Miriam, then?"

"Some of them arrived after she died," I said. "And the letter I found in their apartment seemed to have been sent to them, not from them."

"Was the handwriting the same?"

"The one in the apartment was typewritten." I repeated it back to him.

Lars touched the watermark. "This is government paper."

"Where does the paper come from?" I did not question that he was correct.

"You sign it out a hundred sheets at a time." He rubbed the paper between his thumb and forefinger. "The paper company has a contract with the government, so this paper is not available to civilians. That is why you need to sign for it."

"So whoever wrote the letters to me works for the government, or at least has access to the paper." That sounded promising. Whom did I know who worked for the government?

"That narrows the field of suspects down to thousands." Lars squelched my hope.

"Not counting the Gestapo men, who else in government thinks I took the life of someone they love?"

"It doesn't have to be someone whose life you took," Lars pointed out. "It could be someone who feels that you ruined his life."

"A much wider field," I said. "Are you on that list?"

He draped his arm across the seat behind me. "I am on the other end. You redeemed mine."

"Did I?" I picked at my glove. It felt as if every single thing I had done to try to help people had backfired. "Before you met me, you were a successful police *kommissar*, a Hauptsturmführer in the SS. Now you are sleeping in a garage."

"Spatz—"

"You were correct to stay away, Lars. I have never loved a man who did not come to grief."

"The banker seems to have ended up in quite satisfactory

circumstances," he said. "Perhaps I should have read the fine print at the bottom of the contract and applied for a position in Switzerland."

I appreciated his effort to lighten the situation and forced a smile. He tucked a strand of hair behind my ear.

I looked into his questioning dark eyes. Dark like Paul's. I wanted Lars to explain his past before I made any decisions. I would regret this action later, but now was all I had. All anyone really had.

I leaned forward and kissed him hard. My teeth clacked against his, and I tasted blood, but I did not care. I wanted to forget everything else.

He curled his hands around my shoulders. "No, Spatz." He pulled back from me. "I won't. Not like that."

Face hot with shame, I fumbled at the door handle. I could not get out of the lorry fast enough.

He kept hold of my shoulders. "Stay. Please."

I dropped my hands into my lap, head down so he could not see my face.

He took my head between his hands and drew me close. "It's me, Lars. And you, Hannah. No one else is here."

He tried to banish Paul's ghost. I doubted that he could, but I nodded. I closed my eyes. I saw Paul's face.

"Look at me," Lars said softly.

I looked into his face and saw the expression that Fräulein Ivona had recognized from across the train station.

"Please?" He traced my lips with his fingertip.

I kissed him then, gently and for a long time, until I wanted to be filled, not emptied. When his lips finally peeled off mine, I had forgotten everything outside the lorry. Steam coated the windows, and he was half naked.

"I surrender," he whispered.

I kissed him. "Looks more like an advance than a retreat."

He kissed my throat. "One touch of your skin and every single resolution disappears."

I arched my neck back. "What resolutions?" I asked breathlessly.

His fingers undid the front of my dress. I had no idea what had happened to my coat, but I did not worry about it. I was far from cold.

"Tomorrow," he whispered. "Time for resolutions then."

I resolved only to enjoy this moment. I had waited years to be with him again.

I caressed his scarred back, and moved my hands lower.

Lars moaned. "Spatz."

I smiled into his shoulder.

He removed the last bit of clothing between us.

Much later, we fell asleep in a jumble of coats on the lorry's leather bench seat.

19

I woke with a start, seeing Paul's empty shirt in my dreams. Lars's arms were tight around me. I could scarcely believe that I lay next to him again, our bodies pressed close together on the small seat. I inhaled mingled scents of leather, cigarettes, oils, and metal tools. I moved my cheek off his chest to look at him. Golden light from the overhead lamp softened the years on his face and rendered the scar on his eyebrow invisible.

He opened his eyes and smiled lazily. "Hello, Frau Schmidt."

The last time he had said that was when I woke up in his arms for the first time. Back then, I had not called him Herr Schmidt, not ready for the intimacy of a marriage in real life instead of on counterfeit papers. Things were much more complicated now, yet I surprised myself. "Hello yourself, Herr Schmidt."

He tightened his arms. I held him close. For a long time neither of us spoke.

He caressed one palm down the length of my back and I shivered. "How did you sleep?"

In answer, I only smiled.

He rolled over onto his side and faced me. Our legs intertwined on the narrow lorry seat. "Where does that leave us now?"

The warm feelings evaporated as I thought about our future. "Tell me about Russia."

"It's not a happy story," he said. "Shouldn't we tell only happy stories in bed?"

"I want us to tell only true stories," I said. "And those are not always happy."

He propped himself up on his elbow. "I've told no one. That has worked so far. Why do you want to know?"

"Why do you not want to tell me?"

He studied my face for a long time before speaking. "I will tell you once. But only once."

"I will take notes."

"I'd rather you didn't," he said. "I'd rather you forget it, as soon as I tell you."

I waited, not certain what to say.

He reached up and switched off the lorry's light. I felt him turn onto his back. I stayed on my side pressed tight against him. "I was arrested almost immediately. At first I thought that your SS friend had missed my name on some list, and that I was arrested for being Lars Lang and my work with the British."

Perhaps my SS friend, Wilhelm, had been wrong. "That was not the reason? Are you certain?"

"Fairly, yes." Irritation sounded in his voice. "I was quite good at my former job, you may recall. I know how interrogations work. The first interrogators were not particularly skilled and made their intentions perfectly clear."

I covered him with his coat. The lorry felt colder now.

"They started with simple physical violence, the kind that can kill the suspect before you get any real information. Careless work." He glided his hand along the coat, making sure that I was covered, too. "Of course, I was barely healed from our encounter with Hahn when I arrived."

I winced. That, too, had been my fault.

"Spatz," he said gently. "It was my own fault I was caught."

He put one arm around me and kept the other behind his head. I suddenly wanted him to stop talking. I did not want to send him back into the Russian prison, but if I stopped him, I might never hear what had happened, and despite what he said, he needed to tell someone, and I needed to know. "Go on."

"They would not have started with that kind of violence if they thought I had anything valuable to tell them, so I decided that the best way to stay alive was to wait out the first round. I stuck to my story of being a German businessman investigating the industry in Saratova."

"How long?"

He settled my head against his chest. I suspected that he did not want me to see his face, even in the darkness. "It's tough to say precisely. I'd say no more than a week."

In the Gestapo warehouse, the interrogators had broken his nose and two ribs in less than a minute. "A week?"

"There's a cycle to it," he explained. "They didn't expect to get information of value out of me, so they were more perfunctory."

Perfunctory? I thought of the scars on his back and flattened my palm over his heart.

"Once they finished, they dumped me in the general prison population. I figured they would either let me rot there, or things would get more interesting."

He did not speak for several seconds, and I kept my head on his chest, listening to his heartbeat. When it had slowed, I said, "Did they get more interesting?"

"Oh yes." He took a shuddering breath. "They did."

"How?"

"First, they sent in a physician to stitch me up and set my various broken bones."

Which bones? I wanted to ask, but I stayed quiet. As lightly as he talked, his heart raced under my ear. I slid my leg across his and held him.

"That showed that they suddenly thought I was of value. You never want your interrogator to believe that you have any value, unless it's so much value that they will release you immediately. Clearly that was not the case."

I stayed silent. He lay still. Together we waited until he got his breathing under control. "After that, as expected, they sent in a team more skilled in extracting information."

I hated to ask the question. "What did they do?"

"Let's just say that I quickly came to miss the simple beatings."

All the time that I had been mourning his death, he had been being tortured. "I am so sorry, Lars."

"It was over a year ago," he said. "I am quite recovered."

His entire body was taut next to mine, and his breaths came rapid and shallow. I stroked my hand in a circle on his chest and, slowly, his breathing eased.

"Once they started using more . . . finesse, I realized that I was in the second stage of the cycle. I had hoped that would never happen, of course."

"What did you do?" I asked.

"I prepared a second cover story. I decided that enough time had passed for me to have reached a breaking point, and I told them that I had been sent by Hahn to do an undercover investigation of Project Zephyr."

"But he did not send you. Hahn was already dead."

He laughed mirthlessly. "Yes, Spatz. I knew that, even though I was not sure of many things by that point. But since I had arrived in Russia little more than a week after his death, the assumption might be that he had given me the order, I had prepared myself, and left. Hahn, of course, could not gainsay it."

"What happened?"

"My story within a story impressed them enough for them to talk to their German allies, and after another short stint in the general population, they released me to the SS."

"What did the SS do?"

"I had expected them to kill me or torture me for details about Hahn's death, which is why I did not try that story earlier." He sighed. "But, oddly enough, they believed that one. They got me a real doctor. I healed for a few months. When I was well enough to leave the hospital, I first took a short leave of absence to take care of a small matter in Russia, then went to Switzerland to see you."

"What small matter?"

"Not today." He rolled onto his side, facing away from me.

"All right, Lars." After hearing him talk about being tortured, I wondered what could be worse. If he did not want to tell me, I could wait. I fit myself against his back and asked. "What happened in Switzerland?"

He slowly rolled to face me. His breath whispered against my cheek. "I was afraid that I was being monitored by the SS, of course, but for me to visit Adelheid Zinsli was a reasonable thing, even though I had told them that I had ended our engagement before I went to Russia."

"You did?" Although the engagement had been fictitious, I was surprisingly hurt.

"It was the only way I could explain why you did not contact me in Berlin when I was in Russia, Spatz."

I felt like a child, and a dull one at that. "Of course. Please go on."

He took in a long breath and let it out slowly.

"Lars?"

"I went to Switzerland to break it off with you."

I jerked my head back from him so hard that it smacked the glove box. "Break it off with me?"

He slipped his fingers through my hair. "Did you hurt your head?"

"W-why?" My head whirled. I had not expected this.

"I was . . . broken, not fit to be in a family. I saw that."

"I would have welcomed you," I said.

"Of course you would have. You would have taken care of me as best you could, without regard to the cost to you." He stroked my hair.

"But—"

"If you had known I was alive, you would have destroyed your life for me. As you risked death for your friend Paul, even though you have not been romantically involved with him for almost twenty years." His muscles bunched.

"I did Paul no favor." I pulled away from him. "And helping you would not have destroyed my life."

"I was a mess, Spatz," he said. "I could not sleep. I could barely eat. I was drunk more than I was sober. I was useless."

"I do not love you because you are 'of use' to me." I forced myself to touch him, to swallow my anger. For now.

He traced a fingertip down my cheek, and I turned to kiss it. "That's why I had to leave." He took his hand back. "Because I was damned if I would drag you and Anton down with me."

"Lars—"

"It's past the point of discussion now."

"It most certainly is not," I said. "But not now."

"Something to look forward to," he said. "The reporter forgets nothing."

I ignored that. "You did not break things off with me. We never spoke. I did not know that you came to Switzerland. What happened?"

He settled deeper into the seat. "I spent a few days seeing if I was followed. When I was confident that I was not, I staked out the newspaper offices, as I did not know where else to find you. I did not have the banker's address."

"I was not living with Boris," I put in.

"I know that now. Or at least I hope I do."

"Lars!"

I heard the smile. "I do."

"Did you find me at the newspaper?" I went there often now that Anton was in school, enjoying the collegial atmosphere. Or at least the collegial atmosphere before Herr Marceau started to resent my political pieces.

"I followed you to the park and saw you and the banker and the woman I assumed to be the nanny with a new baby." His words sped up. He must be anxious to get through this part. "Boris and Anton played football and were happy together. You seemed content playing with the baby. I assumed that it was yours, and that you had married him."

We visited Boris on weekends so that he and Anton could spend time together. I sometimes stayed to play with the little girl that Anton called his sister. "I did not marry him, and that baby is not mine."

"I know that now," he said. "But at the time it seemed logical. You had assumed me dead, perhaps mourned for a time, and moved on with your life. With the life you would have led had I never recruited you to courier for me. The life you should have led. I thought it would be easier if I did not reopen any old wounds you might have had and let you continue to think me dead."

"Those wounds never closed." I grazed my fingertip over the scar on his eyebrow. "I mourned you every day until I saw you in Poland."

He shifted, and the seat squeaked. "I could not provide for you as he could. I could not father Anton as he could. I still can't."

"How do you know what I want?"

"I know what you need," he said. "You didn't need me."

I swallowed another argument. "After you inadvisably left Switzerland—"

He chuckled. "Yes?"

"What did you do next?"

"I returned to Berlin and drank myself out of the SS, whored myself out of Berlin—" I flinched. He kissed the top of my head. "I'm sorry, Spatz."

I lay still. It hurt to hear him say it, but no more than the rest of it. The thing that hurt the most was that he had left me.

"I read your articles. When I heard that you were going to Poznań, I adjusted my route and went there to keep an eye on you, little knowing how much danger you would find. You know the rest."

"I think you may be leaving out as much as you are telling."

He sat up suddenly. Cold air blew across my bare skin. I sat next to him and pulled the coat over us. I wondered what our lives would have been like if I had fallen in love with him in my twenties. Could I have lived the domestic life of a policeman's wife, as my friend Bettina did? I tried to imagine us leaving for work in the morning, coming home at night, and not worrying about being arrested or killed. I could not picture it, and I reminded myself, he had been a Nazi when I met him. I had hated and feared him at the time. Besides, for many years after I had left Paul and realized that I did not wish to be married, I had closed the door on the thought of falling in love, until I met Boris. Even if Lars and I had met in our twenties, we would not have fallen in love.

He adjusted my upside-down coat across my shoulders, fingertips lingering on my collarbone. A slight contact, but electric.

I had fallen in love with him two years ago, unexpectedly and against my better judgment. The feelings had not gone away when I thought him dead, or when I saw him again in Poland with Fräulein Ivona. Whether I liked it or not, I still loved him. A better question was what I intended to do about it.

"At Paul's last night," I said. "When I woke up and looked at you, you did not recognize me."

"What do you mean?" His heart beat faster. He must know I could feel it.

"What happened to you?"

He stared into the windshield as if the answer might be hidden in the dark garage. "I don't know."

"I have worked with shell-shocked soldiers—"

"Sometimes I'm somewhere else." I felt his hand outside the coats clench into a fist.

"Where?" I spoke as gently as I could.

"I don't know." His tone was anguished. "My body is still there, functioning, but my mind is in a fog. I . . ."

"Does it happen often?"

"Not like it used to. It's better, but I can't promise that . . ."

"That what?"

"That I won't end up back there in the fog." He pulled me close. "I've never hurt anyone, not during those moments. If I thought that I would hurt you, that I could hurt you, I would stay away. I promise you that."

"You already made good on that promise," I said bitterly.

He put one hand on the crown of my head. "It was the best I could do."

"What is the best you can do now?"

"I think I can stay. I'm better," he said. "I can sometimes sleep more than a few hours. I am mostly sober again. Sometimes I can see through the . . . episodes, and stop them."

"How do I know you won't leave—?"

"Because." He cleared his throat. "It would kill me to leave you again."

I heard truth in his words. "Can we build something where no one leaves? And no one dies?"

He swept me into a rough hug. "God help us, Spatz."

I held him.

Eventually, we lay back down on the lorry's seat. He rearranged the coats over us. I stroked my hands along his body, exploring the things that had changed in the last two years. He had so many scars now. I began to kiss them, one by one.

He arched under my lips and moaned softly. I smiled.

A weight fell against the outside of the lorry. Knuckles pounded the window glass.

20

Lars snatched his gun off the dashboard and pointed it at the lorry's window. With his other hand, he pushed my head down against the seat.

"Lang? Is that you?" called a male voice with a Russian accent. "What the hell are you doing here?"

Lars's shoulders relaxed, and he lowered the gun to his side. I ducked my head under my coat collar. Safe from danger, but not from embarrassment.

Lars sat abruptly. A gust of cold air shot into our nest. I drew my coat high around me. He slung his coat over his shoulders, put a finger to his lips, and rearranged my coat.

He cranked down the window. "Good morning, Herr Populov. I stopped by for a bit of sleep."

"Can't spring for a hotel anymore, Lang?" Herr Populov laughed. "Hope he paid you in advance, Fräulein."

I gritted my teeth and kept my face hidden, wanting him to simply go away.

"I paid her plenty in advance," Lars said. "She's my wife."

What a lovely introduction. I stifled a groan. I would have to meet Herr Populov now, and under the worst of circumstances. I sat up, careful to keep myself covered by my coat. My cheeks burned. What would my mother have said about me being caught naked on the front seat of a lorry and being mistaken for a prostitute, even with a man who was allegedly my husband? My father would have beaten me so hard, I could not have sat down for days. Then again, he had done that often, and for less.

"Spatz, I'd like you to meet Herr Populov, the man who kindly extended us his hospitality last night. Herr Populov, my wife, Frau Lang."

I stretched my good hand across Lars. Herr Populov shook it with his calloused one. "I'm sorry, Frau Lang. I meant no offense. I'll go wait in the office."

"My son is sleeping in there," Lars said.

"Son?" Herr Populov looked as if the roof had caved right in on his head. I imagine I looked no better, but Lars seemed to be enjoying himself.

"If you could give me a few minutes," Lars said. "I will meet you by the front door, and we can all pretend that this didn't happen."

Herr Populov's face retreated. Footsteps echoed off the walls of the cavernous warehouse. The overhead light snapped on, and the front door closed with a bang.

"Sorry, Spatz," Lars said.

"You do not look particularly sorry." I felt around on the floor for my clothes.

He handed me my slip. "I am not particularly sorry to be here now. Perhaps it shows."

He kissed me gently on the lips, and I had to smile at him. "Embarrassed, yes. Sorry, no." I wriggled my cold slip over my head and finger-combed my hair.

"My god," he said. "You are beautiful."

"I probably look a sight!"

He gathered me into his arms. "A more beautiful sight I have never seen."

We stared at each other like love-struck teens.

He cleared his throat. "I'd better get shaved and go talk to Populov before he comes back."

"I want to be dressed the next time I meet him," I said. "So, go."

He climbed out of the lorry and shut the door.

I resumed my search on the lorry's floor. My clothes were scattered, and it took me some time to find them and get dressed. I lifted Paul's shirt off the steering wheel and hung it over my arm before stepping into my cold shoes and hurrying across the concrete floor to the office.

I stood next to Anton's makeshift bed and studied his face, relaxed in sleep. I folded Paul's shirt and added it to my bag. "Anton?"

"Here." He yawned loudly.

"We have to leave now, so that the shop can open for business."

Lars emerged from the washroom, wiping shaving cream off his face. "My apologies, Frau Lang." He kissed me on the nose and was gone, leaving behind the scent of his eucalyptus shaving cream.

Anton rubbed his eyes and sat. "Are you two pretending to be married again?"

"After a fashion." I handed him his shoes and pointed to the washroom. "And if it comes up outside, Lars is your father."

Shaking his head, he trudged over to the washroom.

I folded his blanket, then packed the nightshirt he had used as a pillow. We had unpacked nothing else.

Anton stumbled back out and leaned against the wall. "What time is it?"

"Almost seven." I stepped past him into the washroom. I looked at the filthy floor and wished for the luxury of waiting for better facilities. Instead, I splashed cold water on my face and hands, and smoothed my hair. I chanced a glance in the mirror. My relaxed face told the story of last night's events in the lorry. I hoped that it would be too dark outside for Herr Populov to notice.

Best to get it over with. I collected our things, and Anton and I walked to the front door.

Herr Populov and Lars stood next to the warehouse. The cherry of Herr Populov's cigarette shone red against the early morning gloom.

Lars took my bag. He ruffled Anton's hair. Anton gave him an aggrieved look, me a warning one, lest I decide that hair ruffling was suddenly acceptable.

"My apologies for the . . . the inconvenience," I stammered to Herr Populov, blushing.

Herr Populov's hearty laugh rolled out. "Not a problem, Frau Lang. Your husband explained to me that you will be here for the next few nights."

"We appreciate the hospitality." I hoped that darkness hid my glowing face.

"Anton," Lars said. "How about you open the door so I can fetch the lorry out here before your mother faints on the grass?"

Anton stepped over to me. "Are you all right?"

"I am fine," I said. "Thank you. But, please, do get the door."

Lars and Anton walked back toward the warehouse door together.

"He's a fine man, your husband," Herr Populov said. "It's an honor to help him, and you and the boy."

"Thank you." I wondered what he knew about Lars. Had they met in Russian prison?

He opened a pack of Sobranies. Russian cigarettes, too. "May I?"

"Of course." I hated the smell, but could hardly tell him what to do at his own warehouse, especially considering my own actions here. "Have you known my husband long?"

"Long enough. He's helped me more than once, if that's what you're asking."

I itched to ask more, but Lars stopped the lorry and stepped down to open the door and help me in. He slid in beside me.

"Breakfast?" Lars asked.

"Places are open this early?" Anton rested his head against the window. "People eat in them?"

Lars chuckled. He waved to Herr Populov as we drove away.

Even at this early hour, lorries had begun to arrive at the warehouses around us. The workers wore mostly blue overalls and shouted greetings to one another. I sank down in the seat, wondering if they were watching me as much as I watched them. Tomorrow, I would wake up earlier. "A tea would not come amiss."

I looked over at Anton. He had gone back to sleep.

"I envy him the sleep." Lars turned off onto a street that led out of the warehouse district. We passed battered brick apartment buildings.

"Me, too."

"I left Populov a list of supplies. He said he will have them by the end of the day, so tonight I can build the compartment."

"Wonderful." I covered my mouth and yawned.

"My apologies for the wake-up call," he said.

"The warehouse experience was not quite up to Hotel Adlon's standards."

"I don't know," he said. "Parts of it were sublime."

I leaned against him. "They were."

We drove in silence. The sky slowly turned dove gray. We stopped near a café as its inside light flickered on. The waitress took chairs off the tabletops. We would have a bit of a wait before she was ready to accept breakfasters.

Lars gestured at the sky. "So, in the cold gray light of morning, do you want me to slip quietly away from this noisy crowd?"

I recognized the Rilke quote. I also knew the last line. "Only if I come, too."

He dropped his arm around me and drew me in close. "Good, Spatz."

Together we watched the waitress bustle around. He rested his cheek against the top of my head. His breath stirred my hair. This moment, this sky, Lars warm by my side, and Anton asleep a meter away. That was what we had.

Paul had nothing. Grief choked out my feeling of peace. I had no right to it.

The waitress unlocked the front door. Lars stirred. I shook Anton. "Breakfast time."

Anton stretched like a cat. Looking at him made me yawn.

In the restaurant, Lars convinced the waitress to give us a large table at the back. All three of us were ravenous and ordered eggs, rolls, meat, and tea. She shook her head, clearly disbelieving that we would finish it all.

But we nearly did. Lars paid and slipped her an extra bill to give us longer use of the table.

He cleared his throat and sat up straight, suddenly looking like a headmaster. I crossed my hands in my lap and assumed my best attentive pupil posture. Anton followed suit.

"I think we need to talk about the implications of what happened to Paul last night," Lars said.

Anton sucked in a quick breath. I put a hand on his shoulder. He promptly shook it off, trying to act the part of a man in front of Lars.

Lars looked at me. "How much do we tell Anton?"

Anton crossed his arms.

"All of it," I said. "He runs the same risks that we do."

Anton raised his eyebrows in surprise.

"Very well." Lars drew a worn black notebook out of his inside coat pocket. "Do you have a pen, Spatz?"

I handed him my fountain pen.

"Let's start with what we know." Lars quickly wrote down the time and cause of death. Anton and I tried to decipher his handwriting upside down as the pen flew across the paper, filling in details of last night's events.

"How long were you a policeman?" Anton asked.

Lars smiled briefly. "I was a *kommissar* in the police for more years than I want to think about. In fact, I was a *kommissar* when I met your mother. I investigated murders in Berlin."

"You can find out who killed Paul?"

"I hope so." Lars tapped the pen's nib against the paper. "But I don't have the resources I'm used to. And I didn't solve every case when I did."

"Really?" Anton sounded surprised.

"I did have the highest solve rate in Berlin," Lars said. "So there is hope for me."

Anton nodded sagely.

"Spatz," Lars said. "This won't be easy for you, but . . ."

"Yes?" I said.

"Do you have a sketch pad, or a notebook?"

I took out my sketch pad, its leaves considerably larger than Lars's notebook.

"I wish I had a photograph," he said. "But we will make do. I would like you to draw me two sketches. One of the kitchen as we saw it when we entered last night. Everything but the body."

"Paul's body," I corrected.

"Apologies." He briefly touched my shoulder. "After you finish that sketch, I would like a sketch of Paul. Add nothing. If you are uncertain, leave it blank."

I dug in my satchel for a pencil and started work. Drawing the kitchen without Paul in it was easier than I had expected. I sketched in the table, bare except for the note that Lars had taken. I cross-hatched in shadows in the corner. One chair was pushed into the table. Another sat at an angle, the third pushed back against the wall, and the final chair held Paul. He had been eating and drinking with his killer. I drew his chair in quick strokes, then moved down to the floor. Broken dishes, an empty glass, and a rumpled pile of tablecloth.

I sketched in the window. The bullet had passed through Paul and pierced the glass. A round spiderweb of cracks radiated from the hole. Undisturbed curtains hung on each side.

Lars and Anton talked quietly next to me. Lars took a statement from Anton. The building door had been locked; Anton had un-locked it. Paul's front door had been left open. Anton thought he might have heard footsteps going up the stairs above him. No one passed him on his way up. I shuddered at the thought that Anton might have met the murderer.

I handed Lars my sketch and started drawing Paul's outline. They pored over the first sketch, discussing its accuracy. I blocked out their voices and concentrated on Paul. He had slumped sideways in the chair, as if he had yanked off the tablecloth but had not had time to raise his arms again. I took a deep breath.

I started with his feet. He wore the old brown slippers he always donned inside. His shoes, I knew, were lined up by the front door. His pants had been darker near the bottom. Wet. He had been out in the rain. Had he walked in the rain with his killer, or let him in later? Whom would he let into his home so late? Not a stranger, surely.

I finished his rumpled shirt, the slump of his shoulder, his empty hands, until all that remained was his face.

I took a long drink of tea.

"If you can't finish it," Lars said. "I—"

"If Paul can die there, I can certainly stand to sketch it." The pencil trembled in my hand when I went back to work. I pretended to be a camera, taking a picture, that I had not loved Paul, that I did not care that he was gone.

I finished the sketch, turned it over, and slid it across the table.

Lars studied the sketch, and I studied him. His eyes darted around the picture, taking in every detail, lingering on some, skipping others.

"What do you think, Herr Kommissar? Give me your report."

He paused, thinking. "Paul had no defensive wounds on his hands or arms. I didn't have time to check elsewhere. Based on the door's condition, I would say that he let his killer in, so it may well have been someone whom he knew."

"Someone he thought he could trust," I said bitterly.

"Or at least someone from whom he did not fear harm," Lars said.

"What will the police think? Will they look for the killer?" Anton looked at my sketch. I turned it over, not wanting him to remember Paul that way.

"I am hopeful that they will write it off as a suicide. That's why I left my gun. If they do, no one will bother to dust the room for prints and find yours, mine, and your mother's."

"But the bullet that killed him will not match your gun," I said.

"We got lucky there," Lars said, and I grimaced. "Considering. The bullet went through his head and out the window. A diligent search may find it, but it just as well may not. I don't expect an investigation. A Jewish man is not one whose death greatly concerns the Nazi police. Even if it did, he had recently lost his wife and child to the deportation. There is evidence that he tried suicide the night before."

I thought of struggling with Paul yesterday, saving his life only so that someone else could take it. I felt his blood-slick wrist under my fingers and remembered closing his familiar eyes for the last time. Lars took my hand.

"Why would someone want to kill Paul?" Anton asked.

"I think that his killer was after me, not Paul," I said.

Anton gasped, and I felt a fool for saying it.

"Possibly," Lars said. "But we cannot be certain of that."

"The note?"

"What if the note was left in Paul's mailbox, or pushed under the door and he put it on the table? And what about the note in the desk?"

"What note?" Anton asked. "I don't remember a note on the table."

Lars took the folded-up note from his inside notebook and looked at me. After I nodded, he handed it to Anton.

"Whose life did you steal?" he asked.

"No one's, except in self-defense," Lars answered for me.

"That is true," I said. "But that does not change the fact that men have died by my hand."

"How many?" Anton asked.

I closed my eyes, but the truth did not go away. "Two."

I opened my eyes. "Put them on the list, Lars."

"I would prefer to start with Paul and Miriam," he said. "I have no idea who wrote the note. Neither do you. It is possible that the killer was trying to punish you, but it is also possible that the note arrived before the killer came for Paul."

I wondered if he believed it, or if he only tried to assuage my guilt.

"Since Paul and Miriam are the ones who are dead." Lars tapped his pen against the notebook. "Let's start with their enemies."

"I have no idea what enemies Paul or Miriam had." Paul had been living mostly in seclusion since the Nazis came to power, avoiding trouble until I came along. "Miriam's family? He was betraying her, and was gone when she was deported."

Lars wrote that down in his precise, cramped handwriting. "Anyone else?"

"Before this visit, I had not spoken to Paul in two years, and we barely spoke then." I clenched my hands in my lap. I had not helped him then or later.

"Who might know more about his enemies?" Lars prompted. I wondered if he cared, or if he sought only to distract me.

"Maria at the *Tageblatt*. Paul's mistress," I said promptly. She would know exactly which rocks to turn over to find Paul's secrets. But would she tell me?

"How does she feel about you?" Lars asked.

I fiddled with a leftover sausage on my plate. "She hates me."

Anton looked at me in shock. I felt flattered that he had thought no one hated me. I wished I felt the same.

"Did she know that you were Adelheid Zinsli? Did she hate you enough to write the letters in Switzerland?" Lars asked.

"She might have known that I was in Switzerland. Paul might have told her I covered the Games in '36. If so, she might have guessed that I was Adelheid Zinsli. Not many female reporters from Switzerland covered the Games."

Lars underlined her name.

"She might have written the letters, but I do not see why. I do not think she would have killed Paul. It seems as if she would have killed me first."

"Perhaps she intended to kill you, but something went awry," Lars said.

Anton's eyes widened.

I pulled a handful of coins out of my pocket and handed them to Anton.

"Could you please fetch us a newspaper?" I pointed to a wizened newspaper seller hunched in a stand outside the restaurant.

Anton knew what I was up to, but he took the coins and tore out the door.

"I think we are frightening Anton," I said.

"Good," Lars answered. "He should be frightened. This is a frightening situation. He would be a fool if he were not frightened. A fool in danger."

Like Paul.

21

"I want to protect him," I said.

"You can't protect every single person in the world, Spatz," Lars said.

"First, Anton," I said. "Then you."

He brushed the back of his hand along my cheek. "What about yourself?"

"I am on the list, too," I said.

Anton dumped the paper on my lap and sat next to me. "Did I miss anything?"

Lars slowly drew his hand back. "No."

Anton's pointy chin jutted, and I knew that he was trying to decide what we had been doing. "Are you two pretending to be married?"

"Lars and I are . . ." What were we?

I could not explain to Anton what we were to each other when I had no idea myself. I began anyway. "It is a complicated situation."

Lars moved to stand next to my chair. Was he leaving us alone so I could explain the situation to Anton?

Instead, Lars dropped to one knee next to me. "Hannah, would you—?"

"That is not how you do that," Anton interrupted. "She's my mother."

Lars took my hand and slipped off the ring he had placed there two years ago. My ring finger felt cold.

So far, no one in the restaurant had noticed. "Lars, you are making a spectacle of—"

"Do I have your permission to ask her hand in marriage?" Lars asked Anton.

I stared at them both, dumbfounded. The waitress eyed us suspiciously.

"Are your intentions honorable?" Anton's expression was as serious as Lars's.

"Nothing but," Lars said.

"Will you take care of her?" Anton asked. "And not abandon her again? Especially with other women."

"Anton—," I began.

"Please, Spatz." Lars held up his palm. He turned to Anton. "I promise."

"Will you keep her out of trouble?" Anton asked.

Lars took my hand again. "I would give my life to keep her safe. But I don't think anyone can keep her out of trouble."

"At least he's no liar," Anton said. "I give my blessing. The rest is up to you, Mother."

Both turned to look at me, Anton's blue eyes expectant, Lars's dark ones frightened. Did he fear that I would say no or that I would say yes?

"It is up to me," I said. "Anton, you are not—"

"Hannah Vogel," Lars interrupted, his voice pitched low so that it did not carry beyond our table. "Will you marry me?"

I took a deep breath. Lars looked ready to faint.

Logically, I should wait. In many ways, I barely knew him. In others, I knew him better than I had ever known anyone. There were a very great many reasons to say no or maybe.

"Yes," I said.

He slid the ring back onto my finger. It felt colder than my skin, but still felt right. He dropped a light kiss on my lips, and I shivered.

"Are you going to eat that?" Anton pointed his fork at my plate.

We laughed. I pushed my plate toward Anton.

He speared my last sausage and ate it in two quick bites.

"From this point on, at least in Germany, we are Hannah and Lars Schmidt," Lars said. "You are Anton Schmidt. Do you understand?"

Anton set down his fork. "Yes, sir."

Smiling gazes of the other customers followed us as we walked out together, Lars holding my arm and Anton on my other side. I was happy to have them close.

Workers in caps and short open jackets jostled by on their way to the warehouse district we had left behind earlier. They were different from the office workers in suits I had passed on my way to Herr Silbert's. They looked more carefree, but also more tired. I wondered how much the Nazis influenced the day-to-day workings in most factories. I imagined that the Nazis were a heavier burden for those in management.

Lars navigated us deftly across the sidewalk to the lorry. Water beaded on its surface from a shower that had passed over while we ate breakfast. Oyster gray clouds promised more of the same before the day was out.

Anton squeezed my hand before he let it go. I looked over at him. "How are you holding up?"

"I want to be a policeman." He bounced on the balls of his feet, excited at the prospect. "Last night Lars told me about some cases that he's worked and—"

"Appropriate conversation for a thirteen-year-old?" I asked Lars.

"Appropriate for this thirteen-year-old," Lars said. Anton smiled.

I swallowed my protest. Considering the alternatives he had recently seen, I could hardly fault Anton's decision to be an honest policeman.

Lars opened the door for me and helped me in. His hand lingered on my side, and I leaned against it. We both smiled.

"Where do we go next?" Anton slammed the door on his side of lorry. "To solve the case."

"I can't work on the lorry until tonight," Lars said. "Our best plan would be to keep our heads down until we get out of Germany."

"I agree," I said. "But I have a few things to do first."

Lars smiled. "Safe things? Like the zoo? Or a quick trip to the cinema?"

I ignored him and unfolded the newspaper Anton had fetched while we were still in the restaurant. The familiar smell of newsprint filled the air.

But that was the only good thing about the newspaper. The headline screamed: JEWISH SWINE SHOOTS GERMAN DIPLOMAT. With growing dread, I read the article. Leaving out the racial outrage, the facts seemed to be that a Jewish teenager named Herschel Grynszpan had shot a German diplomat named Ernst vom Rath in Paris to protest the treatment of his family at Zbąszyń.

I read excerpts aloud. Lars's face grew more serious with each word. I felt as if the world had just shifted. More restrictions on Jews in Germany. A ban on Jewish children attending German schools. A ban on Jewish newspapers. The suspension of all Jewish cultural activities.

A turning point.

"If vom Rath dies," I said, "there will be terrible reprisals against Jews in Germany."

"We had best get out before that diplomat dies," Lars said. "After those reprisals, they'll surely increase security at the borders."

I wished that the lorry were already complete.

"It might not be as bad as that," Lars said. "He might live."

A few straggling workers passed by the lorry, hurrying to get to work before it rained again.

"Even if that young man's gunshot does not kill him, someone else's will." I refolded the newspaper and dropped it on the lorry's floor. "It is the perfect opportunity for the Nazis to exact their revenge for the fictitious crimes of the Jews. They will not let a chance like that pass."

A flash of recognition flitted across Lars's face. He had just thought of something, and I realized what. "Last night's note. Let me see it."

Reluctantly, he handed it to me.

I unfolded it and read it again. It said: *The Jews are not done murdering though, are they?*

I looked at Lars. "Do you suppose the letter writer meant this attack in Paris?"

"It seems paranoid," he said. "How could he know of a shooting in Paris? The newspapers did not report the attack on vom Rath until this morning."

I could tell that he argued only for argument's sake; he was worried, too. "When did the Nazi leadership know it? Or the Gestapo?"

"I don't know, Spatz."

"Let's find a telephone booth," I said, "and I will see."

Lars drove slowly down the wet street. Telephone booths were not so close together as in tonier neighborhoods, but we found one.

I dropped in coins and asked for the newspaper. Lars and Anton stood next to the booth. Anton was deep in some complicated story, pausing only to give Lars a chance to nod to show that he was still listening.

I called the newspaper for a quick rundown of the Grynszpan story. He had shot vom Rath at five thirty yesterday evening, only a few hours before Paul's murder. If the news had reached Germany by then, it probably reached only the highest levels of the Gestapo. So, either the person who killed Paul was very highly placed, or the note could not possibly refer to vom Rath's shooting. Someone highly placed would have waited and killed me last night, instead of bothering with letters.

Herr Knecht himself came on the line. "Frau Zinsli."

"Good morning. What did the embassy say?" I asked.

He sighed, a long windy exhalation that told me the news was bad. "They are not inclined to help you, but I am exerting pressure. It may take a few more days."

"Thank you," I said. "I am sorry to have dragged the paper into this."

"A daredevil reporter trapped in Nazi Germany will be a top story," he said. "Once you get back out. Keep a journal."

Ever the newsman. "I shall."

"In the meantime, try to stay out of trouble. Call immediately if your situation changes."

"I intend to."

"Good girl," he said. "Keep your chin up. We'll get you out of there, eventually."

I thanked him again and rang off. If something went awry with Lars's plan with the lorry, I hoped that Herr Knecht might help us escape, although it seemed less likely with each call.

I stood alone in the phone booth. I had two things that I needed to do for Paul. This was least important, but perhaps most dangerous. But I owed it to Paul. That and much more besides. I braced myself against the wooden side of the booth and dialed the *Berliner Zeitung*.

I asked the chirpy secretary for Maria, giving my name as Petra Weill, which would make Maria angry enough to take my call. She would hate the thought of anyone poaching on her Peter Weill pseudonym.

"Yes?" Maria asked peremptorily as soon as she got on the line. I relished the familiar sound of her irritation.

"Petra Weill here," I said. She would recognize my voice.

"How kind of you to telephone, Petra." Sarcasm overlaid her words. "To what do I owe the pleasure?"

"I have news for you."

When she paused, I knew she tried to decide whether I might have useful information. I forced a carefree tone. "It has been such a long time, but I remember the good times we had, you and I, and our good friend Paul?"

"Fine," she said flatly.

What else could she say? By bringing up Paul's name, I had reminded her that I knew enough to cause her trouble. "Where should we meet?"

"Let's have dinner tonight at the restaurant where I broke the strap on my shoe. What's it called?" she said.

She had once broken the strap on her shoe when we were at the Ufa-Palast am Zoo movie theater. We were standing in line to see Marlene Dietrich in *The Blue Angel*. Maria had been furious about the broken strap. She probably would have gone straight home if she had not been too jealous to leave us alone at the cinema. It had been an unpleasant night. She wanted me to meet her there. The restaurant was code so that no one overhearing the call would know where she was headed.

I played along. "I remember. The restaurant was called the Angel."

"Exactly!" she said. "I'll see you there at around seven."

So, we would meet in the theater at the Palast am Zoo during the showing closest to seven. I rang off.

Lars and Anton practiced boxing moves on the sidewalk. I did not like to see Anton fight. But he had good reach, and Lars appeared to be giving him solid tips about increasing his punching power.

I had one more thing to do for Paul. I had to explain his death to his father. I called, and Herr Keller asked that I meet him at Saint Hedwig's, the largest Catholic church in Berlin.

I stepped into the brisk fall air. The boxers had taken off their coats and sparred in rolled-up shirtsleeves. Their faces glowed from the exercise.

Anton gauged my reaction. "Bad news?"

"The newspaper confirms that vom Rath was shot last night, probably too late for our note writer."

"That's good news," Lars said.

"You made three calls." Anton crossed his arms. "I counted."

"You will make a fine detective one day," I said.

"The second call?" he persisted.

"Later," I said.

"The third call?" Lars shrugged his coat back on.

"To Paul's father. I must go meet him now."

Lars put his hand on the small of my back. I savored how it felt there.

"Why must you notify them yourself?" Lars said. "It might be dangerous, and the police will have informed his parents of his death."

"The police." I swallowed. "The police told them that their son committed suicide. His parents are practicing Catholics."

"I thought that Paul was Jewish," Anton said.

"Half Jewish, but he was raised Catholic," I said. "His mother was born Jewish, and that is enough for the regime, even though she converted to Catholicism when she married Paul's father. Catholics believe that you go to hell if you commit suicide. I cannot let his parents add that to their grief."

"Where are you meeting?" Lars asked.

"Saint Hedwig's."

He stared off into the distance. "It's a bad idea."

"Regardless," I said.

"You'll never win when she uses that voice." Anton pulled his coat back on. "Even if you are married."

A muscle twitched under Lars's eye. "Thank you for the tip, Anton."

"Would you care to come with me?" I patted Lars's arm.

"I would like to follow up on Paul's death." Lars donned his fedora again.

"What does that mean?" Anton asked. "How do you follow up?"

"If I were still in the police force, I would interview the suspects, see if they had alibis for the time of Paul's death, and check those alibis. Check their fingerprints against the scene. Check their weapons to see if they matched the bullet that killed Paul. Talk to the people in Paul's building. Look for eyewitnesses. Go over the scene again and see what else I could find."

"Can you do all that?" Anton asked.

A woman dressed all in blue walked by, carrying two shopping bags from Wertheim, a formerly Jewish-owned department store. Like everything else, it had been Aryanized. She paid us no heed.

"No, but I can consult with someone who has."

"Who?" Anton clearly wanted to get going. I wished that he were not so enthusiastic about looking for a killer, but I said nothing. The alternative might be a child properly frightened out of his wits. Better for him to think that there were things that he could do.

"Whom can you consult with?" Anton repeated.

"An old friend," Lars said. "He works for the police."

"May I come, too?" Anton asked.

"I'm afraid not," Lars said. "I have to do this by myself."

We separated and agreed to meet back at Friedrichstadt subway station, not far from the church, in a few hours.

Anton and I took the subway to Saint Hedwig's. He told me all about his shooting trip with Lars and the boxing techniques he had just learned. I pretended to listen, my mind already with Paul's father.

Across the square stood the cathedral. It had been modeled after the Pantheon in Rome. My brother always called it "the Catholic breast." When we neared the curved cathedral, I interrupted Anton. "We will go in separately. You go in first and sit in a pew on the left-hand side. I will come in a few minutes later and, if I can, I will sit on the right-hand side a row behind you. I can see you, and you can see me without too much trouble. But do not look at me. Wait quietly until you see me get up to leave. Then follow. Do you understand?"

"Will you be long?" Anton's eyes darted around the square, suddenly looking for enemies.

"I do not know." I stopped. Cooing pigeons flew around us. Errant feathers floated to the ground.

"What if something bad happens?" Anton looked into the gray sky as if he expected a soldier to appear there.

"I doubt that anything will." I put a reassuring hand on his shoulder. "If it does, take the side door. Meet up with Lars as we planned. He will know what to do." By the time he met up with Lars, it would most likely be too late to do anything, but Lars would get Anton out of Berlin safely.

Anton looked as if he knew that, too. "But—"

"This is the time to be a scout," I said. "And bring back reinforcements. Scouts do not enter the battle. That is not their mission."

He dropped his eyes, and I knew that he understood, and hated it.

He walked ahead of me and disappeared into the cathedral. I dreaded losing sight of him, even for a minute, but I counted to sixty and followed him through the arched doorway.

22

I walked slowly around the inside of the church, aware of Anton every second. My eyes were drawn to the curved ceiling, with its strong ribs and the circle of light at the top. I wished I could have told him that Lorenz Adlon, owner of a hotel where Anton had once stayed with his purported grandmother, was buried in the cemetery in the back. Herr Adlon died in a car accident. A devout monarchist, he refused to enter the Brandenburg Gate using the middle line, as that was once reserved for royalty. For his pains, he had suffered two car accidents at the Brandenburg Gate, the final one fatal. It was exactly the kind of story that Anton enjoyed.

I kept an eye on his blond head, which faced obediently forward, as I searched for Herr Keller. When I was certain that he was not there, I sat at a pew to wait. I curled my hands around the aged oak back of the pew in front and breathed in the smell of stone dust and the lingering traces of incense. My thoughts turned to Ruth, the child that Paul had loved, in spite of her parentage. She was too young to remember him long.

Where was she? Paul had told me that she was with someone who could provide more for her than he could. Was that true? I did not entirely trust his judgment, and I would rest easier if I could see her safe and sound for myself.

Would Herr Keller know? I prayed so. I said a prayer for Paul, too.

I hoped that he had found peace, and I promised him, as I had promised his wife, that I would help Ruth if I could.

A figure sat next to me. I unfolded my hands and sat back to look at him. Herr Keller looked so much like Paul that tears jumped into my eyes. He had aged much in the past ten years and looked as if he had not slept, but his familiar brown eyes studied me with curiosity and suspicion.

"Good evening, Fräulein Vogel." His deep voice was quiet.

"Hello, Herr Keller." I held out my hand, and he took it. He shook it once, then held on to it.

"Why are you here? Paul said that you escaped. Proud of you for it, he was."

"I am here only for a few days." I hoped. "I want to talk to you about your son."

"I suppose you heard that he's dead? Took the coward's way out, the police tell me."

"They are wrong." My words swelled in the empty space.

"You know better than the police? They said he'd tried the night before, too. I always knew they'd kill him before this ended."

"I—" I cleared my throat. "I was there the night before, and he did try. I bandaged his wrist. By the next morning, he knew that what he had done was wrong, that he had to take care of Ruth. He said he would make sure she was safe."

"Why would Ruth not be safe?" He let go of my hand and lowered his eyebrows.

I kept going. I would never get through it if I stopped. "The night that he died, I was the first one to come upon his body and—there was no gun in the room. He could not have shot himself without a gun."

Herr Keller raised his long elegant hands to his face and ran them down his cheeks. "You told this to the police, I imagine?"

"I cannot."

He put both hands on the back of the pew in front of us and gripped it tightly. "Don't suppose you'll tell me why not?"

I shook my head.

"You always were a closemouthed one." He leaned back. We sat together in silence. Anton bowed his head in front of us. From what I could tell, he read the Bible.

"Still, my son loved you. Should have married you. Hard to imagine now, but we worried that you weren't Catholic. I wasn't so happy when he dated that hard number from the newspaper. She turned out all right, in the end, I think."

I did not think that Maria had turned out all right, but I did not contradict him.

"In the end, when he married, it was a Polish girl. Turned him into a devout Jew. He would have been better off letting you turn him into a Protestant or an atheist, or whatever it is you are."

"Herr Keller—" I did not know how, or if, to defend Miriam or myself.

"Where's his wife got to? I visited the apartment to—to collect some things, but no sign of her."

I briefly told how she had been deported to Poland and died there.

"Little Ruth?" he asked. "Is she in Poland, too?"

"No. Paul said he knew where she was. Did you speak to him in the last few days? Did he tell you?"

He squeezed the pew so hard that his knuckles whitened. "Not in the last few weeks. Not since Ruth's second birthday. How did he lose track of her? Do you know where she is? Is she safe?"

"Paul thought she was safe." I wished I had a better answer.

Herr Keller's grip on the pew did not loosen. "Have you told the police?"

"I cannot."

"I will," he said. "Today."

That might open an investigation into Paul's death. But if there was a chance they might find Ruth, it had to be done.

"My wife and I adore that girl. Bundle of trouble she is. Parents always fighting over her. Her mother wanted her to be a little lady.

Paul wanted to let her run a little wilder, feel the mud between her toes."

I studied tall arched windows. They had beheld much grief since they were built, and they were likely to see much more. "Do you know where she might be? Perhaps with Miriam's family?"

"They're all dead, so far as I know," he said. "This whole Nazi business has gone too far. I've been trying to convince Paul to leave for years. He wouldn't budge. But we'll take Ruth out, Frau Keller and I, if you bring her to us."

They had been good parents to Paul. Ruth would be safer with them than hiding in a box being smuggled across the Swiss border, and I worried that Lars's shell shock was not something that a young girl should see. Anton probably should not either.

"If I find her," I said, "and I can, I will bring her to you."

"Bless you." He wrapped his arm around my shoulder and drew me close. He smelled like Paul. He felt like Paul. I closed my eyes and pretended that he was.

I sat back up before I started to cry. "What about Miriam's friends?"

"I don't know of any," he said. "She spoke only Polish, so we never had a proper conversation."

Miriam and I had had only one conversation, too, where I promised her to help Ruth. So far, I had failed at that.

"About Paul." He paused.

"Yes?"

He drew a packet of letters tied with a green ribbon out of his pocket. I recognized my handwriting on the envelopes. Love letters that I had written to Paul twenty years before. He had saved them all this time. Herr Keller handed me the packet. "I found these in the cupboard in the bedroom. I couldn't go into . . . the kitchen."

I turned the envelopes over in my hands, a lump in my throat. I had been so young, battered by my childhood and Walter's death, but still so much more hopeful than now.

"I didn't think you would want anyone to read them," he said. "So I took them. Paul would want you to have them."

I stroked my thumb down the stack. I had purchased the cream-colored paper and envelopes in Herr Silbert's shop, long before I was a reporter and before his first arrest for forgery. Memories and these pieces of paper were all that remained of Paul for me. That and his little girl, Ruth.

I turned into Herr Keller's arms and cried for Paul. For the years we had, for the years we had lost, and for all the years he would never see.

Eventually I wiped my eyes and sat back up. "I am sorry."

"Don't be," he said. "It's good to know he'll be missed."

"Thank you for the letters." I blew my nose on my handkerchief.

A priest in a cassock stopped at the end of our pew. He inclined his balding head toward us. "Herr Keller?"

"Everything is fine, Rector," Herr Keller said. "She is an old friend of Paul's."

"You have my condolences," the rector said. "Paul was a good man."

He turned and walked silently toward the altar. "Was that Rector Lichtenberg?"

"A friend to Christians and Jews," Herr Keller said. "He has spoken out against the mistreatment of the Jews since the beginning."

A brave stance, and one that not many Catholic or Protestant priests were prepared to take under Hitler. I hoped it would not get him killed.

"Who would want to kill Paul?" he asked. "He was a good boy. Doing the best he could."

I had hoped that he would have an answer to that question. Paul was not a man who accumulated enemies. Unlike me. "Do you know anyone who might have had a grudge against Paul, or against Miriam?"

He looked at me sharply. "I thought you said that she died in childbirth."

"I am taking nothing for granted," I said.

He ran his hands down his face again. "I don't know who would want to kill either one."

I had little idea either. But both of them were dead.

"If you find out who killed him," he said raggedly, "tell me. Please."

"I will." I gripped the letters tightly.

"And, please, find Ruth. She loves our house. My wife and Ruth have so many tea parties together." He swallowed heavily. "She has her own set of dishes with butterflies on them. For her birthday I bought her a matching set for her house."

An image out of the sketch I had drawn flashed in my mind. A plate on the floor with a butterfly on it. Had Ruth been at the table when Paul was killed? Or, perhaps, I was remembering it wrong. I had to go back and see. But I could not drag Anton back there. If it was a murder scene, I might be able to get past the policemen on my own, but not with Anton in tow. "But first you must do me a favor."

"Anything."

I pointed to the back of Anton's head. "Take him to the Friedrichstadt subway station in two hours. He will be met by a man named Lars."

"Why can't you do it yourself?" He tilted his head to the side, waiting for an explanation.

I could give him none. "It is an uncertain world, Herr Keller."

"If this Lars isn't there?"

"He will be."

He studied me for a good long time before nodding. "It's for Paul, isn't it?"

"And for Ruth."

"Let's get started," he said. "And thank you for coming to tell me that Paul did not commit suicide. It will be a comfort to his mother, as much as anything can be right now."

I stared into the older version of Paul's eyes. He turned away.

"Anton," I called softly.

He turned his head, surprised.

"Come here."

He walked back to us.

"Herr Keller," I said, "I would like you to meet Anton."

They shook hands and looked at me.

"I have an errand to run," I began.

"No." Anton shifted his feet wide apart, a fighting stance.

"Herr Keller will take you to the subway station. I will meet you and Lars there."

"I want to go with you." Anton's eyes widened. I knew he was afraid.

"It is nothing dangerous," I said. "Merely complicated."

"Are you at least taking Lars?" he pleaded.

"No. And try not to worry. It is not dangerous." No more so than anything else.

"When I'm older, I won't let you," he said.

"I have to." I hugged him hard and kissed him on the forehead. "Stay here for at least five minutes."

I watched him struggle with his desire to disobey me. In the end, I saw him relent. "All right."

"I love you," I said.

"I love you, too."

I dropped my hand to his shoulder and squeezed it before walking out the door.

I crossed the square and boarded the subway, trying not to cry. I hated to leave him, but I dared not take him with me. It felt good to be on my own again, running risks that affected only me.

23

I found an empty bench on the subway. The car held only a few passengers. Most people were at work for the day. I had only a few hours, so I had to plan this carefully.

A man sat too close to me on the bench. I raised my head to glare at him. Lars.

"Wouldn't it be more convincing if you pretended you knew me?" He leaned in close and kissed my cheek. Even such a trivial contact caused my heart to beat faster.

"Where did you come from?" I whispered, and gave him a faux welcoming smile. He must have followed me. How dare he?

"Where's Anton?" He dropped his arm along the back of the seat.

"Safe. Now, why did you follow me to the cathedral? That seems rather dishonest."

"Less so than ditching Anton and, presumably, me so you can strike out on your own?"

I had no good answer to that. "What did you find out?"

He looked around the empty car before answering in a hushed voice. "Paul's death is considered a suicide. No investigation."

Unfortunate for Paul, but lucky for us, as our fingerprints were everywhere and who knew how many people had seen us coming and going out of his apartment.

"If there is no investigation, it means that there is no police guard on his apartment," I said. That would make things easier.

"Dangerous ideas are running through your head." He shifted his arm on the back of the seat to cup my shoulder.

"I want to find evidence of where Ruth ended up." I sat very straight. "I promised her mother, and I would have promised her father, too."

He tipped his hat up. "I thought you said Paul thought she was better off where she was."

"That was only hours after he tried to commit suicide." I stared out at the concrete wall sliding along centimeters from our window. "I do not know how accurate his assessment was."

"And?" He drew out the word as if to indicate that there were many responses to inaccurate assessments.

"I will feel better if I know for certain that he was correct."

He let out a long breath and settled into the seat. He disagreed, but would not argue further. Fine with me.

"Why did you follow me?" I tapped his knee.

"I followed you because I wanted to see if anyone else followed you. I did not expect you to come out alone."

"Did anyone follow us?"

"Not so far as I could tell." He leaned back and crossed his legs. "So, where are we going? Alexanderplatz?"

"You are going to Friedrichstadt subway station to meet Anton, as scheduled."

"I have a bit of time yet." He tilted his hat forward over his eyes and pretended to sleep, but I knew better. As angry as I was at him for following me, I was glad to have him along.

We reached Alexanderplatz station and climbed the stairs holding hands. It was the first time we had held hands in years, and I quite liked it. I felt hopeful that we could sort things out in Switzerland.

As we walked around Paul's apartment building, hand in hand, I filled Lars in on my conversation with Herr Keller. "He wants Ruth, if we find her."

"You won't take her?" Lars doubled back. He seemed to be count-ing people on the street.

"She is not mine to take." I slowed to keep pace with him.

He raised his eyebrow.

"If she had no one else, I would take her," I admitted. "Who would not?"

Lars squeezed my hand. "I suppose I should be grateful that you take in strays."

"Are you a stray?" I leaned over and kissed his cheek.

He slid an arm around my waist. "More than you know."

We had completed our trip around Paul's building. Nothing seemed amiss.

"Windows in the building across the street can look into Paul's. Anyone could be in there, and we would not know. There is no safe way to do this," Lars said. "Let me go in alone."

"Or you let me do it." I put my hands on my hips.

He shook his head. "Which one of us has the most experience with crime scenes? Which one of us has the most training? Which one of us was a policeman and a soldier?"

He was correct, but I did not care. He read my expression, and his face softened. "Fine, Spatz. You win."

"If someone is watching the apartment," I said. "The most logi-cal place is the front, so we can take the back way in."

We used the entrance from the cellar. Once inside, he drew his gun and stuck it under his coat. He insisted on going up the stairs first, with me steps behind. We made it to Paul's apartment without incident.

He checked each room. I went straight to the kitchen, drew the curtains, and turned on the light. Paul's blood still stained the wall. I stared at it, transported to last night. If we had arrived only min-utes earlier, he might still be alive.

I turned my back on the chair where Paul had died and surveyed the room. Nothing had been cleaned up. Someone had kicked a path through the dishes, probably to remove Paul's body, but otherwise everything was untouched.

Back to the broken window and chair, I squatted on the kitchen floor and examined broken crockery. A broken plate, a glass. I sucked in a breath in surprise. "Lars!"

He came in at a run, gun held in front of him.

I picked two pieces off the floor and fitted them together. It was a child's plate with a butterfly on it. I held it up for Lars. "A child's place setting."

Lars picked up a tiny bowl, cup, and spoon. The bowl, too, had a butterfly on it.

"Ruth was here," I said. "Eating dinner with her father." I lifted a piece of broken glass in my gloved hand. "And a woman."

"A woman?" He took the piece from me.

"Lipstick stains." I pointed. "Near the top rim."

"He could have had dinner with Ruth and the woman, but they left before he was killed," Lars said.

"Or he had dinner with them, the woman shot him, and Ruth watched." My head throbbed. I struggled not to be sick.

"Or that." He checked his wristwatch. "We have fifteen more minutes before we need to leave to get Anton."

I sifted through the rest of the dishes, but found nothing else of note. In the living room, I could not find the picture of Ruth or her birth certificate. Had the killer taken them? Or had Herr Keller?

A cursory search of Ruth's bedroom revealed that her clothes were as they had been when I left, yesterday morning. Whoever took her had not packed any of her things. But if they had just shot Paul and saw us running for the building, they would have known that there was no time.

When I came out of the room, Lars stood in the living room reading a letter from a pile. I looked over his shoulder. It was in Polish.

"You can read Polish?" I asked, surprised.

"Polish is similar enough to Russian that I can make out a bit of it. Nothing seems significant."

"How fluent is your Russian?"

"Fairly," he said. "I had a great deal of free time to practice it, although considering where I learned it, I doubt that it is drawing room Russian."

I touched his back.

He put the letters back on the desk. "Did you find anything?"

"None of Ruth's clothes are missing."

As we walked out into the hall to the door, I noticed that the green blanket was gone. I hoped that Ruth had it with her, and that she was still alive.

We crossed into the rear courtyard where Anton had played football and marbles and into the adjoining building, through it to the street behind. We walked a few blocks before circling back around to Alexanderplatz subway station. I bought the tickets, because Lars kept his gun drawn but hidden by his coat until we were on the train.

Once the subway doors closed, he stuck his gun into his waistband, put his hand on the small of my back, and directed me to a seat. The subway car was too full to talk, and I had nothing to say.

The killer had taken Ruth.

We had to find her. Lars slipped an arm across my shoulders. I dropped my head against him. He stroked my hair gently, over and over. He knew how worried and terrified I felt.

We arrived at the Friedrichstadt station early. He led us to an empty corner and leaned me up against the wall as if to kiss me.

"Spatz?" he asked. "Are you all right?"

"No," I said. "Some woman murdered Paul and took Ruth. Who knows where Ruth is, and what they have done to her."

He slid his arms around my waist and bent his head close to mine. "We'll find her, if we can."

"The only woman I can think that he might have let in so late is Maria," I said. "But I cannot see why she would kill Paul, or take Ruth."

"Are you going to meet her?" He asked the question, but his taut expression said that he knew the answer.

"At seven," I said. "At the Palast am Zoo."

He closed his eyes.

"If she killed him, I want to know," I said. "If she did not, she deserves to know that he did not commit suicide. That he did not choose to leave her."

"Impeccable at logic." He kissed the tip of my nose. "Terrible at risk assessment."

"Sometimes," I said, "that works to your advantage."

"Not so frequently as you may think."

I glanced once around the bustling station. Everyone seemed to be going about their business and ignoring us. "I am meeting her."

"I expected nothing less." He tucked my hair behind my ears. "If she plans to shoot you, her best chance is while you're still on the street, so she can run afterwards. If she plans to knife you, however, she's best going into the theater with you, so she can stab you in the dark and leave before the film is over."

"She would not have killed Paul," I said. "And she will not kill me. She is vicious but cowardly."

"Be that as it may," he said. "How about you get there early and go in? We will follow. I'll sit in the row behind you. A few seats in. I want you on my left side, in case I need to use my gun."

A shiver of fear ran through me. "All right."

He pulled me closer. I put my arms around his neck.

His lips almost touched mine when he spoke. "If I begged you not to go, would you change your mind?"

My heart hammered so erratically that I had trouble concentrating on his words. "No."

"I didn't think so." He kissed me gently on the lips. "I never thought we would spend our wedding night like this."

"It is not our wedding night." Propriety demanded that I move out of the circle of his arms before things became too heated in the subway station. I rested my head on his shoulder.

He threaded his fingers through my hair, and I nestled deeper in his shoulder.

"I put the ring on your finger this morning. Or have you forgotten?" he said.

"I do not think that is legally binding—"

"It's binding in every way that counts." He kissed me on the lips, and I forgot that I was frightened and sad and that we were in a public building. He pulled back and traced my lips with his fingertip. I smiled.

Behind him, Anton and Herr Keller strode through the door. I slipped out from under Lars's outstretched arm and hurried toward them.

Relief flashed across Anton's face, quickly replaced by a scowl. "Hello."

I thanked Herr Keller and promised to tell him what I found out about his granddaughter. I already lied, as I did not tell him what I had discovered at Paul's apartment and my worries that Ruth was with his murderer. I did ask if he had taken Ruth's birth certificate. He had not.

Lars led us aboveground. Rain drizzled, and Lars opened an umbrella. He and I crowded under it, but Anton stayed outside its circle, shoulders stiff with fury because I had left him with Herr Keller.

"The lorry is a few blocks up," Lars said. "On the way, Anton, please give me a report on your mission."

"Mission?" Anton's delicate eyebrows lowered suspiciously.

"Your mother sent you there to see if Herr and Frau Keller would make good parents for Ruth. What is your assessment?"

Anton's shoulders relaxed. I could see him thinking that he had not been sent away. He had been sent on a mission. Lars had defused the situation.

"I liked them." Anton moved under the umbrella. "They were very sad, but they were kind to me. Frau Keller made me a special dinner, and they had pictures of Ruth up on the walls."

"That sounds promising," Lars said. "Thank you for the report."

Anton smiled at Lars. "What's the next mission?"

"Protection." Lars explained how things would work at the theater. Anton listened earnestly. Watching them together, I understood why Lars was a good leader. Anton would follow him anywhere. Even with his ring on my finger, would I? I had never followed a man before.

I bade them farewell and took the stairs down to the Zoologischer Garten subway station. I threaded through the crowd, taking the exit near the movie theater. Dark came early to Berlin in November. Neon tubes outlining the theater's arches and roofline glowed eerily through the evening mist.

The clouds had finally released their store of rain, so I walked across shiny wet cobblestones to queue up. Lars and Anton arrived and queued up, too. Four people were in line between us.

I pretended that I did not notice them as I scanned the film start times to find the film starting closest to seven. *Thirteen Chairs* with Heinz Rühmann. How delightful. The film must be based on the similarly titled 1928 novel by the Russian writing team Ilf and Petrov. Apparently the Nazi regime had not noticed that Ilf was Jewish. That thought cheered me. I spoke a little loudly when I purchased my tickets, so that Lars would know what movie I saw.

I let the usher lead me to an end seat near the back. I did not see Maria, but I did not expect to. I expected her to arrive late and sit next to me as if by accident. Fortunately, the show had been out for weeks. The half-empty theater would make it easier for us to speak unobserved.

Lars and Anton arrived and sat behind and to my right, as Lars had said they would. They were so close that I could hear their conversation. I heard Anton list off the Heinz Rühmann films he had seen. Far more than I had taken him to. Did he go with Boris and Nanette, or was he sneaking out with schoolmates?

While I wondered about that, I studied other patrons. A young couple in the back looked eager for the lights to go down so that they could turn their attention properly to each other. I once sat back there myself with Walter and did not begrudge them. Other seats held more sedate couples and solitary older women like me. Heinz Rühmann, with his cleft chin and ready smile, was a German cinema idol. I had met him in all his charismatic glory once, briefly, when my friend Sarah worked on hats for his film *Those Three from the Gas Station*. A Jew, she certainly would not be allowed to work on films at UFA today. I caressed the dress I wore, one of hers, and felt grateful that my borrowed papers had got her safely to New York.

A propaganda reel flickered to life. Preparations were in place for a fifteen-year celebration of Hitler's Beer Hall Putsch tomorrow, on November 9. Hitler had taken only fifteen years to go from Stadelheim Prison to the Reichstag. I had certainly accomplished nothing so grand in the last fifteen years.

Finally the film started. I settled in to watch. Heinz Rühmann's expressive face filled with dismay when he learned that his rich aunt had left him only thirteen chairs in her will. *Be careful, Heinz,* I told him. *Everyone conceals something.* Heinz did not listen to me and sold those thirteen chairs anyway.

I smelled rain and cigarette smoke. Maria.

"Excuse me." She stepped on my feet and took the seat next to mine. She was now between Lars and me. Perfect.

24

"Hello," I whispered to Maria. I glanced at her small leather purse. Too little to hold anything but a small gun or a knife. I felt better.

She took off her hat and raincoat, showering me with cold raindrops. She still wore her dark hair in a bob, and it still did nothing for her severe schoolmistress's face.

"What do you want?" Maria could make even a whisper sound angry.

"Do you know where Ruth is?" I said.

"Paul knows." She fiddled with the hat in her lap. "We talked about it yesterday afternoon."

So, while I had been visiting Herr Silbert, Paul had been with Maria. Perhaps the glass with the lipstick on it was hers. "Where did you meet?"

She snorted and watched Heinz discover that one of those thirteen chairs he had sold contained 100,000 Reichsmarks, thus starting the frantic search that would propel the film forward.

"At a hotel," she said finally. "And that's all I'll say."

If true, then it was not her lipstick. But if she had shot Paul, she would lie. "Where is Ruth?"

"If Paul wants you to know," she whispered. "I imagine he'll tell you himself."

Once I told her that he was dead, I might get no more information from her. I shifted in my velvet chair. Out of the corner of my eye, I saw Lars reach into his coat. I forced myself to look more relaxed. "Did he also tell you that he tried suicide?"

Her mouth dropped open slightly. He had not told her.

I relayed a quick version of events, ending with bandaging his wrist, and omitting Lars entirely. I downplayed the seriousness of the wound, even as I remembered the blood everywhere.

"Always there to comfort him, aren't you?" she hissed.

"What do you mean by that?"

"You know exactly what I mean." She leaned so close that I felt her stale cigarette smoke breath on my cheek. "Even though you've moved to Switzerland and are living with some banker getting fat on chocolate, it's always you."

"Paul and I have been over for two decades." I moved away. "This is about his daughter."

"It is, is it?" Her sharp features contorted into a snarl. "When you told him that his wife was dead and his daughter was missing, whom did he turn to?"

"The sofa, as I recall." I struggled to keep my voice down. "You left as fast as you could make it out the door."

"You," she whispered. "He turned to you. He's barely seen you in seven years, but it was still you."

"Paul's like a brother to me."

"A brother that you used to sleep with?"

We had strayed far from my entreaties for Ruth. "Please, Maria, help find Ruth. I will be gone in a few days, and with any luck, you and I will never see each other again."

She pursed her too-thin lips. "That would be too much to hope for."

"This is more important than the enmity between you and me. This is about a lost little girl," I said. "Ruth. Did Paul give you a name?"

She scowled. "I don't have a name. Paul said he would meet with the people who had Ruth after we parted, but he did not say who or where. Why don't you ask him yourself?"

If she did not know, how would I find out whom he had met with on the night of his death?

We sat together and watched the film. I struggled to figure out a way to break the news of Paul's death to her. I knew that I was stalling as I watched the audience laugh when Heinz found and destroyed all the chairs one by one, until he found the final chair in an orphanage. Maria glared at me as soon as Heinz entered the orphanage.

"You picked the film," I whispered.

She snorted again.

I watched Heinz, but spoke to Maria. The film was almost over. "One more thing—"

"Good god, isn't there always?"

I had to tell her. If I did not, it might be weeks before she learned of Paul's death. He would not have wanted that. "Maria—"

"Where's Paul?" she asked. "I went by his apartment this morning, but it was locked."

"Last night," I began. "Paul—"

"Did he take Ruth and leave?" She pinned me with her intense gaze.

"I do not know if he found Ruth." I turned in my seat to watch her face. "But—"

"He left without me, didn't he?" She sounded more hurt than angry.

How could I tell her that he was dead, here, in the middle of the theater? But the darkness was probably the best place to tell her. Would I tell her that he had been murdered, or stick with the police's suicide theory?

My mind raced. She could view a copy of the police report deeming his death a suicide. If I told her otherwise, she might start an investigation. She, too, was a crime reporter. She had her own sources.

She stopped pretending that she watched the screen. "Enough, Hannah. Tell me where he is."

"Last night I went to Paul's," I began. "And he—"

"Stop." She held up a palm like a traffic policeman. "I don't want to hear the rest."

"All right," I said.

She turned her hat around and around in her lap. "He's dead, isn't he?"

"I am sorry, Maria." I had no better words than that, as much as I wished for them.

It hurt to see how hard she tried not to cry. In her own way, she had loved him. And I was likely the only one who knew that. Because their relationship had been a secret, she would have to conceal her grief from everyone. I wished that I had picked a better place to tell her. It felt spiteful to have told her here.

"All that worry over a child that wasn't even his." She crushed her hat between her hands. I did not think it would be salvageable. "I never understood it."

"Not his? You are certain?" The man in the locket who looked so much like Ruth must be her father. Paul had said that he was no friend or relation.

"He never told you, did he?" Her tone held satisfaction, even in grief. If she had been in Poland, I could have seen her killing Miriam. But she was with Paul in Germany. "A few years ago we had a fight, and she seduced him away from me. When she told him she was pregnant, he married her."

"Who was the father?" Did he have Ruth? Did he kill Paul? And perhaps Miriam as well? Lars moved his hand toward the front of his coat again. I forced myself to sit back.

"Paul never knew. But he knew enough biology to know it wasn't his when Miriam gave birth to a beautiful blond baby six months after their wedding instead of eight." She spat the words out savagely. Poor Paul.

Paul had raised someone else's child with a faithless wife. I stopped blaming him for having an affair with Maria, even as I faulted his taste. "Why did he stay married to her?"

"Are you so naïve?" She jeered. "She asked him to stay married to her, for the baby's sake, and he did. He thought that his German passport might afford them some protection. That child that wasn't his was always more important to him than me. The second one probably wasn't his either, but he would have loved it more than he did me, too."

I saw the sorrow behind the anger. "Maria, I—"

"Save your pity, Hannah," she said, "and yourself. Get out while you still can."

She walked out of the theater, holding herself carefully erect, as if she expected, with every step, to fall. I let her go.

Hearing the movie nuns describe how they would use the money to help the orphans made Heinz and his partner in crime realize that they could not in good conscience recover the money. The film ended with Heinz becoming rich off a hair tonic he had invented. A random event, but at least virtue was rewarded, and we had a happy ending all around. I should be so lucky.

I waited for the lights to come up before leaving. Out of the corner of my eye, I saw Lars and Anton stand to follow me and kept my pace slow enough that they could keep me in sight. I walked through the lobby like a spinster who needed to get home to feed her cat— quick but not suspiciously so. I took the stairs down to the subway, meandered along the platform, and climbed out a different exit. I waited. I knew that Lars would find me. And he did.

He looked at my face and drew me into a long embrace. "I'm sorry, Spatz."

I took a deep shuddering breath, and another. I would not cry here. I stepped back and hugged Anton briefly.

"Does she know where Ruth is?" Lars asked.

"No. But she thinks Ruth might be with her real father."

Lars tightened his lips. "Do you have a name?"

I shook my head. It made no sense. If her father had killed Paul last night and taken her, why was there lipstick on the glass? If he had Ruth, why bring her to Paul's apartment only to kill him?

"Let's get to the warehouse," Lars said. "I want to start working on the compartment as soon as I can."

I had no better suggestion, so I nodded.

On our way to the warehouse, we drove through the Jewish quarter. Lars pulled over next to a man with a lorry heaped high with household goods. Chairs, boxes, bags, a bicycle, and more were tied in with rope. A FOR SALE sign was tacked to the side of the lorry. What could Lars possibly want to buy off him?

Lars turned off the engine and went to talk to the man. We followed.

"Is it all your stuff?" Anton pointed.

"It is." The man ran one hand down his curly white beard. "We're leaving as soon as I have enough money together to buy gas."

Crowded in the front seat of the lorry, a woman in a black dress who looked young enough to be his daughter and three children stared glumly at us. I was reminded of the refugees in Zbąszyń. "You are not going to Poland, are you?"

He folded his hands in front of him. "Holland."

Lars examined the man's bald tires. "You won't get far on those. Especially if it rains."

"So, buy something and pay me extra." The man chuckled, then grew serious. "We'll have to buy new tires when they blow out. We must be out of Germany before that diplomat in Paris dies."

"Do you expect reprisals?" I asked.

"I'm a Jewish man living in Hitler's Germany," he said. "How could I expect otherwise?"

Lars pointed to the back of the lorry. "How much for the mattress?"

I smiled tiredly. He had promised to make sleeping in the warehouse more comfortable.

The old man and Lars haggled about the price.

"Just pay him what he asked," I told Lars. He needed the money to get his family away.

Lars looked ashamed. He drew out his wallet.

I walked to the front of the car and peeked in at the woman and children. Anton stayed with Lars. The woman's dark eyes studied me curiously.

"Good evening," I said.

She answered in Dutch. I had a strong feeling that she also spoke German, but chose not to.

"Safe journeys." I hurried back to Lars and Anton.

Anton untied the tarp so they could load the mattress. He clambered into the back of our lorry and surveyed the mattress's position, tugging it back and forth as if it were a deadly serious job.

Lars whispered in my ear. "I'm sorry that I have nothing better to provide for our wedding night."

I slipped my arms around his waist. "What could be better than a magical carriage to spirit us out of Germany?"

"That it shall be. I promise that as soon as we get out of this god-forsaken mess, I will give you a proper wedding night."

"I only want a real husband."

He kissed me on the forehead. "Soon. Our simple life together will start soon."

I look skeptically into his dark eyes. "Do you think we will ever achieve simple?"

He chuckled. "Simpler?"

"Simpler would be wonderful."

He kissed me on the lips, and I suddenly did wish for a proper wedding night. Immediately.

Someone coughed. I reluctantly drew back. Lars held me a second longer, then turned to pay the man for the mattress. Together we refastened the tarp and drove to the warehouse.

The warehouse was dark and looked empty, but again Lars left us in the lorry while he scouted it out. This time he left me the Vis pistol.

25

"Clear." Lars opened the door and helped us out. Cold from the concrete floor seeped through my shoes. The warehouse felt colder than last night.

I sent Anton to brush his teeth while I crawled around the back of the lorry, making up the bed with the linens and blankets Lars had purchased when he bought the mattress. Lars climbed in next to me, expression impenetrable in the gloom.

"Are your supplies here?" I spread a blanket across the old mattress.

"They are. If all goes well, I can get the box built tonight. Tomorrow, I'll ask Herr Populov to stay late and help me attach it to the lorry."

"I can help."

"You can't," he said. "It's too heavy. I'll need at least two other men."

I folded the blanket back for Anton.

"Tell me what happened in the theater," Lars said.

I told him.

"If her father does have her, he has a better claim to her than Paul's parents." He tucked the blanket under the mattress at the bottom, cracking his knuckle on the metal bed of the lorry.

He held it up for me to kiss, and I did. His hand smelled like gun oil.

"He does have a better claim on her, Spatz," he repeated.

I held his hand between mine. "Unless he murdered Paul."

"Unless that." He sat next to me in the dark. "How do you plan to find him, as I imagine you do?"

"Perhaps he is the doctor that Reuben told Anton about. Or that doctor knows who he is." I knew I sounded crazy. I had no proof. "Maybe he killed Paul to get to Ruth. After all, he took her before."

"How do you know that?" Lars kept his voice gentle, but I heard the skepticism that underlay his words.

"I will show you."

We crawled out from under the tarp that covered the back of the lorry. I took the scrap of white fabric from my satchel and gave it to Lars. "I found this on the hinge of the cupboard where Ruth was hiding. I think it is a piece of a lab coat."

He studied it. "Perhaps."

"If he wore a lab coat, he must have been an Aryan doctor," I said.

Anton walked up and perched on the tailgate. "Why?"

"Because Jewish doctors in Germany are forbidden from practicing medicine. Some probably still do, but I doubt that they walk around in lab coats."

"Sounds reasonable," Lars said.

"Probably very few Aryan doctors make house calls in the Jewish quarter." Excited, I spoke more quickly. "And I have a friend, a doctor, who might know their names."

"The woman who stitched you up last time?" Lars asked.

"Yes." Frau Doktor Spiegel. I thought about visiting her tonight, but knew that she liked to go to bed early and asking her for favors in the middle of the night was a mistake.

Anton and I bedded down in the lorry while Lars went to work building the compartment. Anton fell asleep easily, but sleep eluded me. I continued to worry about Ruth. Either she was with her father, or with the person who murdered Paul. Perhaps they were one and the same. And how to explain the lipstick on the glass?

Eventually I fell into a restless sleep. I awoke with my heart pounding. I had dreamed of finding Paul dead. I heard men talking and quickly slipped into my dress and shoes. Not intending to be caught in a state of undress again, I had left them by the side of the mattress the night before. I crept to the end of the lorry and listened through the tarp.

The voices spoke Russian. Lars and Herr Populov. Lars seemed to be asking for something. Herr Populov seemed reluctant to give it. Was he asking for help to install the compartment when the shop closed again tonight? Whatever it was, Lars pressed him, and he agreed.

I roused Anton, and we went to breakfast at a different restaurant from the day before. Afterwards, we drove to the Jewish quarter. Lars decided to rest in the back of the lorry while Anton and I went to talk to Frau Doktor Spiegel. First I stopped by her favorite bakery to pick up rugelach. Their cinnamon scent filled the lorry's cab.

Anton fixed his best beseeching eyes on me.

"One," I said. "The rest are for Herr and Frau Doktor Spiegel."

He fished out a pastry and took a satisfied bite.

"You just had breakfast," I pointed out.

"I'm always hungry for treats." He spoke around the rugelach.

He was. I reparked the lorry just outside the Jewish quarter in a sunny spot. Hopefully that would warm up the back a bit for Lars. He had looked exhausted after breakfast, having traded last night's sleep for finishing the compartment. We would install it after Herr Populov's shop closed at six and be in Poland before bedtime. As much as I wanted to find Ruth, I dared not endanger Anton another moment.

That left me only one day for sleuthing.

I picked up the brown bag of rugelach. Together Anton and I walked into the Jewish quarter. Fresh graffiti jeered from the buildings. Boards covered more windows. I wondered if it was the result of everyday anti-Semitism or if it was in response to vom Rath's shooting. If he died, I feared much worse than rocks through windows.

We hurried through unnaturally quiet streets to Frau Doktor Spiegel's ground-floor apartment. It looked the same as always. The lace curtains were perfectly aligned on either side of her front window. The building's smooth stone front had been cleaned during the Olympics, and its tan surface was cheery in the morning light.

Anton brushed crumbs off his shirt while I rang the bell. The blue and white sign near her door that advertised her services as a doctor was gone, but the brass door handle and bell were still brightly polished.

Frau Doktor Spiegel answered the door herself. Her hair was now more gray than black, and her dark eyes looked tired. She had aged ten years in the last two.

"Fräulein Vogel?" She scrutinized me. "You look better than last I saw you."

Last time I went to visit her, I had just been hit by a car and was bleeding from a head wound. "That is no great feat," I said. "You, too, look well."

She harrumphed. "What a charming liar you make. Who is this?"

I put my hand on Anton's shoulder. "Anton. We brought breakfast."

She stepped out of the doorway. "Come inside, then. I just made tea."

I followed her back to her kitchen and set the rugelach on her long mahogany table. She handed me an absinthe green translucent glass plate, and I arranged the pastries on it.

"Have one," she said. "You as well, Anton. Although it looks by the crumbs on the corners of your mouth that you started early."

He wiped his mouth. "My apologies. I didn't know how many people there would be to share it with."

She busied herself setting out teacups, a pot of cream, and a sugar bowl, all made of the same peculiar glass. "Just me."

"Where is Herr Spiegel?" I asked, surprised.

"Dead," she said. "They arrested him a year ago. He didn't last a month in the camps."

A memory of Herr Silbert's emaciated frame flashed in my mind. "You have my condolences."

"Thank you."

I poured tea for the three of us. She sat and put a rugelach on her plate. But, although I knew it was her favorite pastry, she did not take a bite.

"Does that glass glow?" Anton pointed to a collection of green glass plates lined up on a shelf above the sink, similar to those she had set on the table.

"In some lights, it does," she said. "It's called Vaseline glass. Uranium makes it glow under certain lights."

"I've heard of that!" He walked carefully over to the plates, as if afraid his mere presence might break them. "Isn't uranium poison?"

"In larger doses," she said. "These days, I think I will die of other causes long before uranium poison would do me in."

He studied the plates.

"My husband used to buy them for me. I kept them crated up because they're expensive, but after he was taken away, I found I wanted to see them every day."

"Do not touch," I said. He would not, but I could not help myself. Sometimes my mother's voice spoke from my mouth.

He swallowed a retort.

"Why are you here, Fräulein Vogel?" she asked. "Not for emergency medical care, I see."

"A social call?" I used the silver tongs to add a cube of sugar to my tea.

"Strange time to be sociable. Vom Rath lingering on the edge of death. Broken windows and new graffiti last night. If he dies, it'll be worse. You're here for something else. As always."

I thought of concocting a story, but decided to try the truth. "Do you remember Paul Keller?"

She patted my shoulder. "I heard about his suicide. You have my condolences. I know that you were close."

I blinked back surprise tears. "We were."

Anton turned from the plates, eyes sad. He sat next to me again and pushed away his plate of rugelach.

"So were you the mystery blond woman and child seen at his apartment when he died?"

My breath caught. We had been seen, too. It had been a close escape on many levels. "Unfortunately, too late. But I am here on his behalf." I explained about Ruth's disappearance and finished with, "Do you know the doctor who might have carried her away?"

She stared into her translucent teacup, as if reading the tea leaves on the bottom.

"Frau Doktor Spiegel?"

"Of course I know him," she said. "He took over my practice, didn't he?"

"Why did he do that?" Anton asked.

"Someone had to. As a Jew, I haven't been able to practice medicine since July twenty-fifth. Another Nazi law. They're trying to starve us out, and most of us would go eagerly if we had a place to land."

I drew back. "About this doctor—"

"I've nothing against him. I'm grateful that he treats Jews. Precious few Aryan doctors do anymore." She slugged her tea like whiskey.

"Could you give me his name?" I asked. "I wish to ask him about Ruth today."

"No." She set the teacup down with a clank. "I think I'll leave him out of this."

"But I heard that he has been offering to buy babies."

"Just one baby, I should think." She turned the cup around on the saucer. "And he has since sorted that out."

"So, one baby is acceptable to sell?"

"He wanted to adopt a baby." She picked up the empty teacup. "His wife is infertile."

"And he cannot formally adopt? Surely an Aryan doctor would have no trouble legally adopting a child."

"The Party wants all good German mothers to bear many children, so they can send them into the new *Lebensraum*." She splashed tea into her cup and onto the table. "He worried that if his wife's infertility were known, it could be used to disadvantage them. As it would if they started formal adoption procedures."

"So, he asks pregnant Jewish women if they will give up their child to him?" I asked. Horrified, Anton clamped his mouth closed.

"I know you think it sounds horrible, Fräulein Vogel, but be practical." She set down her full cup of tea and shook her finger at me to emphasize her points, as she used to when she taught. "If he can identify an adoptive mother before she delivers, he can send his own wife out of the country for the pregnancy and birth and she can come back with a baby, and no one the wiser. The baby will be much better off with a German physician than being raised as a Jew in Hitler's Germany. And that is where we all live. Hitler's Germany."

I sat back in my chair and studied the eerie green dishes. If I did not find out what had happened to Ruth today, I would never know. I tried to formulate a better argument, but once Frau Doktor Spiegel made up her mind, she was rarely swayed.

"I will help you," she said. "Don't fear."

I sat forward so suddenly, my chair legs clacked against the floor. "How?"

"I'll give you the name of the girl's father."

I gaped at her. Anton did, too.

"Don't look so surprised. Doctors talk, although we were both discreet about this, and not only for poor Paul's benefit."

Poor Paul, indeed.

"His name is Heinrich Stauffer." She scratched the address on her old prescription pad and handed it to me. "Here's his office address. He's married and in the Party, so don't expect a warm welcome."

I puzzled out the address. Her handwriting, never good, had not improved with age. "Wilhelmstrasse? He works—"

"At the Ministry of Propaganda and Enlightenment," she interrupted. "The irony is not lost on me."

Ruth's father worked, probably indirectly, for Joseph Goebbels. I could see how a relationship with a Polish Jew would be complicated. How could he care for Ruth? I folded the scrap of paper and handed it back to her. I could not take the paper with me; it had her name on it. "Do you think he has her?"

She shrugged. "With Miriam and Paul gone, the doctor would have taken her there. What happened after, I can't say."

I finished my tea in one gulp. "We must be—"

"Leaving now that you have what you needed?"

Half standing, I stopped.

She laughed heartily. "The expression on your face, Fräulein Vogel."

"I . . . that is we . . . this evening—"

"I quite understand." She handed Anton his half-eaten rugelach. "As always, you are on a tight schedule."

I sat down again. "What are your plans? Will you stay here?"

"Not a second longer than I must." She wiped her hands on her napkin. "Which appears to be many more seconds than I would like."

"You would leave everything behind?"

She gestured around the empty apartment. "What everything?"

Perhaps I could help her as I had not helped Paul. Lars's compartment was big enough for her and Anton. "Will you be here this evening? I can make no promises, but I might have a solution to your problems."

"Better than Paul's?" she asked.

So she believed the suicide story as well. "I hope so."

"I'll be here," she said. "I have nowhere else to go."

26

Back at the lorry, I checked to see that Lars was still there. Feeling ridiculous, I paused to make sure that he was breathing, taking nothing for granted since Paul's murder.

Anton and I piled into the front seat, and I eased into the busy street. It hurt to shift with the cast, but I hated to ask Anton to shift for me in this kind of traffic.

"Are we going to see Ruth's father now?" Anton asked.

I was not certain if he was coming. "I am."

"Did you love Paul?"

"Yes." I gripped the wheel. "We were close friends for many years."

We had left the Jewish quarter. The absence of graffiti made everything feel safer.

"Did you love him more than Lars?"

I halted to let a group of girls dressed in the brown uniforms of the League of German Girls cross the street. Every one of them was younger than Anton.

"Did you?" he asked again. Sometimes, he reminded me of myself.

"I loved him longer than Lars." The girls reached the cobblestone sidewalk. We lurched forward again. I gritted my teeth and shifted into first. "I almost married Paul twenty years ago."

"Why didn't you?"

None of the reasons I had listed twenty years ago made sense now, especially knowing that Paul would have been protected from the Nazi government if I had. He would have known the parentage of his children. I would have insisted that we emigrate years ago. And he would still be alive. "I do not know."

"How can't you know something like that? Do you know why you agreed to marry Lars this morning?"

I shifted into second and hoped I could stay there for a while. "I think I understand that less than why I did not marry Paul."

He groaned. "How am I supposed to ever understand?"

I shook my head. "I do not think you are supposed to. I cannot claim that I do."

He crossed his arms and stared moodily out the window. I resisted the urge to tousle his hair and instead drove straight to the government offices in Wilhelmstrasse. The buildings here were cleansed of graffiti and soot. They looked clean enough to eat off, despite the filth that they contained.

Not wanting Lars to be caught sleeping next to a government office, which might have more thorough police sweeps, I drove past the Ministry of Propaganda and parked several blocks away, in a residential district.

I left my old Hannah Vogel and Adelheid Zinsli passports, and the Vis, in the glove box. The only identification that my satchel contained was my, now properly stamped, Hannah Schmidt passport. Venturing into a Nazi edifice without proper papers was suicidal. But the passport would hold up. Herr Silbert's work had always been reliable.

I brushed my hair and applied a fresh layer of pink lipstick while trying to decide what to do with Anton. In the end, I decided to take him with me, so that I could watch him. He would probably tail me if I left him alone in the lorry.

"You are Anton Schmidt," I said. "If anyone asks, your passport is at your aunt's house. You are Swiss, and not Jewish."

"I am ready." He used the accent he had acquired in Switzerland and immediately lost when we returned to Berlin.

"It is no game," I said. "Do exactly as I say."

"Don't I always?"

"No. That is why I am making the point."

"I understand," he said.

Together we walked to the new Ministry of Propaganda. Its stark lines said that its purpose was serious, with no time for frills, and the sharp angles told of the importance of order to the new regime. The eagle topping the walls looked ready to drop his stone swastika on our heads.

I presented my papers to a stern-looking man in uniform whose bushy eyebrows looked weighted down with invisible rocks. Beetle-brown eyes sized me up and found me wanting.

"I am here to see Herr Stauffer." I stood as straight as I could, acutely aware that I was much shorter than he. "On personal business."

The man's eyes flicked from my breasts to Anton. "Upstairs, second office on your right."

He had a visitor log, but did not ask me to sign it, and I did not mention it. Instead, I hurried up the imposing stairs. Did Herr Stauffer entertain so many women in an average workday that they no longer bothered to keep track of them? That gave me something to work with.

Tall ceilings swallowed the sounds of our steps. I put a hand on Anton's sleeve. "When we get to his office, I will go in and sit down without being asked. If there is a second seat, you sit as well. Otherwise stand directly behind my seat with your hands on the back. Do not move from that position or say a word unless I tell you to. Understood?"

"Yes," he said. He looked serious, and grown up.

We turned right at the top of the stairs. I opened the second door without knocking and strode in as if someone expected me. The room contained a small metal desk, lines of gray filing cabinets, a typewriter, and a rooster of a man with a barrel chest and a cockscomb of red hair cut bristly short. The man from the locket. His fingers hung motionless above typewriter keys.

I dropped into the chair in front of his desk uninvited. Anton stood behind me, as it was the only free chair in the room.

The man swept his report into a drawer and stood. As I suspected, he was barely my height.

"What are you doing here?"

I said nothing and kept my face stony. Let his conscience tell him.

He studied my face, then Anton's. "He's not mine," he said. "I don't remember you."

I clenched my teeth, angry for Miriam, and for Ruth. They were only two in a long line of women and abandoned children. "Fortunately," I said icily, "that is true. I am here for a child who is."

"Preposterous!" His face reddened.

"A Jewish child."

He sat down. The flash of terror in his eyes told me that Frau Doktor Spiegel had named the correct man. Then he deserved everything he got.

"We can discuss this here." I spoke slowly so that he would feel the weight of each word. "Or we can discuss it at the courthouse. I believe that the Nuremberg Laws were fully in effect when you impregnated a young Jewish woman in early 1936."

He gulped. "That is—"

"A crime punishable by prison or hard labor, which might include a stint in a concentration camp." Let this Nazi think about the consequences of his own laws.

"You have no proof," he said weakly. "No proof at all."

"I do," I lied. "Eyewitnesses, diaries, papers, medical statements."

He dropped his face into his square hands. "How much do you want?"

"Knowledge," I said. "To start."

Anton's hand twitched on the back of the chair, but he said nothing.

Herr Stauffer raised his head to look at me. His freckled face had gone blank. I was glad that he had his hands where I could see them.

"Where is the child now?" I asked.

"An orphanage." He bit his chapped lips.

"Aryan or Jewish?" I spoke like an interrogator.

"I'll not tell you that." He glared at me.

If it was a Jewish orphanage, he would have told me the name. So he must have delivered her to an Aryan one. At least he had done something to make things easier for her. "Another law broken, I suspect." I did not keep the disdain from my voice. "But for the sake of a child." It had been for his own sake.

"What do you want?" He sounded calmer now. He had adjusted to the situation. I had to keep him off guard.

"Why did you take her to an Aryan orphanage?" I stressed the word *Aryan*, to remind him that I knew it, and if I turned him in, things would go even worse for him.

"There was nowhere else to take her." He worried his lower lip. "I couldn't find that Jew that Miriam married."

Paul.

"What about keeping her? You are her father." She was better off in an orphanage than with him, but someone should remind him of his responsibilities.

"Impossible! I tried to explain that to the damn doctor. I told him what I would have to do, where I would have to take her, but he didn't care."

Because there were no better options for Ruth than an Aryan orphanage, with her mother dead in a refugee camp, and Paul nowhere to be found. The doctor must have told Paul where Ruth was on the night that he tried to commit suicide. Paul, too, had thought an Aryan orphanage would offer her the protection that he could not.

In the end, Paul had changed his mind and fetched her home. And his killer had her now. The man in front of me had not killed Paul. Stauffer would have been thrilled to dump his illegitimate child on Paul. But what about Miriam?

Herr Stauffer fidgeted with a piece of blank paper on his desk. The watermark looked familiar. Government paper, the same as on my notes. And Miriam's.

"I have a letter typed on this stationery, threatening the mother of the child." I clipped out each word.

He scooted his chair back from me.

"Would a police investigation find that it came from that type-writer?" I knew it would, as did he.

His eyes shifted down to the typewriter and back up. "I have no idea what you are talking about."

"The letter threatens to end things," I said. "And now she is dead."

His freckles stood out in sharp relief in his suddenly pale face. "Miriam, dead?"

"In a refugee camp in Poland," I said.

Tears welled up in his eyes. "The baby?"

"Dead, too," I said. "A stable is no place to deliver a baby."

He lowered his head. He seemed genuinely upset over Miriam's death, in spite of his bold talk earlier.

"What did she want from you that you would not give her? Money?"

He shook his head.

"You are Aryan, are you not?"

He did not raise his head. "Completely."

"She wanted you to claim your daughter." I did the horrific Nazi calculation in my head. "If the child had two Aryan grandparents, then she would be classed as a Mischling, not a Jew."

Paul had only one Aryan parent, Miriam had zero. Not enough to save Ruth.

"She was born one month too late." He directed his words down at his desk. He still would not look at me. "If she had been born before the end of July in 1936, then she would have been a Mischling, but she was born in late August. I tried to tell Miriam. I could not help her. But she would not listen."

"And?"

"I paid her." He sounded numb now, as if he was past caring. "I gave her money to leave so that she could have the other baby somewhere free. But the only place that she could go was Poland, and she would never go there."

I remembered Paul's words. "What happened to Miriam in Poland?"

He spread his hands wide. "Horrible things. It's why she came here. And then I met her, and everything got so complicated."

"She died there," I said. "In Poland."

He gulped back a sob. "She always said that Poland would kill her quicker than the Nazis ever would."

"Did you have a hand in that?"

"Me?" He blew his nose on a crisp white handkerchief. "If I had wanted to kill her, I would have done it here. No one would investigate the death of another Jew in Germany."

I studied him. His words seemed true, but even if they were not, I would not come to the root of them here. If Miriam was murdered, I might never know. I thought back to the mysterious translator in the stable. What had become of her?

I stood so suddenly that Anton almost tipped my chair over. "I am done with you, for now. But I am watching you. If you do not change your behavior, I will turn you in. I have heard that Oranienburg is lovely this time of year." Just a quick reminder of the concentration camp near Berlin where he might be sent.

He flinched.

I swept out with my head held high, my shoulders square and angry. Anton was so close behind me that I worried he would tread on my heels. "Not a word," I told him.

We made it past the disapproving officer by the door and walked several blocks before I cut left and circled back toward the lorry.

"All right, Anton," I said. "You may speak again."

"I had no idea you could lie like that!" He looked at me with admiration. "He was terrified!"

I hated to hear his enthusiasm over my skills in deception. "Unfortunately, that is probably all the punishment he will ever receive for abandoning his daughter."

"You should have shaken some money out of him."

"Anton!" Shocked, I stopped walking.

"For Ruth," he said. "She probably needs it more than he does."

"Blackmail is . . ." I wound down. I had blackmailed him for information, if not for money. "For life and death, I will do it. But not for cash."

That was a fine distinction to make, and I was not certain that Anton agreed, but he held his peace.

We stopped at a telephone booth on the way to the lorry. I called the newspaper again. Herr Marceau answered on the first ring.

"It is I," I said. "No names."

"I have news for you." He paused uncertainly.

"Is it good?" I asked, although I could tell from his tone that it was not.

"No—"

"First answer a question for me." I glanced up and down the nearly empty street. I had assumed that the Gestapo monitored the telephones near the ministry, but I could not be certain about this one either. "Could you look at the envelopes of the letters I received and tell me where they were postmarked?"

"Berlin, but—"

"I know that, but do they have anything on them to indicate where in Berlin?"

"The police have them," he said. "Now, be quiet and listen."

"Go ahead." I paused at his tone, worried about the reasons behind it.

"A woman called today to leave a message for you. She claimed to be the one who has been sending you the letters. I spoke to her myself."

I sagged against the wood and glass side of the booth. The letter writer had escalated to calling. Anton looked at me worriedly. "A woman?"

"She said that if vom Rath dies, so will the little girl. She wants you to know that it's your fault, as it was the day before yesterday."

My throat was too dry to speak. It was her lipstick on the glass.

She had killed Paul. She had Ruth, and she planned to kill her, too. I cleared my throat. "Why?"

"I asked her that, too. She said that you know why. You murdered someone whom she loved."

Frau Röhm had once thought that I killed her son and had been willing to kill Anton in revenge, but what other woman could link me to Ruth, Paul, and Berlin? I discounted Maria. She might have killed me, but she would never have killed Paul. And as much as I hated her, I did not believe that she would kill Ruth either.

"What was she talking about?" He sounded more perplexed than accusatory. Even Herr Marceau did not think me a killer. Except, I was.

"I never murdered anyone," I said. Self-defense was not murder. A fine line, but all I had to cling to. "I have no idea what she meant."

"She certainly seemed angry at you," he said. "She felt wronged."

I gripped the black Bakelite receiver, trying to think. "Can you find Herr Knecht?"

"I will see." He put the phone on the desk with a clunk. While I waited, I thought about Paul. The woman he let in the night he was murdered was someone he trusted. Someone he did not think would ever harm him. Regardless, she had chosen him because of me. Guilt over having brought Paul into the line of fire welled up in me. No matter who had killed him, it was my fault.

Cold fury overrode the guilt. His murderer had killed an innocent, and threatened to kill another. I would stop her. Or die trying.

"I'm back," Herr Marceau said. "I could not find Herr Knecht."

"Could you please—?" I cleared my throat again. "Could you please stay by the phone for more messages? All day, even into tonight? I hate to ask—"

"I'll stay," he said. "Of course."

"I am going to try to find the little girl," I said. "As soon as I can, I am coming home."

"We miss you," he said. "Be careful."

I thanked him and broke the connection. Did Herr Marceau have a heart, or a deeper agenda? I left my hand atop the phone box.

A woman caller. Maria? Paul would certainly have let her in. But I could not picture her killing him, and certainly not taking Ruth. Did Paul entertain other women visitors late at night? Or had it been someone who looked like Maria? Or like me?

I took a deep breath. The person I could think of who looked the most like me was Fräulein Ivona. That seemed ridiculous. She was somewhere in Poland. But it was a lead to follow, and I had no others. She and Lars had been together less than a month, and I did not think that her feelings for him were deep enough to kill just to hurt him. But I could be wrong about that. I had been wrong about every-thing else. I turned toward the door, and Anton. I had to think. I had to set aside my anger and guilt to save Ruth.

The timing, I told myself. Start with the timing. The letters started a month ago, before Fräulein Ivona met Lars. So what had happened a month ago? Fräulein Ivona's mother died. Perhaps, then, she had started writing me letters and sought out Lars and their meeting had not been a chance encounter in a bar, as Lars thought.

But why? Did she blame us for her mother's death? I had never killed another woman. Had Lars? She had said that her mother had been ill. I did not see how we could be responsible for that. Perhaps her mother told her something before she died.

The other person who became agitated with me a month ago was Herr Marceau. I had only his word that there had been a woman caller. Was he trying to frighten me into leaving Berlin? But how could he know about Ruth's disappearance? Or perhaps this woman was related to his beloved actress in Berlin.

Anton knocked against the glass. I pushed the door open and stepped into the cold afternoon.

"What happened?" he asked. "You look like a horse rode over your grave."

"Truer than you think," I said. "We have to get back to the lorry."

27

I walked him there too quickly for either of us to speak. I was out of breath when we arrived. A rumpled and tired-looking Lars leaned against the back of the lorry.

I filled him in on my conversation with Herr Marceau. Lars did not believe that it was Fräulein Ivona. Logic, passion, or self-deception?

"Give me another name, Lars," I said. "One other woman who sought us both out?"

"I don't know," he said. "That does not mean that the name doesn't exist. Why would Ivona go to these lengths?"

"Why would anyone?" I put my hands on my hips. I could think of no other suspect, and neither could he.

"What about Ruth's father?" He ran his fingers through his mussed hair, and I felt sorry for him. He was exhausted, he had done nothing but work to get us all to safety, and he could not have known about Fräulein Ivona either.

I told him of my encounter with Stauffer, the only other lead we had.

"What is Fräulein Ivona's last name? Did you know?" She had presented herself to me as Fräulein Ivona, so I had assumed that was her surname, but now I knew it was her given one.

"Of course I know! It was Fischer," he snapped. "Ivona Fischer."

Fischer was one of the most common surnames in Germany. "Did you ever see her passport or identity papers?"

"I was sleeping with her," he barked. "Not interrogating her."

"More's the pity." I bristled at his tone. "So you have no proof that her name was, in fact, Fischer?"

"I did see a student identification card," he said. "There was no picture. But everything that she told me fit in with the file my colleague checked for me. Ivona Fischer is not your culprit, no matter how jealous you may be."

"This has nothing to do with your philandering." I stepped closer to him. "I am trying—"

"Arguing won't solve anything." Anton took my arm and pulled me back a step.

"How about," Lars said coldly, "I visit the Berlin address from her file? I have it in my notebook. Perhaps she is even there. If not, will childhood photographs convince you that she is who she says and that she has no connection to this affair?"

He opened his old notebook. I watched him flip past the list of suspects, remembering the names of those who had died because of me: Hahn, Bauer, and two unnamed Gestapo agents in the warehouse, plus the two by the side of the road. I wished that I had never met any of them.

We drove to the address without speaking. Anton pressed himself against the door and stared out the window, probably wishing he did not have to be in the cab of the lorry either.

Lars stopped the lorry and wrenched up the parking brake with such force that I worried he might yank it out entirely. He stomped up the drive of a well-kept house.

"Please stay here," I told Anton.

"I have no wish to follow you." He took out his platypus and began to shape it.

I hurried after Lars.

He rang the bell. A young woman with long dark hair tucked into a bun answered the door. A black cat twined around her ankles.

"Yes?" she said in a high-pitched, almost childish voice.

"We wish to speak to Ivona Fischer," Lars said.

"That's me," she said.

Lars took a quick step back.

"Do you work for the department of road building?" I asked.

"I do," she said. "Is something wrong? I only work part-time. I was told not to come in today."

Lars was unable to take his eyes off her.

"Nothing wrong," I told her. "I just wanted to confirm that you made your donation to the Winter Relief Fund."

"But I did!" She shifted nervously from foot to foot. "I can give again."

"Not necessary. Thank you." I took Lars's arm and walked him back down the path to the lorry.

I had seldom seen him so shaken.

"We need to find another telephone booth," I said. "I know someone who might be able to find out Fräulein Ivona's last name."

He nodded. He seemed to have lost the power of speech.

I found a telephone box on a busy shopping street. Anton insisted that I leave the door open so that he could hear. Lars crowded next to him.

While the operator worked on the connection, I wondered if the man I was trying to reach had changed his number. Much might have changed since he gave it to me in the Olympic Village two years ago. The phone rang through.

Now I could only hope that he was home for lunch.

"Lehmann," said a deep voice. I almost cried with relief.

I thought how to play it. He might not recognize my voice, so I used a variation of my brother's name. "This is Ernestine. I am in town for a few hours and—"

"Wondered if I had spare time over lunch? So you called me at my home?" Wilhelm asked. "Naughty girl."

I hoped that Anton could not hear what he had just said. "How about we meet outside the restaurant where I had lemonade last time and then . . ."

A short pause, then Wilhelm said, "The one with your favorite cowboy?"

He had guessed correctly. "You know how I feel about cowboys."

He chuckled. "Give me half an hour. I need to get a hat."

I rang off.

"I am meeting an old friend," I said to Lars. "He might help us."

"Who?" Anton asked.

"Wilhelm Lehmann," Lars said. He had met Wilhelm as part of my brother's murder investigation. And he had heard both sides of my conversation.

"I remember him!" Anton said. "He gave me a ride up the stairs and told me stories, and he was in that meeting. The one where . . ."

The one where I was shot. "Yes. Him."

I turned to Lars. "We need to drive to Haus Vaterland. I am meeting Wilhelm out front. You and Anton must stay out of sight."

"I don't like leaving you alone," Lars said.

"Wilhelm might get spooked if you are there." He certainly would not tell me much with Lars listening.

"I want to spook him a little," he said. "To keep you safer."

"If you cannot bear it, follow me. But out of sight. I would be interested to know if anyone follows Wilhelm. I will stoop down and pretend to fix my shoe when you should pick me back up."

"Spatz—"

"I would not have to do this if you could verify Fräulein Ivona's last name." A mean thing to say, and I regretted it. But it was true. "I am not going to let Ruth die without trying to save her."

He held his finger under his eye, on the muscle that twitched when he was angry. "As you wish."

He dropped me a block from Haus Vaterland. He pulled into traffic and disappeared. I trusted him to keep track of me unseen, in spite of our squabble.

I walked in a seemingly aimless fashion down the Kufürstendamm. I noticed how shops on this fashionable street took great pains to advertise their German-ness, probably to ingratiate themselves with the Nazis to protect their windows. I passed signs advertising German restaurants, a German candy store, and a German store that sold umbrellas and luggage.

I stepped into a German tobacconist's next to Haus Vaterland to wait for Wilhelm. The scent of pipe tobacco reminded me of my father. He had usually been happy while smoking his pipe in the evening. Before he got to his third or fourth drink.

I walked between glass cases of pipes, cigarettes, and tobacco. A mural of an exotic-looking tobacco plant covered the wall behind the counter. A dapper man puffed on his pipe, a perfect advertisement for his wares.

I stopped next to a life-size wooden carving of an Indian. Brick red paint covered his face and hands, the wooden feathers on his headdress were brown tipped with white. The costume was wrong, as Anton would have pointed out.

"How may I help you, Fräulein?" the clerk asked. "Cigarettes, perhaps?"

"I do not smoke," I said automatically.

"Filthy habit for a woman." He stroked his long mustache.

I suppressed a smile. It was an equally filthy habit for a man. "I am looking for a pipe for my father."

The shopkeeper lifted out a tray of expensive pipes and set them on the display case. The shelves behind him showcased brightly packaged cigarettes.

I angled my body so that I could see Haus Vaterland and, hopefully soon, Wilhelm. I picked up a smooth briar pipe. My father would not have liked it. He liked the feel of a meerschaum.

As if reading my mind, the salesman stroked his finger along the foam-white surface of a meerschaum pipe. "This one is popular with our older customers."

I pretended to study it. A horse was carved into it, and my father had liked horses. If he had been alive still, the meerschaum would have been his favorite. Clearly, the salesman knew his business.

I spotted Wilhelm's tall blond form half a block away and waited for him to draw closer.

"I must think on it a bit," I said. "But that horse pipe is lovely."

"You can't do better than that," the shopkeeper said. "Solid crafts-manship. It'll last a lifetime. If you have boys, perhaps one of them might use it later."

"Indeed." I intended to prevent Anton from smoking as long as I could. "Excuse me."

Wilhelm looked startled when I stepped out of the tobacco store into his path, but he swept me into a hug all the same. I had quite forgotten how tall he was. As tall as my brother had been. They had been a handsome couple.

"To what do I owe the pleasure?" he asked.

"Trouble," I said.

He slipped my hand into his arm. We strolled down the street as easily and companionably as if we had done it a thousand times. Women in fashionable clothes walked by us. Very few women wore makeup or trousers, as that was discouraged by the government. It was hard to believe that the Nazis were able to find time for fashion edicts. Yet, they did.

"How are Frieda and the baby?" I looked up at him. He was a man now, although still a young man in his mid-twenties, but I re-membered him as a teen, blue eyes uncertain and gawky limbs crash-ing into things, hoping that my brother would notice him and fall in love with him. And Ernst had, almost too late.

"Frieda is tiresome," he said. "By tonight she will be very jealous of you."

"The way you spoke to me on the telephone, I can hardly blame her."

"Stirring up a little jealousy in her for another woman will do her good," he said.

We passed the German luggage store. The shop window contained open red umbrellas with swastikas on them. I looked back at Wilhelm. "Your child?"

"It's a boy, as I hoped," he said. "I named him Ernst."

For my brother. My eyes teared. Wilhelm had loved my brother very much. "He would be proud of that, I think."

He barked out a laugh. "Proud of me married to a woman when I should have been with him? Not likely."

To that I had no ready answer. We strolled to the end of the block and turned to walk back. We stopped in front of the plate glass window of a fashionable dress shop. The dresses were boxy, utilitarian, and there were no trousers for women in the store at all. Nazi fashion, again. I studied Wilhelm's reflection in the mirror. He was grown up, to be sure, but still so young. I remembered how young I had once been, even when I thought myself grown, and all the boys I had nursed back to health after the men in charge had sent them to play and die at war. Would that be Wilhelm's fate, too?

"Tell me your troubles," he said. "Mine bore me."

"I need to know if there is anyone with a first name of Ivona who might be related to the men who died in the warehouse in 1936." Back then, he had checked their files for me, and mine and Lars's, to see if we were under investigation for those murders. He might be able to look at them again.

"I don't need to check for that," he said. "Which is just as well, since I can't."

"Why not?" I stopped, suddenly worried.

"My friend in Records has been reassigned." He pulled me closer to him to let group of young women enter the dress store. One of them eyed him appreciatively. He touched the brim of his uniform cap, and she giggled.

I made a *tsk*ing sound. "You are married to one woman, out with another, and making eyes at still a third."

We were well away from everyone else. "And for all that," he said, "I'm not interested in any."

I nodded ruefully. "You said you did not need to check for an Ivona. Why not?"

"I remember it. It's an unusual name. Dirk Hahn's daughter was named Ivona."

My heart raced. I was correct. Fräulein Ivona had targeted me because she thought I had killed her father. And I had.

I knew my enemy now. This was my first real lead. Now that I had named her, I would catch her. She would pay for what she had done, somehow. And Ruth would walk free. I hoped.

Wilhelm steered us down the sidewalk, but I no longer saw the bright shops. I was thinking about Ivona Hahn. How had she known to come after me? The letter. Herr Marceau had quoted it to me when I phoned in the orphanage story, but I had given it little thought after. What had he said? *He wrote her and said that he would meet with you that day.* Hahn must have written a letter, either to Fräulein Ivona or her mother, telling her of the meeting he was to have with me on the last day of his life. The meeting from which he had never returned.

Paul and Ruth had not earned her wrath, but I had.

"Before my friend left, I checked your files again, and Lang's. They noted you as residing in Switzerland and separated from your fiancé." He chuckled. "I rather thought it wouldn't last with Lang. Did it at least end well?"

I thought of Lars's activities over the past years and said nothing.

"According to the file, after he left you, he was arrested in Russia." Wilhelm walked faster than I, and I found myself taking extra steps to keep up. "He spent over a year in a Russian prison, before being traded to the SS for a Russian political prisoner."

I felt relieved that his story tallied with what Lars had told me and chastised myself for a lack of trust in Lars. "Oh."

"He was apparently quite badly tortured, and spent several months in an SS hospital near Munich." I sensed that even Wilhelm did not want to talk about Lars's experiences in prison.

"Did he?" So, it had taken him months to recover enough to make his mystery trip to Russia.

Wilhelm guided us around an old woman carrying a vase wrapped in brown paper before speaking again. "He left the SS and seemed to fall off the map. Are you still in touch?"

"I have no idea where he is now," I said. "But I am curious."

Accurate, if not entirely truthful.

"He had quite a time in Russia, did you know?" We stopped at a traffic light.

"I did not know." At least not until last night.

He hesitated. "Do you want to?"

"Not particularly." I longed to ask for details, but I could not snoop on Lars that way. I would have to wait until he was ready to tell me. If he ever was.

We crossed the street to circle the Kaiser Wilhelm Memorial Church, which sat like an island on the Kufürstendamm, across from Haus Vaterland. Wilhelm stopped to stare at the grand rose window. Last time I had stood here I had admired it myself, shortly before I entered the church, and Frau Röhm told me that Anton had been killed. A lie, but one powerful enough to almost destroy me.

Wilhelm pulled on his lip, as he had when he was thinking since he was just a boy. "I don't know, Hannah."

"About what?"

He leaned in close, and I wondered what Lars would think. "About it all."

He glanced around the square. I followed his gaze. No one close. Or at least no one who seemed to be watching. "Wilhelm?"

"I'm sick to death of the whole thing." He sounded sad, and a little angry.

He had a love of the dramatic, but this time the emotions felt true. I waited.

"You were correct. About the Nazis. I used to see just the strength and pageantry. Now—" He spread his strong fingers out as if casting a net and drawing it in. "Now I see behind it. I see the weakness. The meanness."

"You do?" He had always been a devout party member.

"When it was a revolution to sweep away corruption, to make Germany strong again, it made sense."

He felt nostalgia for the early days of Nazism. "Did it?"

"I know it never made sense to you. But it did to me. Now it doesn't."

I almost felt proud of him.

"I'm married to a woman I don't love to satisfy a party I don't believe in." He spoke more to the church than to me, as if confessing. "He'll know."

"Who?"

"Little Ernst." He seemed surprised that I could imagine him speaking of anyone else. "When he gets older. He'll know I don't love Frieda, and that she doesn't love me. That it's based on lies and rot. I can't bear the thought of him looking at me and knowing. I want to leave it behind and be authentic again. Divorce Frieda and start over."

We crossed the street and entered the park.

"What does Frieda think?" We walked among bare trees now, sometimes hidden from view. I wondered what Lars thought of that.

"I don't know what Frieda thinks. About anything. I sometimes think we've never exchanged a single honest word."

"What if you start?" I asked.

"If only it were so simple."

I had no answer for that. Nothing was simple anymore.

"Enough self-pity." He ran one hand through his thick blond hair. "Now, in case anyone is watching me, I'd like to establish a useful reason for this meeting."

He gave me what from a distance must have looked like a passionate kiss. I hated to think of Lars's reaction to that.

He moved his mouth away from mine. "The idea that I'm meeting an attractive blond piece over lunch is too good an opportunity to pass up."

"I am flattered," I said, rather breathless. "But I have always been far too old for you."

"Your most important quality is that you are a woman, and a mysterious one at that."

He positioned a tree between us and the street, and stayed close. I was concealed, but he was mostly visible. It must look like a quick tryst in the trees, barely discreet. I leaned back against the tree trunk, hoping my shoes would not get muddy. I imagined that Lars must be livid, but then again, he had slept with a raft of women since we parted, so he had no right to be jealous. On the other hand, I would have to explain it to Anton. We kept our heads close together.

"Do you have an address for Ivona Hahn?" I asked.

"I don't remember one. I think she lived with her mother."

"Can you get me her file?"

He moved closer. "As I said before, I don't have the access to the file room that I once did."

His tone told me that it would make no sense to argue. Besides, I suspected that Fräulein Ivona was too smart to take Ruth to her own home, in case Lars or I knew someone who could find it.

We talked about my brother and the old days. Eventually, he stepped back and adjusted his suit. I brushed off the back of my dress.

"Maybe next time we should rent a hotel room." He picked a piece of bark out of my hair.

"I am hopeful that there will not be a next time."

"Aren't you always?" He smiled. "If there is, we shall rent a room."

I had to smile back. "How extravagant!"

He kissed the top of my head. "I have to get back to work."

"Well, that was certainly quick."

He gave me a lazy smile. "I got what I needed, and so did you."

"I suppose that is the best one can expect of any rendezvous."

"Take care of yourself, Hannah."

We embraced. I held him for a long while, wondering if it would be the last time.

"Until we meet again." He gave me a mock salute.

As I watched his tall, strong form lope off, I wondered what would become of him. Germany marched toward war. Chamberlain would not keep handing Hitler territory forever, even if he had traded those bits of Czechoslovakia easily enough a little more than a month ago. The Sudetenland and Austria would not suffice for Germany's former corporal. Eventually someone would have to fight back. I hoped that Wilhelm would not be sacrificed on a battlefield for the Nazi cause, one he no longer believed in.

I walked slowly back to the street. Once I reached the sidewalk, I bent to fiddle with my shoe. Anton darted over.

Without Lars.

28

I stood and nodded to Anton.

Where was Lars? How jealous was he? Would it keep him from believing what I had uncovered about Fräulein Ivona?

"That was not what it looked like," I said to Anton.

"I understand." He fiddled with something in his pocket. "It's the most logical thing for a man and woman to do in the woods in the middle of the day."

Sometimes I forgot how much he must have learned in his years with his prostitute mother. "But we did not."

He laughed. "I know, but Lars doesn't. His head got very red. He looked as if he would explode. He said we are to meet him at the Wild West Bar. He will join us soon. He's going to follow Herr Lehmann first."

I imagined that he needed to calm himself, too, and was grateful for the reprieve. I was also impressed that he had thought to choose the Wild West Bar. Years ago, I had vowed to take Anton there if we ever returned to Berlin together. I suspected that this might be our only opportunity.

Rain drizzled down. I hurried across the square. We stopped at the traffic light. "That was the first traffic light installed in Europe," I said. "In 1924, a few years before you were born."

He studied it with interest. "How do you know?"

"I came to marvel at it," I said. "It was news."

"A stoplight?" He shook his head in disbelief.

"Technology marches on," I told him. "Someday your child will be amazed that you rode in something as old-fashioned as a zeppelin."

We crossed with the light and walked toward the curved front of Haus Vaterland. I had rarely come to this building of themed restaurants when I lived in Berlin. Since I left, it had practically become my home away from home. I had met Wilhelm at the Wild West Bar to exchange information in 1934 and Lars at the Türkische Café in 1936.

We paid our entrance fee, trotted up the ugly staircase, and marched through swinging saloon doors into the Wild West Bar. It had changed little since 1934. Anton gaped as a cowboy in a ten-gallon hat strode over. I smiled to see Anton happy.

"Howdy, ma'am," the cowboy said in English. He touched the brim of his felt hat with two fingers and a thumb. Anton was enchanted.

"A table for three," I said.

"Follow me." He stepped past a brass spittoon to a round table with poker chips and playing cards painted on it.

He pulled out my rough-hewn wooden chair, and I sat. Anton scooted his chair forward and studied his painted cards.

"I win," he said. "Full house. Three jacks and a pair of deuces."

"When did you learn to play poker?" I asked.

The cowboy handed me a menu full of American specialties and left.

"At riding school," Anton said. "Back of the stable."

"I am glad to hear that they are broadening your education."

"You don't sound glad." He counted his painted chips.

"You do not play for money, do you?"

He shook his head. "Not yet. No money."

"That is not so reassuring," I said.

The waiter returned. "Something to wet your whistle?"

Our waiter in 1934 had used just those terms.

Anton ordered a High Noon, lemonade with a shot of cola. It sounded terrible. I had a tea, straight up.

Lars slid in next to me and ordered a Schultheiss beer with no Western pretense.

The waiter sauntered off.

Lars picked up his menu without meeting my eyes. He barely glanced at the menu before dropping it on the table.

"Poker," Anton said, pointing to the cards.

Lars looked at his cards and moved to my other side.

"Why did you move?" Anton asked. "I already have the best hand."

Lars pointed to his first cards. "A pair of aces and a pair of eights. That's called the 'dead man's hand' because that's what Wild Bill Hickok was holding when he was shot."

"How do you know that?" Anton asked.

"I make it my business to know things." Lars gave me a meaning-ful look.

"Sometimes," I said. "Things slip through. Wilhelm said—"

The waiter returned and set down my thick mug of tea, Anton's tin one frothing over with a fizzy brown mixture, and Lars's familiar beer glass.

"Know what vittles you'll be needing?" The waiter hooked his thumbs in his braces and leaned back as if he had just jumped off his horse on the trail.

Lars and I each ordered a plate of beef stew. Anton asked for the pork and beans with sourdough biscuits.

I decided to ask Lars a few questions before revealing Fräulein Ivona's identity. I expected that to render him speechless, at least for a while. "Was Wilhelm followed?"

"Inexpertly. By his wife." Lars drank a long swallow of beer.

"He is married?" Anton asked.

"And he has a little boy," I told him. "Did anyone else follow him?"

"Not that I could see. I tailed him after you parted as well. His wife left when you started your performance in the woods."

I blushed and looked over his shoulder at a cactus. "That is all it was."

"What information did you extract from him?" Lars clipped off each word angrily.

"Ivona's last name is Hahn."

Lars rocked back in his chair. He looked as if he might be ill on the table.

I drank my strong tea and waited for him to collect himself. Anton stared at his painted poker chips.

The waiter clanked tin plates in front of us. The beef stew looked better than I had expected. I tasted it. Salty, but edible. I took a few bites, watching Lars.

Anton pretended to ignore both of us and swabbed his biscuit through the sauce on his pork and beans. I supposed that was standard manners in the Old West and said nothing.

"Lars?" I asked. Finally, he had outwaited me.

He pushed his plate away untouched. "I'm sorry, Spatz."

I pulled a handful of coins out of my pocket and handed them to Anton. "Please select a song on the player piano and stay next to it until the song ends."

Anton jumped to his feet, clearly eager to have a good excuse to get away from the argument he knew must be coming. He hurried across the room. Seconds later, a Western-style song plonked away.

"I should have checked further," Lars said. "I didn't, and that's landed us all here."

"Hopefully there will be time for self-recrimination later," I said. "Now we need to find Ruth. What do you know about Fräulein Ivona?"

"I knew her only three weeks," he said. "I did a quick check on her file and it seemed fine. We shared drinks, meals. I slept with her because she resembled you."

I winced.

"I'm sorry. I'm sorry. I'll say it a thousand times if you like."

"I do not like it." I spoke too loudly. I brought myself back under control. I had to stay calm. "Please, I want to focus on Ruth and only Ruth. Where would Fräulein Ivona take her?"

"I don't know," he said. "Hahn is dead. I don't know where her mother lived."

I kept my voice even. "Do you know where Hahn lived?"

"Yes." He tapped his spoon against his tin plate. "But his wife did not live with him. I went back to his apartment after I was released from the hospital, as part of my sanctioned but unofficial investigation into his death. His apartment had long been rented to someone else."

I stopped his spoon from tapping. "Did you find out much about his wife or daughter in your investigation?"

His lips thinned. "Obviously not. They were not suspects in his death."

Across the room, Anton fed another coin into the piano. He looked like he wanted to stay there all day. I wanted to join him.

"She said that her mother died recently. Do you know where?"

Lars looked at me in surprise. "Her mother is dead?"

"She told me her mother died a month ago." I thought back to her words in front of Doktor Volonoski's fireplace. "It is no more reliable than anything else she said, but the letters started then, too. It did not seem like a lie at the time, but—"

"Many things didn't seem like a lie at the time," he muttered angrily. "Can we get her file? That should have some facts in it."

His faith in the accuracy of Nazi record keeping was disconcerting. "Wilhelm cannot. What about your sources?"

He studied the untouched stew congealing in front of him. "Doubtful."

"We have to assume that she will kill Ruth." My voice wavered. "As she killed Paul."

"If she favors her father, she is sadistic enough to want us to suffer as long as possible before she kills us," he said. "So Ruth is probably safe."

I did not point out that she could already have killed Ruth while still continuing to torture us. I did not want it to be true. "You know her better than I."

"I don't think I know her at all," he said. "But I know that she's a fervent anti-Semite. She worshipped her father, and he was a devoted Party man." He ticked off the point on his thumb.

I waited for him to keep counting. He knew more than he thought. I hoped.

He raised a finger. "And she's a clever strategist. Assuming someone else's identity because she thought I might check. Writing you the letters to lure you here. Those are all thought-out maneuvers. Whatever she's doing, she's doing it carefully."

The song ended, but Anton quickly dropped in another coin. The waiter watched us with interest. "What else do you know about her?"

Lars took a deep breath. "She's a crack shot. We went hunting together a few times."

"I wonder why she did not shoot you?"

"Why did she start with me?" Lars asked. "Why not you?"

"You were easier to find. Hahn's colleagues might have told his daughter where you were. You are probably listed as one of the last people to speak to him, so it would not be unreasonable for her to use that as a pretext to want to speak to you. Or perhaps she thought that you might be easier to control."

He grimaced. "As I was. I led her straight to you. The minute you arrived in Poland."

She was no fool, and clearly determined to get us both.

"That makes it my fault," he said. "All of it."

"You could not have known."

"Couldn't I?" he said savagely. "It's my job to know."

I touched his shoulder, but he shook off my hand. The third song ended. Quiet expanded through the room. Anton was out of coins. He looked to see if he should come back. I gestured him over, and we finished our lunch.

The day passed in a frenzy of useless activity. We visited Hahn's old apartment. Lars talked his way in again, but found nothing. I called the newspaper every hour, but they had no more messages.

Evening came with no answers. The sun set, and darkness rolled in. Still we drove around Berlin. We had no idea how to find Fräulein Ivona and Ruth, but when we were moving, it at least felt like we were doing something.

At eight thirty that night, the radio announced that Ernst vom Rath had died of wounds inflicted by a vicious Jew. They called for two minutes of radio silence. Once it was over, they announced that the Führer had said that no official actions would be taken against the Jews, but that citizens could use their own judgment. Everyone knew what that meant. Lars pulled the lorry to the side of the road.

I brought my hands together under my nose and rocked back and forth. We had lost Ruth. Fräulein Ivona might already have killed her.

"The newspaper," Anton said. "Let's call them again."

I called them again. Lars hovered outside like a nervous parent. Anton stayed in the lorry.

"Thank god," Herr Marceau said as soon as he heard me.

"She called?" I dreaded hearing what she might have said.

"She said that 'the Jew bastard in Paris chose Ruth's fate but—' "

I gripped the phone tightly. "But what?"

"She says that she'll trade you for the girl."

Lars studied my face. I pressed the receiver tight against my ear, hoping that he could not hear. But I knew he already had.

"Where?" I said.

Lars shook his head. I turned so that I could not see him.

"I don't think you should go, Frau Zinsli." I heard the crackle of Herr Marceau shuffling papers, his nervous habit. "It's probably a trap."

Of course it was a trap. A trap that she had baited with something that she suspected I could not resist. I could not let Ruth die without trying to prevent it. "Where?"

He gave me the address of the warehouse where Hahn had died. She intended to kill me there. It was the perfect place to do it. Dark, deserted, and the right site for an act of revenge.

"Do you know where that is?" Herr Marceau asked.

"Yes." I still had nightmares about it. I had watched Hahn die there a hundred times in my sleep. In some dreams, I died there myself. To think I once thought that dreams do not come true.

"Call the police," he said. "Send them there."

I almost laughed. The police would not listen to an anonymous tip. "Thank you, Herr Marceau. Is there anything else?"

"Good god, isn't that enough?"

I swallowed. "More than enough."

I broke the connection and turned to Lars.

"You can't go," he said quickly. "She intends to kill you."

So, he had overheard the entire conversation. "If I stay away, she kills Ruth."

"If you go, she'll kill you both," he said. "I won't allow that."

"You do not allow or forbid me to do things, Lars." I knew he was frightened for me. I was frightened for me, too. But that did not change what I intended to do.

Anton got out of the lorry and jogged over.

"I cannot live with myself if something happens to Ruth because of me," I said. "You know that."

"She knows it, too." Lars jammed his hands into his pockets.

Anton took my hand. "What's going on?"

"You explain it to him." Lars stalked off. Perhaps a walk would calm him down.

"Anton," I began. "Fräulein Ivona called the newspaper and left a message."

I had to think of someplace safe to stash him. Herr Keller's, perhaps?

"What message? Is Ruth all right?" He could tell how serious things were.

"She said—"

Before I could finish the sentence, the lorry roared into life.

Lars drove off and left us alone in the dark.

I ran a few steps before realizing the futility of trying to catch him on foot. I stood in the street cursing him until I remembered Anton.

He stared at me with his jaw hanging open, too surprised to speak. He was getting quite an education this trip.

As soon as I calmed down enough to think, I called a taxi. While we waited, I explained to Anton that Lars had gone to get Ruth from Fräulein Ivona, and we were following.

"How do you know?" Anton asked. "What if he just left?"

That had not occurred to me. I shook my head. "I just do."

In my heart, I knew that Lars had realized the futility of arguing and taken matters into his own hands. If someone had to walk into a trap, he chose himself. I viewed his action with equal parts of love and fury.

Anything that was going to happen would have happened before we arrived. And I did not think I could bear it if another man I loved died for me.

The taxi driver did not want to take us to a warehouse so late at night, but agreed after I said that I would double his fare, which took every pfennig I had. When we arrived, the taxi dropped us off and disappeared with the squealing of tires.

I pushed Anton behind me, drew the Vis from my satchel, and approached the warehouse.

Lars stepped out of the shadows. "Don't bother."

I holstered the Vis. If he did not need a gun drawn, I probably did not need one either.

"God damn you!" I yanked Lars into a tight embrace. He was alive. That was the most important thing.

Lars gave me a quick smile. He pulled us both back toward the lorry, practically shoved us in, and drove off. Only when the warehouse was well behind us did he speak.

"She never showed up," he said. "She left you a note on the front of the warehouse door. I've checked around. I don't think she went inside."

He handed me a folded sheet of white paper written in the blocky printing of the letters I had received at the paper. I turned on the overhead light and held the paper where Anton could not see it. The watermark matched the other letters that Fräulein Ivona had sent.

My dear little Frau Zinsli,

You have been a wilier prey than I expected. I can see why Lars and my father were attracted to you. Both underestimated you, but I won't make their mistake.

I learned much about you, my dear, in the scant time we were together. I once thought to turn you in to the Gestapo so you could face the justice of the Reich.

But now I know that it will be worse for you to hear of the little girl's death. I can only imagine how the death of your friend must haunt you.

That was an accident. I intended to wait for you there, but he wanted to protect you, so . . . I panicked afterwards and took the girl, but it turns out that was my best decision of all.

She looks so very Aryan, doesn't she? Aryan enough to support a charge of blood libel. It has been a long time since the Jews have paid for their crimes. After tonight, we will rain down misfortune on all the Jews in Berlin.

Don't worry. I'm not yet done with you. Or that annoying son of yours. Or Lars.

Until later,

I

I dropped the letter back in Lars's lap, wanting it as far away from Anton as possible. I turned off the overhead light and took Anton's hand. If she could, Fräulein Ivona would make good on her threats. She would kill Ruth, and she would kill Anton.

I stared into the blackness rushing toward us on the other side of the windshield. We would never be safe from her. She intended to torture me by killing my loved ones, then me. How could I find Ruth? How could I protect Anton?

"Where are we going?" Anton asked.

"To Populov's warehouse," Lars said. "In a few hours, I'll have the compartment installed. We can get out of Germany and decide what to do somewhere safe."

"What about Ruth?" Streetlamps slid by outside, but beyond that, there was little to see. He drove so fast, I worried that a policeman would stop him.

"I am so sorry, Spatz, but there is nothing that we can do. We've spent the whole day thinking and searching. We don't know where Ivona is."

"She mentioned blood libel." I kept my voice even with an effort. I did not want Anton to know how frightened I was.

"What's blood libel?" Anton asked.

"Blood libel is an accusation that Jews kill Christian children to use their blood in their Passover bread," I said.

"Is it true?" he asked, aghast.

"No," I said, "but thousands of Jews have been murdered because of it. Which means the results are real, even if the accusation is not."

"What does it mean for Ruth?" Anton pulled his knees up to his chin.

It meant that Fräulein Ivona intended to kill her, probably drain her blood into a bowl, and leave the body somewhere where the Jews would be blamed. But where?

"Well?" Anton hugged his knees and looked at me.

"A synagogue," I said. There was little I could do to shield him from the truth now. "She intends to kill Ruth in a synagogue and leave her body there to be discovered."

"Assuming that were true." Lars looked behind us again, probably checking to see if we were being followed. "There are nineteen synagogues in Berlin."

"How do you know that?" I asked.

"I was in the SS." He took a quick left turn and I grabbed the dash to keep from plowing into him. "You did not think we counted?"

"Which synagogue would she pick?" I asked Lars. It was a slender hope, but it was the only one that we had.

"I've no idea," he said. "It never came up in conversation."

"Bronislawa Hahn died a month ago," I mused.

"I doubt that they had a service in a synagogue for her," Lars said.

"Of course not," I snapped. "She was Catholic."

"How do you know that?" he asked, surprised. "Did Ivona tell you that she was Catholic?"

"Did she ever say that she was Catholic?" I asked Anton.

He shook his head. "Not to me."

I thought back to our conversations. Lars kept driving. Fräulein Ivona had never mentioned her religion. Most Berliners were Protestant, so why did I think she was Catholic? I ran over the things she had told me about herself, her father, and her mother. The nuns. "She said that the nuns were very kind to her mother before she died."

"Nuns?" Anton asked.

"Only Catholics have nuns." I had an idea. "Take us to Saint Hedwig's Hospital."

"Why?" Lars asked.

"There are two Catholic hospitals in Berlin with nuns in attendance. Saint Hedwig's is next to the Neue Synagogue. The largest synagogue in Berlin."

Lars turned right so abruptly that Anton slammed into the door.

"Are you all right?" I asked.

He sat up. "I am not made of glass."

"She might not be there," Lars said.

But we both knew that it made sense. "It is a place to start. And it is all we have."

"Have you ever been inside?" Lars asked.

"Of course. It is a Berlin landmark. You have not?"

"I've never been in a synagogue. Why would I go?"

His SS past rankled. "Because it is beautiful."

"Yes, Spatz," he said. "I'm certain it is. Could you describe it for me? Especially the entrances and exits."

I closed my eyes. "The front door is on Oranienburgerstrasse. After you enter, you come into a large hall. There are stairs on both sides to the women's section upstairs. If you stay downstairs and head for the back, there are a couple of smaller halls before you get to the main one. Stools on either side with an aisle up the middle. At the back is the Ark. The Ark is on a kind of stage. With her flair for the dramatic, I think that is where she would . . . take Ruth."

"Windows?"

"Yes. Windows line both sides of the main hall. I think there is a side entrance on the left halfway down, and a rear entrance that opens onto the back, near the Ark and the room where weddings are performed."

"I'll go in through the back," Lars said. "It's closest to the Ark. I won't have to go through the whole open hall."

"Fine," I said. "I will follow."

"This is not something for a civilian," Lars said. "She is armed. She has a hostage."

I did not pretend to mull that over. Logically, he was correct, but I had no intention of waiting in the lorry and hoping for the best. I took the Vis out of the glove box and awkwardly checked that it was loaded with my left hand, wishing again that I had the use of my right arm.

29

We sped down Oranienburgerstrasse. Shouting men thronged the sidewalks. They had heard Hitler's veiled call to arms, too.

Lars drove past them and on to the synagogue.

"Right there!" I pointed.

He mashed on the brakes, and the lorry stopped so suddenly, it stalled. He started it again and drove more decorously past the opulent Moorish-style synagogue.

A crowd had gathered there. A group of men, some in uniforms and some in civilian clothing, milled on the sidewalk. Many carried torches. Mounted police had joined them. A gray and a chestnut horse shifted in the crowd. A fire truck passed us and parked. We drove past the crowd before parking behind another Opel Blitz lorry.

I craned my neck around to study the mob. "They are going to burn the synagogue."

"Why do they have a fire truck?" Anton asked.

I looked at the buildings built flush against the synagogue. It was horrible, and it made perfect sense, if one thought like a Nazi. "Those buildings are not Jewish-owned, I suspect. They will let the synagogue burn, but they will try to save the buildings around it."

"This complicates matters." Lars tapped his fingers against the steering wheel.

I reached over Anton and opened his door. We climbed out into the cold night. If Ruth was in the building, Fräulein Ivona would be found soon. We had to go in now.

No one in the mob noticed us. They probably thought that we had come to enjoy their spectacle of hate.

"Anton," I said. "Stay with the lorry."

He did not look any more pleased about this news than I had when Lars told me the same thing. "But—"

"You must cover my retreat," Lars said. "When we come out, we might not have much time."

Anton nodded, and I was again struck by how easily Lars convinced him to follow orders. I wondered what Lars had tricked me into against my better judgment, but came up with nothing. I had known what I was doing all the time, for better or for worse. Lars handed Anton a gun.

"If you see Ivona," Lars said. "Shoot her."

Anton's eyes grew round. He hefted the gun in his hands, looking young. I wished again that I had left him in Switzerland.

"No." I took the gun away from him. "Just run."

I had formulated a plan for him in the lorry. I gave him quick directions to the Swiss embassy. "Stay out front. If I am not there in two hours, go in and tell them that you are a Swiss citizen named Anton Zinsli. You sneaked across the border on a dare. Tell them to call Boris. He will get you out."

Lars looked impressed with my plan for Anton, but in truth it was sheer desperation. On top of everything else, I was not certain that Boris could get Anton out, even with his expensive lawyers. Boris himself was wanted by the Gestapo, but I knew he would do everything that he could. If things went that badly, he was the best hope that Anton had.

"I'll steal one of those horses." Anton gestured to the police mounts now tethered a short distance away, riders gone to join the mob. I gave him a worried look. He had stolen horses once before, on a dare.

"Don't do anything fancy," Lars said. "Just run."

I gave Lars's gun back to him and stuck the Vis in my pocket. It pulled my dress out of shape, but I had no belt to tuck it into. I glanced once more at the shouting men brandishing torches.

"Spatz," Lars said. "Stay here. Please."

I was not a lady out of the Middle Ages, ready to send a knight into battle for me. I would run the risks he did, or I could never live with myself after. We both knew that I had no intention of staying. Two of us might be more successful than one. Our lives, and Ruth's and Anton's, might depend on that success.

"Stay on my left, and let me go in first," he said finally.

That I would do.

I hugged Anton hard. "We will be back soon."

He sucked in his lower lip as he always did when he tried not to cry, and held out a hand for Lars to shake.

Lars shook his hand. "Mind the retreat, Anton. I truly need you here."

I hoped that would be enough to keep Anton in place.

Lars started toward the synagogue. As I had been told, I stayed on his left side.

The crowd clearly readied itself to storm the synagogue, but they were more organized than I had expected. They behaved more like a unit of soldiers than like a mob. A man in front exhorted them for patience. Even though he wore no uniform, I sensed that he was their commanding officer.

We circled the outside of the crowd, slipped around the block and to the back of the synagogue. Through the back window, a light flickered. The eternal flame. Soon, I predicted, it would be extinguished.

I gripped Lars's tense arm. "She does not expect us. With the noise of the crowd, we may slip in undetected."

He drew a stag-handle knife with a dull nickel blade out of his boot. It was short, about twenty centimeters from handle to tip; half of that was blade. "It's a trench knife. I've had it since the War." He handed it to me handle first. "I keep it sharp."

I weighed it in my palm. I had no boot to stuff it into. Instead, I carefully slipped it blade first into my cast at the wrist. He winced. It slid in easily, stopping before my elbow. Uncomfortable, but reassuring, rather like my relationship with Lars.

"If you have to," I said, "could you kill her?"

He hesitated. "I will do what I have to do to keep Ruth safe. Or you."

I did not believe him. He had some kind of feelings for her, whether he admitted it or not. And those feelings might be enough to make him pause. I knew the cost of killing a human in cold blood. I still woke screaming from nightmares where I killed Hahn, and I would never again forget the face of the Gestapo man lying in the gravel next to the car, but if it came down to it, I would do what had to be done. Killing Hahn had saved my life and the lives of who knew how many others. Killing Fräulein Ivona to save Ruth came with a cost that I would pay. But hopefully, it would not come to that.

A shadow crossed in front of the eternal flame. Someone was inside the synagogue. Fräulein Ivona?

We crept to the imposing back door. Not so dramatic as the front, it was still twice as tall as I. I tried the handle. Unlocked. Lars shouldered past me and opened it. The shouting of the crowd was quieter here, but still loud enough to mask our approach.

I slipped off my shoes and left them by the back door. The hard stone, cold under my feet, rendered my footsteps soundless.

Lars was ahead of me, moving sideways through the oval-shaped room, his boots quiet, too. I followed close behind until we stood in the back corner of the main hall. Arched ceilings soared above us. Light from the eternal flame cast a dull glow. It burned around the corner.

I turned left toward the light. Ruth lay on her back atop the Ark, a few meters away. She wore a simple white dress and shiny patent leather shoes. Her long blond hair hung across her face. I hoped that she was still alive. Next to her sat a ceramic bowl with a razor next to it. Next to that a Luger. There was no sign of Fräulein Ivona.

"Ruth?" I whispered. She turned her head toward me, eyes shin-

A CITY OF BROKEN GLASS 309

ing in the candlelight. She was alive. I sighed with relief. I beckoned for her to come to me. As quietly as I could, I crept closer.

Out of the corner of my eye I saw Lars motion for me to stop. I did.

Ruth sat up and looked behind her. Fräulein Ivona stood there with the Luger pointed straight at me. She had been kneeling behind the Ark. With the other hand, she scooped up Ruth and held her in front of her like a shield. She balanced Ruth in the crook of her elbow. In her hand glittered the razor.

"Hello!" Fräulein Ivona cried cheerfully. "This could not go better!"

I could not shoot her without harming Ruth. I was no marksman. But Lars was.

She pressed her elbow harder against Ruth's throat. "I can crush her trachea. I did it to a pig once."

A shot whistled past my head. Lars. He missed.

In almost the same instant, Fräulein Ivona swiveled the Luger toward him and shot. He thudded to the floor. *Please,* I begged silently, *don't let Lars die.*

Before I had time to react, the Luger was aimed at me again.

"Drop the Vis," she said. "We don't want the girl to be hurt early."

I complied, eyes never leaving Ruth. She stared at me with wide eyes, too frightened to speak. "Please, Fräulein Ivona. She is only a child."

"She is only a Jew." She tightened her grip on Ruth. The child gasped for air.

"She is just a little girl." I took one slow step toward them, then another. Unless Lars was seriously wounded, he would try again. But could he shoot her, in spite of his determined words earlier? I did not believe that he had missed by accident, even if he did not know it.

"Don't come any closer," she said. "I can crush her throat long before you reach me."

Ruth whimpered and twisted. Fräulein Ivona was correct. Ruth would be dead before I made it to her. I stopped.

"Be still," she said sharply. Ruth went limp. "I chloroformed her earlier. I'll do it again soon. She won't feel a thing. It will just be like going to sleep."

Tears trickled from Ruth's eyes, but she stayed very still.

"How about we work out a trade?" I said. "Let the girl go, and I will come up there unarmed and lie down on the Ark in her place."

Ruth gaped at me.

"I don't need you here," she said. "I need a child."

I swallowed. I had to save Ruth. Nothing else mattered.

"This isn't mere sport, like hunting." She shook Ruth. "When they find the child's body and the basin of blood next to her, it will start a pogrom like we haven't seen since the Middle Ages."

I feared that the world was poised to see that anyway.

Fräulein Ivona shook her head, hair still perfectly combed. "My father will see that I am strong. He will be proud of me. At last."

"Ivona," I said softly. "Your father is dead."

She glared at me. "By your hand. You'll be on this altar soon enough. My father was a great man, and his death won't go unavenged. Then he will forgive me for my weaknesses."

Two deaths on my conscience. "It was self-defense. There is nothing to avenge."

Fräulein Ivona tightened her grip on Ruth, and the little girl cried out. "It might have meant nothing to you, but not to me."

I calculated the distance between us again. I would not make it before she killed Ruth. "Fräulein Ivona, your father—"

Something smashed through the side window several meters away. Broken glass crashed to the floor. Ruth flinched. I smelled gasoline. I looked to see what had come through the window. A bottle, and stuffed in its neck was a flaming piece of fabric.

"It has begun." Fräulein Ivona smiled beatifically and reached for the razor. I tensed. If she moved that razor toward Ruth's throat, I would have to intervene, no matter the risk.

"The police know that Ruth is missing," I said desperately. "They have already started an investigation. They will identify her body and know that she is Jewish, not Aryan. Your plan is flawed."

A wooden chair ignited. Then another.

Fräulein Ivona laughed. "Such a clever tongue."

"It speaks the truth," I said. "Let her go. She and I will leave by the back door. No one need ever know that we were here."

Fräulein Ivona gestured around the room with the razor. "I think you put too much faith in the police. They won't investigate her disappearance. They don't care."

Fire crackled behind me. Fräulein Ivona looked past me at the flames, as transfixed as she had been in the doctor's office. This distraction was my only chance.

I charged her and grabbed the Luger. Its barrel was still hot from shooting Lars. With one twist, I yanked it out of her hands and threw it into the burning synagogue.

Fräulein Ivona rolled Ruth down toward the razor in her left hand.

I pushed my cast between Ruth's throat and the razor. With the other hand, I yanked Ruth out of Fräulein Ivona's grasp and dropped her to the floor. She ran into the smoke.

Before I could follow, the razor sliced through my cast and clanked against metal. The trench knife.

I ripped the knife out of my cast and slashed her upper arm, aiming for the brachial artery. The blow knocked her down to the side.

We grappled. She was younger and stronger than I, but the blood spurting out of her arm weakened her. As I had hoped, I had severed the artery.

"You will bleed out in under a minute," I told her. "Stop."

She lay still, probably because she had lost too much blood to struggle further. I thought of two nights ago when I had held Paul's blood in. I had saved him, only for her to kill him. I wanted to let go, but I pressed hard against her severed artery. I could still save her, as I had saved Paul.

Behind us, the wooden seats in the synagogue crackled with bright flames. Acrid smoke billowed toward us. I stifled a cough.

"Ruth?" I called. No answer.

"What now?" Fräulein Ivona asked.

"If I let go, you die," I said. "Stay still, and you might live."

She laughed. "I didn't think you had it in you to be a killer."

"I am no killer."

"But you are," she said. "You murdered my father."

My good hand began to go numb. "Self-defense."

Her lips curved into a pale smile. "Everyone's a killer."

Not far away, Ruth coughed weakly. I wished I knew how near the flames were, but I could not afford to look.

"He is hurt," Ruth's childish voice called. "Like my *Vati*."

She had watched her father die. Ruth would carry that memory for the rest of her life. I glanced back into the smoke, searching for Ruth.

The second I was distracted, Fräulein Ivona twisted out of my grip.

Blood pumped out of her shoulder, drenching her white shirt. I struggled to put pressure on her wound, but it was too late. She went limp under me.

I coughed. My eyes teared in the smoke.

"Ruth?" I called. "Lars? Where are you?"

"Here!" piped up Ruth.

I followed the sound of her voice. She stood next to a crumpled form. Lars.

I pulled Lars's coat back. Blood stained his chest. I grabbed the cloth covering the Ark with my casted hand. The ceramic bowl fell to the ground and shattered. Ruth yelped, but she kept hold of Lars's hand. I felt the edge of the cloth, sturdy and hemmed. It would not tear so easily as Paul's worn pillowcase had.

I held it in one hand and turned my attention to Lars. Flickering light from the eternal flame revealed a bullet hole below his left clavicle. Blood frothed out. I heard a sucking sound when he breathed. The bullet had punctured his lung.

His dark eyes watched me from a face gone pale as ashes. I kept my face impassive so he would not know how frightened I was. I slid one hand under his armpit and around to his back. No exit wound.

I reached behind me for the trench knife and used it to cut the edge of the cloth, then tore off a strip.

"Good girl, Ruth." While I talked, I made a quick bandage for Lars. "In just a minute, we can go and visit your *Opa*. Can you wait one more minute?"

She stuck the corner of her green blanket in her mouth and nodded. I folded the bandage quickly. Fräulein Ivona's slice through my cast had made it easier to move, if more painful.

"Ivona?" Lars coughed and blood stained his lips.

I glanced back to where she lay unmoving on the floor. Her chest no longer rose and fell.

"Departed." I hated to say *dead* in front of Ruth. She had already seen too much death in her short life.

Lars knew what I meant.

"Not your fault." I lay the bandage on his chest. "Mine."

"Sorry."

"Me, too." She was correct. I was a killer. She and her father had set up the circumstances, but I had killed. Three times. "Now, hush."

He nodded.

"Breathe out and hold your breath."

He complied. As soon as the air was out of the lung, I tied the bandage tight across his chest.

"Breathe," I whispered.

He did. The wound sounded mostly closed, for now. I kept both hands pressed against it. Smoke filled the synagogue. I could see barely a meter in front of me. If I did not get him to a doctor soon, he would die. Even if I did, he might die anyway.

Lars put his hands on top of mine and pressed on the bandage. He jerked his head toward Ruth. I took my hands away, and he kept applying pressure.

"Ruth?" I asked. "Are you hurt?"

She shook her head. I patted her all over quickly, just to be sure.

Blood streaked her once white dress, but it was Lars's. Physically, she was unharmed. That at least.

How could I get them out of the synagogue before it burned down? Flames filled the main hall. Something else crashed through the window. Glass rained onto the floor.

"Take Ruth," Lars coughed.

He knew how futile it would be to try to save him, too. But how could I leave him? I cradled her against my chest and stood. If I left him, he would die. If I did not, we might all die.

30

I set Ruth on her feet. I saw the reflection of the flames behind us in her eyes.

"Ruth?" I said. "Hold on to my dress and don't let go. Can you do that?"

She gripped a fistful of my skirt.

I bent my legs, draped Lars's arm over my shoulder, and hoisted him to his feet. I knew that if he'd had any breath, he would have argued. But he did not.

We stumbled to the back door of the synagogue. Ruth doggedly kept hold. The heat of the flames beat against my back. Smoke boiled around us.

Ruth coughed. She wiped her eyes with her green blanket. But she did not let go.

A few more steps and we reached the door.

"Ruth," I said. "Please push on it for me."

She opened the door. I dragged Lars through.

I gulped deep breaths of the fresh air. The grass felt cool on my bare feet.

Lars sagged against me. I had no time to catch my breath. I hauled him one step, then another. Anton waited with the lorry. All we had to do was get there.

My legs threatened to give out. Ruth hung on my dress, adding her little weight to Lars's. Just a few more steps.

I stopped and raised my head to look for the lorry. It was where we had left it. "Anton?" I called softly.

He did not answer.

I hauled Lars closer.

Smoke curled out of the cab of the lorry.

It was on fire.

I lowered Lars to the ground. Ruth clung to me like a monkey. I hefted her onto my hip and ran to the lorry.

A broken bottle rested on the floorboards. Flames licked the bottom of the dash. I smelled gasoline. Where was Anton?

The mob rushed the burning synagogue. No one paid us any heed.

"Anton!" I screamed.

"Here!" he called.

Shadows approached, too big to be Anton. "Where?"

"Mother?" Anton led a chestnut horse out of the darkness. Next to it was the dapple gray. He had stolen the police horses, just as he said he would. I wanted to kiss him. "When the lorry caught fire, I knew we would need something else."

"Good." For this, I would not lecture him later.

"Where's Lars?"

"Wounded." I handed him Ruth. "This is Ruth."

He held her on one hip. "Hello, Ruth," he said softly. "Do you like horses?"

She nodded.

I took the leather reins and led the gray to Lars. Well trained, the animal flared its nostrils at the smell of blood, but did not bolt.

When I hefted Lars upright, he groaned. Anton hurried to help. Together we hoisted Lars on my mount. Anton held him on the horse while I swung up behind. Lars slumped in front of me, but he had enough strength to keep his seat, at least for a while. He seemed to breathe better sitting up. Anton got Ruth on the other horse on his own.

Even though barely conscious, Lars settled into the rhythm of the horse. I hoped that the riding of his childhood might save his life now. We galloped through the grounds of Saint Hedwig's Hospital like something out of a Karl May book.

"No," Lars said weakly. "Questions."

He was correct. I could not ride up to the hospital on stolen police mounts with a gunshot victim and a child in a bloody dress. We would all be arrested. I turned my horse's head toward the Jewish quarter. I knew only one doctor who would help without asking questions.

Behind us, the synagogue blazed, but the fire truck already strove to put it out. I hoped that they would save it.

We galloped down cobblestone streets, turning heads. Anton rode close to my right flank, holding Ruth's waist with one hand and the reins with the other. As always, he was most agile and at ease on a horse.

"Frau Doktor Spiegel's!" I yelled above the wind. He nodded. He rode confidently, as if we were out for a quick canter in the woods.

Lars, on the other hand, barely managed to stay in the saddle. I dropped the reins from my left hand and held him against me, hoping I could stay balanced.

Anton watched the reins fall and moved his horse ahead of mine. Smart boy. Instead of swerving off, my horse followed his lead. I trusted that Anton could control both horses.

I wrapped both arms around Lars and threaded my fingers through the gray's mane. I felt Lars fighting to keep his balance, but I also felt his strength ebbing. We were close, but I did not know if we would make it.

We rode past crowds ranged on the edges of the Jewish quarter. They carried lit torches and baskets of rocks. Stones flew through shop windows. Looters were already inside others, throwing items into the street. The horses' hooves crunched in the broken glass.

I gripped the gray more tightly with my knees.

We galloped to Frau Doktor Spiegel's street, a few blocks from the edge of the Jewish quarter. The mob had not ventured so far in yet. A hurricane lamp burned in her front window, but otherwise the apartment looked deserted. Streets stretched dark as far as I could see. Someone must have cut the power to the entire Jewish quarter. Telephones, too, I imagined. But we had nowhere else to go.

Anton jumped off his horse before it stopped moving, and helped Ruth down. He grabbed my reins and steadied the gray with one hand and soft words. A wobbly Ruth clung to his shirt.

Frau Doktor Spiegel's door opened. "Fräulein Vogel?"

"I cannot get him down on my own."

They steadied Lars while I slid off. Together, she and I carried him toward the apartment.

"The horses," I called to Anton. "Send them off."

He slapped their rumps, and hooves rang against the street as they trotted away, probably heading home to their nice quiet stables. I envied them.

Anton took Ruth's hand and led her inside.

"The kitchen," Frau Doktor Spiegel said.

We got Lars up on the table. I stripped off his coat and stained shirt. Blood soaked my makeshift bandages. "He has a gunshot wound to the lung. The bullet is still in there."

"Get me a torch!" she ordered. "By the sink."

Anton found the electric torch and clicked it on. When he shone the beam on Lars, I feared that he was already dead. My heart stopped. After all this time, I had come to view him as indestructible. That, no matter what, he would endure. But he was just a man.

Outside, the mob grew louder. They were only a few streets away.

"He's not dead yet, Fräulein Vogel!" Frau Doktor Spiegel snapped. "Can you assist me here, or should I haul him back out to die in the street?"

I fumbled with his bandages. "I have never had problems assisting."

"You've also never looked at one of your patients the way you just looked at him, not even Paul."

Lars's lips moved into a faint smile. He was still conscious.

"Once he is well, he will be insufferable." I kissed his blue lips, hoping my words would be true.

She pulled a vial with three white pills out of her brassiere. I worked on preparing Lars for surgery. "What is that?"

"It's my opium," she said. "I keep it there. In case of emergency."

She studied it, face ghostly in the glow of the electric torch.

"What emergency?" Anton asked.

The same emergency that Paul faced. She kept that opium so that when things became unbearable, she could commit suicide. "Frau Doktor?"

She removed a pill and stuck it in Lars's mouth. "I suppose this is an emergency as well."

His chest was fully exposed. She doused her instruments with carbolic acid, and we began work. Anton sat on the floor, holding Ruth. He told her a story of Winnetou and his sister Nscho-tschi in the Wild West. I had never been more proud of him.

I held the light with one hand and assisted with the other while she took out the bullet and stitched Lars up. Side by side, we both worked as quickly as we had under fire in the war. It was the same. If the mob outside found her practicing medicine on an Aryan, they might well kill us all.

But she finished before they arrived.

We moved Lars into the bedroom. I stayed with him while Frau Doktor Spiegel and Anton cleaned the kitchen. No one could see the bloody instruments and cloths, or they would know that she had broken the law to save his life.

Ruth sat on the floor next to me with both arms wrapped around my legs. I stroked her back with one hand, and held Lars's hand with the other. He was a fighter. He was still alive. He would not die now. But as I knew from many battlefield surgeries, he very well might later.

Frau Doktor Spiegel appeared in the doorway. "Clean yourself up, Hannah. I can't have you covered in blood when they get here. They're close."

She handed me a wet towel and a clean dress. I changed and wiped myself as clean as I could, then dropped the bloody items into a bag she held.

"Take this to the back courtyard. Dump it with the rest." She handed Anton the bag. He ran.

I sat next to Lars and adjusted the blankets, pulling them to his chin.

"I want to transfuse him," she said. "He's lost too much blood. Now that I don't need you standing . . ."

"Of course." My blood type was O. Because I was a universal donor, I had spent the last year of the War perpetually anemic from emergency blood donations.

"I'll fetch my—"

Something crashed through the front window. Ruth yelped. Anton rushed into the room.

"There is brandy in the front room," I said. "Bring it now."

He was back quickly, bottle in hand.

The front door splintered open. Did they have an ax? Frau Doktor Spiegel went toward the sound.

I sprinkled brandy on Lars, then hid the bottle under the bed.

In the living room, something hard smashed against the walls. Glass broke and crashed to the floor with each stroke.

"Get behind me," I told Anton. "And hold Ruth."

He scooped her up in his arms and stood near Lars's head. I stepped in front of them, although I could do little against an organized mob.

I pulled my Hannah Schmidt passport out of my satchel and took Lars's from his back pocket. It seemed dry. I wished I could check to see if it had bloodstains.

Two men in SA uniforms stormed into the room. Both were tall. I could only hope I would be able to convince them to let us go. They glared at me.

"What are you doing?" I trembled with fear, but they expected that. It would have been suspicious otherwise.

"We're teaching you filthy Jews a lesson." One spit on the floor.

"I am not Jewish," I said. "I am not even German. I am Swiss."

They both stopped. During the Games in 1936, the storm troopers had been issued orders not to harm foreigners. I could only hope that they had similar orders now. In the front room, a different soldier yelled at Frau Doktor Spiegel. Glass crashed to the floor.

I walked over and handed my passport to the soldier who had not spit on the floor. He turned on a torch and examined it, studying the last stamp, the false one from Zbąszyń. He pointed his light at my eyes. I squinted.

"I am sorry, Frau Schmidt," he said. "This is not a safe place to be tonight."

I silently thanked Herr Silbert.

The soldier shone his light on Lars and the children. Something thudded against the floor in the front room.

"Those are my children, and that is my husband." I hoped that Ruth would stay quiet.

"Does he have identification? If not, we must arrest him. All Jewish men between the ages of sixteen and sixty are being arrested tonight."

"He is Swiss." I handed him Lars's passport. My hands shook. He would not survive the trip to a concentration camp.

"How old is the boy?" The soldier jerked his thumb toward Anton.

"Thirteen." I grabbed Anton with one hand. He was tall for his age, and I had no identity papers for him at all. His Anton Zinsli passport was back in the hotel in Zbąszyń.

What if the soldier demanded proof? I would not let Anton go without a fight, even if I knew it was futile. I could not win a battle against the two soldiers, but it might buy Anton enough time to run out the back door. If he would go.

The soldier directed the torch at Anton's face. I held my breath. I loosened my grip on Anton's arm and steadied myself.

I turned my back to the soldier and mouthed, *Swiss embassy,* to Anton.

He understood what I said, but looked mulish. *Oh please,* I begged silently. *Just this once, son, do what I say. I would hate to throw my life away for nothing at all.*

The soldier gave a brief nod. "Tall one," he said, "but you're not sixteen."

Anton was spared.

The soldier studied Lars's false passport. My heart beat hard in my throat. Like everyone in the Jewish quarter tonight, I had no recourse but hope. Actually, I had more. I had hope and forged Swiss passports. Would that be enough?

Behind me, I heard Anton and Ruth's quick breathing, and Lars's slow breaths. I was grateful that Lars, at least, would sleep through whatever came next.

The sound of tearing fabric came from the front room. Were they ripping up the drapes?

The soldier passed the beam of the torch across Lars's pale face. "Why is he in bed?"

"I—" I dropped my gaze to the worn Persian rug. "He— overindulged and passed out."

The soldier took a step toward the bed and sniffed. The smell of brandy was strong there, as I had hoped it would be.

"My advice, miss," he said calmly, "is to get him and the children out of here as soon as you can."

"Yes, sir," I said. "When will it be safe to travel?"

"I think we will be at this all night," he said.

"I see."

"Stay near the bed," he said. "I'll let that alone, as a favor to the Swiss."

I stood between the children and the soldiers, my arms centimeters out from my sides, as if that could protect them.

He flicked his truncheon casually at the wall toward Frau Doktor Spiegel's wedding picture. So much younger than now, she stood proudly next to her husband, surrounded by family and friends. In the back right corner, Paul smiled out from a different time. The truncheon shattered the glass. The soldier flipped the picture out of its frame, tore it in half, and dropped it on the floor.

He swiped a pair of reading glasses off the dresser and ground them under his heel. Ruth whimpered. I covered her eyes, hoping to keep her from seeing as much as I could. Anton watched every movement. And I could do nothing about that. I drew him close to my other side.

The soldier dumped each drawer. I was grateful that Frau Doktor Spiegel was not here to see him stomp on her underthings, although by the crashing coming from the kitchen, things were no better there. He opened the closet door and began methodically removing everything, breaking what he could.

The thorough way he destroyed her possessions was more terrifying than mob violence would have been. He did it efficiently, like a familiar job. He had orders.

He spotted the electric torch in Anton's hand. Anton offered it up to him, but he shook his head. "I'll assume that it's Swiss."

Ruth stared at him, as nonplussed as the rest of us.

"My apologies for disturbing you, Frau Schmidt," he said.

I gaped. I had no response for his polite address in the midst of his destruction.

He touched his cap, turned on his heel and left, taking his companion with him. I let out a long breath. I left the children on the bed with Lars and went to check on Frau Doktor Spiegel.

The noise had not prepared me for the extent of the damage. Every picture had been removed from the wall and had its glass smashed. Her books had been ripped from the shelves. Torn pages littered the floor.

They had even sliced open the upholstery on her sofa and slashed the rug on the floor. My bare feet stepped carefully around the glass. I thought of my own shoes, lined up by the synagogue door.

In the kitchen, her precious Vaseline glass collection lay in shards. I shone the torch around. They had even broken the jars of jam and honey.

Through her broken front door, I watched them move on to the next house, remembering the soldier's words. They would be at this all night.

She knelt on the floor, one fist pressed tight against her heart.

"Frau Doktor?" I hurried to stand next to her.

She stood. She held a long black tube with large needle at one end, a smaller at the other. "They broke my transfusion glass, of course, but we can do a direct one. I'm old enough to remember how."

She gestured at the wrecked apartment. "This will wait, but I think my patient will not."

I followed her into the bedroom, awed by her matter-of-fact courage. She had watched everything she owned destroyed in front of her. If Lars's wounds had been discovered, she might have been executed on the spot, and still she kept moving.

I lay on the bed next to Lars. Anton held the torch while she stuck the large needle into my arm, the small one into Lars's. Ruth covered her eyes.

"Hold the light on my watch." Frau Doktor Spiegel took my pulse, trying to calculate how much of my blood had flowed into Lars. Without a glass to measure, it was the best that we could do.

Eventually, she pulled out both needles and taped a strip of gauze over my arm, then his. His color looked better. I took his pulse as soon as I could move my arm. Weak but steady.

"Yes," she said, reading my expression. "It looks promising for him."

"Now I need to get him out of Germany." The burnt-out lorry was back at the synagogue, and useless to us regardless. Yet none of us could stay here for long.

"Fräulein Ivona drove Lars's old lorry to the synagogue," Anton piped up. "I saw it by ours."

I remembered the Opel Blitz that was parked in front of us.

"Are you certain it is the same one?" I asked. That lorry had a finished compartment, because she had stolen it from Lars. Anton had ridden in it when he crossed the Polish border.

"Yes," he said. "It had an extra gas tank, the fake one. And it had a dent in the tailgate."

"Wait here," I said.

Over Frau Doktor Spiegel's protestations, I left them all in the apartment to fetch the lorry, borrowing Anton's shoes for the trip.

Light-headed from the blood donation, I stumbled down glittering streets.

All of Berlin seemed to be covered in broken glass. In every direction, columns of smoke marked where synagogues burned.

Weeping old men, women, and children lined the street. Lorries rolled by filled with Jewish men. Many bore the marks of SS fists. The men's next stop would be the concentration camps. Paul, at least, had been spared that.

I quickened my step, swerving around the remains of a grand piano. Boys just a few years older than Anton stood next to it, hacking at the ebony wood with hatchets. I looked up. Someone had pushed the piano out of a third-story window. The cloth that once covered it had caught on a shard of glass and fluttered like a flag of surrender.

Unnoticed in the confusion, I reached the synagogue without incident. The fire department had put out the blaze, and a policeman stood guard in front of the building, stopping further vandalism. Destruction raged around him, but he stood firm. He caught my eye and I bowed my head in thanks. Whoever he was, he had risked much to keep this one building safe.

I clomped to Lars's old lorry. I opened the driver's door and felt in my pocket.

I did not have a key.

I would have to sneak into the synagogue and see if I could find Fräulein Ivona's purse. I glanced back at the policeman, wondering how I could get past him.

I reached inside and felt the ignition, just in case Fräulein Ivona had left them there for a quick getaway. My fingers touched the key. I blew out my breath in relief.

I started the lorry, returned to Frau Doktor Spiegel's, and loaded everyone inside. Lars and Frau Doktor Spiegel rested in the back on a mattress; the children huddled together on the front seat. Lars was still completely unconscious. She had given him enough opium to knock out a horse.

We drove out of the Jewish quarter into well-ordered neighborhoods where nothing had been disturbed. Moonlight reflected off intact windowpanes. The night was quiet here, everyone sleeping, everyone safe. None of them knew what horrible crimes were being committed just a few miles from their soft pillows.

The Kellers owned their own house. I parked in front. "Say good-bye to Ruth, Anton."

He gave her a quick good-bye, and she ducked her head shyly.

"I will be back soon, Anton," I said. "After that it is straight on to Switzerland."

"I've heard that before." He chucked Ruth under the chin.

"This time," I said. "It is finally true."

I lifted her out of the front seat and paused near the bed of the lorry. "Is everything in order, Frau Doktor Spiegel?"

She chuckled. "In this neighborhood, it certainly is."

"Is Lars—?"

"He is as well as can be expected. As am I." She held up her wrist-watch. "Stopped. The men must have broken it. I didn't even notice. Remember how I said I would not stay a extra second?"

I nodded.

She shook her wrist. "My second's up. Stopped with the watch."

"After we get across—"

"Palestine," she said. "Even if I have to ride there in the back of another lorry. I expect they need doctors there, too."

Ruth rested her head against my shoulder.

"Get that little one into bed," Frau Doktor Spiegel said. "It's very late. We all need a rest."

"*Jawohl*, Frau Doktor."

She gave me a tired smile.

Relieved that she had a plan that did not involve the rest of the opium, I hurried up the walk with Ruth on my hip. She looked around excitedly, clearly recognizing the yard.

I rapped on Herr Keller's door until footsteps stomped down the hall. He flung open the door. "What is it that cannot wait until a decent hour?"

"Opa!" Ruth wriggled out of my arms and ran to him. He swept her into a hug and turned to me, disbelieving.

"Take good care of her," I said.

Tears spilled down his cheeks. "You are an angel."

"Leave Germany as soon as you can," I said. "Promise?"

"I promise," he said. "Of course, I promise."

I lifted Miriam's locket's delicate chain over my head. "Ruth?"

She stared at me, arms still locked tight around Herr Keller's neck. "Yes?"

I draped the chain over her head. She gripped the locket with tiny fingers.

"It is from your mother," I said. "She wanted me to give it to you."

I kissed her once on the top of her head. She smelled like smoke, blood, and horses. The smells of war.

"Good-bye," she said.

I turned and hurried back to the lorry.

The drive ahead promised to be long.

Alexanderplatz. Central police station for Berlin through World War II. Also called "the Alex."

Bella Fromm. A German Jewish aristocrat who worked as a reporter in Berlin in the 1920s and 1930s. Her fascinating diaries have been published as *Blood and Banquets: A Berlin Social Diary*.

Bernhard Lichtenberg. Rector of Saint Hedwig's Church who spoke out against the treatment of the Jews during the Nazi regime. He was arrested for "abuse of the pulpit and insidious activity" for praying for the Jews. He died while waiting to be sent to Dachau concentration camp.

Blood libel. A false accusation that Jews use the blood of Christian children in religious rituals. There have been more than 150 recorded cases of blood libel accusations, which have resulted in the deaths of thousands of Jews. These accusations continue today.

Ernst Röhm. Early member of the National Socialist party and close friend to Adolf Hitler, often credited with being the man most responsible for bringing Hitler to power. Openly gay.

Ernst vom Rath. German diplomat in Paris shot on November 7, 1938, by Herschel Grynszpan. Grynszpan was protesting the deportation of his parents and sister to Zbąszyń. Vom Rath died on November 9, 1938. News of his death led to Kristallnacht.

Évian Conference. Conference held in July 1938 to determine how to respond to the burgeoning number of Jewish refugees from Germany and Austria. Although much sympathy was expressed, most countries refused to accept more refugees.

Gestapo. Abbreviation for Geheime Staatspolizei (Secret State Police). The official secret Nazi police force. It was formed in 1933, and investigated treason, espionage, and criminal attacks on the Nazi party and Germany. In July 1936, the Gestapo and the regular police force were merged. The Gestapo had various departments, including one dedicated to "the Jewish question."

Hauptsturmführer. Rank in the German Schutzstaffel (SS) equivalent to captain.

Herschel Grynszpan. Polish refugee in Paris, France, who, at age seventeen, shot German diplomat Ernst vom Rath to protest the deportation of his family from Germany and their treatment in Zbąszyń. He was held until the Nazis occupied Paris; then he was transferred to Germany. He allegedly died sometime in 1945, although the manner and date of his death are unknown.

"Horst Wessel Song." Anthem of the Nazi party. The lyrics were written by Horst Wessel, a Sturmabteilung (SA) commander in Berlin. He was killed by Communists in 1930, and the song later became the official anthem. Since the end of World War II, the music and lyrics have been illegal in Germany and Austria.

Hotel Adlon. Expensive hotel in Berlin, built in 1907. It quickly became known for its vast wine cellars and well-heeled clientele. On May 2, 1945, the main building was burned to the ground, either accidentally or deliberately, by Russian soldiers. The East German government opened a surviving wing as a hotel, but demolished it in 1961 to create the no-man's-land around the Berlin Wall. A new Hotel Adlon was rebuilt on the original location and opened on August 23, 1997.

Kommissar. Rank in the police department similar to a lieutenant.

Korn schnapps. Strong German alcoholic drink.

Kristallnacht. "Night of Crystal" or "Night of Broken Glass" refers to a series of state-sanctioned attacks on Jews in Germany and Austria on November 9, 1938, and November 10, 1938. According to the Holocaust Museum, 267 synagogues were destroyed, 7,500 Jewish businesses were destroyed, and at least 91 Jewish people were killed. An increased number of rapes and suicides were also recorded. Many view these actions as the beginning of the Holocaust.

League of German Girls (*Bund Deutscher Mädel*). The female branch of the Nazi youth movement. The male branch was called the Hitler Youth (*Hitler-Jugend*).

Mischling. A term created in the Nuremberg Laws to define which German citizens would be considered Jewish. If a Jewish person was not practicing Judaism and was not married to another Jewish citizen, he or she would be considered Jewish if they had at least three Jewish grandparents. A person with two Jewish grandparents (like Ruth in this novel) was considered Mischling of the first degree. A single Jewish grandparent made one Mischling of the second degree. These legal distinctions could, and often did, mean the difference between living through the war and being deported to a concentration camp.

National Socialist German Workers' Party (Nazi Party). Party led by Adolf Hitler that assumed control of Germany in 1933.

Nuremberg Laws. Anti-Semitic laws announced at the Nazi Party Rally in Nuremberg in 1935. These laws defined who was considered a Jew (someone with three or four Jewish grandparents). The laws then prohibited Jews from marrying or having sexual relations with "Germans of non-Jewish blood," forbade Jews to hire German domestic workers under the age of forty-five, forbade them to display the German or Reich flag or the national colors, and stripped German Jews of their citizenship. More anti-Semitic laws soon followed.

Obersturmbannführer. Rank in the SS equivalent to lieutenant colonel.

Paragraph 175. Paragraph of the German penal code that made homosexuality a crime. Paragraph 175 was in place from 1871 to 1994. Under the Nazis, people convicted of Paragraph 175 offenses, which did not need to include physical contact, were sent to concentration camps, where many died.

Pfennigs. Similar to pennies. There were one hundred pfennigs in a Reichsmark.

Reichsmark. Currency used by Germany from 1924 to 1948. The previous currency, the Papiermark, became worthless in 1923 due to hyperinflation. On January 1, 1923, one American dollar was worth nine thousand Papiermarks. By November 1923, one American dollar was worth 4.2 trillion Papiermarks. Fortunes were wiped out overnight. In 1924, the currency was revalued and remained fairly stable until the Wall Street crash in the United States in 1929. When the novel takes place, one American dollar was worth approximately 2.49 Reichsmarks.

Schutzstaffel (SS or Blackshirts). Nazi paramilitary organization founded as an elite force to be used as Hitler's personal bodyguards. Led by Heinrich Himmler.

Spatz. Sparrow. A German term of endearment.

Sturmabteilung (SA, Brownshirts, or storm troopers). Nazi paramilitary organization that helped intimidate Hitler's opponents. Led by Ernst Röhm.

Sturmbannführer. Rank in the SS equivalent to major.

Treaty of Versailles. A peace treaty that negotiated the end of World War I between Germany and the Allied powers.

UFA (Universum Film AG). Principal film studio in Germany during the Weimar Republic and World War II. UFA went out of business after World War II, but now produces movies and TV shows.

Winnetou. The Apache brave hero in a series of bestselling books written by German author Karl May. Originally published in the late 1800s, the novels are still very popular today.

Zbąszyń, Poland. Town on the border with Nazi Germany where Polish Jewish refugees were deported between October 27 and October 28, 1938. As in the novel, refugees were housed in stables, the flour mill, and other locations.

Author's Note

My books are often inspired by major historical events, so I feel an obligation to get the history right or to explain why I deviated from it. *A City of Broken Glass* sprang from the real-life events of the deportation of the Polish Jews from Germany and the ensuing Kristallnacht Pogrom of 1938. I stayed true to historical events whenever possible, but sometimes the emotional truth of the story required small changes.

The deportations of the Polish Jews from Germany to Zbąszyń, Poland, took place on October 27–28, 1938. To meet the refugees the morning after they arrived, Hannah would have had to have been there on October 29, 1938. Because I wanted her to bear witness to both the immediate aftereffects of the deportation and Kristallnacht on November 9–10, I changed the historical timeline in the story. I carefully avoided giving specific dates in the novel until she wakes up on the fifth of November so that my readers would not put wrong dates to the earlier events.

Just as Hannah reports, the refugees in Zbąszyń were housed in stables and a flour mill, among other places. The stories she hears of people walking back and forth across the border in the rain while being beaten and shot at are taken from actual survivor accounts.

I don't know how the Polish government numbered the refugees, or even if they did, but I wrote a prisoner number on Miriam's arm as a foreshadowing of what would come when such numbers would be tattooed into the arms of prisoners in concentration camps.

The Neuen Synagogue on Oranienburgerstrasse was not destroyed on Kristallnacht but, as Hannah witnesses, it was set afire and desecrated. A German police lieutenant named Wilhelm Krützfeld intervened after the synagogue was set alight, drawing his pistol and placing himself between the mob and the building. He also ordered the fire department to extinguish the fire, which they did, in spite of standing orders not to put out any burning synagogues. That's why Hannah sees them working to control the fire—because, in spite of the danger, one man stood up and made a difference.